Queens of Romance

*A collection of bestselling novels by
the world's leading romance writers*

**Two fabulous novels on a wedding theme
from international bestselling author**

JESSICA
STEELE

"Jessica Steele's latest is a delightful read. The
characters' chemistry and depth
add to the romance."
—*Romantic Times* on *A Paper Marriage*

"Jessica Steele's latest is delightfully
packed with emotions and warm,
tender characters…"
—*Romantic Times* on
An Accidental Engagement

100 Reasons to Celebrate

We invite you to join us in celebrating
Mills & Boon's centenary. Gerald Mills and
Charles Boon founded Mills & Boon Limited
in 1908 and opened offices in London's Covent
Garden. Since then, Mills & Boon has become
a hallmark for romantic fiction, recognised
around the world.

We're proud of our 100 years of publishing
excellence, which wouldn't have been achieved
without the loyalty and enthusiasm of our
authors and readers.

Thank you!

Each month throughout the year there will
be something new and exciting to mark the
centenary, so watch for your favourite authors,
captivating new stories, special limited
edition collections…and more!

JESSICA STEELE

Engaged to be Married?

Containing

A Paper Marriage
& An Accidental Engagement

M&B™ and M&B™ with the Rose Device
are trademarks of the publisher.
Harlequin Mills & Boon Limited, Eton House,
18-24 Paradise Road,
Richmond, Surrey TW9 1SR

Engaged to be Married? © by Harlequin Books S.A. 2008

A Paper Marriage and An Accidental Engagement were
first published in Great Britain by Harlequin Mills & Boon
Limited in separate, single volumes.

A Paper Marriage © Jessica Steele 2003
An Accidental Engagement © Jessica Steele 2003

ISBN: 978 0 263 86657 5

025-0308

Printed and bound in Spain
by Litografia Rosés S.A., Barcelona

A Paper Marriage

JESSICA STEELE

The
Queens of Romance
Collection

MILLS & BOON
100 YEARS
a pure reading pleasure

Dear Reader

I have had a long and happy association with
Mills & Boon. It began with that first lunch
with Frances and Pat, then the chief editor and
chief copy editor of the company. This was after
I had entered several stories in a short story
competition Mills & Boon were running at
the time.

Later, on acceptance of my first novel, I had
lunch with Alan Boon, a man of great charm.
There were many trips to London for lunch after
that, all splendid and most joyful affairs.

Apart from leaving home to journey to London,
I have made many other trips in relation to my
writing. Trips overseas to places as diverse as
Italy and China, Siberia, Japan and Peru. I had a
splendid time in Mexico and thought Egypt and
its antiquities absolutely breath-taking.

I have just returned from Switzerland where I
have been doing a little research for my next
book – my eighty-seventh for Mills & Boon.
Normally I do my research trips on my own, but
for the Swiss visit my husband was able to come
with me, so it was an especially enjoyable trip,
and such a pleasure – as is being an author for
such a wonderful company.

Jessica Steele

Jessica Steele lives in the county of Worcestershire with her super husband, Peter, and their gorgeous Staffordshire bull terrier, Florence.

Any spare time is spent enjoying her three main hobbies: reading espionage novels, gardening (she has a great love of flowers) and playing golf. Any time left over is celebrated with her fourth hobby, shopping.

Jessica has a sister and two brothers and they all, with their spouses, often go on golfing holidays together.

Having travelled to various places on the globe researching background for her stories, there are many countries that she would like to revisit. One of her most recent trips abroad was to Portugal where she stayed in a lovely hotel, close to her all-time favourite golf course.

Jessica had no idea of being a writer until one day Peter suggested she write a book. So she did. She has now written over eighty novels.

**Jessica Steele has a new novella,
Hired: His Personal Assistant, out as part of
The Boss's Proposal, published in May 2008,
part of our special centenary programme.
Don't miss it!**

CHAPTER ONE

LYDIE was in worried mood as she drove her car in the direction of Buckinghamshire to her family home. Something was wrong, very wrong. She had known it the moment she had heard her mother's voice over the telephone.

Her mother never rang her. It was always she who rang her mother. Lydie had held back from asking what was wrong—her mother would tell her soon enough. 'I want you to come home straight away,' Hilary Pearson had said almost before their greeting was over.

'I'm coming next Tuesday for Oliver's wedding on Saturday,' Lydie reminded her.

'I want you here before then,' her mother stated sharply.

'You need my help in some way?'

'Yes, I do!'

'Oliver…' Lydie began.

'It has nothing to do with your brother or his wedding!' her mother snapped sharply. 'The Ward-Watsons are more than capable of seeing to it that their only daughter gets married in style.'

'Dad!' Lydie cried in alarm. 'He's not ill?' She thought the world of her father. She occasionally felt that fate had dealt him a raw deal when it had selected her sometimes acid-tongued mother for the mild-mannered man.

'Physically he's as fit as he always has been.'

'You're saying he has a mental health problem?' Lydie asked in alarm.

'Good heavens, no! He's just worried, not sleeping well, he's…'

'What's he worried about?'

There was a moment or two of silence. 'I'll tell you that when you get here,' her mother eventually replied.

'Why can't you tell me now?' Lydie pressed.

'When you get here.'

'You can't leave it there!' Lydie protested.

'I'm certainly not going to discuss it over the phone.'

Oh, for heaven's sake! Who did her mother think was listening in? 'I'll ring Dad at his office,' Lydie decided.

'Don't you dare! He's not to know I've been in touch with you.'

'But…'

'And anyway, your father no longer has an office.'

'He…' What the Dickens was going on?

'Come home,' her mother demanded crisply—and put down the phone.

Lydie's initial reaction was to dial her mother straight back. A second later, though, and she accepted that to ring her would be a waste of time. If her mother had made up her mind to tell her nothing, Lydie knew from experience that she would get nothing more from her until her mother was ready.

Despite her mother's 'Don't you dare' Lydie dialled her father's business number. She need not tell him anything of her mother's call, just say she'd called to say hello prior to seeing him again when she arrived at her lovely old home next week.

A few minutes later and Lydie began to feel seriously worried herself. There was no ringing out tone from her father's firm; his number was a ceased number. '…your father no longer has an office' her mother had said.

At that point Lydie put down the phone and went in search of the woman whose employ she was due to leave next week. Though Donna was more like the sister she had never had than an employer. She found her in the sitting room with one-year-old Sofia and three-year-old Thomas. They looked such a contented family and Lydie knew she was going to feel quite a pang when she left the family she had been nanny to for the past three years.

Donna looked up. 'Did I hear the phone?' she asked with a smile.

'My mother rang.'

'Everything all right at home?'

'How would you feel if I left a week earlier than we said?'

'Today?' Donna queried, her smile disappearing. 'I'd hate it.'

'You'll be fine on your own; I know you will,' Lydie assured her bracingly.

That had been some hours ago. Lydie drove into her home village and realised she had been an infrequent visitor just lately to the home she so loved. Beamhurst Court was in her blood, and it had been a dreadful wrench to leave Beamhurst five years ago when at the age of eighteen she had gone to begin her career as a nanny.

Her first job had not worked out when the husband had started to get ideas about his children's nanny that had not been in her terms of employment. She had left to go and look after Thomas, Donna and Nick Cooper's first child, while they followed their careers.

Donna had suffered a quite terrible bout of the baby-blues following the birth of her second child, Sofia. While she was surfacing from that she had started to get very depressed at the thought of returning to work. It had been her husband Nick who had suggested that unless she desperately wanted to keep on with her career, given that they would not be able to afford a nanny and would have to let Lydie go, they could otherwise manage quite adequately without her income.

'What do you think?' Donna had asked Lydie.

'Which would make you happier?'

Donna thought, but not for very long. 'I've always felt a bit of a pang at missing out on Thomas's first couple of years,' she answered. That, simply, decided the matter.

Lydie had been due to leave next Tuesday, when she went home for her brother's wedding the following Saturday. She knew it would not be long before she found another job but, having been so happy with the Coopers, and on edge most of the time with her previous employers, she was in no rush to accept the first job offered.

She turned her car in through the gates of Beamhurst Court and love for the place welled up in her. She stopped for a brief while just to sit and look her fill. Beamhurst would one day be handed down to her brother, she had always known that, but that did not stop the feeling of joy she felt each time she came back.

But her mother was waiting for her, and Lydie started up her car again and proceeded slowly up the drive, starting to get anxious again about what it was that worried her father so, and what it was that caused his business telephone line to be unobtainable.

She left her car on the drive, knowing that her father was her first priority. She would not be looking for a new job until she knew what was happening here. Using her house key, she let herself in and went in search of her parents.

She did not have to look far; her mother was in the hall talking to Mrs Ross, their housekeeper. Lydie kissed her mother and passed a few pleasantries with Mrs Ross, whereupon her mother said they would have afternoon tea in the drawing room.

While Mrs Ross went kitchenwards Lydie followed her slim stiff-backed mother into the drawing room. 'You took your time getting here!' her mother complained tartly, turning to close the door behind them.

'I had to pack. Since I was leaving anyway there didn't seem much point in going back next week to collect my belongings,' Lydie answered, but had more important matters on her mind. 'What's going on? I rang Dad's office and—'

'I specifically told you not to!' her mother interrupted her waspishly.

'I wouldn't have mentioned you'd phoned me! If I'd had the chance! His number's unobtainable. Where's Dad now? You said he no longer has an office. But that's impossible. For years—'

'Your father no longer has an office because he no longer has a business!' Hilary Pearson cut her off.

Lydie's lovely green eyes widened in amazement. 'He no longer…!' she gasped, and wanted to protest, to believe that her mother was joking, but the tight-lipped look on her parent's face showed that her mother saw no humour in the situation. 'He's *sold* the business?' Lydie questioned.

'Sold it! It was taken away from him!'

'Taken! You mean—stolen?' Lydie asked, reeling.

'As good as. The bank wanted their pound of flesh—they took everything. They're after this house too!'

'After Beamhurst!' Lydie whispered, horrified.

'Oh, we all know you're besotted with the place; you always have been. But unless *you* can do something about it, they'll force us to sell it to pay them their dues!'

'Unless I…' Already Lydie's head was starting to spin.

'Your father paid out enough for your expensive education—totally wasted! It's time for you to pay him something back.'

Lydie was well aware that she was a big disappointment to her mother. Without bothering to take into account her daughter's extremely shy disposition, Hilary Pearson had been exceedingly exasperated that, when Lydie's exam results were little short of excellent, she should take on what her mother considered the menial work of a nanny. Lydie still had moments of shyness, and was still a little reserved, but she had overcome that awful shyness to a very large extent.

She stared at her mother incredulously. Pay back! She hadn't asked to be sent to an expensive boarding school. That had been her mother's idea. 'There's that few thousand pounds that Grandmother left me. Dad can have that, of course, but…'

'You can't touch that until you're twenty-five. And in any case we need far more than that if we're not to be thrown out like paupers.' Thrown out! Of Beamhurst! No! Lydie could not believe that. Could not believe that things were as bad as that. Beamhurst Court had been in the Pearson family for generations. It was unthinkable that they should let it go out of the family. But her mother was going angrily on, 'I've told your father that if the house has to go, then so shall I!'

'Mother!' Lydie exclaimed, on the instant angry too that when, by the look of it, her father should need his wife's support most, she should threaten to walk out on him. Anything else Lydie might have added, however, remained unsaid when Mrs Ross brought in a tray of tea and set it down.

While Hilary Pearson presided over the delicate tea cups, Lydie made herself calm down. Her last visit home had been four months ago now, she realised with surprise. Though with Donna only then starting to get better, but still feeling down and unable to cope a lot of the time, she had wanted her near at hand should everything became too much for her.

Taking the cup and saucer her mother handed to her, Lydie sat down opposite her, and then quietly asked, 'What has been happening? Everything was fine the last time I was home.'

'Six months ago,' her mother could not resist, seemingly oblivious that she was out by a couple of months. 'And everything was far from fine, as you call it.'

'I didn't see any sign…'

'Because your father didn't want you to. He said there was no need for you to know. That it would only worry you unnecessarily, and that he'd think of something.'

It had been going on all this while? And she had known nothing about it! She tried to concentrate on the matter in hand. 'But he hasn't been able to think of anything?'

Her mother gave her a sour look. 'The business is gone. And the bank is baying for its money.'

Lydie was having a hard time taking it all in. By the sound of it, things had been falling apart when she'd been home four months ago—but no one had seen fit to tell her. They had always had money! How could things have become so bad and she not know of it? She could perhaps understand her father keeping quiet; he was a very proud man. But—her mother? She was proud too, but...

'But where has all our money gone?' she asked. 'And why didn't Oliver...?'

'Well, naturally Oliver's business needed a little help.' Hilary Pearson bridled, just as if Lydie was laying some blame at her prized son's door. 'And why shouldn't your father invest heavily in him? You can't start a business from scratch and expect it to succeed in its first years. Besides, Madeline's family, the Ward-Watsons, are monied people. We couldn't let Oliver go around looking as though he hadn't a penny to his name!'

Which meant that he would take Madeline to only the very best restaurants and entertainment establishments, regardless of cost, Lydie realised. 'I didn't mean Oliver had—er—taken the money,' Lydie endeavoured to explain, knowing that her brother had started his own business five years ago and that, her father's firm doing well then, he had put up the money to set his son up in his own business. 'I meant why didn't Oliver say something to me?'

'If you cast your mind back, you'll recall that Oliver and Madeline were on holiday in South America the last time you were home. Poor Oliver works so hard; he needed that month's break.'

'His business is doing all right, is it?' Lydie enquired— and received another of her mother's sour looks for her trouble.

'As a matter of fact, he's decided to—um—cease trading.'

'You're saying that he's gone bust too?'

'Must you be so vulgar? Was all that expensive education lavished on you completely for nothing?' her mother grumbled. Though she did concede, 'All companies work on an overdraft basis—Oliver found it just too much of a struggle. When he and Madeline come back from their honeymoon, Oliver will go and work in the Ward-Watson business.' She allowed herself the first smile Lydie had so far seen as she added, half to herself, 'I shouldn't be at all surprised if Oliver isn't made a director of the Ward-Watson conglomerate before he's much older.'

All of which was very pleasing, but this wasn't getting them anywhere. 'There won't be any money coming back to Dad from Oliver, I take it?'

'He'll need all the money he can lay his hands on to support his wife. Madeline *is* used to the finer things in life, you know.'

'Where's Dad now?' Lydie asked, her heart aching for the proud man who had always worked so hard. 'Is he down at the works?'

'Little point. Your father has already sold the works to pay off some debts—he's out of a job, and at his age nobody's going to employ him. Not that he would deign to work for anyone but himself.'

Oh, heavens, Lydie mused helplessly, it sounded as though things were even worse than she had started to imagine. 'Is he out in the grounds somewhere?'

'What grounds? Any spare ground has been sold. Not that, since it's arable land only, it made a lot.' And, starting to build up a fine head of steam, 'Apart from the house—which the bank wants a slice of, which means we have to leave—your father has sold everything else that he can. I've told him I'm not moving!' Her mother went vitriolically on in the same vein for another five minutes. Going on from talk of how they were on their beam-ends to state that if they had only a half of the amount the Ward-Watsons were forking out for their only daughter's fairy-tale wedding, the bank would be satisfied.

'Dad doesn't owe the bank very much, then?' Lydie asked, but before she could start to feel in any small way relieved, her mother was giving her a snappy reply.

'They're his one remaining creditor—he's managed to scrape enough together to pay off everybody else, plus most of his overdraft. But—today's Tuesday, and the bank say they have given him long enough. If they aren't in receipt of fifty thousand pounds by the end of banking on Friday—they move. And so do we! Can you imagine it? The disgrace? A fine thing it's going to look in Oliver's wedding announcement. Not "Oliver Pearson of Beamhurst Court", but "Oliver Pearson of No Fixed Abode". How shall we ever—?'

Her mother would have gone on, but Lydie interrupted. 'Fifty thousand doesn't sound such a fearfully large amount.'

'It does when you haven't got it. Nor any way of finding it either. Apart from the house, we're out of collateral. How can we borrow money with no way of repaying it? Nobody's going to loan us anything. Not that your father would ask in the circumstances. No, your father overextended himself, the bank won't wait any longer—and now *I* have to pay!'

Lydie thought hard. 'The pictures!' she exclaimed after a moment. 'We could sell some of the family—'

'Haven't you been listening to a word I've said? Haven't I just finished telling you that everything, everything that isn't in trust for Oliver, has been sold? There's nothing left *to* sell. Nothing, absolutely nothing!'

Her mother looked closer to tears than Lydie had ever seen her, and suddenly her heart went out to her. For all her mother had never been the warmest mother in the world to her, Oliver being her pride and joy, Lydie loved her.

Lydie went impulsively over to her. 'I'm sorry,' she said gently, taking a seat next to her on the sofa. 'I'm so very sorry.' And, remembering her mother saying only a short while ago that it was time she paid something back for the expensive education she had received, 'What can I do?' she asked. While the amount of her inheritance was small, and nowhere near enough, Lydie was thinking in terms of asking to have that money released now and not two years hence, when she would attain the age of twenty-five, but her mother's reply shook her into speechlessness.

'You can go and see Jonah Marriott,' she said clearly. 'That's what you can do.'

Lydie stared at her, her green eyes huge. 'Jonah Marriott?' she managed faintly. She had only ever seen him once, and that was some seven years ago, but she had never forgotten the tall, good looking man.

'You remember him?'

'He came here one time. Didn't Dad lend him some money?'

'He did,' Hilary Pearson replied sharply. 'And now it's his turn to pay that money back.'

'He never repaid that money?' Lydie asked, feeling just a touch disappointed. He had seemed to her sixteen-year-old eyes such an honourable man—and she knew he had prospered greatly in the seven years that had elapsed.

'Coincidentally, the money he borrowed from your father is the same amount we need to stay on in this house.'

'Fifty thousand pounds?'

'Exactly the same. I can't impress on you enough that if the bank don't have their money by Friday, come Monday they'll be making representation to have us evicted. I'd go and see him myself, but when I mentioned it to your father he hit the roof and forbade me to do anything of the sort.'

Lydie could not imagine her mild-mannered father hitting the roof, especially to the wife he adored. But he must be under a tremendous amount of strain at the moment. No doubt he himself had previously asked Jonah Marriott to make some kind of payment off that loan. There was no way her father's pride would allow him to ask more than once. But to…

Her thoughts faded when just then the drawing room

door opened and her father walked into the room. At least the man was tall, like her father, white-haired, like her father, but Lydie was shocked by the haggard look of him.

'Daddy!' she whispered involuntarily, and went hurriedly over to him. There was a dejected kind of slump to his shoulders which she found heartbreaking, and as she looked into his worn, tired face, she could not bear it. She put her arms round him and hugged him.

'What are you doing here?' he asked, putting her aside and sending her mother a suspicious look.

'I—thought I'd give Donna a chance to see how she'll cope without me,' Lydie invented, quickly hiding her shocked feelings. 'I'll give her a ring later. If she's okay I'll stay on, if that's all right with you?'

'Of course it's all right,' he replied with assumed joviality. 'This is your h...' He turned away and Lydie's heart ached afresh. She just knew he had been thinking that this was her home, but would not be for very much longer. 'Your mother been bringing you up to date with everything?' he enquired, his tone casual, but pride there, ready to be up in arms if his wife had breathed a word of his troubles.

'This wedding of Oliver's sounds a bit top-drawer. Are they going to have a marquee—you didn't finish telling me, Mother?'

Over the next half-hour Lydie observed at first hand the proud façade her father was putting up in front of her, and her heart went out to him. Looking at him, seeing the strain, the worry that seemed to be weighing him down, to go and see Jonah Marriott and ask him to repay the money he had borrowed from her father seven years ago did not seem such a hard task. Particularly as, if memory served, that money had only been loaned for a period of five years anyway.

'Your room's all ready for you.' Her mother took the conversation away from the wedding. 'If you want to go and freshen up,' she hinted.

'I've things to attend to in my study,' Wilmot Pearson commented before Lydie had answered. 'It's good to see you, Lydie. Let's hope you'll be able to stay.'

No sooner had he gone from the room than her mother was back to the forbidden subject. 'Well?' she questioned. 'Will you?'

Lydie knew what she was asking, just as she knew that she did not want to go and see Jonah Marriott. 'You're quite sure he hasn't paid that loan back?' she hedged. Her mother gave her a vinegary look. 'Perhaps he can't afford to pay it back,' Lydie commented. 'All firms work on an overdraft basis, you recently said so,' she reminded her mother, but, still shaken by the haggard look of her father, wondered why she was prevaricating about going to see Jonah Marriott.

Her mother chose to ignore her comments, instead scorning, 'Of course he can afford to pay it back—many times over. His father made a packet when he sold his department stores. Ambrose Marriott might be one tough operator but I can't see him giving to one son and not the other—and the younger Marriott boy hasn't done a day's work since the deal was done. They're all sitting on Easy Street,' her mother said with a heartfelt sigh, 'and just look at us!'

Lydie glanced at her parent, and while the last thing she wanted to do was to go and ask Jonah Marriott for the money he owed to her father, she knew that the time for prevaricating was over. She looked at her watch. Half past four. She had better get a move on. 'Do you have his number?'

'You can't discuss this with him over the telephone!' her mother snorted. 'You need to be there, face to face. You need to impress on him how—'

'I was going to ring his office for an appointment,' Lydie interrupted. 'He's hardly likely to see me without one.' And if he guesses what it's about he'll probably say no anyway!

'I don't want your father to catch you. You'd better make your call from your room,' Hilary Pearson decided. And, not allowing her daughter to consider changing her mind, 'I'll come up with you.'

'Marriott Electronics,' a pleasant voice answered when up in her old bedroom Lydie had dialled the number.

'Mr Marriott please,' Lydie said firmly, striving with all she had to keep her voice from shaking. 'Mr Jonah Marriott,' she tacked on, just in case Jonah had taken other members of the Marriott clan into the business.

'One moment, please,' the telephonist answered, but even though Lydie's stomach did a tiny somersault at the thought she might soon be speaking to the man she had seen only once but had never forgotten, she did not think she would be put through to him as easily as that.

Her stomach settled down when the next voice she heard was a calm and pleasant voice informing her, 'Mr Marriott's office.'

'Oh, hello,' Lydie said in a rush. 'My name's Lydie Pearson. I wonder if it's possible for me to have a word with Mr Marriott?'

'I'm afraid Mr Marriott's out of the office until Friday. Is there anything I can help you with?' Pleasant, polite, but Lydie knew she was getting nowhere.

'Oh,' she murmured, then paused for a moment, very much aware of her mother's tense gaze on her. 'I wanted to see him rather urgently. Um—perhaps I should ring him at home,' she pondered out loud, knowing in advance that she had small chance the woman—his PA, most probably—would let her have his private number.

'Actually, Mr Marriott is out of the country until late on Thursday evening.'

Oh, grief, she wanted this over and done with. 'I'll ring again on Friday,' Lydie said pleasantly, and rang off to be confronted by her mother, who wanted to hear syllable by syllable what had been said.

'We're going to lose the house!' Hilary Pearson cried. 'I know it! I know it!' And Lydie, who had never before seen her mother in a state of panic, began more than ever to appreciate how very dire the situation was—and she started to get angry—with Jonah Marriott.

'No, we won't,' she said as calmly as she could. 'I'll go and see Jonah Marriott on Friday, and I won't leave his office until I have the money he owes Dad.'

Lydie had no chance in the two days that followed to have second thoughts about going to see Jonah Marriott. With her father seeming to grow more drawn and careworn by the hour, not to mention her mother's endless insistence that Lydie was their only hope, Lydie knew that she had no choice but to go and see him.

Consequently, whenever the voice of reality would butt in to enquire what made her think anything she might say would make him promise to repay that money—he had let her father down; what difference did she think her appeal would make?—her emotions, her love for her parents and the calamity they were facing, would override the logic of her head.

Which in turn, over the days leading up to Friday, caused Lydie to grow angry again with Jonah Marriott. That anger turning to fury with him when she thought of how her father had lent him that money in good faith, and how Jonah had so badly let him down.

Her fury dimmed somewhat, though, whenever she recalled her only meeting with the man. She had occasionally helped her father in his study during her school holidays, and had known that someone was coming to the house in the hope of borrowing some money. It had gone from her mind that day, though, until she had come home and found him sitting in the drawing room of their home. She had been sixteen, a thin, lanky, terribly shy sixteen-year-old.

'Oh, I'm s-sorry,' she had stammered, blushing to the roots of her night-black hair. 'I didn't know anyone was in here!' He hadn't answered, but had done her the courtesy of rising to his feet. She had blushed again, but had felt obliged to ask, 'Are you waiting for Daddy?'

The man had superb blue eyes, quite a fantastic blue, she

remembered thinking as he'd looked directly at her and commented in that wonderful all-male voice, 'If your daddy is Mr Wilmot Pearson, then, yes, I am.'

Her knees by that time were like so much jelly. But, at the same time, she could not help but think how ghastly it must be for him to have to come and ask to borrow some money, and, while she wanted to fly, she found she wanted more to make him feel better about it. 'I'm Lydie,' she stayed to tell him. 'Lydie Pearson.'

'Jonah Marriott,' he answered, and, treating her as a grown-up, his right hand came out.

Nervously, she shook hands with him, her colour a furious red as their hands met, his touch firm and warm. But still she could not leave him without trying to make him feel better. 'Would you like some tea, Mr Marriott?' she asked him shakily.

He had smiled then, and she had thought he had the most wonderful smile in the world. 'Thank you, no, Miss Pearson,' he had refused politely—and she had blushed again, this time at the dreadful thought that he was perhaps teasing her.

Just then, though, her father had come in. 'Sorry to keep you, Jonah. That phone call has settled most everything.' And, with a fond father's look to his daughter, 'You've met Lydie—soon to tear herself away from her beloved Beamhurst and go back to school again after the summer break!'

'You'll miss her when she's gone, I'm sure,' Jonah answered with a glance to her, and Lydie had blushed again.

'I'll see you later,' she mumbled generally, and fled.

And so had begun a giant-sized crush on one Jonah Marriott. But she had not seen him later or ever again. That had not stopped her from finding out more about him. He had been in his late twenties then, and already had a thriving electronics business. From bits she had gleaned on separate occasions from her mother, from her father, and also from her brother Oliver, who at one time had gone around with a crowd that included Jonah's younger brother Rupert, she knew that Jonah was the elder son of Ambrose Marriott. Their father owned several department stores, and Jonah had felt obliged to go and work for his father. When Rupert had finished university, and had declared that there was nothing he would like better than to start work in the business, Jonah had felt free to leave the family business and start up his own company.

His father had not liked it, so Jonah had borrowed from the bank to get started. He had gone from success to success, but still owed the bank when he had wanted to expand his company. The banks had lent him as much as they could—it had not been enough. Too proud to ask his own father to lend him money—he had approached her father, a well-known businessman, instead.

The rest was history, Lydie fumed when, after a very fitful night's sleep, she awakened on Friday morning. Her father had lent Jonah Marriott fifty thousand pounds. Jonah Marriott, her idol for so long, had never paid him back. And Lydie was going to do something about it—this very day!

Had she experienced the smallest doubt about that, then that very small doubt evaporated into thin air when she went down to breakfast and saw that, while she had slept only fitfully, her father looked like a soul in torment and appeared not to have slept at all.

'And what are you going to do today?' he forced a cheerful note to ask. And she wished that she could tell him, Don't, Dad, I know all about it. But her father's pride was mammoth, and she could not take that away from him. Time enough for him to know when she came back from seeing Jonah Marriott and was able to tell him—if all went well—that Jonah would ring her father's bank and tell them, hopefully, that he would take on his debt.

'I haven't seen Aunt Alice in ages,' she answered, Aunt Alice being her mother's aunt, in actual fact, and therefore

Lydie's great-aunt. 'I thought I might take a drive over to see her.'

'You're picking her up for the wedding next week, aren't you?'

'She doesn't want to stay away from home overnight.' Lydie tactfully rephrased part of what her great-aunt had written in her last letter.

'We, your mother, Oliver and me, are going to a hotel overnight, as you know. Your mother's idea,' he muttered, but added dryly, 'Hilary will be sorry her aunt won't be staying here.'

Lydie grinned. She thought Aunt Alice brilliant; her mother thought her a stubborn pain. Lydie was not grinning after breakfast, though. Dressed in a smart suit of powder blue, her dark hair pulled back from her delicate features in a classic knot, she got out her car ostensibly to make the twenty mile drive to her aunt's home in Penleigh Corbett in the next county.

While facing that she did not want to make the journey to the London head office of Marriott Electronics, since make it she must, she wanted to be early. For all she knew she might have to wait all day, but if Jonah Marriott was in the building and refused to see her, then, since he had to come out at some time, she was prepared to wait around to speak to him on his way out.

Her insides had been churned up ever since she had opened her eyes that morning, but the nearer she got to London, the more her churning insides were all over the place.

When the traffic started to snarl up she found a place to park her car and made it to the Marriott building by foot, tube and lastly taxi.

But once outside the building she experienced the greatest reluctance to go inside. For herself, perhaps having inherited her father's massive pride, she would have galloped in the opposite direction. Only this wasn't for her; it was for him.

Lydie had to do no more than recall her father's drawn look at breakfast and she was pushing through the plate-glass doors and heading for the reception desk.

The receptionist was busy dealing with one person and there was someone else waiting. 'Mr Marriott's PA is on her way down to see you.' The receptionist put down the phone to pass on the message to the suit-clad man she was dealing with.

Lydie closed her ears to the rest of it, her glance going over to where the lifts were. One started up and, from the changing numerals, she saw that the lift was making its way down from the top floor.

Without being fully aware of it, Lydie edged over to that lift. When the doors opened and a smart-looking woman of forty or so stepped out, and with a smile on her face went over to the man at the desk, Lydie stepped in and pressed the button for the top floor.

She knew she could quite well have got it wrong, but if her hunch was right, that had been Jonah Marriott's PA. If she had just come down from the top floor, then, to Lydie's mind, on the top floor was where she might find Jonah Marriott.

The lift stopped; she got out. She felt hot, sick, and knew that this was the worst thing she was ever going to have to do in her life. Instinct took her to the end of the carpeted corridor. With what intelligence her emotions had left her, it seemed to her that the man who was head of this corporation would have his office well away from the sound of the lift going up and down.

There were doors to offices on either side of the long corridor. Lydie ignored them and at the bottom of that corridor turned round a corner which opened out to show two doors blocking her way. Lydie hesitated, but only for a moment. She was by then starting to feel certain she had got it all wrong. Somehow, churned up, anxious, worried, she had got it all wrong, all muddled; she knew that she had. She went forward and, placing a hand on the handle to the door to the right, she paused for about half a second, then turned the handle.

Shock as the door swung inwards and she saw a man seated at a desk in front of her kept her speechless and motionless. He looked up, and as colour surged to her face so, his glance still on her face, he rose from his chair and began to come round his desk and over to her.

She was five feet nine inches tall, he looked down at her and—to her utter astonishment—commented, 'Still blushing, Lydie?' He remembered her, her blushes, from seven years ago?

'I'm L-Lydie Pearson,' she heard herself say inanely from somewhere far off.

'I know who you are,' he answered smoothly. 'Come in and take a seat,' he invited, and as she took a couple of steps into the room he closed the door behind her and touched a hand to her elbow.

In something of a daze she found she was seated on a chair some way to the side of his desk before she had got herself anywhere near of one piece.

'Haven't I changed at all in seven years?' she asked, her head still a little woolly that he had so instantly recognised her.

'I wouldn't say that,' Jonah replied pleasantly, his eyes flicking a glance over her still slender, but now curving deliciously in all the right places, shape. 'Elaine, my PA, made a note that a Lydie Pearson phoned last Tuesday. I recalled one black-haired, green-eyed Lydie Pearson with one hell of a superb complexion. It had to be you.' He paused, and then, while she was feeling a touch swamped that he thought she had a superb complexion, 'You're still Lydie Pearson?' he enquired.

Having thought she had her head more together, Lydie wasn't with him for a moment or two. 'Um...' she mumbled, then realised what he was asking. 'I'm not married,' she answered, and, with a quick glance to his ringless left hand, 'It doesn't look as if anybody's caught you either.'

His rather splendid mouth quirked upwards at the corners slightly. 'I have very long legs,' he confided.

'You sprint pretty fast at the word marriage?'

He did not answer. He didn't need to. 'So, how's the world treating you?' he asked.

Lydie looked away from his fantastic blue eyes and over to his laden desk. He had not been expecting this visit and from the look of his desk was extremely busy catching up on a backlog of work. Yet he seemed to have all the time in the world to idly converse with someone he barely knew, someone he had only ever clapped eyes on once—and that was seven years ago.

'Er—this isn't a social call,' Lydie stated abruptly.

'It isn't?' he questioned mildly—when she was sure he must *know* that it wasn't.

She experienced an unexpected urge to thump him that surprised her. She swallowed down that small burst of anger, but only when she felt marginally calmer was she able to coldly state, 'My father seems not to have fared as well, financially, over the last seven years as you yourself appear to have done.'

Jonah nodded, every bit as if he already knew that—and that annoyed her—before he coolly commented, 'That's what comes from constantly bailing out that brother of yours.'

How dared he blame Oliver? 'Oliver no longer has his own business!'

'That should make things easier for your father,' Jonah Marriott shot back at her, cool still.

Honestly! Again she wanted to hit him. 'My father's own business has gone too!' she retorted pithily, and saw that at last Jonah Marriott was taking her seriously.

'I'm very sorry to hear that. Wilmot is a first-class—'

'So you *should* be sorry!' she interrupted hotly. 'If you'd had the decency to honour that debt…'

'Honour that debt?' Jonah queried toughly, just as if he had not the first clue what she was talking about.

'You're trying to say that you have totally forgotten coming to my home seven years ago and borrowing fifty thousand pounds from my father?'

'I'm hardly likely to do that. If it wasn't for your father—'

'Then it's about time you paid that loan back!' she interrupted his flow hotly. And, suddenly too het-up to sit still, she jumped to her feet—to find Jonah Marriott was on his feet too, and was standing looking down on her. She saw him swiftly masking a look of surprise—at her nerve, no doubt. But she cared not if he thought she had an outrageous sauce to burst in on his busy morning without so much as a by your leave and demand the return of her father's money. Her father's peace of mind was at stake here. 'If my father doesn't have that fifty thousand pounds by the end of today's banking,' she hurtled on, 'we, that is my mother and father, will lose Beamhurst Court!'

'Lose…'

But Lydie was too angry to let him in. 'Beamhurst Court has been in my family for hundreds of years and my father has until only today to see that it stays in the family!' she charged on.

'You're exaggerating, surely?' Jonah Marriott managed to get in evenly, his eyes on her angry face, her sparking green eyes.

'I love Beamhurst! Does it look as if I'm exaggerating?' she erupted. But calmed down a little to concur, 'It's true my father invested heavily in Oliver's company, but my father didn't know his own firm was going to suffer a downturn.'

'So he borrowed as much as he could from the banks, putting Beamhurst Court up as collateral,' Jonah took up. 'And when your brother's firm went belly-up, and your father settled his son's creditors, there was nothing left in the kitty to settle his own debts.'

'You know this?' she asked, starting to feel her anger on

the rise again that he should be aware of the situation and still refuse to repay her father.

'I didn't,' Jonah replied, defusing her anger somewhat. 'From what you've said, that seems the most likely way it went.' And disconcertingly he asked, 'And what's your brother doing in all of this?'

Lydie did not care for his question. It weakened her argument. Her father was distraught—while Oliver did nothing. 'He... I haven't seen Oliver. I only came home on Tuesday,' she excused, and defended her elder brother. 'Oliver's getting married a week tomorrow. There's a lot to arrange. He's staying with his fiancée's people to help with any last-minute problems they...' Her voice trailed away.

'Let's hope he makes a better job of it than he made of his business,' Jonah commented, but, before she could take exception, 'Big do, is it?'

Lydie could have done without that remark too. In the instance of her family being on their uppers—and she was coming to realise more and more that her father constantly financing her brother's business was largely responsible for that—it did seem a bit over the top to have such a pomp of a wedding.

'The bride's parents are paying for everything,' she felt obligated to admit, her pride taking something of a hammering here. 'Look, we're getting away from the point!' she said snappily. 'You owe my father money. Money he needs, *now*, if he is to remain in the only home he has ever known, the home he loves.'

'Fifty thousand pounds will assure that?' Jonah asked, doubting it.

'My father has sold everything he can possibly sell in order to meet his debts. All that remains is an overdraft of fifty thousand pounds at the bank that he knows, and they know, he cannot find—nor has any likelihood of finding. They have given him until today to try to find that money anyway. He cannot,' she ended, and her voice started to fracture. 'A-and he looks t-terrible.'

Abruptly she turned away from Jonah, knowing that her emotions as she thought of her dear distracted father had brought her close to tears. She went to stare unseeing out of the window and swallowed hard as she fought for control. Her pride would never survive if she broke down in front of this hard man.

When she felt she had control she turned towards the door, knowing instinctively that she had pleaded her father's cause in vain. It had been a long shot anyway, she realised. Had Jonah Marriott the smallest intention of repaying that money, he would have done so long before this.

She took a step to the door—but was halted when Jonah, having not moved from where she had left him, stated, 'Obviously your father doesn't know you've come here.'

Lydie turned. 'He's a proud man,' she replied with a tilt of her head.

'His daughter's pretty much the same,' Jonah said quietly, his eyes on her proud beauty.

She wished she could agree. Albeit she had not come to the Marriott building for herself, she had not been too proud to come here today—even if that money was still owing. 'Should you ever bump into my father, I'd be obliged if you did not tell him I came here,' she requested coldly.

For answer Jonah Marriott went round to his desk. 'I won't—but I think he'll know,' he drawled, to her alarm. And, even while she was instantly ready to go for Jonah Marriott's jugular, he was opening a drawer in his desk, taking out a chequebook, and asking, 'Who do you want the cheque made out to, Lydie?'

'Y-you'll pay?' she asked, shaken rigid, but in no mind to refuse—no matter how little he offered. He did not answer but picked up his pen. She went over to stand at the other side of his desk. 'My father. Would you make it out to my father, please?' she said quickly, before he could change his mind.

It was done. In next to no time the cheque was written and Jonah was handing it to her across the desk. Hardly daring to breathe, lest this be some sort of evil game he was playing, Lydie inspected the cheque. It was made out to Wilmot Pearson. The date was right. The cheque was signed. But the amount was wrong. Jonah had made it out for fifty-five thousand pounds!

'Fifty-*five* thousand…?'

'The bank will be adding interest—daily, I don't doubt. Call it interest on the debt.'

He meant his debt, of course. Feeling stunned, then beginning to feel little short of elated, Lydie looked up and across at him. She was about to thank him when she looked at the cheque again and noticed that it was not a company cheque, as she would have thought, but a personal cheque—and a large chunk of her elation fell away. Anybody could write a personal cheque for fifty-five thousand pounds, but that did not necessarily mean there was any money in that bank account. Was this some kind of sick joke Jonah Marriott was playing, to pay her back for her impertinence in daring to walk unannounced into his office and demand he paid what he owed?

'There's money in this account to meet this amount?' she questioned.

'Not yet,' he admitted. Though, before her last ray of hope should disappear, 'But there will be…' he paused '…by the time you get to your father's bank.'

'You're—sure?' she asked hesitantly.

Jonah Marriott eyed her steadily. 'Trust me, Lydie,' he said quietly—and, strangely, she did.

'Thank you,' she said, and held out her right hand.

'Goodbye,' he said, and, with that wonderful smile she had remembered all these years, 'Let's hope it's not another seven years before we meet again.'

She smiled too, and could still feel the warm firm pressure of his right hand on hers as she waltzed out of the Marriott building and into the street. She remembered his blue eyes and…

She pushed him from her mind and concentrated on what

to do first. She had half a notion to ring her mother and tell her the outcome of her visit to Jonah Marriott. Lydie then thought of the cheque that was burning a hole in her bag. She had been going to take it straight to her father, to tell him everything was all right now. To tell him that Jonah Marriott had paid in full, with interest, the money he had owed him for so long. But, with Jonah saying that the funds would be there by the time she got to her father's bank—presumably all that was needed was for Jonah to pick up a phone and give his instructions—would it not be far better for her to bank the money now and tell her father afterwards?

Lydie decided there and then—thanking Jonah for the suggestion—that she would bank the money before she went home. Yes, that was much the better idea. As things stood she had plenty of time to get home, hand the cheque over to her father and for him to take the cheque personally to his bank. But who knew what traffic hold-ups there might be on the road. Much better—thank you, Jonah—to bank the cheque first and then go home.

Having found a branch of the bank which her father used, it was a small matter to have her father's account located, the money paid in, and to receive the bank's receipt in return.

Oh, Jonah. Her head said she should be cross with him for his tardiness in paying what was owed. But she couldn't be cross. In fact, on that drive back to Beamhurst Court, she was hard put to it not to smile the whole time.

The house was secure and, although with not so much land as they had once owned, it was still in the hands of the Pearsons. While her father was unlikely to start in business on his own account again, he no longer, as Jonah had put it, needed to bail her brother out ever again either. Her mother had hinted that her father had been looking into the possibility of some consultancy work. Surely all his years of expertise were not to be wasted.

Optimistically certain that everything would be all right

from now on, Lydie drew up outside the home she so loved and almost danced inside as she went looking for her parents. Had today turned out well or hadn't it? She understood now why, when she'd asked Jonah not to tell her father she had been to see him, Jonah had replied, 'I won't—but I think he'll know.' Of course her father would know. The minute she told her proud father that his overdraft was cleared he would want to know where the money had come from. Jonah would not have to tell her father— she would. She could hardly wait to see his joy.

'Here you both are!' she said on opening the drawing room door and seeing her parents there—her father looking a shadow of his former self.

Her mother gave her a quick expectant look, but it was her father who asked, 'How was your great-aunt Alice?'

'Actually, Dad, I lied,' Lydie confessed. 'I haven't been to see Aunt Alice.'

He gave her a severe look. 'For someone who has lied to her father you're looking tremendously pleased with yourself,' he remarked. 'I trust it was a lie for the good of mankind?'

'Not exactly,' she replied, and quickly opening her bag she took out the receipt for the money she had paid into his bank account. 'I went to see Jonah Marriott.'

'You went—to see Jonah Marriott?' he asked in surprise. He took the folded receipt she held out, opened it out, read the very little that was written there, but which meant so much, and—his face darkened ominously. 'What *is* this?' he demanded, as though unable to believe that an amount of fifty-five thousand pounds had been paid into his account.

'Your overdraft is cleared, Dad.' She explained that which he seemed to have difficulty in taking in.

'Cleared!' he echoed, it passing him by completely just then that she knew about his financial problems, and his tone of voice such that, had she not known better, Lydie would have thought it was the calm before the storm.

'I went to see Jonah Marriott, as I said. He gave me a cheque for the money he owed you. I paid it into your bank on my—' She didn't get to finish.

'You did *what*?' her father roared, and Lydie stared at him in astonishment. Her mild-mannered father *never* roared!

'You n-needed the money,' she mumbled anxiously— this wasn't at all how she had imagined it. 'Jonah Marriott owed you fifty thousand pounds—I went and asked him for it. He added five...'

'You went and *asked* him for fifty thousand pounds?' her father shouted. 'Have you *no* pride?'

'He owed it to you. He...'

'He did *not*,' her father cut her off furiously.

'He—didn't?' Lydie gasped, looking over to her mother, who had told her that he did, but who was now more interested in looking at the curtains than in meeting her eyes.

'He does not owe me anything!' her father bellowed. 'Not a penny!' Lydie flinched as she turned her head to stare uncomprehendingly at the man who, prior to that moment, had never raised his voice to her in his life. 'Oh, what have you done, Lydie?' he asked, suddenly defeated, and she felt then that she would rather he shouted at her than that he should sound so utterly beaten. 'Any money Jonah Marriott borrowed from me was paid back, with good interest, more than three years ago.'

CHAPTER TWO

'HE PAID you back!' Lydie gasped. And, reeling from what her father had just revealed, 'But Mother said—' Lydie broke off, her stricken gaze going from her mortified father to her mother.

This time her mother did meet her eyes, defiantly. But it was Wilmot Pearson who found his voice first, and, transferring his look to his wife, 'What did you tell her?' he demanded angrily.

'Somebody had to do something!' she returned hostilely, entirely unrepentant.

'But you knew Jonah Marriott had repaid that loan—repaid it ahead of time. I told you. I clearly remember telling—'

'*Mother!* You *knew*?' Lydie chipped in, horrified. 'You knew all the time that that money had been repaid—yet you let me go and ask Jonah for money!' Oh, how she had asked him. No, Please will you lend us some money? but 'This isn't a social call' she had told him shortly, and had gone from there to suggest he didn't have any decency and that it was about time he paid that loan back—when all the time he already had. And she had thought he looked a bit surprised! No wonder! 'Mother, how could you?'

Her mother did not care to be taken to task, and was at her arrogant worst when she retorted, 'Far better to owe Jonah Marriott money than the bank. At least this way we get to keep the house.'

'Don't be so sure about that!' Wilmot Pearson chipped in heavily—and uproar broke out between her parents for several minutes; he determined he would sell the house to pay Jonah Marriott and her mother said her father would

32

be living elsewhere on his own if he did, and that
Beamhurst was to be preserved to be passed down to
Oliver. It was painful to Lydie to hear them, but when her
mother, retorting that at least they wouldn't be opening the
doors to the bailiffs come Monday morning, seemed to be
getting the better of the argument, her father turned and
vented his frustration out on his daughter.

'He—Jonah—he gave you a cheque, just like that, did
he? You told him you wanted that "loan" I made him
back—and he paid up without a murmur?'

'He—um—said he had never forgotten how you helped
him out that time. He was grateful to you, I think,' Lydie
answered, starting to wish that her mother had never
phoned her last Tuesday.

'So he gave you fifty-five thousand pounds out of gratitude and without a word that he had already settled that
debt? How the devil do you suppose I'm going to pay him
back?' her father exploded, and in high temper, 'Why *ever*
didn't you bring that cheque home to *me first*?' he demanded. 'Why in the world did you *bank it* without first
consulting me?'

Lydie felt she would have brought the cheque to her
father, had not Jonah Marriott put the idea of banking it
first into her head. And suddenly she began to get the feeling that, one way and another, she had been well and truly
manipulated here. First by her mother, very definitely by
her mother, and secondly by Jonah Marriott himself.

'*Well?*' Her father interrupted her thoughts.

'It seemed the best way to do it,' she answered lamely.
'If there had been any sort of a traffic snarl-up I could have
been too late for the bank here. And I knew—' thank you,
Mother '—that the bank wanted their money by today.'

'And they've got it—and it's for certain they'll hang on
to it!' he stated agitatedly. 'There's absolutely no chance
they'll let me have it back again.' He sighed heavily. 'I'd
better go and see Jonah.'

'I'll go!' Lydie said straight away, as she knew she must.

'*You,*' her father erupted, 'have done enough! You can stay here with your mother and dream up your next scheme.'

That comment was extremely unfair, in Lydie's opinion, but she understood his pride must be hurting like the very devil. 'Please let me go?' she pleaded. He hesitated for the merest moment, and Lydie rushed on quickly, 'You're not the only one with any pride,' she added—and all at once her father seemed to fold.

He looked at her, his normally quite reserved daughter who, up until then, had caused him very little grief. 'None of this has been very easy for you either, has it?' he queried, more in the calm tone she was familiar with. And, relenting, if reluctantly, 'We'll go and see him together,' he conceded.

That wasn't what Lydie wanted either. 'I'll go and ring him,' she offered.

'Not go and see him?'

'I'll probably have to make an appointment first.' In this instance of eating extra-large portions of humble pie, it seemed more diplomatic to try and get an appointment first rather than to go barging straight into his office.

'We'll make the call from my study,' Wilmot Pearson declared, and, giving his wife a frosty look in passing, for which, since her home was for the moment secure, she cared not a jot, he and Lydie went from the drawing room and to his study.

She was glad that her father allowed her to make the call and did not insist on doing that himself, but her insides were on the churn again as she dialled the Marriott Electronics number.

Again when she asked to speak with Mr Jonah Marriott she was put through to his PA. 'Hello, it's Lydie Pearson…'

'Oh, good afternoon,' the PA answered pleasantly, before Lydie could continue. 'I missed seeing you this morning.' And Lydie realised that plainly Jonah must have made some comment to his PA about her visit—probably something along the lines of Don't ever let that woman come in here again—she's too expensive. Lydie hoped he hadn't revealed the full content of her visit to his confidential assistant. 'I'm afraid Mr Marrriott's at a meeting. If you would like to leave a message?'

Blocked. 'I should like to see him some time. Later this afternoon if that's possible.'

'He's flying to Paris tonight, but...'

Something akin to jealousy gave Lydie a small thump at the thought that he would be dallying the weekend in Paris. Ridiculous, she scoffed. But she began to realise she had inherited a little of her mother's arrogance in that she would beg for nothing. 'I'll give him a call next week. It's not important,' Lydie butted in pleasantly, wished the PA an affable goodbye, and turned to relay the conversation to her waiting father. 'Try not to worry, Dad,' she added quietly. Having been set up by her mother, she was not feeling all that friendly towards her, but attempted anyway to make things better between her parents. 'And try not to be too cross with Mother; she only did what she did to help.'

Wilmot Pearson looked as if he might have a lot to say about that, but settled for a mild, 'I know.'

The atmosphere in the house was not good for the rest of the day, however, and Lydie took herself off for a walk with a very great deal on her mind. She still felt crimson around the ears when she thought of the way she had gone to Jonah Marriott's office and demanded fifty thousand pounds!

Oh, heavens! But—why on earth had he given it to her? Not only that, but he had made sure his cheque was banked and not returned to him with a polite note from her father. 'There's money in this account to meet this amount?' she had asked him. 'There will be...by the time you get to your father's bank,' he had said, as in Make haste and get there—and she had fallen for it!

Lydie carried on walking, not knowing where she was

emotionally. With that money in the bank her father had some respite from his worries—and he sorely needed that respite. Against that, though, since it was she who had asked for, and taken, that money, regardless of where she had deposited it, she was beginning to realise that the debt was not her father's but hers; solely hers.

Feeling quite sick as she accepted that realisation, all she could do was to wonder where in creation she was going to find fifty-five thousand pounds with which to repay him? That question haunted her for the remainder of her walk.

She returned home knowing that adding together the second-hand value of her car, the pearls her parents had given her for her twenty-first birthday and her small inheritance—if she could get into it—she would be lucky if she was able to raise as much as ten thousand pounds!

She went to bed that night knowing that Jonah Marriott's hope that it would not be another seven years before they met again must have been said tongue in cheek. He must have known she would be on the phone wanting to see him the moment she discovered his loan from her father had been repaid long since. Jonah Marriott, without a doubt, had told his PA to inform her when she rang that he could not see her.

Why he would do that, Lydie wasn't very sure, and conceded that very probably he'd given his PA no such instruction. It was just one Lydie Pearson feeling very much out of sorts where he was concerned. Him and his 'Obviously your father doesn't know you've come here.' It was *obvious* to her, *now*, that Jonah knew her father would have soon stopped her visit had he the merest inkling of what she was doing.

Lydie spent a wakeful night with J. Marriott Esquire occupying too much space in her head for comfort. Oversexed swine! She hoped he was enjoying himself in Paris—whoever she was.

The atmosphere in her home was no better when she went down to breakfast on Saturday morning. Lydie saw a whole day of monosyllabic conversation and of watching frosty glances go back and forth.

'I think I'll go and see Aunt Alice. Truthfully,' she added at her father's sharp look.

'While you're there for goodness' sake check what she intends to wear to the wedding next Saturday,' her mother instructed peevishly. 'She's just as likely to turn up in that disgraceful old gardening hat and wellingtons!'

Lydie was glad to escape the house, and drove to Penleigh Corbett and the small semi-detached house which her mother's aunt, to her mother's embarrassment, rented from the local council.

To Lydie's dismay, though, the sprightly eighty-four-year-old was looking much less sprightly than when she had last seen her, for all she beamed a welcome. 'Come in, come in!' she cried. 'I didn't expect to see you before next week.'

They were drinking coffee fifteen minutes later when, feeling quite perturbed by her great-aunt's pallor, Lydie enquired casually, 'Do you see your doctor at all?'

'Dr Stokes? She's always popping in.'

'What for?' Lydie asked in alarm.

'Nothing in particular. She just likes my chocolate cake.'

Lydie had to stamp down hard on her need to know more than that. Great-Aunt Alice was anti people discussing their ailments. 'Are you taking any medication?' Lydie asked tentatively.

'Do you know anybody over eighty who isn't?' Alice Gough bounced back. 'How's your mother? Has she come to terms yet with the fact dear Oliver wants to take a wife?'

'You're wicked,' Lydie accused.

'Only the good die young,' Alice Gough chuckled, and took Lydie on a tour of her garden. They had lunch of bread, cheese and tomatoes, though Lydie observed that the elderly lady ate very little.

Lydie visited with her great-aunt for some while, then, thinking she was probably wanting her afternoon nap, said she would make tracks back to Beamhurst Court. 'Come back with me!' she said on impulse—her mother would kill her. 'You could stay until after the wedding, and—'

'Your mother would love that!'

'Oh, do come,' Lydie appealed.

'I've got too much to do here,' Alice Gough refused stubbornly.

'You don't—' Lydie broke off. She had been going to say You don't look well. She changed it to, 'You're a little pale, Aunty. Are you sure you're all right?'

'At my age I'm entitled to creak a bit!' And with that Lydie had to be satisfied.

'I'll come over early next Saturday,' she said as her great-aunt came out to her car with her.

'Tell your mother I'll leave my gardening gloves at home,' Alice Gough answered completely po-faced.

Lydie had to laugh. 'Wicked, did I say?' And she drove away.

The nearer she got to Beamhurst Court, though, the more her spirits started to dip. She was worried about her great-aunt, she was worried about the cold war escalating between her parents, and she was worried, quite desperately worried, about where in the world she was going to find fifty-five thousand pounds with which to pay Jonah Marriott.

And, having thought about him—not that he and that wretched money were ever very far from the front of her mind—she could not stop thinking about him—in Paris. She hoped it kept fine for him. That made her laugh at herself—she was getting as sour as her mother.

'Aunty doesn't look so well,' Lydie reported to her mother.

'What's the matter with her?'

'She didn't say, but...'

'She wouldn't! Typical!' Hilary Pearson sniffed. 'Some man called Charles Hillier has been on the phone for you.'

'Charlie. He's Donna's brother. Did he say why he phoned?'

'I told him to ring back.'

Poor Charlie; he was as shy as she had been one time. But while to a large extent she had grown out of her shyness, Charlie never had. He had probably been terrified of her mother. Lydie went up to her room and dialled his number. 'I'm sorry I was out when you rang,' she apologised. She was very fond of Charlie. He was never going to set her world on fire, but she thought of him as a close friend.

'Did I ring your mother at a bad time?' he asked nervously.

'No—she's a little busy. My brother's getting married next Saturday.' Lydie covered the likelihood that her mother had been rude to Charlie if he had been in stammering mode.

'Ah. Right,' he said, and went on to say he had planned to ask her to go to the theatre with him tonight, and had been shaken when he'd rung Donna to hear that she had already left Donna's home. 'You're helping with the wedding, I expect,' he went on. 'Would you have any free time? I've got the tickets and everything. I thought we'd have a meal afterwards and you could stay the night here, if you like. That is… You've probably got something else arranged?' he ended diffidently.

'I'd love to go to the theatre with you,' Lydie accepted. 'Would it put you out if I stayed?'

'Your bed's already made up,' he said happily back, and she could almost see his face beaming.

Lydie went to tell her mother that she was going to the theatre with Charlie Hillier and would not be back until mid-morning the next day.

'You're spending the night with him?'

'He has a flat in London. It could be quite late when we finish. It seems more sensible to stay than to drive home afterwards.'

'You're having an affair with him?' her mother shook her by accusing.

'Mother!' Honestly! Charlie wouldn't know how to go about an affair. Come to think of it, Lydie mused whimsically, neither would she. 'Charlie's just a friend. More like a brother than anything. And nothing more than that.'

Lydie went back upstairs and put a few things into an overnight bag. Charlie had overcome his shyness one time to attempt to kiss her, but had confessed, when they'd both ended up mightily embarrassed, that he had kissed her more because he thought he ought to than anything else. From then on a few ground rules had been established and they had progressed to be good friends who, on the odd, purely spontaneous moment, would sometimes kiss cheeks in greeting or parting. She had stayed at his flat several times with Donna and young Thomas before baby Sofia had come along. But over the last year Lydie had a couple of times comfortably spent the night in his spare bedroom after a late night in London.

The play Charlie took her to was a light-hearted, enjoyable affair. 'Shall we get a drink?' he asked at interval time.

For herself, she wasn't bothered, but felt that Charlie probably wanted one. 'A gin and tonic sounds a good idea,' she accepted, and went with him to mingle with the crowd making their slow way to the bar.

They eventually entered the bar, where she decided to wait to one side while Charlie got the drinks. But Lydie had taken only a step or two when all of a sudden, with her heart giving the oddest little flip, she came face to face with none other than Jonah Marriott!

He stopped dead, his wonderful blue eyes on the riot of colour that flared to her face. 'I thought you were in Paris!' she blurted out, surprised at seeing him so unexpectedly causing the words to rush from her before she could stop them.

'I came back,' he replied smoothly.

She could do without his smart remarks. It was obvious

he had come back! 'I need to see you,' she said tautly—
by no chance did she intend to discuss her business where
they stood. But suddenly she spotted something akin to
devilment in his eyes and knew then that if he answered
with something smart—That's what they all say—she was
going to hit him, regardless of where they were.

He did not say what she expected, but instead drawled,
'Monday, same time, same place,' and they both moved
on.

She felt unnerved, unsettled, and wished it were Monday,
when she would march into his office and demand to know
why he had given her a cheque for fifty-five thousand
pounds! She was glad when Charlie returned with their
drinks.

But Lydie started to feel worse than ever when she
abruptly realised that to demand why of Jonah wasn't relevant. What was relevant was to make some arrangement
with him to pay him back. Her spirits sank—how? With
that question unanswered, she flicked a glance around—her
gaze halting when she spotted Jonah. He was not looking
at her but over in their direction, at the tall manly back of
her dark-haired escort. Her glance slid from Jonah to the
stunning, last word in perfection blonde he was escorting.
And she'd thought her spirits couldn't get any lower!

Not wanting Jonah to catch her looking in his direction,
Lydie tore her eyes away from the sophisticated blonde.
'How's business?' she asked Charlie.

'We've got a new woman at the office—she started a
couple of weeks ago,' he said, and went red.

'Charlie Hillier!' Lydie teased. 'You're smitten.'

He laughed self-consciously, and she smiled affection-
ately at him. 'Well, she is rather nice.'

'Are you going to ask her out?'

He looked horrified. 'Heck, no! I hardly know her!'

Dear Charlie. He had been a frequent visitor to his sister's home, but Lydie had known him a year before they

had begun to graduate from more than an exchanged hello and goodbye.

She did not see Jonah again that night, and had a late supper with Charlie and went to bed. They shared toast and eggs for breakfast, and Lydie drove home to Beamhurst Court with her head on the fidget with thoughts of her great-aunt, her parents and a man who appeared to enjoy escorting sophisticated blondes to the theatre. Had he taken the blonde with him to Paris?

She awoke on Monday in a state of anxiety. 'Couldn't sleep?' her father asked when she went down to an early breakfast.

She didn't know about couldn't sleep—he did not look as if he had slept at all! She looked at his weary face and knew she should tell him that she was going to see Jonah Marriott, but somehow she could not. 'I thought, with Mother wanting Aunt Alice to look smart on Saturday, that I'd better make an effort and get myself a new outfit,' Lydie announced. And, seeing that her father looked about to remind her of a very important phone call they had to make, 'I thought,' she hurried on, 'that while I'm in London I'd call in at the Marriott building and make an appointment for us to see Jonah. He was abroad somewhere last week, so I suppose he's still got a lot of catching up to do and will be too busy to see me today.' She was lying to her father again, and hated doing so, but this, seeing Jonah, she felt most strongly, was something she had to do on her own.

But her father was nobody's fool. 'How did you manage to get an appointment with him last Friday? He would have been catching up then too.'

'On Friday I thought he owed you money. I didn't bother to make an appointment. I just sort of barged my way in.'

Her father looked appalled. 'You...' he began.

'Please, Dad,' she butted in. 'I was wrong. I know it. Which is why I feel I have to do it the right way this time.'

'I can ring from here. He...'

'I know I've embarrassed you by going to see him at all.

But please try to understand—I need to be involved here. I can't let you take over from me.'

Her father grunted. But, muttering something about being determined to see Jonah at the first possible opportunity, he agreed to allow her to make the appointment.

Lydie was walking into the Marriott Electronics head office building when she started to half wish her father was with her. She felt sick, shaky, and she heartily wished this imminent interview were all over and done with.

She rode up in the same lift, walked shakily along the same corridor and turned round the corner without an earthly idea of what she would say to the man. Eating humble pie did not come easy.

Outside his door, she paused to take a deep breath. She knew she was ten minutes earlier than she had been on Friday, but she was too wound up to wait for ten minutes of torturous seconds to tick by.

She put her right hand on the door handle and took a deep breath, and then, tilting her chin a proud fraction, she turned the handle and with her heart pounding went in.

Jonah Marriott was not alone, but was mid-instruction to the woman Lydie had seen step out of the lift last Friday. He looked up and got to his feet to greet her. 'Lydie,' he said and, turning to his PA, introduced them to each other.

'We've spoken on the phone,' Elaine Edwards commented with a smile, and obviously aware of this appointment, even if Lydie was early for it, she picked up her papers, said, 'I'll come back later,' and went through into her own office and closed the door.

'Enjoy the play?' Jonah asked, taking Lydie out of her stride—she had intended to pitch straight in there with some ''The debt is mine but I can't pay''-type dialogue.

'Very much,' she answered, with barely an idea just then what the play had been about.

'Take a seat,' he offered. 'Was that your steady boyfriend?'

'Er—what? No. Um—I see him sometimes,' she replied,

wondering what that had got to do with anything, though she would not have minded asking if the blonde were his steady. Not that she was terribly interested, of course.

She took the seat he indicated and opened her mouth, ready to put this conversation along the lines it was to go, when, 'Coffee?' he asked, and she knew then that she was not the one in charge of how the conversation went—he was. He was playing with her!

'No, thank you,' she refused, her tone perhaps a little less civil than it should be in the circumstances. 'When I came here last Friday I was under the impression you had not honoured the debt you owed my father. I…'

'So I gathered,' Jonah replied, having retaken his seat behind his desk, leaning back to study her.

She did not care to be studied; it rattled her. 'You should have told me!' she flared. 'You *knew* you had repaid that loan!

He smiled—it was a phoney smile. 'I knew I would end up getting the blame.'

Just then guilt, embarrassment, and every other emotion she had experienced since seeing him again last Friday after seven years, all rose up inside her, causing her control to fracture. 'And so you should!' she snapped. 'You set me up!' she accused hotly.

The phoney smile abruptly disappeared. He cared not for her tone; she could tell. '*I* set you up?' he challenged. 'My memory is usually so good, but correct me if I'm wrong— did I ask you to come here, dunning me for money?'

Dunning! Put like that it sounded awful. Her fury all at once fizzled out. 'I *trusted* you,' she said quietly. 'Yet you, the way you hinted that I should pay the cheque into my father's bank straight away, made sure I did just that.'

Jonah Marriott eyed her uncompromisingly. 'Would you rather I had not given you that cheque?' he questioned toughly. 'Would you prefer that your father was still in hock to his bank?'

She blanched. It was becoming more and more clear to

her that Jonah Marriott was much too smart for her. He knew, as she had just accepted, that by taking the money from him she had allowed her father some respite. At least there wasn't a ''For Sale'' notice being posted in their grounds that morning. 'Why did you give me that money?' she asked. 'And why make it pretty certain that I'd bank it first and tell my father afterwards?'

Jonah shrugged. 'Seven years ago your father's faith in me, his generosity, made it possible for me to successfully carry out my ideas. From what you told me on Friday, Wilmot was in a desperate fix with no way out. Without a hope of repaying any financial assistance, I knew there was no way he would accept my help.'

That was true. Lydie sighed. She felt defeated suddenly. 'My father wanted to see you as soon as possible. I said, since I was coming to London today, that I'd make an appointment and that we would both come and see you.'

Jonah eyed her solemnly. 'You lied to him?'

'I'm not proud of it. Until last week, when I told him I was going to see a great-aunt but came here instead, I had never lied to my father in my life.'

Jonah nodded. 'I can see reason for you lying to him about coming here the first time—obviously either your brother or your mother has been bending your ear with falsehoods too—but why lie to your father about coming here today?'

'Because—because he's been a very worried man for long enough. It's time somebody else in the family took some of the load.'

'Namely you?'

'It was I who asked you for that money. I who—er—um—borrowed it, not him. The debt is mine.'

Jonah stared at her for some long moments. 'It's yours?' he queried finally.

'My father didn't ask for the money. Nor would he. As you so rightly said, he wouldn't—not for something he couldn't see his way to pay back.' She broke off and looked into a pair of fantastic blue eyes that now seemed more academically interested than annoyed. 'The debt is mine,' she resumed firmly, 'and no one else's. I've come today to...' her firm tone began to slip '...t-to try and make arrangements to repay you.'

He looked a tinge surprised. 'You have money?' he enquired nicely.

Lydie swallowed down a sudden spurt of ire. Was she likely to have taken money from him had she money of her own? 'I intend to sell my car and my pearls, and there's a small inheritance due in a couple of years that I may be able to get my hands on—but otherwise I have only what I earn.'

'You're working?' he enquired.

He was unnerving her. 'I'm between jobs at the moment,' she answered shortly. 'I was leaving my job this week anyway, but left early when my mother telephoned last Tuesday and—' Lydie broke off and could have groaned out loud. Jonah Marriott was a clever man. From what she had just said he would easily deduce it had been her mother who had told her that he had reneged on his debt to her father.

Jonah did not refer to it, however, but asked instead, 'What sort of work do you normally do?'

'I'm a nanny. I look after children.'

'You enjoy it?'

'Very much. I thought, once Oliver's wedding is out of the way, that I'd look around for something else.'

'In the same line?'

Lydie gave him a slightly exasperated look, and was wondering what his questioning had got to do with her repaying him when it all at once dawned on her it had *everything* to do with it. She was proposing to pay him back fifty-five thousand pounds—out of her earnings. 'Actually—it, the job—it pays quite well,' she offered—rather feebly, she had to admit.

He smiled again, that smile she had no faith in. 'Even

so, I don't know that I want to wait thirty years for you to save up.'

'You can't put the debt at my father's door!' she erupted fiercely, her lovely green eyes at once sparking fire.

He stared at her, unsmiling, for several long moments. 'I have no intention of doing that,' he stated.

'You accept that the debt is mine, and mine alone?'

'You're determined to take the—er—debt on as your own?'

She did not have to think twice about it when she thought of her poor dear father's haggard face, his shoulders bent with worry. 'I am,' she said. 'I'll make arrangements to…'

'You have a plan?'

'No,' she had to confess. 'But I…'

'Don't go selling your car or your jewellery,' Jonah advised, it seeming plain to him, evidently, that she hadn't any idea how to meet her debt.

'I don't know how else to begin to make a start on repaying you.'

Jonah leaned back, studying her as if he liked what he saw. 'Perhaps I can come up with something,' he remarked.

It was her turn to stare at him. 'You'll—think of something?' she queried eagerly.

He afforded her a pleasant look. 'Leave it with me.'

Leave it with him? That was much too vague! She'd been fretting about it all over the weekend. She needed this sorted out now. 'You've no idea now?'

'I'll need to think about it.'

'When will you let me know?' The sooner they had matters arranged, the sooner she could make future plans—perhaps she could find work on her time off. Anything extra would be welcome, the sooner to pay off that colossal debt. 'If you could tell me this week some time?' she hinted. 'I'd—'

'Let's see,' he cut in pleasantly. 'Today's Monday—I should have some idea by, say, Saturday.'

'You'll tell me on Saturday?' she asked urgently. Then

remembered, and cried, 'Oh—I'll be at Oliver's wedding on Saturday!'

That smile she didn't trust a bit was in evidence again. 'I'll see you there,' he informed her.

'You're going to...? You've had an invitation?'

'I'm sure you'll remedy that oversight,' Jonah Marriott answered coolly.

Lydie stared at him in disbelief. 'You want to go to Oliver's wedding?' Why, for goodness' sake, would he want to do that? There was only one way to find out. 'Why do you want to attend?' she questioned suspiciously.

'I like weddings,' he replied without a blink. 'Provided they're someone else's.'

Lydie eyed him hostilely. Why would he want to gate-crash her brother's wedding? She thought of her beloved father, in his own private hell, and her eyes widened. 'You wouldn't embarrass my father?'

Jonah's smile abruptly disappeared. 'I have the greatest respect for your father,' he told her sternly.

She thought she could believe him. But, even so. 'I'd better sign something to the effect that it is I who owe you that money,' she suggested.

Jonah's harsh manner departed. 'I think I can trust you, Lydie,' he said evenly.

She had previously believed she could trust him—and had been set up for her pains. 'It isn't for you. It's for me,' she told him bluntly.

He looked back at her, his chin thrusting just that aggressive fraction forward. '*You* don't trust *me*?' he said coldly. 'You think, after the discussion we've just had, that I'll forget everything we've said, and that I'll send the debt collectors after your father?' Stubbornly she refused to back down. Silently a pair of obstinate clear green eyes stared into a pair of cold blue eyes. Then Jonah Marriott opened a drawer and drew out a sheet of paper. He dropped the paper down in front of her and without another word uncapped his pen and handed it to her.

He hates me, she thought, but was unshakeable in her resolve. That cheque had been made out to her father. She took the pen from Jonah and after a moment's thought wrote.

I, Lydie Pearson, in respect of the fifty-five thousand pounds borrowed from Jonah Marriott and paid into the bank account of Wilmot Pearson, hereby agree that the repayment of that fifty-five thousand pounds is my debt alone.

She read through what she had written and, while she felt lawyers might phrase it a little differently, she believed it said what she wanted it to say: that the debt was nothing to do with her father. Before she signed it, and purely as a courtesy, she turned the paper round so Jonah should read what she had penned.

It did not take him long. Though, when she would have taken the paper back and signed it, he took the pen from her hand and in his strong writing added something. Then, as she had, he turned it round for inspection. 'The fifty-five thousand pounds to be repaid at the direction and discretion of Jonah Marriott,' she read.

Lydie was not very sure of the ground she was on here, but, having stubbornly held out to have something in writing, she did not think she could start nit-picking about any wording now.

Without looking at him, she took the pen from him and signed her name at the bottom, and then added the date. She handed both pen and paper back to him, and watched while he recapped his pen and stood up. He was a busy man; her appointment with him was over.

'I take it you'd like a copy?' he queried.

Since the idea of that piece of paper absolving her father of the debt was her idea, she didn't know how Jonah could ask. In fact, she thought the original should be hers.

She stood up, chin tilted. 'Please,' she answered shortly.

He smiled that smile she was beginning to hate. 'I shall look forward to Saturday,' he said.

With that she had to be content. She would see him on Saturday—now how was she going to wangle him an invitation? And what possible excuse could she use for wanting him there? And what, in creation, was she going to tell her father?

CHAPTER THREE

LYDIE thought and thought all the way home. But she still had not worked out what to tell her father when she was heading up the drive of Beamhurst Court. She wanted to stick as close to the truth as possible, but doubted that her father would be impressed that his near to penniless daughter had claimed his debt as hers. He just would not stand for that.

The first person Lydie met on going indoors was her mother. Oh, grief. Her mother had not seemed very friendly towards Jonah Marriott when she had spoken of him. Lydie just knew she was going to ask quite a few vitriolic questions when Lydie said she wanted him to be invited to Oliver's wedding.

But there was a smile on her mother's face. 'Oliver's home,' she beamed, Oliver was home; all was right with the world. 'Did you leave your shopping in your car?' Shopping? 'Your father said you were going in to London to...'

'Oh, I couldn't see anything I liked.' Heavens, was there no end to the lies she had to tell?

'Nothing?' Her mother looked askance. 'In the whole of London?'

'You know how it is,' Lydie began uncomfortably, but was saved further perjury when Wilmot Pearson emerged from his study. Saved, that was, of lying further—to her mother.

'I'll go and see Mrs Ross about this evening's meal,' Hilary Pearson declared, and Lydie knew that whatever they had been going to have was about to be changed to something Oliver was particularly partial to.

51

In normal times she and her father might have exchanged wry smiles. But these were not normal times, and there was not a smile about either of them as her mother went to see their housekeeper and her father held his study door open—indicating that Lydie join him in there.

He was not interested in how she had fared on her shopping expedition, but as soon as they were in his study and he had closed the door he at once asked, 'When do we see Jonah?'

'We don't,' Lydie answered, but added hurriedly as her father's brow creased, 'I was lucky. I managed to see Jonah today.'

'You've s—'

'He was able to spare me a few minutes out of his busy day.'

'You told him that I wanted to see him?'

'Of course.' She was glad she hadn't had to lie about that.

'So you've made an appointment for me to...'

'Well, not exactly.' Her father was starting to look exasperated with her, and Lydie hurried on. 'He said you mustn't worry.'

'Not worry!' Wilmot Pearson stared incredulously at her, and Lydie rushed in again.

'He said to forget about the money.' What was one more lie?

'Forget it?' her father echoed, and, his pride to the fore, 'That I will not!' he stated vehemently.

'Oh, Dad, please don't...' she said helplessly.

And at her totally wretched tone he calmed down to stare at her. 'What...?' he began. She wriggled, mentally writhed, and knew she should have stayed away from the house until she had some convincing lie worked out. Though, the way things were, she felt it would be some time next week before she could come up with anything halfway convincing to relieve her father of his worry. 'Spit it out, Lydie love,' he coaxed, when she was still stumped.

'It's—difficult,' she said after a struggle.

'What is? I owe Jonah Marriott money and have to see him to discuss it. What's difficult about that?'

'That's just it! I don't want you to see him.'

Wilmot Pearson was a fair and just man. And, in respect of his two offspring, indulgent, and prepared to do everything he could for their health and happiness. Which was perhaps why he tempered what was obvious to him—that, regardless of what his daughter wanted, he and his pride demanded he meet with the man to whom he was in debt—and asked, 'Why don't you want me to see him, Lydie?' Oh, help. She racked her brain, but no good reason would come through. 'Why is it difficult?' he persisted.

'It's—difficult for me.'

'What's difficult for you?' he asked with what she thought was a father's admirable patience.

'Don't—er—don't make things difficult for me, Dad,' she said at last.

'For *you*?' he took up. 'Difficult for you? How?' he questioned. She could feel herself going pink, but it was more from feeling awkward and inadequate that she had no answer for him than anything else. But her father spotted her high colour and, having already noted that she seemed embarrassed to be having this conversation, 'Good Lord!' he exclaimed. 'You're blushing!' And, plainly looking for reasons for her blush, 'Surely—you haven't—fallen for him?' he pondered.

And suddenly, her brain racing, Lydie was ready to grasp at any straw her father gave her. 'Is—is that so astonishing?' she asked, hoping, when she couldn't meet her father's eyes, that he would think her shy of discussing this topic with him.

He thought about it. 'Well, I suppose not,' he to her surprise decided. 'You had a giant-sized crush on him when you were a teenager...'

'You knew about that?' she asked, astounded, at last able

to meet his eyes. But, looking quickly away, she assured him, 'It isn't a crush this time, Dad.'

'Oh, baby,' he said, his own problems for the moment forgotten. 'But you hardly know him! Apart from seven years ago, you've only seen him twice recently.'

'Three times, actually. I saw him at the theatre on Saturday.'

'You went to the theatre with him?' he questioned. 'On *Saturday*, when you knew I wanted to see—'

'It wasn't like that,' she interrupted hurriedly. She didn't want her parent pursuing that track, but hoped he would think her reserve of old had reared its head, causing her to be unable to tell him anything about it either yesterday when she'd come home or at breakfast that morning. 'But anyhow,' she plunged on, grabbing at the fact that her father had taken one look at her mother and that had been that for him, 'how many times did you have to see Mother before you knew it was the real thing?'

With relief, Lydie saw her father had taken everything she said as gospel. They were away from the subject of that money anyway, and she guessed from his expression that he was recalling that his dear Hilary had not returned the compliment and fallen in love with him at first sight. She had taken some wooing, from what Great-aunt Alice had told her.

'And how does Jonah feel about you?' her father asked with a father's natural concern.

'I—it's too early to say,' she answered, winging it, playing it by ear—desperately glad Jonah Marriott wasn't a fly on the wall, listening to all of this. 'B-but he wanted to take me to dinner this coming Saturday.'

'He asked you for another date?' Lydie could feel herself colouring up that she had allowed her father to believe she had dated Jonah last Saturday. 'You didn't come home on Saturday night!' her parent remembered, looking a little shaken. And, while colour scorched her cheeks at that implication, she was thankful for once that hostilities were still prevailing between her parents, otherwise her mother would have told her father that their youngest was having a sleepover at her friend Charlie's.

'I had to tell Jonah that I couldn't have dinner with him because I'm unsure what time Oliver's wedding celebrations will go on until,' Lydie said in an embarrassed rush. 'Er—Jonah asked if he could—er—come to the wedding too.'

Her father looked at her solemnly for a second or two, and then he smiled. 'Well, that sounds as if he's keen enough,' he declared encouragingly. Lydie smiled faintly, very much confused that, purely in her father's interests, she had been able to make up this fantasy. 'You'd better ask your brother to see he gets an invitation.'

Lydie stared at her father. Agreed, she had been in very much of a lather, but it had been that easy? She was staggered. Well, that part of it had gone better than she had anticipated, but, 'And you won't say anything to Jonah? At the wedding, I mean. About the money?'

'It would hardly be appropriate,' he admitted. 'But you must see, Lydie, that I shall have to discuss it with him some time.'

She supposed she had known that. Her father was an honourable man. 'But not now, not until some other time. I think he's away this week,' she lied on the spur of the moment. 'Some conference or other. Abroad somewhere.'

'It will have to wait until next week, then,' her father agreed. But, looking at him, Lydie thought that although he was obviously still very much burdened, he suddenly did not seem to appear so hunched over as he had.

It was good to have Oliver home. He was a bit muddle-headed sometimes, but loveable—either because of or despite that. 'Lydie!' he exclaimed when she and her father left the study and went into the drawing room. 'How's life?' he asked, coming over and giving her a hug.

'Can't complain.' She grinned. 'Looking forward to Saturday?'

'To tell you the truth, I'll be glad when it's all over and Madeline and I can go off and be by ourselves. Such a fuss! I tell you, if it were left to me we'd just nip into a registry office somewhere and do the deed—but Mrs Ward-Watson will have none of it.'

'Of course she won't,' his mother chipped in. 'These things have to be done properly, Oliver. The Ward-Watsons can't have their only daughter sneaking off somewhere as if they've got something to hide.'

Oliver, it appeared, had endured more than one lecture on the subject and did not fancy another, even if it was from his adoring mother. 'Any sign of you trotting up the aisle yet, Lydie?' he asked, more to take the limelight away from himself than anything.

About to say no, that she was more interested in children than grown men, Lydie just then caught her father's glance on her. 'I...' she said, and faltered.

'You've gone red!' Oliver teased.

'Leave her be,' her father cut in. But, instead of making things better for her, succeeded in making her want to fall through the floorboards when he added, 'Though there is someone you could invite to your wedding.' Oliver looked at him, interested; her mother looked at him questioningly. 'Lydie's just started seeing Jonah Marriott. It would be a kindness if Mr and Mrs Ward-Watson sent him a wedding invitation.'

Oh, mercy! Lydie glanced to her mother, who was looking at her in total disbelief. 'How long's this been going on?' she asked sceptically.

'Lydie went to the theatre with him on Saturday,' Wilmot Pearson answered for her.

'I thought you went with Charlie somebody-or-other?' Hilary Pearson challenged her daughter.

'I—er—didn't think you—um—cared for Jonah,' Lydie answered, making out she had been lying then about her theatre date with Charlie, but pink with embarrassment that she was lying now.

'What have you got against Jonah Marriott, Mother?' Oliver chipped in.

'I'm going for a walk,' Lydie said—cowardly, but it saved her telling a whole load more lies—even if she did seem to be getting rather good at it.

Oliver, who was not seeing his fiancée that evening, seemed to spend most of his time on the telephone to her, but he made it to the table at dinnertime and seemed quite blissful.

Lydie was glad he was there. Her mother could not help that he was her favourite and Lydie was perfectly happy that it was so. Particularly that evening when, her mother finding yet more matters to quiz him over, it rather took any inquisitive questions away from Lydie herself.

'Jonah should get his invitation in the post tomorrow, by the way,' Oliver informed her at one point. 'You were still out walking when Madeline rang, but Dad was able to give me his address.'

'Oh, thanks,' she mumbled, glad her father had been able to find Jonah's address. She hadn't a clue where he lived.

Oliver and her parents were going to stay overnight in a hotel near his bride's home on Friday. This so they should not have far to travel the next day. The wedding was not taking place until the afternoon, so Lydie would have plenty of time in which to go and collect her great-aunt Alice. But there were days to be got through before Friday.

Uncomfortable with lies, but seemed called upon to tell them at every turn, Lydie wanted to keep as much out of her parents' way as possible. Which was why, on Tuesday, she did take herself off shopping for a wedding outfit.

She had some very nice outfits in her wardrobe, several of which would have been suitable, and she fretted for an absolute age about spending money she should give to Jonah Marriott. Then she decided that what she would spend would be a drop in the ocean compared with what she owed him. And somehow—and she was sure it had more to do with keeping out of her parents' way than the fact that Jonah would be a guest at the wedding—it seemed a good idea to shop for something new.

She returned to the home she so loved with several large glossy carriers. 'You really have been to town,' her mother quipped when she went in, and was as delighted as Lydie had been at the lovely deep coral suit and its accessories she had purchased.

Oliver was unable to keep away from Madeline the next day, and left early and came home late. But he declared on Thursday that Mrs Ward-Watson had said they could cope very nicely without his assistance from then on—and Madeline, it seemed, had a hundred and ten things she must attend to before the 'big day'.

'Which leaves me having to ask my little sister to come and have a drink with me down at the Black Bull.'

'Since you ask so charmingly,' she accepted. Oliver's present friends were scattered around the country, apparently, but since some of them were converging on the same hotel tomorrow he was having his stag 'do' then—with strict instructions not to get up to anything too outrageous.

'Have you and Madeline decided where to live yet?' Lydie asked when sitting in the Bull with a gin and tonic. Oliver took a swig of his pint.

'Didn't Mother tell you?' He laughed sunnily at the thought that that must be a first. 'Madeline and I are having a place built in the grounds of her parents' home.'

'Will you like that?' Lydie queried slowly, her feelings more and more for her brother, whose life seemed to be being taken over by the Ward-Watsons.

'You bet your life I will,' he declared stoutly. And, misinterpreting her entirely, 'I'd much rather have something new and up to date.'

That shook her more than somewhat. 'You wouldn't rather have something with a bit of history to it?'

'Like Beamhurst?' He shook his head. 'No, thanks! All Dad's ever done is chuck money at the place. It's no wonder he's skint! That place costs a mint to keep in good repair.' And while Lydie stared at him, incredulous that he didn't seem to appreciate that their father was 'skint', as he called it, for no other reason than that he'd had to wade in there and rescue his son from his debts, Oliver went blithely on. 'I told him on Tuesday, when Mother was bleating on about my inheritance, that if my inheritance included the white elephant Beamhurst I'd be just as happy to be left out of the will. Drink up,' he said, 'I'll get you another.'

He left her sitting stunned, and went up to the bar while Lydie tried to accept that just because she loved the old house it did not necessarily mean that Oliver had to. Even if he had been brought up there. By the sound of it, too, Oliver was quite cheerfully unaware that, through the mismanagement of his business, their father was in an extremely severe financial situation. As she had been sublimely unaware of the parlous state of their father's finances, so—incredibly—had her brother been! True, with Oliver getting engaged and wanting to be out of the house and off somewhere with Madeline all the while, it was doubtful that he had been in the house for more than half an hour at a stretch. But...

With her brother so excited and happy, and so looking forward to marrying his Madeline, now did not seem to be a good time to acquaint him with a few pertinent details.

It was a relief to wave goodbye to her parents and brother on Friday morning—a relief to be in the house with just her and Mrs Ross. No need to start getting uptight lest she be called on to evade some truth or other—or even tell a downright lie. And what lies she had told, albeit in the interests of her still very worried-looking father. Those lies had been told ultimately for her mother's peace of mind too.

But Lydie was plagued by the thought that, come Saturday, she was somehow going to have to make it appear that she and Jonah had been 'intimate friends' and that they were well on the way to being 'an item'. Oh, save us!

Then, should she be able to overcome *that* mighty obstacle—without Marriott Esquire being or becoming aware that he had been designated her 'beau'—she had to learn what he had come up with in respect of the fifty-five thousand pounds she owed him. One way and another Lydie could not say that she was looking forward to her brother's wedding all that much.

Saturday dawned bright and beautiful and Lydie decided to go and call for her great-aunt in plenty of time. She was about to leave the house, however, when Charlie Hillier rang. 'I thought you might like to come and have a meal with me,' he said straight away, sounding just a hint not his normal self.

'When were you thinking of?' Lydie asked. He was a friend; she sensed something was troubling him.

'Tonight would be good.'

'Charlie! It's my brother's wedding today! I can't.'

'Sorry, I forgot. Tomorrow, then? Come to dinner.'

Fleetingly she thought of how she was supposed to be dating Jonah Marriott. Could she pretend to her parents that her date tomorrow was with him? Oh, Lord, she was getting herself into all sorts of bother here! 'I'd love to, Charlie,' she said quickly. 'Er—is anything the matter?'

He was silent, and she could almost hear him blushing when, all in a rush, he blurted out, 'That new woman—the one I told you about—Rowena Fox—she's asked me out!'

Poor Charlie, Lydie mused as she drove to her great-aunt's house. He was in one almighty flap. Without a doubt he would not mind at all going out with the unable-to-wait-to-be-asked Rowena, but with astonishing lack of self-confidence just knew something would go wrong if he did—and that Rowena would never stop laughing at him. Charlie was in urgent need of some confidence-bolstering. That, Lydie knew, would be her role tomorrow. Meantime, there was her brother's wedding to attend.

'Will I pass muster with your mother?' Alice Gough

asked, ready and waiting when she answered the door to her great-niece.

'You look terrific!' Lydie beamed, admiring her great-aunt's silk dress and straw hat.

They did not leave straight away, Alice decreeing, 'I've made some sandwiches. We might as well eat them now. The formalities and photographs at these dos take for ever—heaven alone knows when we'll eat again.'

They were at the church in good time, and were ushered into their pew immediately behind Lydie's parents. Lydie smiled encouragingly as her rather strained-looking brother, who was seated in front of her parents with his best man, looked over his shoulder to her. Her mother too had turned in her seat, and Lydie saw her mother give her great-aunt the once-over—and spotted great-aunt Alice doing likewise. Both appeared satisfied, and Lydie and her great-aunt took their seats and awaited the events.

Lydie didn't know how her brother's insides were that morning, but hers were very definitely on the fidget. Why did Jonah Marriott want to come to the wedding anyway? Him and his, 'I like weddings. Provided they're someone else's.' He wasn't remotely interested in this particular wedding. He just wanted to make her sweat, that was all.

She was not too clear why he would want to make her sweat. What was clear to her was that she had never felt so on edge. She hoped he wouldn't come, that he would fail to turn up—and then realised that, should he not come, she would be the one left looking a fool. The things she'd invented to get him an invitation!

Lydie's great-aunt Alice had the seat nearest the aisle so that, being shorter than Lydie, she should have a good view of the wedding procession when it arrived. But Lydie's thoughts were more on Jonah Marriott, and her growing certainty that he would not come. She started to quite hate him—making her look a fool like that. Heaven alone knew what fresh lies she would now have to tell to cover his non-appearance.

Suddenly, though, she became aware that a tall man had strolled up the aisle and was standing at the entrance to their pew. She looked over to him, and her insides somersaulted. She was not sure her heart did not give a little flip too. He had come.

Their eyes met. He looked superb. Tall, immaculately suited, those fantastic blue eyes—not to mention he was extremely good looking—and sophisticated with it. 'Lydie,' he greeted her.

She flicked her gaze from him for a moment, and found her voice. 'Jonah, I don't think you know my great-aunt, Miss Alice Gough. Aunty, Jonah Marriott, a fr-friend of mine.'

'Pleased to know you, Miss Gough.' Jonah pleasantly shook hands with her and then moved into the pew to go in front of Lydie and take a seat beside her. Whereupon he bent close to her ear, and asked, 'Where's the boyfriend?'

Oh, help! All at once it struck Lydie like a bolt from the blue that, somehow or other, for today's purposes, she was going to have to tell Jonah that *he* was her boyfriend! Oh, heavens. Yet she just couldn't have him mingling with her family and referring to someone else as her boyfriend.

'Er...' she began, but was so overwhelmingly conscious of him sitting so close to her, and of what she must say to him, that she could get no further.

'Er?' he prompted—and her newly discovered thumping tendency was on the march again.

She would have liked to move her head away from the close proximity with his, but she could not afford to have anyone else hear what she had to say. 'I—um—need to talk to you—rather urgently—on that subject,' she said in a low voice.

'Shall we go outside?' he asked blandly, obviously picking up that she did not wish to be overheard.

She gave him a speaking look—she really was going to thump him before this wedding was over. 'For the purposes of today, and until I can explain,' she said through gritted teeth, '*you* are my boyfriend.'

His head came closer, and to her amazement he brushed aside her night-dark hair and planted a kiss on her cheek. 'Forgive me, darling,' he murmured, 'I forgot to do that when we said Hello.'

Thump him? She'd like to throttle him! Her insides were having a fine old time within her. He was playing with her; she knew that he was. And, having designated him her boyfriend, there was not one darn thing she could do about it!

She moved her head out of range, and gave him an icy look. He smiled. Lydie gave her attention to the printed Order of Service they had each been handed. 'Do you know these hymns, Aunty?' She concentrated on her great-aunt instead.

'Backwards,' her great-aunt replied. 'Is it serious?'

'What?'

'You and your man?'

Oh, grief. Lydie found she had the utmost trouble in lying to her great-aunt. 'I'm working on it.' She played for safety, saw and heard Alice Gough smile and then actually giggle, then the strains of Richard Wagner hit the air, and everyone got to their feet.

The ceremony was lovely. The bride looked radiant, and Lydie felt a lump in her throat as she witnessed her only brother being married. She saw her mother trying to be surreptitious as she reached for her handkerchief, and Lydie felt choked again when she spotted her father take a comforting hold of her mother's hand. Her father might have been very out of sorts with her mother all this week, with verbal communication between them at a minimum, but that did not mean they did not still care deeply for each other.

As they had always been going to have to—provided Jonah turned up, that was—he and her father met up with each other as they mingled outside of the church. 'How are you, Wilmot?' Jonah at once greeted her father, extending his hand.

Her father shook hands with him. 'I'm in your debt, Jonah. I think we should meet.'

Jonah nodded, his eyes on the man who had been a stone heavier and a lot healthier-looking the last time he had seen him—three years ago. 'May I call you?' Jonah asked.

'If you would.' And, turning to his wife who had appeared at his elbow, 'You remember Jonah?'

'Isn't it a perfect day?' Lydie's mother commented, evidently still uncertain whether to like her daughter's escort or not.

Jonah smiled politely, and looked at Lydie, 'Quite perfect,' he replied to her mother.

There was no time then, or for some while, in which Lydie could explain to him why she had let her family believe that she and he were dating. But while Jonah was undoubtedly waiting, and she did not lose sight of the fact that she had some explaining to do, Lydie noticed that her great-aunt had started to wilt, and her great-aunt became her first priority.

The wedding reception was being held at the bride's home, Alcombe Hall. But when Lydie and her great-aunt started to walk the quite some distance to where Lydie had been able to park her car, Jonah took charge and offered, 'My car's right here, Miss Gough.' And, before Lydie could say a word, he had opened up the passenger door and was helping Alice Gough in. Then Jonah was turning to the slightly stunned Lydie, his expression bland, but something indefinable lurking in his eyes. 'See you shortly, dear,' he said, and Lydie knew then that if he made the smallest attempt to kiss her cheek in parting she was definitely going to thump him.

She took a step away. He got the message and he drove off, and Lydie mutinied like crazy. First of all Marriott had arrived at the church *after* her, yet had still somehow found a favoured parking spot, and secondly that was *her* great-aunt he had just gone off with, not his.

By the time she had reached her car, though, Lydie was starting to wonder what in thunder was the matter with her. She should be grateful to him that, whether or not he too had spotted her great-aunt's look of weariness, he had saved her the need to walk quite some way. Lydie recalled how Jonah had said he had the greatest respect for her father. That had been evident in the manner in which he had spoken to him—and she *was* grateful to him for that.

So, it appeared that there was nothing the matter with Jonah other than that he was enjoying himself hugely at her expense—she could still feel the imprint of his mouth against her cheek. And why wouldn't he enjoy himself at her expense? He might have asked to be invited to this wedding, but he hadn't asked to be nominated her boy-friend. Which then brought what was the matter with her down purely to nerves. Fact one, she found him extremely unsettling. Fact two, she owed him all that money. Fact three, she hadn't even got a job yet, and any time now he was going to tell her his idea for how she should begin to pay him back.

Lydie pinned a smile on her face on arriving at Alcombe Hall. She joined Jonah and her great-aunt, who appeared to be getting on famously, and who had waited for her before tagging on to the procession waiting to shake hands and congratulate the bride and groom.

After which Jonah found a chair for her aunt and, with waiters hovering, accepted refreshment for the three of them. With everyone in happy spirits time went by, with more photographs—a good number having been taken at the church—and guests chatting and renewing old acquaintances until it was time for the meal and the speeches. But at no time did it seem the right time for Lydie to have a private conversation with the man who was, whether he liked it or not, her man-friend in particular that day.

Jonah had been placed in between Lydie and her great-aunt at the meal table, and Lydie had to give him top marks that he saw to it that her great-aunt was not neglected. He was attentive to her too, pleasant and affable, but it was still just not the place in which for them to discuss what they had to discuss.

Nor was there any space later, when the meal was at an end and all the speeches over and the guests started to move about. Because by then Lydie was thinking in terms of getting her great-aunt Alice home. She knew the dear love had enjoyed the wedding, but sensed she had had enough. And was certain of it when modern music started issuing forth from one of the rooms and her great-aunt visibly winced.

'You look worried?'

Lydie looked up to see Jonah addressing her. 'I think I should take Aunt Alice home, but...' She didn't have to finish.

He nodded understandingly. 'I'll come to your car with you when you're ready.'

Lydie supposed the drive of Alcombe Hall was as good a place as any on which to have their discussion. But it took them some while in which to say their courtesy fare-wells.

By then all Lydie could think of was that her great-aunt seemed to sorely be in need of rest and quiet. 'Take my arm, Miss Gough,' Jonah suggested when at last they were out on the drive. 'This gravel path is very uneven in places.'

'I'll go and bring the car up, you stay there,' Lydie attempted, but Alice Gough would not hear of it. They went very slowly to Lydie's car, and Lydie could not help but notice how heavily Aunt Alice leaned on Jonah. 'You'll stay and enjoy the rest of the—er—festivities?' Lydie asked him, for something to say as they progressed to her car. 'You—um—said you liked weddings,' she reminded him.

She looked across at him. His answer was to grin—and something happened in her heart region. Lydie did not speak to him again until they had safely assisted her great-aunt into the front passenger seat and, on their way to the driver's door, had walked to the rear of the car. And there Lydie halted. Jonah halted with her.

'I'm—sorry about you having to pretend to be my boyfriend today.' Having got started, she apologised in a rush.

'What was all that about?' he asked solemnly, and she was glad he was taking her seriously.

'Even now I'm not sure quite how it came about,' she confessed. 'When I got home, after seeing you on Monday, I had to own up to my father that I'd seen you and that you'd said he wasn't to worry about the money. That you'd said he was to forget about it. I know, I know—I lied again,' she inserted hurriedly. 'But my father's a very worried man, and he's hurting badly over this.'

'Hurting?' Jonah repeated. 'I'm sorry to hear that.'

'Anyhow,' she rushed on, 'he was adamant he would *not* forget about it, and, I don't quite know how, but he was insisting on seeing you—he still is—and I was saying something about it being difficult, that... Well, you know and I know that the debt is mine—' She broke off to take a look inside the car and with relief saw that here greataunt was not fidgeting to go home but had nodded off to sleep. 'Anyhow, I said something to the effect that I didn't want him to see you.'

'And he, naturally, wanted to know why?'

She nodded. 'He insisted on knowing why. I again said it was difficult.'

'You were floundering.'

'I'm new to this telling lies business.'

'You seem to be doing exceedingly well at it.'

She did not thank him for that comment, and said in a rush, 'I was getting very hot under the collar by this time. Dad—um—noticed my warm colour and was certain I was blushing because... Well, he seemed to think I...' she faltered '...that I had fallen for you.' She was feeling very hot under the collar again by this time. 'Well, to be honest, I rather led him to think that,' she felt she had to confess.

She had no intention of telling this sophisticated man of her father's comments about the crush she'd used to have on him. 'Well, what with one thing and another,' she rushed on, 'and I wasn't thinking, just working on instinct, I kind of gave my father the impression that I was seeing you— backed up by the fact you wanted to come to Oliver's wedding. He—um—seemed to think that made you—um—a bit keen on me,' she ended, her voice tailing off lamely.

'You *do* appreciate that I'm not in the running to be anyone's "steady"?' Jonah asked gravely.

'Don't flatter yourself!' she snapped pithily, up in arms in a second.

He smiled that insincere smile, and her right hand itched. 'Having established that fact,' he commented, 'there seems little more to say.'

'Just a minute!' She halted him when she thought he might be thinking of walking away. 'We were going to discuss what you'd been able to think of in terms of me paying you that money back.'

'You want me to tell you now, how—?'

'Please,' she interrupted; she had waited nearly a week to hear. 'My own idea is to get a couple of jobs and make regular payments…'

'What sort of work were you thinking of?'

'Anything I can find. Nannying during the day, night-time too if I can find something. But, generally, I'm prepared to do anything.'

He eyed her steadily. 'Anything?' he questioned. 'You said anything?'

Of course, anything. He had saved her parents from having to move out from Beamhurst Court. 'Anything,' she agreed. But added quickly, 'Anything legal, that is.'

His mouth picked up at the corners—involuntarily, she rather thought. But he sobered, and asked, 'How old are you?'

She was sure he knew how old she was, but answered, 'Twenty-three. Why?'

He shrugged. 'Just making sure that anything I propose is quite legal—amongst consenting adults.'

She stared at him. 'I'm not too sure I like the sound of this,' she told him cuttingly.

He seemed amused, and she added awaking shin-kicking tendencies to her head-thumping tendency list. He looked from her to bend and look into the car, where her great-aunt, Lydie saw as she followed suit, was starting to stir from her doze. 'You know where I live,' Jonah began as he straightened up.

'I don't, actually,' Lydie told him.

Jonah took out his wallet and extracted his card, and handed it to her. 'You'd better come and see me tomorrow—at my London apartment.'

'Tomorrow? Sunday? At your home?'

'Yes to all three,' he replied, and she knew he was playing with her again.

'But I thought we were going to get something settled today.'

'Don't you think it would be kinder if you took your great-aunt home?'

He was right, of course, but it annoyed Lydie that he was presuming to tell her how to look after her great-aunt, even if he *was* right. Lydie looked at his card and saw that he had an address in London and he also had a house—Yourk House, to be precise—in Hertfordshire.

But she wanted this settled and done now. 'I can come and see you tonight?' she offered.

'Hmm, that might interfere with my plans for this evening,' Jonah answered pleasantly.

'Tomorrow will be fine,' Lydie said quickly, a funny sensation hitting her stomach that he was obviously seeing some elegant blonde at any time now. 'What time?' she asked. 'I can be with you just after breakfast.'

'I like to have a lie in on Sundays,' Jonah replied nicely. She'd like to bet he did! 'Let's see,' he contemplated. 'Come early evening.'

She was having dinner with Charlie tomorrow. 'I have a date tomorrow,' she was pleased to let him know.

'Really, Lydie! Two-timing me so soon?' he mocked.

She supposed she had earned that—he hadn't asked to be designated her boyfriend that day. But she waited. Though, when he did not suggest another time, she realised that he clearly expected her to cancel her date. 'What time early evening?' she capitulated.

'Shall we say—seven?'

'Seven,' she agreed, and turned from him.

He was there at the driver's door before her to—sardonically, she thought—open her car door for her. He wished her now awake great-aunt a pleasant journey home, and took a step back.

He had not closed the door, however, when Alice Gough's voice floated clearly on the air. 'What a very nice man, Lydie. He'll make some girl a wonderful husband.'

Suddenly speechless, Lydie looked from her great-aunt to where Jonah was standing with a look of mock horror on his face. Looking straight up at him, Lydie was glad to find her voice. 'Thank heaven it won't be me!' she tossed at him, and, slamming the door shut, she put her foot down and got out of there.

CHAPTER FOUR

WITH her great-aunt cat-napping for most of the way to Penleigh Corbett Lydie had plenty of space in which to reflect on the day. Though it was not thoughts of her brother and his lovely bride which occupied the major part of Lydie's mind, but Jonah Marriott.

Why he had wanted to come to the wedding was as much a mystery to her as ever. But come he had and, she had to admit, he had done nothing to let her down. Though that didn't alter the fact that she still had that sword of fifty-five thousand pounds dangling over her head. Heaven alone knew what Jonah would come up with—and would he be prepared to wait while she earned enough to pay him back?

Lydie drove at a sedate pace and it was a little after seven when they reached her great-aunt's home. Lydie went indoors with her, and was concerned enough about her great-aunt's lack of colour to suggest she wouldn't mind keeping her company overnight.

'That *would* be nice!' Alice Gough exclaimed. 'I don't see nearly enough of you, Lydie.'

Feeling a touch guilty that, for all she wrote regularly to her great-aunt, she could have visited her more often than she had, Lydie made a mental note that, no matter in which part of the country she would end up working, she would make all efforts to visit her more frequently.

They discussed the day's events, with Alice Gough asking, 'When are you seeing Jonah again?'

'Tomorrow,' Lydie answered truthfully, and her aunt smiled serenely.

'I think you'll do very well together,' she commented.

Lydie opened her mouth to state that there was nothing

serious between her and Jonah Marriott, but her great-aunt was looking ready to doze again, and Lydie thought it might be a better idea to talk in terms of going to bed.

Aunt Alice decided she had eaten enough that day to last her a week and required nothing more than a warm drink. She insisted on making it herself, but did allow Lydie to make up her own bed. Eventually Lydie said goodnight to her but, not ready for sleep, she stayed downstairs.

Lydie pottered about, tidying up the kitchen and idly thinking of how her parents had decided to stay an extra night at their hotel. Out of consideration for their housekeeper, who was expecting her to return, Lydie got out her mobile phone and rang Mrs Ross to say she would not be home until tomorrow.

Next Lydie sat down to think about her meeting with Jonah the next evening. She was seeing him at seven, but owned she was feeling more than a shade uneasy about that meeting. Nor was she too thrilled either that, when he full well knew she had a date tomorrow night, the arrogant devil, without thinking about it, expected her to cancel it!

Well, she jolly well wouldn't cancel it, she thought mutinously. Surely the business they were to discuss—her repaying that colossal sum of money he had given her—would not take all evening? To her way of thinking, their meeting should be all over and done with by seven-thirty.

Then Lydie remembered the effortless way Jonah had of sparking her to annoyance, and of generally upsetting her. If the same thing happened in their half-hour discussion tomorrow, would she feel at all like leaving his apartment and going on to Charlie's? Charlie wanted dinner and sympathy over his problem with the forward Rowena Fox. Lydie understood his excruciating shyness. She had suffered similarly—still did hit a wall of shyness occasionally—but in the main had outgrown the affliction. So, while she had every sympathy with Charlie, and the shyness he unluckily had never outgrown, she could not help but ponder if, after a half-hour business session with Jonah—whom she suspected was a tough business negotiator—she would feel up to the task of boosting up Charlie's basement-level confidence.

Another five minutes of tugging at it and she picked up her phone. 'I can't make tomorrow after all, Charlie,' she told him straight away.

'Ooh, Lydie!' he wailed. 'What am I going to tell Rowena on Monday?'

'Do you want to go out with her?'

'Well, yes, I suppose I do. But—'

'But nothing, Charlie. Has she, Rowena, been out with any of your colleagues?'

'Not that I know of. Several have asked her, but so far as I know she turned them down.'

'So what does that tell you?'

Charlie thought for some seconds. 'I don't know,' he said at last.

Lydie had to smile. Charlie was older than her, but she felt like some agony aunt. 'It tells you she likes you.'

'But I'm tongue-tied when she's around—awkward; especially with women.'

'Which is precisely why she wants to go out with you and none of the others.'

'Why?' He didn't get it.

'Well, I'm only guessing here, but I'd say she has probably had enough of over-confident—um—perhaps pushy types. Maybe she feels more comfortable with someone who isn't wise-cracking all the time.'

'Do you think so?' Charlie asked in wonder.

Lydie had no real idea, but now wasn't the time, in this exercise of building up his self-esteem, to admit it. 'You've known Rowena for three weeks now. Rowena has known you for those same three weeks. Do you think she would have asked you out, in preference to any of the others, if she was not a little taken by your non-pushy manner?'

He thought about it for a little while. 'Shall I go, then, do you think?' he asked.

Dear Charlie. He had already agreed that he wanted to go out with Rowena. 'I think you should,' she assured him.

There was a pause while Charlie thought about it. 'Do you—do you think I shall have to kiss her?'

Oh, Charlie! 'You're twenty-eight, Charlie Hillier,' Lydie told him severely. 'And I am not your mother.'

He laughed, and they said goodbye the best of friends. To Lydie's way of thinking, with Rowena in charge of this date, she would let him know if she was expecting to be kissed. All he had to do was just be his loveable shy self.

Lydie was pleased to see on Sunday morning that after a good night's rest her great-aunt was looking so much better. With nothing pressing to get home for, Lydie stayed with her until after lunch, and then made her way back to Beamhurst Court.

With the time coming ever nearer when she must get ready to go to Jonah Marriott's apartment, a familiar churned-up feeling started to make its presence known. Lydie went upstairs to shower and to think what to wear. She had spent a little time last night in trying to build up Charlie's confidence—she wished someone would come and build up hers.

She was under the shower, so did not know that her parents had returned home until, dressed in a pale green trouser suit, her raven hair loose about her shoulders, Lydie went downstairs and heard sound coming from the drawing room.

With her shoulder bag in one arm, car keys in hand, she opened the door to find her parents relaxing there. 'Just off out?' her father asked with a smile for her.

'I'm going to see Jonah,' she answered.

'I wonder you bothered to come home,' her mother chipped in slightly acidly, and, as Lydie looked questioningly, 'Mrs Ross said you didn't come home last night.'

'I didn't think Aunt Alice looked too well,' Lydie explained.

'She looked all right from what I could see!'

'She seems to tire very easily,' Lydie explained.

'What do you expect?' Hilary Pearson demanded. 'She's eighty-one!'

Eighty-four, Mother! 'You didn't think she looked a little pale?'

'We're all a little pale. And likely to remain so,' her mother went on sniffily, with a baleful look to her husband, 'until this whole sorry mess is resolved.'

Lydie glanced over to her father, who was looking pained and tight-lipped. She felt that her mother could be kinder to him, but knew she could not interfere. Now seemed as good a time as any to be on her way. 'I'll see you later,' she said, adopting a cheerful tone.

'Would that be tonight or tomorrow morning?' her mother asked sourly.

And, while Lydie thought her mother meant that by the time she got in that night her parents would be in bed, her father was saying, *'Hilary!'* in his newly found cross manner, causing Lydie to realise her mother was assuming that her daughter might spend the whole night with Jonah Marriott. Without another word Lydie left them and went out to her car.

She was driving out through the gates of Beamhurst Court before it all at once struck her what had brought on her mother's rancid comment. Her mother had not associated her non-return home last night with Aunt Alice, but had associated it with Lydie first dropping off Aunt Alice and then going to stay overnight at Jonah's apartment! Mrs Ross must obviously have commented to her that, with all of them being away, she'd had the house to herself last night. Her mother had, Lydie could see now, put two and two together—and had got her sums wrong. Lydie thought she had as good as told her mother that she hadn't come home last night because, concerned for Aunt Alice, she had stayed the night with her. Jonah, Lydie realised, had probably not gone back inside Alcombe Hall after seeing her and her great-aunt to her car.

Lydie groaned, the words 'tangled web' and 'deceive' floating about in her head. She began to wonder what she had started. Though, in fairness to herself, knew that she would never have gone to see Jonah in the first place if her mother hadn't misled her the way she so dreadfully had. But as her thoughts drifted on to her father, and how he was hurting inside, Lydie knew that, whatever it cost, she could not regret any of what she had done.

Her insides were in turmoil when she arrived at the smart building where Jonah had his apartment. She approached the security desk—and was expected. In no time, tummy butterflies turning into vampire bats, Lydie found herself at his door.

Almost as soon as she had rung the bell, Jonah opened the door. 'Come in, Lydie,' he greeted her, his glance flicking over her long-legged shape in her trouser suit, her long dark hair and green eyes. 'I should have known you wouldn't be bridesmaid.'

His comment took her totally out of her stride. 'W-why?' she asked, to her own ears sounding as witless as she suddenly felt. He was casually dressed—and dynamite with it!

'You're much too beautiful,' he replied as they ambled into his drawing room. 'No bride would want such competition.'

'It strikes me you know too much about women,' Lydie replied, some of her wits returning. Did he really think her beautiful?

'Alas, true,' he sighed. 'Can I get you a drink?'

'No, thank you,' Lydie replied primly. She wanted to keep a clear sharp head here. There would be figures to discuss and, she owned, she was not much of a business woman.

'You'll take a seat, I hope?' he invited urbanely.

Lydie glanced around the gracious room with its sofas, its luxurious carpeting, its pictures. She walked over to a high-backed chair and sat down. 'This probably won't take long,' she began. It was as far as she got.

'You're anxious to keep your date?' Jonah asked, not sounding too pleased about it—as though he would be the one to decide how long it would take.

'Actually, no,' she replied coolly—outwardly cool, at any rate. Already she could feel herself starting to boil. 'I cancelled—in your honour,' she added sarcastically.

Water off a duck's... 'You enjoyed the wedding?'

Lydie stared at him, almost asked what that had to do with why she was there—but abruptly realised that Marriott was in charge here, and there wasn't a thing she could do about it.

'Very much,' she replied with what control she could find. 'You?' she asked sweetly. 'You have a penchant for other people's weddings, I believe.'

She thought the corners of his mouth tweaked a little—as though she had amused him. But he did not smile and she knew herself mistaken. 'Have you been in touch with your aunt this morning?' he asked solemnly.

'Aunt Alice was a little tired yesterday, but she looked more her old self this morning,' Lydie informed him.

'You've seen her?' The man missed nothing. 'You went over to see her? She told me she lives in Oxfordshire.'

'It's not so far away. Though I didn't have to travel; I stayed overnight with her.'

Jonah stared at her, but she had no idea what she expected him to say, and experienced familiar thumping tendencies when he remarked, 'You've gone a fetching shade of pink, Lydie.' And accused, 'Now, what guilty secret are you hiding?'

'I'm not guilty about anything!' she denied—thank you, Mother! But when he just sat there waiting, she somehow—and she blamed him for it—found she was blurting out, 'My m-mother got hold of the wrong end, and instead of her two and two adding up to her believing I stayed the night at Aunt Alice's, as I intended, she seems to think I—er—spent it with you some...' Her voice tailed off. But, feeling extremely warm suddenly, she knew her hopes that having had his explanation he would leave it there were doomed to failure.

'And why would your mother think that?' he determined to know.

'I hate men with enquiring minds!' she erupted.

'Which probably means you're in the cart here, little Lydie,' he commented pleasantly. But insisted, 'Why?'

Lydie gave him a huffy look. 'I'm not here to discuss that!' she told him—a touch arrogantly, she had to admit.

Little good did it do her! He just waited. And she saw that if she wanted to get down to talking facts and figures, which she did, then the sooner she told him, the sooner they would get down to the nitty-gritty of how much per month he would expect from her salary.

She sighed heavily, but realised there was nothing for it but to make a full confession. 'If you *must* know,' she started, gone from merely feeling warm to roasting, 'I stayed over with Charlie the previous Saturday…'

'Charlie?' he interrupted. 'Charlotte?'

Lydie gave him a peeved look. 'Charlie—Charles.'

'You're saying you—slept over—at his place?' Jonah asked, his expression grim suddenly. 'He was the man you were at the theatre with?'

Lydie nodded. 'I do sometimes stay when—'

'Spare me the gory details!' Jonah cut in harshly. And reminded her, 'You were telling me why your mother should think I—entertained—you here last night.'

Entertained! That was a new name for it. He was not smiling. 'Well…' she began, and did not want to go on, but knew, blast him, that she had to. 'Well, you know most of it,' she suddenly exploded. 'It was after…when I got home last Monday, after seeing you in your office. Dad seemed to get the impression that you and I were an item…'

'An impression which you gave him.'

'Oh, shut up!' Lydie snapped, irritated. 'Anyhow, Dad seemed to think I'd fallen for you…'

'Because, for some obscure reason, that is what you let him believe.'

'If you don't stop interrupting I shall never get this out!'

'I won't say another word.'

Lydie borrowed one of her mother's sour looks and bestowed it on him. He did not so much as flinch—she'd have to get more practice. 'Anyhow, my father said something about me hardly knowing you, and how I'd only seen you twice recently, and I said it was three times, that I'd seen you at the theatre on Saturday. People are always misinterpreting me!' Lydie shrugged, feeling totally fed up by then. 'Anyway, Dad suddenly remembered how I hadn't come home on Saturday night—and there you have it.'

'He believes you spent the night with me?' Jonah asked, amazed.

Never had she felt more uncomfortable. 'Yes,' she mumbled, but went quickly on, 'After that, getting you a wedding invite was small beer.' She did not like the fact that, having come to an end, all Jonah did was stare at her long and hard. 'So there it is!' she fumed. 'And perhaps now we can get down to the details of how I'm going to repay my debt to you.' Her voice softened. 'I don't mean to sound ungrateful, Jonah. I am grateful to you; I really am. It's just that everything's been a bit nightmarish recently, and I've been called upon to tell lies which less than two weeks ago I wouldn't have dreamed of uttering.'

Jonah's harsh look all at once seemed to soften. 'Poor Lydie,' he murmured, and, relenting, he smiled a smile that rocked her, then said, 'Let's make a pact to always be truthful with each other.'

'I'd like that—I think. Even if it's—er—embarrassing?'

'Even if,' he stated.

'Fine,' she said, 'I agree.'

'So, for a start, you'd better dump Charlie.'

'Dump Charlie?' she exclaimed incredulously. 'Charlie's my friend!' she protested.

'Dump him!' Jonah instructed, his manner totally unyielding.

'Why?'

Jonah did not look as if he would answer, but after some cold seconds replied, 'All this is about money paid into your father's bank account—with no conditions on my part. You have created conditions in order to save your father more embarrassment. And I understand that. But, since you have claimed me to your family as your boyfriend and— not to be too impolite—your overnight lover—' as if he cared about being impolite, she fumed '—what you must understand is that I can't have you running around town staying overnight with some other man.' And, having succinctly explained that, he ended heavily, 'So, dump him.'

She could have told him that Charlie was not her friend in the boyfriend sense—but, hang it all, a girl had to have some pride. 'Do I go around telling you to dump your women-friends?' she protested instead.

'You're in no position to tell me to do anything,' Jonah replied bluntly, and, as the truth of that hit home, the fire went out of her. That was until, his tone more giving, he added, 'But, since I must be fair over this, I have to tell you I don't have any women-friends.'

'Much!' Lydie erupted. 'That was a mirage I saw you with at the theatre the other Saturday, was it?'

'I don't usually go around explaining myself, but with our total honesty clause established I don't mind telling you that my theatre date with Freya was one made before you claimed me.'

Lydie gave him a hostile look, but, as she recalled the stunning blonde, she found her curiosity needed to be satisfied. 'You won't be seeing her again?' she asked, then realised that sounded much too personal and as if she was interested, and added hurriedly, 'Not that it's any of my business.'

'True,' Jonah agreed, 'it isn't.' But went on to confide, 'I'm a bit jaded with the hunt, if you'd like more truth.'

Her eyes widened. 'You've given up women?'

His lip twitched. 'That wasn't what I said,' he corrected her. Then proceeded to send her rigid with shock, by continuing, 'From what you've said, it doesn't sound as if your parents will be too upset should you spend next weekend with me.'

First Lydie went scarlet, and then pale. Then realised that he could not possibly be suggesting what she thought he was suggesting. 'Er…' she mumbled, but found she was stumped to say more.

Jonah smiled—that insincere smile that she hated. 'I'm going to Yourk House, my home in Hertfordshire, next Friday evening. You can come with me,' he decided.

Lydie stared at him, a drumming in her ears. 'W-what for?' she found the breath to ask.

That insincere smile became a twisted grin. 'Use your imagination, Lydie,' he suggested charmingly.

This wasn't happening to her! It couldn't be happening to her! This sort of thing didn't happen to her! She strove valiantly to *block* her imagination. 'I'm not much of a cook,' she managed.

'You won't be spending much time in the kitchen,' Jonah assured her pleasantly. And when, dying a thousand deaths, she just stared at him, 'Oh, by the way,' he said, getting up and going over to an antique desk where he collected up a piece of paper, 'your copy of the agreement we made,' he informed her nicely, and, coming back, handed it to her.

Lydie took it from him and with a thundering heart read the part written in his hand—''The fifty-five thousand pounds to be repaid at the direction and discretion of Jonah Marriott'. She swallowed hard, and could remain seated no longer. 'This is how I'm to repay you?' she charged, looking him straight in the eye. 'By being your pl…?' She faltered. 'By becoming your plaything?'

'Plaything?' His innocent expression did not fool her for one minute. 'For fifty-five thousand you'd be a pretty expensive plaything, wouldn't you agree?'

'What, then?' she demanded.

'Let's say that, ponder on the problem though I have—and I have to confess I'm not too enamoured of the idea of you working night and day nannying to—um—clear accounts—I have been unable, as yet, to come up with anything.'

'You think my going away with you this weekend might give you some ideas?' As soon as the words were out she blushed.

'Oh, yes,' he answered, his mouth picking up at the corners, his eyes on her crimson face. 'You could say that.'

He was teasing her, tormenting her—and he held all the high cards, and she didn't like it. But she had had his money, and her father was one very worried man.

'Why?' she challenged. 'Why do I have to come with you?'

'Why not?' he answered. 'As of now you no longer have a boyfriend—presumably your ex-boyfriend knows none of your financial business…?'

'Of course not!' she butted in. 'As if I'd tell anyone of the fix my father was in!'

'So what else would you do with your weekend?'

'Begin looking for a job for a start!'

'Don't do that. Not just yet. Let's get all this settled first. You'll feel much better about everything once we've had chance to fully probe into the whys, wherefores and all the possibilities of all this.'

'You're trying to tell me that to investigate possible areas, ways of my repaying you, is what this coming weekend is all about? And don't forget we have a "complete honesty" clause,' she reminded him.

'Would I lie to you, Lydie?' he asked smoothly. And she knew that was as far as she was going to get, particularly when he said, 'I'll finish work early on Friday, and call for you around six.'

'That won't be necessary, I have the address!' she exclaimed quickly, and saw him hide a smirk that, from what she had just said, she had agreed to spend the weekend with him.

'I'll drive you...' he began, but she was shaking her head.

'Sorry to be blunt, Jonah,' she butted in, while wondering why on earth she was apologising, 'but I would much prefer that you kept far away from my home.'

She had thought he might be offended, but he was more understanding than offended when he quietly replied, 'I saw for myself how drawn your father is, how he's suffering in all of this, Lydie, but I shall have to see him, talk to him some time.'

She felt awkward. She did not like Jonah's suggestion for the weekend any more now than she had ten minutes ago, but the great respect Jonah had for her father was there for her to see, and—mentally anyway—she had to thank him for it.

'I know,' she agreed. 'But not just yet. Not until we've got something worked out.'

He accepted that, or appeared to. 'Until Friday,' he said. She moved to the door, their meeting over. He walked with her. She looked at him as he opened the door for her to go through. Wonderful blue eyes met hers full on, and her heart seemed to go into overdrive. Then he grinned, a grin full of devilment. 'Try not to fret, Lydie,' he bade her. 'Who knows? You might have a fun weekend.'

'Did I tell you the one about flying pigs?' she snapped, and went quickly from him.

Her thoughts were intensely agitated on her drive home. She remembered thinking on the outward drive about how her father was hurting inside, and how she knew that, whatever it cost, she could not regret any of what she had done. That thought haunted her all the way back to Beamhurst Court—she'd had no idea then just how much it was going to cost. She was spending the weekend with Jonah at his home in Hertfordshire—he was not expecting her to cook.

Lydie was still in mental torment when she awakened on

Monday morning. She swung first one way and then the other. Perhaps Jonah did not have in mind what she thought he had in mind. Wishful thinking? He had never made a pass at her, had he? And apart from shaking hands and giving her that kiss on the cheek in church on Saturday— and she rather thought she had asked for that, telling him he was her boyfriend—he had never touched her. Certainly he had not given her the smallest hint that he might be thinking in terms of her being his bed companion.

Oh, grief! Even thinking about it made her go hot all over. By the sound of it Jonah had wearied of the chase, but it had to be faced—he was still one all very virile male. And, while she had no evidence that he even fancied her— and surely she would have picked up some clue somewhere along the line—was she so naïve as to believe that this weekend had nothing to do with—bed?

Oh, heavens, she was having kittens just thinking about it, and found that the only way she could cope was by trying to believe that nothing of a sexual nature was going to take place between them that weekend. Jonah had said that, in the absence of him being able to come up with a plan of how she should repay him, they could spend time this weekend probing possible ways in which she could start making repayments.

Well, she couldn't think of anything, and if he wasn't enamoured of her nannying night and day in order to repay him she had no idea what his superior business brain might come up with—even if this coming weekend should stretch on to Christmas.

Lydie went down to breakfast and found her parents already in the breakfast room. But there was such a strained atmosphere that, coupled with guilt and fear, plus apprehension in case one of her parents should ask a question which might call for an embroidered answer, she just grabbed up a banana and, uttering something about washing her car, left them.

Jonah was on her mind the whole of the time while she

washed and wax-polished her car. She should start looking for another job. Jonah didn't want her to do that, not just yet, he had said, when to her mind the sooner she started earning, the sooner she would start to repay him.

She went indoors and decided to ring Donna, her friend and ex-employer. Donna had been nervous of coping without her, but, while Donna had her phone number, Lydie had felt it better to leave it a while before ringing her.

'How is everybody?' Lydie asked when Donna answered.

'We're fine. Though I almost rang you several times.''

'I knew you'd cope beautifully,' Lydie said confidently.

'Which is more than I did. But we seem to have settled into something of a routine. How did the wedding go?'

Guiltily Lydie realised that she'd had so much else on her mind she had almost forgotten about Oliver's wedding—was it only two days ago? 'It was super,' she told Donna. 'Madeline looked lovely.' Unbidden, the memory winged in of Jonah saying yesterday, 'I should have known you wouldn't be bridesmaid. You're much too beautiful'.

'...job yet?'

'Sorry?'

'I was asking if you've got any work lined up yet. Only Elvira Sykes is back—you remember her? Well, she's home from Bahrain, and is desperate to have you if you're interested. She's constantly asking me for your phone number, which I keep telling her I've mislaid.'

'I haven't any work plans at the moment,' Lydie hedged.

'I'll tell her you're taking a long vacation and that if she isn't fixed up by the time you get back you'll give her a ring.'

They chatted on comfortably until one of the children started yelling, then said goodbye. Lydie wandered over to her bedroom window and, glancing out, saw that her father was mowing one of the lawns. Her heart went out to him— they had always employed a gardener, but apparently her father had had to let him go.

She saw her mother come out of the house, then spotted her mother's car on the drive; she was obviously off to some coffee morning, good works, or shopping. She got into her car without attracting Wilmot Pearson's attention. Lydie saw none of the affection between them that had been there on Saturday, when her father had taken a hold of her mother's hand.

Lydie consoled her disquieted feelings by musing that they had probably discussed their plans for the morning over breakfast, and, anyway, had her mother called to him her father would never have heard with the engine of the sit-on mower going at full pelt.

Then the phone rang and Lydie came away from the window. On the basis that her mother was out, her father was out of hearing and Mrs Ross was probably busy, Lydie, though assuming the call would not be for her, went and answered it.

The call was not for her, but that did not stop her heart from picking up its beat when she heard Jonah Marriott's voice. 'Hello, Lydie,' he opened. 'Is your father there?'

'You want to speak to him?' she asked sharply.

There was a pause at her sharp tone. 'If you've no objection,' Jonah replied smoothly.

She wasn't having this. 'What do you want to speak to him about?' she demanded. 'And don't tell me it's none of my business, because—'

'Oh, my word, what a little protector you are,' he cut in mockingly, but sobered to instruct, 'Put your hackles down, Lydie. I promised your father I'd be in touch. I'm just ringing to let him know I shall be out of the country for most of this week.'

Lydie calmed down a trifle. 'I'll tell him,' she said.

'He's not around?'

'It would take me ages to get him—he's mowing the lawn near the end of the drive. It would take me some minutes to get there—and you're a busy man.'

'And you're so considerate of my time.'

He wasn't going to speak to her father, no matter how sarcastic Jonah Marriott became. 'I'll give him your message,' she answered.

'We'll talk next week, your father and me—when you and I come back from Yourk House.'

Her insides did a flip. 'I'll—tell him,' she promised.

'And I'll see you Friday.'

She swallowed hard. 'I'll look forward to it,' she lied.

'What happened to "always truthful with each other"?'

There was no answer to that. 'Goodbye, Jonah,' she said, and quietly put down the phone to find that she was trembling. And that was from just speaking to him! Heaven alone knew what she would be like on Friday!

She felt in need to do something positive, so went and showered off from her car-cleaning endeavours, and changed into jeans and a tee shirt, and then went to see her father. He was still sitting on the mower, but stopped the machine when, almost up to him, he spotted her.

'Jonah phoned,' she informed him. 'He wanted to speak to you...' Her father was off the machine with the speed of a man thirty years younger and Lydie hurriedly halted him. 'He's gone now!' Her father's face fell. 'But he asked me to tell you that he'll be out of the country for this week, but that he'll talk with you next week.'

Her father looked defeated suddenly. 'This can't go on,' he said, and seemed so utterly worn down that she just could not take it.

And she, who found lying abhorrent, was rushing in to tell him, 'Actually, Dad, Jonah has some proposition to put to you which he said will be—er—the answer.'

Her father brightened a little. 'He has?' he questioned, a little life coming back into his defeated eyes. 'What is it?'

'He wouldn't say,' Lydie went on, and even while her head was screaming, Stop it, stop it, don't say any more, she heard her own voice saying cheerfully, 'But whatever it is Jonah is certain—subject to your agreement, of course—that his proposition will be the answer to all your worries.'

'He said that?'

How could she say otherwise? More life was coming into her father's face. 'You know Jonah,' she answered.

'I certainly do. I've thought and thought until I wondered if I was going mental, and I can't see a way out of the hole I'm in. But if anyone can think up a way, I'd lay odds Jonah, a man with more up-to-date business know-how than most, would be the man to do it.' Already, in the space of seconds, her father was starting to look more like the father she knew. He had hope. 'Jonah wouldn't tell you more than that?' her father pressed. And at the urgency of his tone the enormity of what she had just done began to attack her.

'Afraid not,' she replied, marvelling that when she had just done such a terrible thing she should sound so cheerful. Somehow, though, she could not regret giving her father that hope. But, knowing she had told enough lies to last her a lifetime, she began to fear he might dig and dig away at her, and cause her to tell him yet more lies. She decided to make herself scarce. 'I was thinking of driving over to see Aunt Alice,' she said, which was true. She *had* been thinking of going to see her—tomorrow. 'I thought I'd go now, before she settles down for her afternoon nap.'

It was a relief to be away from the house, where unthought lies seem to pour from her as if of their own volition. Though when she thought of how her worried father's dead eyes had come to life on hearing that Jonah had thought up something, Lydie still could not regret it.

At worst her father would be back where he started when next week he and Jonah had their talk and Jonah told him that he had no answers. But at best—and that was the part Lydie could not feel too dreadful about—her tormented father had hope. His spirits had lifted, she had seen it happen. And now, for a whole week, while his financial worries would still be there to plague him, her lies had in effect lifted that dark ceiling of depression that hung over him night and day.

Her own spirits lifted when she found her great-aunt tending her beloved garden and, while still a touch pale, looking in otherwise good health.

Guilt over the lies she had told was lurking, however, and over the next few hours more guilt arrived in great swathes to torment Lydie. Oh, what had she done? Given her father a little peace of mind, but for what? Somehow she was going to have to own up to him before he and Jonah had that talk next week.

It was guilt and a feeling of not wanting to take away her father's peace of mind—not just yet anyway—hadn't he suffered enough?—that kept her away from Beamhurst Court until Thursday. She and her great-aunt enjoyed each other's company and it was a small thing for Lydie—who had with her only the clothes she stood up in—to rinse through her underwear to dry overnight and borrow one of her great-aunt's blouses.

'You're sure you have to go,' Alice Gough asked, but immediately apologized. '"More wants more",' she quoted. 'I'm a selfish old sausage. Love to your mother,' she said sweetly, to make Lydie laugh, and laughed herself, and Lydie hugged her and kissed her and said she would come again soon.

Lydie drove home, her few lie-free days with her great-aunt over, and two very big questions presenting themselves. One, however was she going to tell her dear father about her lies? The other, how on earth could she get out of going to Jonah Marriott's Hertfordshire home tomorrow?

The answer to the one question, she realised the moment she saw her father, was that she just could not confess. How could she? He was looking so much better than he had. How could she shatter that ray of hope he was clinging on to?

The only answer, as she saw it, was to give her father a few more days of feeling that little bit better about every-

thing. Unfortunately, she could find no answer to her reluctance to go to Yourk House to meet up with Jonah tomorrow. Unless there was some devastating earthquake in
Hertfordshire, an area not known for devastating earth-
quakes, she would have to go.

It rained on Friday. The weather matched Lydie's spirits.
Her heart might be beating twenty to the dozen whenever
she thought about staying at Yourk House that night, that
weekend, but she packed a bag for the trip without enthusiasm.

Since she could not just disappear for the weekend without giving her parents some idea of where she was going—
and Lydie had to admit that to lie and say she was staying
the weekend with Aunt Alice had crossed her mind—Lydie
owned up that she was meeting Jonah at his Hertfordshire
home.

Her mother's lips compressed, but she said nothing, and
Lydie's father looked as though he might say something to
the effect that perhaps Jonah might bring her home. But,
clearly believing that if she was meeting him at his home
then it must mean Jonah was flying in from abroad and that
Lydie would be driving her own car to meet him, he said
nothing. But Lydie did not miss that her father seemed
buoyed up with hope.

It was, of course, unthinkable that anyone else should
know of their problems, and her mother, being the chair-
person of an antiques society, was chief organiser in setting
up a meeting that evening. Lydie was grateful that her father was going along for support and that both her parents
left the house around five. She would not have to see them
again before she left—her conscience and the lies she had
told were getting to her.

Jonah had suggested he would pick her up at six and she
had turned down his offer, but she decided that six was as
a good a time as any for her to set out. With weekend bag
in hand, she went down the stairs. But, having wished their

housekeeper goodbye, Lydie was about to leave the house when the phone rang.

With hope in her heart that it was Jonah, ringing to cancel the weekend, Lydie went back to answer it. It was not Jonah but Muriel Butler, her great-aunt's neighbour, ringing to say that Miss Gough had been taken ill and that the doctor was with her now.

'What's wrong?' Lydie asked quickly, all thought of Jonah and everything else gone from her head.

'It's her heart, I think. I saw her collapsed in her garden from my upstairs window. She's had one or two little turns recently. But this looks serious.'

Lydie didn't wait to hear any more. 'I'm on my way,' she said, and was.

With her thoughts concentrated solely on her great-aunt, Lydie had been tearing along for about fifteen minutes when it suddenly dawned on her that the sleek black car that had been behind her had been there for the last five of those minutes. It was a car that could have easily outrun hers, and as easily have overtaken her, yet the driver seemed content to stay tucked in behind her. Then it was that Lydie realised she knew that car. It was the same car that had taken Aunt Alice from the church and to Alcombe Hall last Saturday. It was Jonah's car!

With no idea of why he was there, only a gladness in her heart to see him, Lydie pulled into the first lay-by she came to. Jonah pulled in behind her.

Intending to stop only to give him the quickest explanation of why she would not be visiting him at Yourk House that evening, and then be on her way, Lydie got out of her car as Jonah left his.

'If you're that eager to see me,' he commented obviously referring to the speed she had been travelling at, 'you're going in the wrong direction.'

'I'm not on my way to see you,' she replied solemnly. 'I can't come after all. My—' It was as far as she got.

'You're not coming!' He seemed more than a touch put

out. 'We agreed…' he began, then spotted her weekend bag reposing on the back seat where, hardly knowing she still had it with her, she must have tossed it when she had raced to her car. And to her consternation he was instantly furious, as he tore into her harshly, 'You never did intend to come to Yourk House this weekend, did you?' And, while she just stood there, blinking at his fury, 'All that guff about preferring I kept away from your home!' he snarled. 'You knew in advance, way back last Sunday, that you wouldn't be home when I called!'

'Don't be—'

'Well, let me tell you, Lydie Pearson.' He chopped her off again, his chin thrust aggressively forward. 'No one cheats on me—*ever*!'

'I'm not—'

'Where are you going?' he demanded, suspicion rife.

But she had had enough, and heartily wished she had never stopped to tell him anything. 'That's none of your business!' she hurled at him angrily, and without more ado stormed from him and got into her car.

Seconds later she was charging on her way. The pig! The perfect pig! Fuming, she kept her foot hard down on the accelerator. She glanced in her rearview mirror—he was right behind her. So much for her telling him it was none of his business! From the look of things, the man who did not like to be cheated was *making* it his business!

CHAPTER FIVE

LYDIE arrived at her great-aunt's house in record time—so too did Jonah Marriott. Her great-aunt did not have a drive or a garage; Lydie parked in the roadside; Jonah parked behind her.

She hurried to Alice Gough's garden gate, and found Jonah there to open it for her. She ignored him and went through, just as Muriel Butler came out of her house and looked over the low dividing hedge.

'The doctor called an ambulance. They've taken Miss Gough into hospital. Heart attack,' she added.

'Thank you for ringing me.' With fear clutching at her, Lydie managed to stay calm. 'Which hospital, do you know?'

Lydie waited no longer than to hear which hospital the ambulance had taken her great-aunt to and, thanking Muriel Butler again, turned and hurried back down the garden path.

All this time, though Lydie supposed it had only taken a minute, Jonah had remained silent. But he was there to open the gate again, and had clearly learned in that minute all there was to learn. He took charge.

'We'll go in my car,' he stated. Lydie was in no mind to argue.

They made it to the hospital in less time than it would have taken in her car. Whereupon Jonah again took charge, finding out where Miss Alice Gough was, and escorting Lydie to the intensive care unit where her great-aunt was still being assessed.

They waited outside—it seemed an awfully long wait— and strangely, despite having felt fairly murderous towards

Jonah in that lay-by, Lydie discovered she was glad that he was there.

He was there by her side when the doctor came from the ward and gave the news that there was not much chance Miss Gough would survive the attack.

Naturally Lydie refused to believe it. 'May I see her?'

'Of course,' he answered kindly. 'She's unconscious, but please go in.'

Somehow Lydie found she was holding tightly on to Jonah's hand. He made no attempt to retrieve his hand but went with her into the ward, where Alice Gough lay looking so pale, and so still. Lydie saw for herself that the doctor had been speaking only the truth.

Lydie sucked in her cheeks not to cry, and let go Jonah's hand to hold her great-aunt's hand. They stayed with her some minutes, then Lydie tenderly kissed her and, with Jonah, went outside.

'I should let my mother know,' she said to Jonah; it hadn't seemed right to her to discuss the matter over her great-aunt's bed.

'I'll ring her,' Jonah offered.

Lydie shook her head. Most oddly, she didn't want Jonah to leave her just then. 'They're not in—my parents. They're at a meeting. My mother will have her mobile switched off.'

'Tell me where and I'll go and get them.'

Lydie looked at him then, and fell in love with him. 'Oh, Jonah!' she cried, and he put a comforting arm about her.

'Be brave, sweetheart,' he urged softly.

'It was only yesterday that Aunt Alice was making me laugh when, as I was leaving, she asked me to give her love to my mother. She laughed too.'

'Remember her that way,' he suggested.

She's not dead yet! Lydie wanted to tell him furiously, and realised then that her emotions were all over the place. 'I'll go and sit with her. Could I ask you to ring Mrs Ross, our housekeeper, and ask her to tell my parents what has happened?'

'Of course,' he replied, and, the use of mobile phones banned in the hospital, he left her to go in search of a landline telephone.

Her parents arrived just after eleven. Jonah greeted them and then left the ward so the three family members should keep their vigil. Lydie's great-aunt died at eleven-thirty, and Lydie said goodbye to her.

She left her, left the ward, and found Jonah waiting outside. He took one look at her and held out his arms. Numbly she went forward. She was still cradled in his arms when her parents left the ward. Her father took charge.

'I'll see to things here, Lydie.' He looked at Jonah; now was not the time to discuss his finances. 'Perhaps you'll see Lydie gets home safely, Jonah?'

'I will,' Jonah answered.

In something of a daze Lydie went with Jonah out to his car. She wanted to weep, but wanted to weep alone. Tears were near. The only way to stem them was to think of something else.

She recalled she was supposed to be going to spend the weekend with Jonah at Yourk House. 'I—er—would you mind if we cancelled this weekend?' she asked in a hurry, not thinking, just talking.

'Consider it done,' Jonah replied calmly. 'I'm sorry I was such an evil brute in that lay-by,' he apologised.

In her view, by being there, staying there with her all these hours, he had more than made up for his evil brutishness. 'You weren't to know I was on my way out to drive to your place when Aunt Alice's neighbour rang to say she had been taken ill.' And, just then noticing the road they were on, 'Could you drive me back to my great-aunt's house, please?'

'You don't want to go home?'

'I—it doesn't seem right, somehow. I can't explain it. It

just feels as if I'd be abandoning Aunt Alice if I went home now. As if I'd forgotten her.'

Jonah altered the car's direction. 'You were always sensitive,' he murmured, and drove her to Penleigh Corbett.

Having been with Jonah through the last many sad hours, having witnessed his attention—not least the way he had held her gently in his arms just now, not saying anything, but just holding her safe—Lydie realised that *he* was far more sensitive than he would want anyone to know.

'Do you intend to stay the night here?' he asked when they reached her great-aunt's house.

'Yes,' she confirmed.

'Would you like company? I don't mean bed company,' he assured her.

'I know,' she answered, love for him welling up inside her. 'I think I need to be on my own.'

He understood, and she loved him for that too. 'You have a key?'

'Third flowerpot from the left.'

There was a light on in the next-door house, and Muriel Butler suddenly appeared with the house key, having locked up after the ambulance had left, her face falling when Lydie told her the sad news.

'I'll stay here overnight,' Lydie added.

'If you need anything, anything at all, I'm only next door,' Muriel offered, but, not wishing to intrude, said goodnight and went back indoors.

'You go in. I'll get your bag from your car,' Jonah instructed Lydie, seeming to remember she had been in such a rush to leave her car she had not waited to lock it. 'Shall I have your car key? I'll lock it up,' he suggested.

Lydie gave him her key and went into her great-aunt's house, where a very short while later Jonah joined her.

'Thank you, Jonah, for...' she faltered '...for being there,' she said.

He came closer, his fantastic blue eyes searching into

hers. 'You'll be all right if I leave you?' Lydie nodded, and swallowed hard on emotion when he placed his hands on her arms and gently placed a kiss on her brow.

She telephoned her home after he had gone. She knew Mrs Ross would be in bed, but her mother always checked the answer-machine when she got in. Lydie left a message letting her parents know where she was. Then Lydie broke down and cried.

She wept for her great-aunt's passing, and for the love she had for her. Much later she was able to find a weak and watery smile through her tears that her great-aunt's passing had shown a tenderness in Jonah which Lydie had never suspected he had.

By morning she had adjusted only slightly that she would never again share her great-aunt's company, nor hear her have a sly, if funny, dig at her mother. Lydie wandered around the small semi-detached house and still felt her aunt's presence there. It was a comforting presence.

It was still early when her parents telephoned. She spoke with both of them, her father telling her to come home when she was ready, and also letting her know that he and her mother would be making all the arrangements about her aunt's funeral. 'I know you were fond of her, but try not to be too upset,' he said, and passed the phone to her mother.

'Are you on your own?' Hilary Pearson enquired, her voice less tart than it had been of late.

The question threw Lydie for a moment, until she recalled all that had gone on—the lie she had let her parents believe that she was not a stranger to spending a night with Jonah.

'Yes,' she answered, feeling slightly amazed that her sharp-as-a-chef's-knife mother should be so easily taken in. Although, on thinking about it, Jonah had been there with her at the hospital, and both her parents had seen her in his arms last night when they had come from Aunt Alice's bedside.

'Well, I expect you'll be seeing Jonah today,' her mother went on confidently, and, repeating what her father had said, tacked on a kindly meant, 'Try not to be too upset,' adding, before she rang off, 'The old dear had a good innings.'

Lydie put the phone down and supposed she should start thinking in terms of going home. But she was not yet ready; she felt restless and unsettled. She tidied round her great-aunt's already immaculately tidy home—Lydie had vacuumed and polished on Wednesday while her great-aunt just 'did a bit in the garden'.

Lydie smiled at the memory, and found more chores to do. By half past nine she had both beds stripped and the washing machine busy. There was a ring at the doorbell. She went to answer it. It was Jonah!

For ageless moments she just stared at him. She had wondered several times that morning if, in the trauma of last night, she had imagined her feelings for him. But with her heart pounding, her insides all squishy just from looking into his sensational sensitive blue eyes, Lydie knew she had imagined nothing. She was in love with him. It was a love that was there to stay.

'I thought you'd be somewhere in Hertfordshire!' she exclaimed, inanely, she felt, as she tried to get herself together.

'I can go to Yourk House another time,' he replied easily. And, those superb eyes studying her, 'I wondered if I could help in any way?'

Oh, Jonah! Sensitive, had she said? He was warm and wonderful—and she had better buck her ideas up. 'My parents have phoned. They're taking care of all the arrangements.'

He nodded, looked at her, and then nicely enquired, 'Do

you know anywhere around here where a man might get a cup of coffee?'

'Oh, Jonah, I'm so sorry!' Lydie exclaimed. He had driven from London—and she had kept him on the doorstep! 'Whatever was I thinking of?'

He smiled kindly, his eyes on her slightly red-rimmed eyes. 'You have other matters on your mind,' he excused.

'Please, come in,' she bade him, and led the way to her great-aunt's sitting room feeling guilty—Lydie was growing no stranger to guilt. While she guessed he had noticed she had shed tears, she had not had thoughts of her great-aunt on her mind when talking to him. 'I'll just go and make some coffee,' she remarked.

'I'll come with you.'

'I've got the washing machine on. I think it came out of the Ark. It makes a fearful racket.'

His lips twitched. 'I can hear it,' he replied, and went into the kitchen with her, where a minute later the washing machine went on to a quieter cycle. 'Going home today?' Jonah enquired casually.

'Later,' Lydie agreed. 'There are a few practical things I should do here first.'

'Such as?'

'Well, somebody's got to sort out Aunt Alice's belongings. I think she would want me to do it...' Lydie shrugged helplessly, feeling very much out of her depth. 'Only it doesn't seem right to me, you know, when it was only last night that she died, to straight away pack up her belongings.' She paused, then confided, 'I really don't want to do it today.'

'Does it have to be today?'

Lydie thought about it. 'Well, I suppose not. Knowing Aunt Alice I'm certain she'll have her rent paid until the end of the month, so I've several weeks before I need hand the keys over to the local authority.'

'Then today you can rest and adjust.'

'I can?'

'You don't have to be in work on Monday, or for several Mondays yet,' Jonah pointed out logically. 'Why not leave it until you've said a formal goodbye to your great-aunt?' Lydie stared at him. It made sense to wait until after Aunt Alice's funeral. By then perhaps she would have adjusted a little. 'It's a sad time for you,' Jonah commented softly, and suggested, 'Spend the day with me?'

Her heart suddenly began to thunder. 'Spend the day with you?' she repeated faintly.

'Prior to your great-aunt's heart attack you were going to anyway.'

'That's true,' Lydie agreed, and rushed in at the gallop, 'I d-don't know what p-plans you had for this weekend, but—but I don't want to spend any t-time in bed with you!'

Jonah stared at her earnest crimson face. Then he tapped her gently on the nose. 'Sweetheart,' he said, 'wait until you're asked.'

Temporarily, she hated him. 'We'll have coffee in the sitting room,' she told him sniffily. What else was she to think he'd had in mind had they gone to Yourk House that weekend? Yet here he was making it seem as if she were some kind of female sex maniac!

The washing machine started creating again. Jonah picked up the tray and they were both glad to go to the sitting room. He waited until Lydie was seated, the coffee on a table by her side, and he took a seat nearby.

'So, what have you in mind?' she enquired, thawing a little, loving him too much to hate him for long.

'Anything you care for,' he replied. 'Take a drive, have lunch out, find a church fête—I might even win you a tin of baked beans on the tombola.'

He made her smile and, while she wondered how he knew about anything so simple and villagey as a church fête, she thawed completely. She knew he would never fall in love with her; she had seen the type of woman he was attracted to and, remembering the sophisticated blonde, Freya, he had been at the theatre with, Lydie knew better than to wish for the moon.

'I...' She hesitated, and just then, even though she knew she would guard with her life against him getting so much as a whiff of her feelings for him, she knew that she wanted his company. 'I'm not fit to be seen,' she replied. No way, other than with sunglasses to hide her red-rimmed eyes, was she going to any restaurant for lunch. 'If you're serious, bearing in mind you've tired of the hunt and that I represent no threat—to either your virtue...' he laughed, and she loved him some more '...or to your bachelorhood, I could fix us some lunch here.' Oh, heavens, how intimate that sounded!

'You said you weren't much of a cook?'

'I lied,' she answered. 'Though, since it wouldn't seem right to me to raid my great-aunt's pantry, anything we get from the village shop will probably be cooked already.'

Somehow, and Lydie could almost pinpoint it exactly, it seemed to her then as if their relationship, friendship, whatever it was, had changed. He seemed even more sensitive than he had previously been and, as they took a stroll up to the village store, Lydie felt she could talk to him about anything. Not that she had any secrets to keep; he probably knew more about her family finances than she did.

It was a fact that they seemed in harmony for once. Talking non-stop on occasions, about any subject that came up, and at other times not talking at all. They were eating lunch of oven heated frozen chicken and mushroom pie, with potatoes, broccoli and carrots, when Jonah asked her about her boyfriends. She did not wish to let the side down, so thought to admit to a few. 'There haven't been too many,' she replied.

'I'm to believe that?' He obviously didn't.

'It took me longer than most to get over the crippling shyness of adolescence.'

He smiled across at her. 'Which makes you a rather special person, Lydie Pearson. When you would have been about sixteen years old, and I came to your house to ask your father for a loan, you must have known why I was there and, despite your desperate shyness, you seemed to want to put me at my ease.'

'I asked you if you would like some tea.'

'You were charming,' he said, and her heart danced. 'What about Charlie?' Jonah asked in almost the same breath, and Lydie stared at him.

'What about Charlie?' she asked, for the moment mystified.

'You were going to give him the "big E",' Jonah reminded her.

'Oh!' she exclaimed, startled. 'I meant to ring him.' She had—to ask him how he'd fared with his office colleague, Rowena Fox.

'You forgot?' Jonah challenged.

She didn't want to fight with him. 'It isn't important.'

'You don't sound too involved?'

'How about you? Given that you're not hunting any more?'

'My last couple of—um—sorties—came to an abrupt end when the words "moving in" first crept into the conversation.'

Lydie laughed. 'That had you running scared.'

'Too right!' he grinned. 'Oh, Lydie, it's good to see you laugh.'

Jonah helped her with the dishes, and helped her through sad reflective moments too when, as happened through the day, the sadness of losing her great-aunt would unexpectedly well up and choke her.

'Your father sold the family business, I believe,' she said unceremoniously at one such moment. She knew Jonah would understand, but she just did not want to cry in front of him.

'The sale was completed four years after your father so very kindly backed my venture into fibre optics,' Jonah agreed, and, going on purely to get her over her sad moment, Lydie felt, 'It was fortunate that when I knew that another day spent in the retail business would drive me out of my mind, my brother, Rupert, showed a keen interest in entering the family firm.'

'You were able to leave and set up in business that went well?'

He nodded. 'Though I have to say that my father didn't take it too well.'

'He refused to back your fibre optic venture?'

Jonah paused, and she felt privileged when he confided, 'My father and I were at odds with each other for a while— I wouldn't ask him for money. In fact,' he went on, 'when later Rupert decided he wanted out of the business too, and my father started to consider the offers he'd many times had for his business and then decided to sell, I didn't expect to receive any money.'

'But you did,' Lydie said softly, knowing it was so.

'I should have known better. Whatever our differences, my father has always been fair with Rupert and me. Rupert received a quarter of the proceeds—so too did I.'

'And you at once paid my father back.'

'But only in money. I owed him more than that. Wilmot had faith in me when the money institutions were saying they'd gone as far as they could.'

They finished the dish-washing and putting everything away with Lydie realising that it was because of that faith her father had shown in him that Jonah had given her that cheque. 'I *will* pay you back—that money you gave me,' she told Jonah sincerely. And, while they were on the subject, 'Have you thought of anything yet? Other than my making monthly payments to you from my earnings?'

'Let's not talk about it today, Lydie,' he answered sensitively.

And she smiled at him, but felt he should know that her father did not take the matter lightly. 'While the debt is mine, I really want you to understand that my father is a most honourable man,' she told Jonah earnestly.

'I know,' he replied quietly.

But that did not seem enough. 'He would have sold the house, but…'

'He was ready to sell Beamhurst Court?' Jonah seemed very much surprised.

'It's all he has left to sell.'

'But it's been in your family for ever!'

'My father was desperate,' she stated. But, as Jonah had confided a little about his father, Lydie felt she could confide about her mother's role in the non-sale of Beamhurst Court. 'It hasn't come to selling yet. My mother is sticking out against selling—she's objecting most strongly.'

'Your mother loves Beamhurst Court as you do?'

'It's not so much that, I think,' Lydie confessed. 'She wants it for Oliver.'

'And does Oliver want it? I heard he was having some five star place built in the grounds of the Ward-Watson home?'

'Unless he drastically changes his opinions, he wouldn't touch Beamhurst with a bargepole,' Lydie answered, guessing that with Oliver and Madeline's plans general knowledge at the wedding, Jonah had picked up a snippet about the new house there. But Lydie was feeling strangely shy all at once. 'You'll be wanting to get off home now, I expect,' she said quickly, feeling very conscious that she had monopolised so much of his time and, while not wanting him to go, feeling guilty because of it.

But it seemed Jonah had nothing pressing that day to get back to. 'Don't give me hints, woman,' he teased. 'Tell me straight out.' She smiled, but could not find an answer. And he asked, 'Do you want to be on your own, Lydie?'

She shook her head. 'No,' she said.

'Then we'll go for a walk,' he decreed.

It was for the most part a silent walk, though Lydie did think to ask, 'What were you doing following me yesterday? I thought you'd be on your way to your Hertfordshire home.'

'I had business in your area. I anticipated you'd leave around six and thought we'd go in tandem—me leading the way in case you got lost. I was tucked in near the crossroads when you shot by. Do you want me to apologise again for being so swinish to you?'

She smiled at him and shook her head, just grateful to have him with her for this short time. They walked on, Jonah busy with his thoughts, and Lydie overcome with sadness on seeing the bench near the church where she and her great-aunt had sat on one of their evening strolls.

She felt saddened that she would never sit on that bench with Aunt Alice again. And, as other memories arrived, saddened that she would not again go with her to some Saturday afternoon function at the village hall. Then, lastly, a feeling of guilt came to trip Lydie up.

She and Jonah were on their way back to the house when a shaky kind of sigh took her, and Jonah caught a sympathetic hold of her hand. 'Bad moment?' he asked kindly.

'Guilt,' Lydie replied unthinkingly.

'All part of the territory when you lose someone you care for,' he assured her.

'Is it?'

He let go her hand and smiled down at her. 'Want to talk about it, Lydie?'

'Oh, you know. Generally I could have visited her more than I did.'

'You stayed overnight with her Saturday,' he reminded her quietly. 'And didn't you say you'd seen her again only on Thursday?'

'I came over on Monday and stayed until Thursday.' Lydie could feel herself going pink as she remembered. She looked up and saw Jonah was looking down at her—he couldn't help but notice her embarrassed colour. She knew then that she had some confessing to do. 'I've done a terrible thing,' she owned.

'Are you likely to go to jail for it?' he enquired lightly.

'Hopefully not,' she answered, and then blurted out, 'I can't stop telling lies. I never used to,' she hurried on. 'Before I took that cheque from you lies and my tongue were strangers. But ever since I just seem to open my mouth and all these lies pour out!'

'Oh, my word—should I worry?'

'I *have* involved you,' she admitted.

His tone did not change. 'Perhaps you'd better tell me what's been going on,' he suggested mildly.

Lydie thought for a moment, and then said, 'I had intended to come and see Aunt Alice on Tuesday last anyway—and that's where some of the guilt I feel comes in— I came on Monday instead. But only partly for Aunt Alice. More specifically, I came on Monday mainly because I was afraid if I stayed home yet more lies would come tumbling out. For the same reason I stayed on here with my great-aunt until Thursday.'

'Afraid to go home?'

'Something like that. I wanted to avoid my tongue running away with me.' Jonah was silent. He was waiting— and she did not want to tell him. But his very silence seemed to be compelling her to go on. 'I've told the most howling lies!' She paused—Jonah wasn't helping her out. 'On Monday. You know, when you rang. Well, I went to give my father your message, that you'd rung and wanted to speak with him, and before I could say more he was ready to sprint back to the house to take your call. Anyhow, I stopped him by saying you were going out of the country but that you'd talk with him next week.'

'So far you don't appear to have told any fresh lies,' Jonah commented dryly.

She was glad to feel a touch niggled with him, but the feeling did not last. How, after what she had done, dared she be in any way annoyed? 'Anyhow, my father suddenly looked so defeated, so at the end of his rope, so as if—as if he's thought himself to a standstill trying to find some solution, that I couldn't bear it. He was saying something about this could not go on, and looked so much as though he was worn to his roots and couldn't take another day of it, so—um...' Oh, grief. 'I couldn't take it, Jonah. I told him—that you had a proposition to put to him that you said would be the answer.'

She ran out of breath, and waited for Jonah's wrath to fall about her ears for her nerve. But, instead of being furious with her, he politely enquired, 'And what is this proposition, Lydie? Am I not entitled to know?'

Perhaps his wrath would have been better, she mused. 'I haven't worked anything out yet. I just wanted him to have some respite from it all. I thought that while you were out of the country, and until the two of you meet—which I can see now that you're going to have to—it might give him about a week of not worrying so much. Give his poor head a chance to get perhaps a little rest.'

'He *was* looking a little less stressed out last night than when I saw him last Saturday,' Jonah acknowledged. 'You'd better tell me word for word exactly what you said to him in my name.'

Lydie felt a bit pink about the ears again at that last bit. 'That's about it, I think,' she replied. 'A spark of life seemed to come to my father's eyes, and I found myself lying—I just couldn't seemed to stop—and telling him that you wouldn't say what your proposition was, but that whatever it was you were certain, if he agreed to it, that your proposition would be the answer to all his worries.'

'And he bought that?'

'He said he'd thought and thought but he couldn't see a

way out of the hole he was in, but that if anyone could then you would be the one to do it.'

'And that was all?'

Lydie, having arrived back at her great-aunt's door without knowing it, thought hard. She shook her head. 'Dad asked if you wouldn't tell me more than that, and, while I couldn't regret having put hope back in his eyes, I started to worry that if he pressured me to say more I might end up telling him even more and bigger lies.'

'So you decided to make yourself scarce.'

'I came here,' Lydie agreed. And, as she knew she had to, said, 'I'm sorry, Jonah. I've behaved disgracefully. But my punishment will be that I must now go home and take that ray of hope from my father's eyes by confessing what an outrageous liar he has for a daughter.'

Whether Jonah accepted her apology she knew not, but he stood looking down at her for long moments, and she would loved to have known what he was thinking. Then, his expression still thoughtful, 'Don't confess anything just yet,' he instructed.

Her eyes widened. 'You've thought of something?' she enquired eagerly, getting used now to the way her heart misbehaved from time to time when she was with him. 'You've thought of some kind of proposition? Some kind of—?'

'Leave it with me,' Jonah cut in.

'You've thought…?'

'Something's filtering away inside the old grey matter,' was all that he would say.

'But…' She started to probe anyway, but could see he wasn't going to be drawn, no matter how much she pressed. So she had to let it go, but did ask, 'You're not mad at me?'

Jonah gave her a hint of a smile. 'Any lies you've told, Lydie, were not for yourself, but to try and make life more bearable for your father than it is just now.' She simply stared at him, marvelling at him understanding. Then he had done away with the subject, and was asking, 'Any chance of a cup of tea before I go?'

They went inside and Lydie made some tea, reflecting that she had never envisaged last Sunday that she would spend time with him this weekend in this way. Thoughts of her great-aunt were never very far away, however, her passing away so recent, and again Lydie thought sadly, if fondly, of her great-aunt.

'I'd better get going before I outstay my welcome,' Jonah said, finishing the last of his tea and getting to his feet. And while Lydie was wishing he would stay for ever, but starting to be positive he must have a date that night, she got up and went to the door with him. 'You've no objection if I attend Miss Gough's funeral?' he asked.

'You don't have to do that,' she said in a rush, already too much indebted to him.

'You ashamed of me?' he asked, his mouth quirking in that way that made her feel all gooey over him.

She shrugged to combat the feeling. 'You scrub up quite nicely,' she told him, and felt pretty wonderful about him when he laughed.

Though he was serious when, standing close to her, he looked down into her smiling green eyes and instructed, 'Try not to worry—I'll think of something.'

Mutely she stared up at him, then didn't know where the Dickens she was when, for all the world as though he could not help himself, Jonah took her in his arms—and kissed her!

The feel of his lips on hers in that oh, so gentle kiss turned her legs to water. She wanted to cling on to him, to return his kiss, to cling on to him for evermore and to never let go.

But jealousy, that stranger to her until now, that foul stranger that perched on her shoulder and from nowhere tormented her that Jonah would probably have his arms around some other woman that night, gave her no option but to push him away from her. 'Sweetheart,' he had said, 'wait until you're asked.'

'Sweetheart,' she said, finding her voice sounding incredibly stern when her legs felt about to collapse, 'I do trust you're not asking?'

For a moment Jonah looked as though he couldn't believe his hearing. Then he burst out laughing. 'You'll know when, Lydie, without having to ask,' he promised—and went.

Lydie closed the door, not knowing whether to laugh or cry. Her heart was still thundering in her ears as she returned to the sitting room and collapsed on to a chair. Jonah had kissed her! Jonah had kissed her, she marvelled. And she, idiot, had pushed him away!

CHAPTER SIX

HER great-aunt's funeral was an occasion Lydie was not looking forward to. But given that Oliver—who had never particularly got on with his mother's aunt—was on his honeymoon and did not attend, it passed quietly and in a dignified manner. Lydie had spotted that Jonah was there, but he did not presume to come and sit in the family pew.

He came over to her in the general standing around afterwards, though, and asked how she was. 'Fine,' she answered, and he was still next to her when her father walked over to them.

The two men shook hands. 'You'll come back to the house?' Wilmot Pearson asked Jonah.

To Lydie's surprise Jonah accepted. He was a busy man and Thursday was a work day. 'Perhaps I could see you at some convenient time after today?' Jonah suggested to him, and Lydie started to get all churned up inside. Plainly Jonah had put his thinking cap on and had come up with something.

'No disrespect to Miss Gough, but today would suit quite well,' her father replied, a further endorsement, if Lydie didn't know it, that her dear father was likely to have heart failure if he had to wait much longer to have a talk with Jonah.

'Whenever you say, Wilmot,' Jonah agreed.

'Until later,' her father said, and went on to talk to family members who, until Oliver's wedding not two weeks ago, he had not seen for some while.

'You've thought of something?' Lydie asked Jonah the moment her father was out of earshot.

'All in good time,' Jonah murmured, and Lydie knew at once she was going to get nothing more out of him.

To show her disgust she walked over to Muriel Butler, whom she just then noticed, and thanked her for attending.

'Such a sad day,' Muriel answered, and they chatted for a few minutes, then, deciding that Jonah couldn't leave her not knowing, Lydie went back to him. By then, though, he had been annexed by her beautiful cousin Kitty.

'I was just telling Jonah how I saw him at Oliver's wedding but you'd whisked him off somewhere before we could be introduced.'

Lydie had always envied her cousin her self-assured air, and wished some of it had brushed on to her. 'You've introduced yourself now, I hope?' She smiled, her manners holding up despite the green-eyed spears that were prodding. Jonah did not look to be at all put out that the beautiful, self-assured Kitty was batting her big brown eyes at him.

At that moment, however, a general move was made to where everyone had parked their cars. The cortège had left from Alice Gough's home, but the family, in the absence of her having close friends, were assembling back at Beamhurst Court. No matter what, on their uppers though they might be, Hilary Pearson was going to have things done properly.

'Want to drive back with me, Lydie?' Jonah asked as Kitty trotted off.

Lydie had come in the lead car with her parents, but it would suit her quite well to drive back to Beamhurst Court with Jonah. 'I'll just tell my father,' she accepted, but discovered that she did not have to tell her father anything. Somehow, and she rather thought she had no one to blame but herself, her parents seemed to believe that she and Jonah had something 'going'. Her father must have assumed she would be driving back with Jonah anyway, because he waved to them and turned and, with a hand on her mother's elbow, escorted his wife down the church path.

Much good did it do Lydie to drive with Jonah. 'What are you going to say to my father?' she asked as soon as they were in his car and moving.

'For the moment,' he replied carefully, 'that must be between your father and me.'

'Don't be mean!' she erupted. 'I've as much right...'

'Stamping your foot, Lydie?' Jonah mocked. But, perhaps bearing in mind that they had just come from her beloved aunt's funeral, 'I don't want you to be more upset—I just feel I have to speak to your father first.'

Not be more upset! Lydie fumed. 'You won't distress him? If I...'

'I hope not to distress him,' Jonah answered—and with that she had to be content.

But she watched. At her home, with her relatives assembled in the drawing room, Lydie watched. She chatted and looked after the more mature members of the family group, but the whole time she knew where Jonah was and where her father was.

She was talking to her mother's cousin when she saw her father look across to Jonah. Kitty had annexed him again but, whatever unspoken signal had passed between her father and Jonah, when a minute later her father left the drawing room she saw Jonah skilfully excuse himself from Kitty and, casually, he strolled from the drawing room too. She knew he would meet her father and they would go to his study.

They were gone for a half-hour. She knew because she had spent that half-hour in either looking to the drawing room door, watching for them to come back, or looking at her watch. What on earth were they talking about all this while?

With her insides churning, her heart seemed to somersault when, together, the two men dearest in the world to her came and stood in the drawing room doorway. She tried to read something, anything from their faces. Jonah's expression was telling her nothing. Her glance went quickly to her father. His expression was telling her little more other than that whatever proposition Jonah had put to him it had not depressed him. He looked more thoughtful than anything—though certainly not down. She started to hope.

Lydie was by then on the other side of the room from where she had been half an hour ago. She went to move across the room, but as she did so, without looking at her but just as if he had known from where he stood just exactly where she was, Jonah moved forward and blocked her way.

She halted, looked up, her glance moving worriedly from him to her father. She opened her mouth, but Jonah, taking a restraining hold of her arm spoke first. 'Let's go for a stroll, Lydie,' he said quietly.

She stared at him, her lovely green eyes still trying to read something in his expression. He was telling her nothing. She looked from him, looked around the room. Everyone seemed comfortable; no one was sitting alone staring into space.

'Yes,' she murmured, and was more churned up than ever. The only reason Jonah could be suggesting a stroll was so that he could tell her what she wanted to know: what the proposition was that he had put to her father.

They left the house and walked up the long drive. They went out through the gates. Jonah seemed to be more deep in thought than ready to let her know of his discussion—his half-hour discussion—with her parent in the study. She did not want to be again accused of 'stamping her foot' and, having learned that she was going to get nothing out of Jonah until he was good and ready, with more patience than he could know, she waited.

They were walking her favourite walk, and she waited until, having strolled down a picturesque lane, the air scented with honeysuckle, they left the lane and turned to where a five-barred gate led into a meadow. It was then that Lydie could wait no longer. She stopped walking; Jonah halted too.

'So?' she asked—a shade belligerently, she had to admit—and realised that the stresses of more than one kind that day were getting to her. 'What have you got to tell me?'

His reply was not at all what she had been expecting. And was in fact totally staggering when, turning to face her, he looked down into her eyes, and, after a moment, very clearly said, 'I've decided—it's time I married.'

Lydie wasn't sure her jaw did not drop. 'But—you don't want to marry,' she argued, feeling sick inside. But, rapidly getting herself together—this would never do—she forced a smile. 'Let me congratulate you, Jonah.' He was going to marry Freya, that lovely blonde creature! Though hadn't he said something about not seeing the blonde again after that theatre date?

'Thank you,' he accepted.

'You've obviously known the lady in question some while?' she fished.

'You could say that,' he replied, adding, when Lydie knew that it was nothing whatsoever to do with her, 'I hope you approve of my choice.'

She didn't; she wouldn't. In fact just then she was ready to stick pins in his choice! Somehow, though, when what she wanted to do was to run and hide herself away to get over this awful blow, Lydie managed to keep control; even her father was for the moment forgotten as she fought to mask that she was falling apart. 'Do I know her?' she asked casually. She was going to hate him if it *was* Freya.

Lydie had felt staggered before. But his answer this time was to shake her to her very foundations, when, looking nowhere but at her, 'You,' Jonah replied succinctly, 'are her.'

Lydie stared at him, disbelieving her ears. Then her jaw very definitely did drop open—it almost hit the ground.

'Me!' she gasped, and, her eyes saucer wide, she just looked at him. 'Are you serious?'

'I wouldn't joke about something like this.'

'Y-you're saying you want to—marry me?' Was that squeaky voice hers?

'That's my plan,' he confirmed, set, determined, everything about him brooking no refusal.

Well, she'd soon see about that! Just because he had now decided it was time he married, he thought he'd have a pot-shot at her—well, could he think again! 'I'm not marrying you!' she told him in no uncertain fashion. Love him she might, but *really*!

'Yes, you are,' he countered, not a bit abashed.

'Give me one good reason why I should,' she challenged hostilely.

'I can think of fifty-five thousand reasons,' he returned coolly—and on that instant her hostility immediately evaporated.

A soft gasp of 'Oh!' escaped her as thoughts of her father rocketed in. 'You've...' Her voice failed her. 'This isn't the proposition you put to my father. It can't be.' It wasn't making sense. 'What sort of proposition would that be? To marry...' She ran out of steam; her brain seemed to have seized up.

Jonah came in to help her out. 'Let's put it this way. We both know that your father is a proud man, an honourable man. Now, you tell me—who would he rather owe money to? An acquaintance or a member—albeit a son-in-law—of his family? An outsider—or an insider?'

Lydie looked from him. She needed space, some time to think. Jonah had out of the blue just hit her with this notion that they marry to make him a member of her family, an insider, and thereby make that money all within the family.

'The debt is mine, not my father's,' was the poor best she could come up with.

'That's not the way he sees it,' Jonah replied. 'Nor will you be able to convince him any other way.'

Lydie knew that he was right, but, 'I can't marry you,' she insisted.

'Your father's peace of mind isn't worth it?'

'Oh, don't, Jonah!' she cried. 'Of course it is,' she said fretfully.

Jonah smiled kindly. 'I wish I could give you time to think about it, Lydie, but your father's expecting us to go back with happy smiles.'

'You've told him you were going to ask me?' She stared at him open-mouthed.

'He has a problem. He has thought and thought and cannot come up with a solution. To my mind this is the only solution for your father. For the moment we leave it that he owes a close family member a sum of money which, in time, I hope he will learn to live with. For my part I have no interest in having that money repaid.'

'But you don't want to be married. You said as much.'

'Can't a man change his mind?'

She supposed he could. 'But—why me?'

'Why not you? Ignoring the fact, for the moment, that by you marrying me I'm hoping to relieve the terrible stress and strain of a man I hold in the very highest regard, for myself I'd be getting a most beautiful wife. And, from what I've witnessed in today's sad circumstances alone, I shall also have myself a most admirable hostess.'

Some of her shock was starting to fade, but she still felt she needed time—time, space to think. She loved him, and now that the idea was settling in her head a little she could think of nothing she would rather do than marry him. But that did not make it right.

And from her father's viewpoint, yes, perhaps he would feel better able to live with owing that money to someone whom she did not doubt he would be pleased to look on as a son. But from her viewpoint—that still did not make it...

'Penny for them?' Jonah asked, and she realised she had

been silent a long time and that he would not mind being let into her thoughts.

'How did my father take it? I mean, I can't see him simply saying "Oh, yes" when you mentioned you'd marry me to make him feel more comfortable about his debt.'

'I hope I wasn't that crude,' Jonah replied, going on, 'From what you've told me you have already given your father the impression that we're keen on each other. I let him think we had grown to love each other, and that I was asking his blessing that I should marry you.'

'Thank you for that,' Lydie said without thinking—she would rather her father thought she was marrying for love in preference to have him thinking she was marrying to make him feel better. Not that he would have stood for that anyway.

'Is that a yes?' Jonah asked quietly.

'No,' she said quickly, but could see how, from her thanking him for letting her father believe it would be a love match, Jonah would think she had agreed. 'That is,' she qualified, 'you've suddenly, in the space of three weeks, gone from running like blazes from the thought of marriage to deciding now that to marry would quite suit you? How do I know that you won't, three weeks into any marriage, just as suddenly ask for a divorce?'

'How can you talk of divorce when I've only just asked for your promise to marry me? Divorce,' he told her firmly, 'is not an option.'

Lydie still needed time, though could quite well see that if Jonah had told her father he was about to propose to her then her father, having noticed their absence, was going to think she had turned Jonah down should they return with nothing to announce. Which in turn would send him tumbling straight down into a pit of stress and depression again.

'Would it—um—this marriage—would it be a n-name only affair?' she asked, embarrassed, but needing to have a few answers now.

'I'm family-minded,' Jonah replied. 'I'm afraid we'd have to do what we have to do to produce a few offspring.'

Oh, heavens! 'Um,' she mumbled, and, more to get herself over some hot-all-over moments than anything, abruptly asked, 'What if—supposing—we find the money?' She was starting to feel confused. And no wonder! But remembering—was it only last Friday?—the way he had aggressively taken exception at the thought of being cheated—'No one cheats on me—*ever*,' he had said—'Supposing you and I were engaged and, and we found we could pay back the money. I'd be cheating you to marry you then—and you wouldn't like that.'

'You're wriggling, Lydie,' Jonah accused, plainly knowing as well as she that she and her father hadn't a hope in Hades of finding fifty-five thousand pounds and paying him back. 'And you'd have to find it pretty quickly.'

'I would?' She stared at him.

He nodded. 'Having decided it's time I married, I can't see any reason to wait.'

Lydie looked at him helplessly. She guessed that was part and parcel of the man—decide upon something, decision made, expedite it. But this wasn't business, this was her future, his future, and while as more shock receded she knew that she could not think of anything she would rather do than be his wife, to see him most every day—it still did not seem right.

'You're sure you want to be married?' she questioned.

'Totally sure.'

'And I'm—"it"—?'

'Don't sell yourself short, Lydie. You're a little bit gorgeous.'

Her heart fluttered. 'I'm trying to be serious here,' she told him sternly.

'You think I'm not?'

'What the alternative?' she asked. 'From my father's point of view, I mean. What's the alternative if I don't marry you?'

Jonah shrugged. 'The money, as your father sees it, will still be his debt. When I spoke with him in his study a while ago, and acquainted him with my plans, I saw that spark of hope in him grow and grow the more we talked. I even felt as we left his study that there was a bit of a spring in his step that hadn't been there before,' Jonah added, then asked quite simply, 'I've made my decision, Lydie, may I now hear yours?'

She needed more time, only there wasn't more time. Her father would be watching for them to come back, would be searching their faces. Could she bear to see that ray of hope die from his eyes? Could she bear to see that hurt, that stress return to his eyes? As her father had said, he had thought and thought and could find no solution. He had great trust in Jonah and had said that if anyone could think up a way Jonah would be the one to do it. Well, he had, and, while it was true it might not be the proposition her father had hoped for, he would as the days went by, learn to live with the fact that his debt was not to a man he himself had once helped, but to his daughter's husband.

Oh, grief. Husband—Jonah! Her legs threatened to give way at the thought. She turned and placed a seemingly casual hand on the top of the five-barred gate, gripping it hard. Then, decision made, she turned back to him.

She looked up into his wonderful blue eyes and took a long steadying breath. 'It seems a bit formal to shake hands on—um—my promise,' she began, 'but I don't think I'm ready for k-kisses just yet.'

Jonah stared down at her for long moments, then raised a hand and brushed a stray something or other out of her hair. 'Your word is good enough for me, Lydie,' he said quietly. And then, oddly, seemed to draw a steadying breath himself at her acceptance of his marriage proposal. But Lydie knew that it was just her imagination gone wild— and no wonder—because his voice was totally matter of fact when, taking a step away from the gate, he suggested, 'We'd better get back.'

Lydie could only agree. Her father would be waiting, watching for their return. She fell into step with Jonah, but they were walking back up the drive when she thought of the sadness of the day, and hurriedly asked, 'We don't have to announce it—our engagement—straight away, do we?'

'It doesn't seem entirely appropriate to announce it generally today,' he agreed.

'Thank you for understanding,' she said softly.

And he looked at her and smiled. 'We'll be all right together, Lydie, trust me,' he said. And she did, and started to feel more on an even keel. 'We'll tell your parents when everyone has gone,' he decided, then seemed to realise that there was a partnership going on here, and added, 'If that's all right with you?'

Lydie had an idea he'd do as he pleased even if it wasn't all right with her, but, since he was going through the motions, 'Fine,' she agreed. Then they were at the steps of Beamhurst Court and her father, who had obviously been on the fidget, strolled, as if casually, out to meet them. 'I've—er—been showing Jonah my favourite walk,' Lydie said, and, as both her father and Jonah looked down at her, for no reason she blushed. Her father looked delighted. 'Can Jonah stay to dinner?' she heard herself blurting out.

'I think that can be arranged,' Wilmot Pearson answered, and for the first time since she had come home from Donna in Norfolk, Lydie actually saw her father grin. She knew then that to agree to marry Jonah had been the right decision. Already her father was starting to get back to being the man he used to be! It seemed incredible that, just to know that Jonah was to be his son-in-law—she would hardly have invited Jonah to dinner if she had turned him down—her father should at once be on the way to being his former self. But, remembering his grin—there were no two ways about it.

Gradually all the relatives trickled away, Kitty being one of the last to leave. Lydie would have quite liked to tell her cousin that the man she was drooling over was, as of today, affianced. But there was an order to these matters, and her parents had to be informed first.

Though, when she'd decided to go upstairs to change out of her mourning clothes, Lydie was on the staircase when she observed that Jonah and her father seemed to making for the study again. In all probability, she realised, Jonah was telling her father she had accepted him.

As, over dinner, she learned was true. Only her mother seemed unaware of what had taken place, and looked at her husband askance when he left the table and came back with a bottle of chilled champagne.

'How do you feel about gaining a son?' he asked her. And, with Hilary Pearson looking as much bemused by this suddenly playful change in the dour husband she had known of late as by what he said, 'Jonah has asked Lydie to marry him,' he added. 'And Lydie, I believe, has accepted.'

'Lydie's accepted…' her mother gasped. 'You're going to marry…'

Loving someone meant that no one was going to say anything against that someone, Lydie at once discovered, even if that someone was more than well able to take care of himself. And, 'Is it such a surprise, Mother?' she could not refrain from butting in.

Her mother recovered well. 'I'm very happy for you both,' she unbent sufficiently to say.

But was not so very happy when, a champagne toast drunk, Jonah let it be known that he was keen to marry as soon as possible.

'These things take an age to organize. A year at least,' his future mother-in-law let him know.

Jonah considered her answer, but not for very long. 'It looks like an elopement, Lydie,' he commented.

'Oh, no! Certainly not!' Hilary Pearson fired shortly. Jonah was unmoved. 'Six months?' she reconsidered.

'Six weeks at the very latest,' Jonah said firmly, and while Lydie was thinking, Six weeks! Grief—six short

weeks! Jonah wanted them to be married before the next
six weeks were out, he was battering down her mother's
defences by stating, 'My mother would love to liaise with
you to give a helping hand.' He did not need to say anything more.

'I'm quite sure I shall be able to manage,' Hilary Pearson
assured him.

Later, as Lydie suspected was expected of her, she went
out with Jonah to his car. 'Six weeks doesn't seem very
long,' she suggested tentatively.

'I don't want to wait that long, but I appreciate your
mother's point of view,' Jonah replied, adding with a smile
in his voice, 'Some board of directors missed a gem when
they didn't snap your mother up.'

After the tensions of the day it was good to be able to
find a light spontaneous laugh. 'Would your mother really
have helped out?' she asked a moment later.

'Try keeping her away!' They reached his car but, while
he opened up the driver's door, he did not immediately get
into the driving seat. Instead he bent inside and extracted
something. It was a small box. He opened it and took out
the most beautiful diamond and emerald engagement ring.
'Shall we see if it fits?'

'You've had this all day!' Incredulous, Lydie stood in
the brilliance of the security lights and just stared at it. 'Oh,
Jonah,' she whispered, her heart all his that, this day of her
great-aunt's funeral, he had sensitively not given her his
ring until now. He slid the ring home on her engagement
finger.

'Come here,' he said softly, and gathered her in his arms.
But, perhaps recalling that she was not ready for his kisses
just yet, he did not kiss her, but just sealed the giving of
his engagement ring to her, and Lydie accepting, by holding her close for long moments. Then he was putting her
away from him, and preparing to get into his car. 'My folks
are going to want to meet you. We'll have dinner with
them. Tomorrow?'

Oh, crumbs! He was serious, then? Although with his ring new, strange on her finger, she rather thought she knew that. 'I'll—er—look forward to it,' she replied politely.

'You're going to have to stop telling lies, Lydie,' Jonah said, but she was pleased to see as he got into his car that he was smiling.

Lydie was a long time getting to sleep that night. Stark reality that hadn't until she was alone had time to settle was there in ample supply. Had it really happened? Was she truly engaged to marry Jonah Marriott? Her fingers went to her engagement ring. It was not a dream. She *was* engaged to marry the man whom she loved with everything that was in her.

And yet—it still didn't seem right. But if she said now that she would not marry him it would mean she would have to go to her father and confess her lies, confess that Jonah had had no proposition to put to him when she had told her father that he had. And, even worse from her father's pride point of view, she would have to admit that she had agreed to marry Jonah solely because he had suggested her father would feel better if his debt was to family and not outsiders.

Lydie knew then that she would go through with this marriage to Jonah. Her father, let alone his pride, had suffered enough. Yet Lydie also knew that she wanted to be married for herself alone. She wanted Jonah to marry her for her, and not because he had decided it was time to marry and saw marriage to her as fitting in nicely with easing the cares of a man he respected. A man Jonah respected so well that he, having repaid his own debt, still believed he owed a lot of his success to.

The trouble was, she loved Jonah so much; but not a word of love had he spoken to her. Hang it, they hadn't even kissed! Not engagement kissed. Though, remembering the day they had spent together last Saturday, and how he had kissed her on parting, thinking about it, Lydie had to be glad he had not kissed her today. Her legs had been ready to fold when his lips had touched hers the last time. How would she have reacted today to the feel of his lips when still in shock from the unexpectedness of his pro- posal?

Lydie finally fell asleep glad she had six weeks in which to grow used to the idea of marrying Jonah. Would six weeks be enough?

They dined with his parents and his brother the following evening. Both Jonah's father and mother were charming, his brother a bit like her own brother in personality, and all three seemed absolutely delighted that Jonah had at last chosen his bride.

Any chance of the next six weeks gliding smoothly by, however, were doomed to failure when the two prospective mothers-in-law met. Lydie's mother wanted matters ar- ranged one way; Jonah's mother wanted to help—her way. Trying to keep the peace between the two of them was running Lydie ragged.

As luck would have it there was just one 'slot' available in her local church on the day Lydie and Jonah had decided upon. Choristers were booked, bell ringers engaged and, after an extensive search, one of the best photographers. Limousines were chartered, caterers given detailed instruc- tions, florists visited, designs chosen and outfits ordered.

Lydie could not believe her mother was so enthusiasti- cally spending money they had not got, and protested ve- hemently again and again as the cost of the wedding rose higher and higher. 'Really, Mother, it's got to stop!' she exclaimed more than once.

'Don't be tiresome!' was her mother's response. 'You're our only daughter. Besides, I'm not going to let that Mrs Marriott think we're paupers!'

That Mrs Marriott! They'd obviously had a sharp exchange of views. 'But we haven't got this kind of money!'

'Oh, for goodness' sake! You're marrying a man worth a mint! Do you think your father and I would let you go to him in anything but the very best?'

Matters might have been helped had Jonah been around for Lydie to talk to. But in his endeavours to get all his work cleared, so they could fly to a secluded sun-soaked island for a couple of months, he was here, there and everywhere. More often than not he was out of the country. Lydie rarely saw him.

He telephoned regularly, though, but she hardly felt she could complain about her lot when, although she was kept busy, he was so much busier. So Lydie silently got on with obeying her mother's 'get this, get that, ring here, ring there' instructions, her 'Don't forget your dress fitting,' and 'No, no, no, you cannot have lisianthus in your wedding bouquet,' and 'Do try and contact Kitty—she's the most tiresome child.' That 'child' was twenty-six and was to be one of Lydie's four bridesmaids because 'You cannot have just Donna!' her mother had exclaimed, horrified.

'Who's going to pay for all this?' Lydie wanted to know, starting to think that Jonah's hint of an elopement was the much better plan. Her question was brushed aside while her mother thought of someone else she really must send an invitation to.

Lydie was glad to get out of the house and drive to her dear great-aunt's home. It was not the happiest task to dispose of her belongings, but at least Lydie had peace and quiet and space to think her own thoughts.

She sighed as she folded away the last of her great-aunt's clothes. It was all getting to be just too much. To avoid further battles with her mother she had agreed to four attendants—three cousins and Donna. And since she had agreed, and because her cousin Kitty was beautiful, and pride decreed that Jonah should not think she was afraid of the competition, Kitty was to be one of them. Her other two cousins, Emilia and Gaynor, were extremely pretty too, as also was Donna.

Lydie waited for the furniture people to come and collect her great-aunt's bits and pieces and then took the keys and a memento of a piece of fine porcelain next door to Muriel

Butler. Muriel had said she would quite like to have Miss Gough's cooker, and would have the keys to enable her to let the service men in to cut off the gas supply prior to reconnecting the cooker in her own home.

'I'll hand the keys in to the council too, if you like,' Muriel offered. 'It will save you having to come back to collect them from me. I've got to go in to pay my rent, and they won't care who hands them in so long as they've got them.'

Lydie had grown to like Muriel, who had always been kind and friendly to her great-aunt. Lydie would not have minded returning—Aunt Alice's home had been a kind of bolthole when things got too stressed at home—but she accepted Muriel's offer.

Lydie then went home to find her father hiding in the summer house. Love her mother as he dearly did, it seemed there were times when he preferred his own company.

'Have you been in yet?'

Lydie shook her head. 'I thought I spotted a figure lurking this way,' she replied, astounded at the change in him since Jonah had told him he wanted to marry her. Talk about bright-eyed and bushy-tailed! Even the expense of her wedding hadn't dimmed that new sharper air about him.

'Um—your dear mother has a lot on her mind. It—er—might be an idea for you to go in quietly.' From that Lydie knew she was in trouble over something. She had an idea what it was.

Her mother was waiting for her. 'Did you ring the florists and countermand my instructions?' she demanded the moment Lydie went in.

'I didn't ring; I called in when I was passing.'

'Deliberately passing! You *know* we agreed we wanted lilies for your bouquet, and—'

'I'm sorry, Mother,' Lydie cut in. Against her better judgement and for the sake of peace, albeit reluctantly, she'd had to go along with everything her mother had decreed must be. But on the issue of her bouquet Lydie had dug her heels in. 'It was *you* who wanted lilies in my bouquet.'

'Better than the red roses Grace Marriott suggested,' Hilary Pearson sniffed.

'I'd prefer to have pink and white lisianthus,' Lydie said, even as she said it wondering why she was being so stubborn.

'I'll have to change everything now!' her mother grumbled. 'The church flowers, the flowers in the marquee. The—'

'Lilies will be lovely,' Lydie said gently, 'everywhere else.'

'Grace Marriott phoned.' Thankfully Hilary Pearson went off on another tack. 'She's thought of someone else she wants to invite!' she complained, when she was adding to the list herself all the time. Grace Marriott's phone call was the subject of her mother's conversation, or rather Grace Marriott's interference was, for the next ten minutes. So that when, mid-way through being harangued about her future mother-in-law's misdeeds, the telephone rang and her mother broke off to order, 'You answer it. I'm much too busy,' Lydie was heartily glad to escape. Her mother went in search of Mrs Ross; Lydie went to answer the phone. It was Jonah!

'Where are you?' Lydie wanted to know.

'You sound as though you need me?' Was that hope she heard in his voice? Fat chance!

'I've managed quite well with not seeing you for more than the briefest occasion,' she answered coolly, to hide that she felt all trembly inside from hearing him. Heaven alone only knew how she'd feel when she was standing beside him, marrying him!

'You're saying you've missed me?'

'I hardly know you!' she retorted pithily. It was a fact. She had seen him so rarely since their engagement he had become a stranger.

'We'll make up for that on our honeymoon,' he said, to

shatter any small amount of calm she might have found.
'What's wrong?' he asked.

Lydie wanted to deny that anything was wrong, but
found she was answering truthfully. 'I suppose, not to put
too fine a point on it, I'm feeling the pressure.'

'About the wedding?'

'To be blunt, between them your mother and my mother
and what I should want and what they *don't* want—and
they're not agreeing about that anyway—are driving me
potty.'

'As bad as that?'

She had to laugh. 'Not really,' she said, ready to apologise for her bad humour. 'I just wouldn't mind having
your job for a while, where I could fly away and leave all
this behind.'

'Are you propositioning me?'

She blinked. 'Pardon?'

'Forgive me. I thought you were suggesting we hid away
at Yourk House this weekend.'

'You're free this weekend?' she queried, her heart starting to thunder. 'You've been so busy...'

'Perhaps we should spend a little time this side of marriage in getting to know each other.'

The idea had instant appeal. Not only would she be away
from her mother's constant supply of something else to
stress her out about, but she would be with Jonah. 'Er—
are *you* propositioning me?' she asked him in turn. But,
nervous suddenly, she went on hurriedly, 'I—um—that is,
later, I know...'

'Calm down, Lydie,' Jonah instructed, a touch of humour
in his voice. 'What are you trying to say?'

She swallowed down her agitation. This was ridiculous.
For heaven's sake, she was marrying the man in two weeks'
time! 'B-basically,' she began chokily, 'what I'm trying to
say is that I'm—er—not read to c-commit...'

There was a pause. Then Jonah was asking, 'As in—
sleep with me?'

'That's about it.'

Another moment of silence followed, then, 'We could have a non-committed weekend at Yourk House?' he suggested.

Oh, yes. She loved him so. Ached so just to see him. 'I'd have my own room?' Why was she prevaricating? For goodness' sake, he'd be telling her to forget it any minute now!

'Non-committed goes hand in hand with you having your own room,' Jonah assured her.

'Oh, Jonah, am I being difficult?' She all at once felt dreadful. 'I'm sorry. You're probably stressed out too!' He said nothing, and she went rushing on, 'Bearing in mind what's between us, I'd like to be friends with you—if we can.'

She could almost see him smile as he rolled the words, 'Friends and lovers,' around on his tongue. And, while her heart was jumping around like a wild thing, 'But not the two together this weekend,' he said softly. 'Do you know, Lydie, I would be honoured to be your friend.'

Her backbone was ready to melt. 'Shall I see you at Yourk House on Saturday?' she asked, striving her hardest to be sensible.

'I'll call for you at your place around six on Friday,' Jonah decided, and, with nothing more to agree on, 'Till then,' he said, and rang off.

And Lydie came away from the phone in something of a daze. It seemed a positive age since she had last seen Jonah, but she was gong to spend the whole weekend with him—which they would use in getting to know each other. She couldn't wait. She absolutely hungered for a sight of him. She loved him so much.

CHAPTER SEVEN

FRIDAY could not come round fast enough, though her mother was not at all pleased that Lydie would not be at home that weekend. 'I just don't know how you can think of going away when there's such a lot still to be done!' Hilary Pearson complained.

Lydie did not want to argue. 'Mother you're such a brilliant organiser,' she replied, which was only the truth. 'You're so far in advance, my being away for the weekend won't make a scrap of difference.'

'There's you wedding dress...'

'I'm collecting it next Wednesday.' And, beating her mother to it, 'And I've arranged with Kitty, Emilia and Gaynor to see them on Thursday about their fittings.'

'Donna...'

'And I'm taking Donna'a dress with me when I go to see her.'

'What if...?'

'And it shouldn't need altering. Donna has spoken personally to the fitter over the phone.'

'It's a pity she can't leave those children for a day to come with you and your cousins on Thursday,' Hilary Pearson said sniffily.

Lydie was ready and waiting and eager to be away when Jonah called for her on Friday. She opened the door to him and saw him standing there tall, broad shouldered, saying nothing but just looking back at her with those fantastic blue eyes. For several speechless seconds while her insides went all peculiar all she was capable of doing was just staring at him. Was she actually marrying this fabulous all-male man two weeks tomorrow? Lydie looked from him and stepped back. 'My parents are out,' she excused them not being there to say hello, 'but I'm all ready.'

Gradually over the drive to Yourk House Lydie started to unwind. She rather thought Jonah had a lot to do with that. 'Still stressed out?' he asked pleasantly as they motored on.

'I'm sorry about that,' she apologised. 'Compared with what you must cope with every day, my getting in a state— stamping my foot, you'd call it—because my mother wants me to carry a bouquet of lilies when I want to carry lisianthus seems quite ridiculous.'

'No, it doesn't,' he denied. 'You're the bride. If you want to carry a posy of dandelions nobody should stop you.' She laughed. She loved him. 'What *are* you carrying?' he asked.

'Lisianthus,' she answered.

'Did I ever tell you that lisianthus are my favourite flowers?'

Lydie laughed again. Lying hound! 'You don't even know what they look like!' she accused.

Yourk House was a lovely old house. It was set in its own grounds and did not appear to have a near neighbour. Lydie stood on the drive with him, and he glanced down at her. 'Come inside and I'll show you around—then you can tell me if you think you could be happy here.'

Lydie knew as soon as she walked through the door that she could be. The house seemed to have a feel about it. It welcomed her. 'We'll be living here after…?'

'When we're married,' he agreed, and dropped their weekend bags down by the bottom of the wide and elegant staircase while he showed her round the downstairs rooms.

Yourk House was not as old as her present home, nor did it have as many rooms as Beamhurst Court, but what it lacked in age and size it made up for in style and comfort.

Upstairs there were five bedrooms and adjoining facilities, and they looked at each bedroom in turn. 'This is the one I thought you'd like this weekend,' Jonah said, opening the door to a large, high-ceilinged airy room.

'It's lovely,' she murmured, and went in, admiring the four-poster bed and the charming furniture. She went over to the window and looked out. It was peaceful and tranquil, and she loved it.

Leaving that room, Jonah took her to see his bedroom, the master bedroom. And she knew that, when they returned from honeymoon, this would be her bedroom too. She would share this bedroom with Jonah. Her mouth went dry and she went to one of the windows in the room. She felt then that she should tell him that she had never slept with a man before—but her throat seemed too locked to tell him anything.

She knew he had come to stand beside her, but when he placed a casual arm about her shoulder, her thoughts just seemed to blank off. 'You're trembling!' She heard his voice somewhere above her head. 'Oh, my—' He broke off, and turned her to face him. She looked up at him; his expression was serious. 'You're—not afraid of me, Lydie?' he asked.

She immediately shook her head. 'No,' she answered truthfully. 'I'm not afraid of you at all.' She smiled at him, he seemed a shade worried and she didn't want that. 'What I am—and I can hardly believe it myself—is shy, I think. I thought I'd grown out of that long since, but...'

Her voice faded when Jonah took her in his arms and held her close up to him. Instinctively she placed her head on his chest, and he held her like that for long wonderful minutes. 'We'll be all right together,' he assured her. 'We've barely seen one another since we became engaged, and we didn't see so much of each other before then.' He paused, and then suggested, 'We'll make up for that this weekend.'

'Agreed,' she said, and, looking up, she smiled, and because she loved him, so as he looked down she stretched up and kissed him, not passionately, but a kiss that was perhaps just a little more than 'friends'. His arms tightened about her.

She pulled back. 'W-was that all right?' she asked shakily.

He smiled. 'Very all right,' he answered, and she started to wonder what on earth had got into her—and stepped back. 'Would you like to look around on your own while I shower and get out of my work clothes?' he suggested. 'Then we'll go out and eat.'

Lydie awoke early on Saturday morning in the room Jonah had shown her to. She lay there thinking of him and marvelling at how well they had got on with each other last night. She had not thought it possible to love him more than she had, but with each new facet she learned of him she fell yet deeper in love with him. He had been a charming dinner companion.

Thinking of the previous evening reminded her that, at some point in one of their many conversations that had rambled all over the place, he had last night, in some throwaway kind of remark, mentioned that nobody had brought him an early-morning cup of tea in bed since the day he had left home for university.

Lydie was out of bed in a flash, pausing for a moment to consider getting showered and dressed first, but then fearing that by then Jonah might be up and about. She tied her cotton wrap about her and tiptoed down the stairs.

A short while later, tea tray in hand, she was coming back up the stairs but was by then having second thoughts. She couldn't do it. It would be like invading his privacy. But why shouldn't she? It would make him smile, and anyway…

In the end, having dithered outside his door for long hesitating seconds, Lydie knocked lightly on his door and went in. 'Lydie!' he exclaimed, awake and starting to sit up. He seemed genuinely pleased to see her.

'Your tea, sir,' she said, and he too remembered their conversation, and grinned.

'Where's yours?' he wanted to know.

'I left it in the kitchen.'

Lydie went over to him, and as he sat there she saw from his broad naked chest that he seemed to favour sleeping in the raw—his top half anyway, and she didn't want to know about anything else. She averted her gaze and placed the tray on his bedside table.

She would have hurried away then, only he caught a light hold of her wrist. 'Come and talk to me,' he urged.

'I...' She looked into his wonderful eyes. 'What do you want to talk about?'

'Anything,' he replied, and moved over to make room. 'Sit here and—' his mouth quirked upwards '—naturally in a non-committed way, let's get—intimate.'

That word 'intimate' shook her a little, but any implication she might have been wary of was negated by his use, in the same sentence, of those words 'non-committed'. So she took that step needed to bring her against the bed.

'Here,' he said, holding out his right arm.

Lydie would have chosen to sit facing him, her feet on the floor, but this was the man she loved, for heaven's sake, and in no time she had disposed of her slippers and was sitting on top of the bed covers with Jonah's right arm about her shoulders. And—it was bliss.

Though with regard to talking about anything, feeling the warmth of his arm about her through the thinness of her light wrap, she could think of nothing else, and certainly nothing to say.

That was until, 'What pretty toes you have,' Jonah observed.

She looked at her pale delicate feet, which looked pretty normal to her. 'Thank you kindly,' she said, and laughed, and commented, 'Peculiar things, feet,' and laughed again at the absurdity of her answer, and was ready to collapse when he dropped a light kiss on her hair—as if he cared for her. 'Do you l-like me?' she asked in a rush, and immediately apologized. 'I'm sorry. I shouldn't have asked that.'

'Of course you should. I'd like to think we could talk about anything at all without embarrassment.' She heard a smile creep into his voice as he went on to ask, 'And would I permanently marry myself to someone I actually *dis*-liked?'

'That—wouldn't be sensible,' she murmured, striving her best to be sensible herself then and there, when his head came nearer, touched hers, and they sat, he under the covers from the waist down, she on top of the covers, with their heads one against the other. 'Er—what shall we do today?' she asked, about the only practical thing she could find floating around in her intellect just then.

'I've made arrangements for us to go and select our wedding rings,' he answered, causing her heart, which hadn't seemed to act normally for some while now, to start leaping about again.

'*Our* wedding rings?' she repeated. 'You're having a wedding ring as well?'

'If you're going to wear a marriage band, it seems only fair that I should,' he answered, and suddenly, after all the weeks of preparation that had been going on, only then did any of it all at once start to feel real.

Lydie pulled a little away from him, tense suddenly, half turning so she could see into his face. 'It's really going to happen, isn't it?'

'Our marriage?' She nodded, her eyes wide as she looked at him. He could, she supposed, have reminded her toughly of her father's despair if their marriage did not go ahead. But he didn't get tough, he instead smiled, and told her, 'Your future mother-in-law and my future mother-in-law will give us hell if it doesn't.'

Lydie had to smile, her tension instantly vanishing. She looked at him, loved him—and knew that this just would not do. 'I'd better go,' she said quickly, and would have manoeuvred herself off the bed—only Jonah took a hold of her hand and held her there.

She gave him a questioning glance. 'There's no hurry, sweetheart,' he murmured lightly, 'but how about we make a start by greeting each day—with a kiss?'

Lydie felt colour flare to her face. He was right, of course. Soon they would be man and wife, in every respect, maybe it was time to break down a few of those shyness barriers, and to skirt the edges of a more intimate relationship.

She looked at him. 'I'd like to,' she mumbled.

'Still lying, Lydie?'

'I'm never going to lie to you again,' she promised solemnly. 'But...' She was starting to tremble; she was wearing next to nothing. It was a new situation. 'I'm a bit nervous, I think,' she confessed. She had kissed him yesterday, but he had been dressed then, and today, now, this minute, he was wearing next to nothing too. It was a new situation and she felt too all over the place. 'Could you do it? The kissing, I mean.'

He stared at her for long moments, then, as if feeling her trembling and not wanting her nervous of him, he gently gathered her in his arms. 'You'll be safe with me, Lydie,' he breathed against her mouth, 'I'll never harm you.'

Oh, Jonah. Their lips met in such a gentle kiss she could have cried from the tenderness of it. She felt quite mesmerised when it ended, and looked deep into his eyes—until she suddenly became aware that her hands were on his hair strewn naked chest, her fingers touching his nipples.

'Oh!' she cried in consternation.

Jonah stared at her, comprehension dawning about what that 'oh' had been all about. 'You haven't had many lovers, have you, Lydie?'

Intimate? They were supposed to be getting to know each other—but she still couldn't tell him of her lack of knowledge in the lover department. 'I'm going,' she said, and leapt from the bed to hurry back to her own room.

She showered and got dressed feeling very much mixed up. Perhaps it was only natural that she should feel a shyness, a reserve, with the man she was going to marry. Theirs wasn't a normal kind of courtship, she knew. But perhaps in the getting to know each other field in normal courtships everyone found there were barriers to be dismantled, piece by piece. Then she remembered that wonderful kiss of not so long ago, and everything else faded from her mind.

They had a toast and coffee breakfast, and Lydie was glad to find Jonah's manner was the same as it had ever been. He was super to be with and she enjoyed every moment of sitting beside him as they motored into town.

They chose matching plain gold rings, and, Jonah taking charge of both rings, they left the jewellers and drove back to Yourk House. Lydie made them a sandwich lunch while Jonah checked the computer in his study for mail.

'I'll show you around the village,' he suggested after lunch, and they walked and talked and talked and walked, and Lydie's heart was so full she just wanted to hold and hold him. Theirs might not be a normal kind of courtship, or a courtship at all, but Jonah seemed to effortlessly be making an effort for them to start off on the right footing.

They dined out again that night. Jonah had a part-time live-out housekeeper who saw to it that Yourk House was kept up to the mark. 'Mrs Allen would have come in this weekend, but I thought we'd manage fine by ourselves,' Jonah confided, going on, 'Doubtless you'll want to organise household matters your own way when we return from our honeymoon. I'm sure Mrs Allen will be pleased to work to suit you.'

'From what I can see, Mrs Allen is doing a first-class job without any input from me. But I'll be glad to talk matters over with her,' Lydie replied, inwardly thanking him for trying to make the transition from daughter of one house to mistress of another smooth for her.

They returned to Yourk House after dinner, Lydie refusing the offer of coffee or any other beverage but offering to make coffee for Jonah if he fancied a cup. He shook his head. 'How are you feeling now?' he asked, once they were relaxing in his drawing room. 'You were a little strung up when I called for you yesterday.'

'It's amazing what a little over twenty-four hours can do,' she replied. 'I must have needed to get away for a short while.' She smiled across at him. 'If I get to feel any more relaxed, I'll fall over.' Jonah smiled too, his glance on her mouth, moving to her eyes, then back down to her lips again. Then Lydie was recalling the way he'd checked his mail in his study before lunch. 'Is there some work you should be doing? Don't let me stop…'

'You're trying to get rid of me,' he accused.

'Not at all!' she answered, but, having enjoyed being with him so much, she started to feel guilty about having monopolised so much of his time. 'I think I'll make tracks for bed,' she decided, and wished she'd kept her mouth shut when he did not argue.

She got to her feet, and Jonah followed suit, walking with her to the door. When he stopped at the door but instead of opening it just stood looking down at her, so Lydie realised that because this weekend together had brought them closer, they were now 'kissing fiancés'.

'Er—goodnight,' she said, and took a step nearer to him, her heart drumming that new beat. She raised her face to his, and he bent, and he kissed her.

'Goodnight,' he answered gravely, and abruptly opened the door for her to go through.

Lydie took another shower before getting into her nightdress and climbing into the four-poster. She and Jonah would be all right, wouldn't she? He was kind, considerate and, while he did not love her—did love matter? And if it did matter that he would never love her, what then? She would still have to marry him. For her father, if not for herself, she would have to marry Jonah.

She fell asleep knowing that above all else, when she and Jonah were married, she must guard against him learning of the love she had for him. Perhaps, given time, Jonah might come to care a little for her, but, remembering where his tastes lay—Freya whatever-her-name-was, for one—Lydie didn't hold out much hope. He was happy to choose someone unsophisticated to be the mother of his children, but when it came to playmates women like Freya would win every time.

Having gone to sleep feeling not all that happy with her thoughts, nor with matters she could do nothing about, Lydie awoke with a start to find that it was morning, and that Jonah was in her room and had just placed a cup of tea down in her bedside table.

Instantly the sun came out for her and she struggled to sit up. 'I thought you liked to lie in on a Sunday morning!' she exclaimed, and felt at once all fluttering inside when Jonah bent down and, his fingers scorching her skin, casually put her slipped shoulder strap back in place.

'You remembered.' He grinned. 'I thought I should return yesterday morning's tea compliment.' And, while her heart played a merry tune within her, 'Hotch over,' he ordered, and as she moved over to make room he sat down on the side of the bed facing her. 'Sleep well?' he asked.

'Like a top,' she replied, having no idea what a top was, but having heard the expression somewhere, and very conscious of the virility of him, the smattering of hair on his chest showing through the neck of his short robe. 'Er—it looks like being a nice day,' she said hurriedly.

'Which reminds me—I have to be in London late this afternoon. I thought we'd have a leisurely morning and have lunch somewhere on the way back to your place?'

'Fine,' she agreed.

'I've a busy two weeks ahead of me and might be a bit pushed to see you. But if anything crops up, or you think of something you feel you may have a problem with, let my PA know. She'll know where to contact me—I'm on the move in foreign climes,' he explained.

'I think my mother's got most everything the way she wants it,' Lydie answered, already starting to feel desolate that he would be out of the country for the next two weeks.

'Apart from your bouquet,' Jonah teased.

'And the invitation list my mother wants closed but keeps thinking of other people we just *have* to invite. Your mother's doing the same, apparently.'

'So I believe,' he commented, revealing to Lydie that she wasn't the only one on the receiving end of motherly gripes. Though his expression had suddenly become stern when he said, 'My mother showed me the latest update to the invitation list your mother faxed her.' His tone had altered and Lydie knew something was wrong, even before he said, 'I wasn't going to bring it up—mainly because I couldn't believe my suspicions. But, since we're talking invitations, who's this Charles Hillier you've invited?'

Lydie stared at Jonah, her spirits taking a dive. 'You know quite well who he is,' she replied solemnly.

'I thought we agreed you were going to dump him?'

'He's my friend!' she protested. 'And I never agreed to "dump" him, as you call it. He's Donna's brother and—'

'And your one-time lover!' Jonah cut her off, somewhat aggressively she thought.

'He's not my lover!' she denied sharply, pulling the bed covers up over her shoulders defensively.

'He was!'

'He never was!' she retorted, outraged.

'You've slept with him!' Jonah replied, his eyes glittering a darker blue.

'Who told you that?' she demanded, feeling amazed. All this because she hadn't obeyed orders and 'dumped' a good friend?

'You did!' Jonah answered curtly, his chin jutting at an aggressive angle.

'When?' she challenged hostilely.

'You said, and I quote, "I stayed over with Charlie"—which meant you'd slept over at his place with him.'

Lydie felt a touch awkward as she recalled how she had known at the time that Jonah had thought Charlie was her boyfriend but from some peculiar sense of pride she had declined to put him straight on that issue.

'If you remember that then you'll also remember I told you people are always misinterpreting me!'

Jonah studied her, his expression unsmiling. 'You're saying now that you did *not* spend the night at his place?'

'I'm not saying that at all!' she denied. 'I've stayed over at Charlie Hillier's place several times when I've been in London and it's been late or more convenient to stay over with Charlie in preference to driving to wherever...' She shrugged. Love Jonah though she did, she did not want this conversation. 'I know you said we should talk of all sorts without embarrassment,' she told him coldly, 'but I'm not happy with this conversation.'

His look said Tough and his voice was terse when, clearly not a man who enjoyed being messed about, 'Tell me straight, Lydie Pearson,' he demanded, 'have you ever had sex with this man?'

She resented his question. The day had seemed to start off so wonderfully—how had it become so ghastly? 'It's none of your business who I had sex with or did not have sex with before you and I became engaged!' she told him haughtily. 'And I'd be glad if you'd get out of my room!'

'I'll get out when I'm ready,' he gritted icily. 'And I'm making it my business!'

'On what basis?' she challenged angrily. Love him she might, but *honestly*!

'On the basis that there'll be no one in that church a week next Saturday with whom I've slept. I should have thought common courtesy would decree you'd do me the same honour.'

Any further argument she might have found collapsed

without trace. It was a pride thing! He was doing her the courtesy of not putting her in the position of having to shake hands with any of his bed-friends; pride demanded that he did not have to shake hands with any of her lovers.

Oh, Jonah! 'I had—when I stayed at Charlie's place—I had my own room,' she admitted at last. 'Charlie and I were never lovers. I slept alone. He is what I told you he is—a friend.'

Some of the aggressiveness left Jonah's expression, but he still did not seem totally convinced. 'You're a very beautiful woman, Lydie,' he commented, and, as if it was the only conclusion that would fit, 'Does this Charlie, your friend, have some kind of a sexual hang-up?' Lydie was about to tell Jonah of Charlie's extreme shyness, but as if remembering her reaction, her consternation of yesterday when she had touched his naked chest, fingered his nipples, plus his surmise that she had not had many lovers, all at once Jonah was staring at her as if with new eyes. 'Or, Lydie, is it you?' he asked.

'W-what?'

'Do you have something against sex?' he pressed.

In view of the fact that they were to be married in under two weeks' time, Lydie supposed it was a fair question. That still did not make her feel any more comfortable with the subject, though.

She dropped her eyes down to the coverlet. 'I w-wouldn't know,' she replied huskily.

There was a pause and, when she would not raise her eyes, movement. And the next Lydie knew, Jonah had moved close and had taken a hold of her hands in his. 'You wouldn't know?' he questioned quietly. And, when she couldn't find her tongue, 'I know you're embarrassed with this subject,' he went on, 'and that traces of the paralysing shyness you've fought so valiantly to overcome still occasionally trip you up, but I honestly think this is a subject we should air.'

'I know you're right,' she whispered. 'And, and I've

wanted to tell you because, because I felt you should know—' She broke off. Even her ears felt a fiery red.

'Know what?' Jonah asked, any aggressiveness gone completely, only understanding there in his eyes when, placing a hand beneath her chin, he raised her head and made her look at him. 'What is it you felt I should know?'

'Oh, Jonah,' she wailed, 'I feel such a fool.'

'Share it with me,' he coaxed gently.

And at his tone, knowing if she went any redder she would burst into flames, Lydie found the courage to tell him. 'I've no idea if I've a sexual hang up or not, because I've—er—I've—um—never tried—um—sex.'

Jonah's reaction was to at first look totally taken aback, and then, still appearing shaken, a warm melting look came into his eyes. 'Oh, sweet Lydie,' he murmured. 'Are you saying you have never—ever—made love with anyone?'

'D-does that make me a freak?'

He smiled. 'It makes you a joy,' he answered, and just sat looking at her for ageless moments until, a wealth of good humour there, 'Given that this is still a non-committed weekend, how do you feel about a little experimenting?' he queried.

'Oh, J-Jonah,' she stammered nervously.

'There's nothing to worry about—I won't let it go too far,' he assured her. And, that smile playing around the corners of his mouth, 'Did we have our morning kiss?' he asked.

Lydie swallowed. 'You've forgotten already?' she attempted, and heard his light laugh. Then, unhurriedly, Jonah was reaching for her.

It was a gentle kiss, at first. She felt his warm touch as he gathered her to him and their lips met. And, more because she wanted to meet him all of halfway in this experiment, Lydie placed her arms around him.

Jonah raised his head to look deeply into her green eyes but, seeing no fear there, only shyness to be nightdress-clad and in his arms, he tenderly laid his mouth over hers again.

Lydie felt his hands warm at her back as they stroked in gentle rhythm. Then his kiss was starting to deepen. It was a heady kiss, and for a moment Lydie was terribly unsure and held back. But because she adored him, and was starting to love these moments of close intimacy, when his arms firmed about her and he held her closer so she moved that little way forward, and held him close.

Excitement started to spiral upwards in her, mingling with love and tenderness for him. He traced delicate kisses down the side of her face, then to her throat, and she clutched at him when he trailed more kisses down to her shoulder.

When he moved the strap of her nightdress down, kissing over her shoulder and down to the swell of her breast, and she felt his lips on that part of her breast that was uncovered, so love for him tangled with modesty and shyness, and she pushed at him slightly.

Immediately Jonah raised his head, drawing back a little, his eyes on her eyes. 'You're still not ready for my kisses, Lydie?' he asked, reminding her of the way, when she had agreed to marry him, she had said she didn't think she was ready for his kisses just yet.

'It isn't that,' she replied honestly. 'I'm just—well—feeling a bit—all at sea. Perhaps I should go and put some clothes on.'

His answer was to smile a teasing kind of smile, 'Oh, Lydie, Lydie,' he murmured softly. 'I don't—hmm—think you're quite getting the hang of this.'

Naturally, as the implication of that remark hit her, Lydie felt pink again. Jonah was meaning that in this instance she should be thinking more in terms of taking clothes off than in putting clothes on.

She took a shaky breath and, looking at him, felt her heart swell with love for him. 'Teach me,' she whispered, and for long, long, rapturous minutes knew utter bliss when tenderly Jonah drew her to him and, after first burying his face in her tousled dark hair, showered her with gentle, exquisite, kisses until she felt she would literally swoon away.

She had never known such a heady feeling like it. And when Jonah drew back to look into her eyes she wanted more, yet more. 'I'm not scaring you, Lydie?' he asked softly.

'I'll let you know when,' she murmured dizzily, and he laughed lightly, and drew her close to him again.

Kiss after gentle, tender kiss they shared, and Lydie's heart was pounding so loud she thought he might hear it. Then gradually a new dimension was entering Jonah's kisses and so, too, was a fire of wanting starting to flicker into life within Lydie.

She pulled back, feeling a little shaken. Instantly Jonah relaxed his grip. 'I *am* scaring you?' he questioned, his eyes studying and serious.

She shook her head. 'I don't think I've any hang up,' she told him honestly.

'Sweetheart,' he breathed, and held her close again, his mouth over hers, sending thrilling darts shooting through her when the tip of his tongue found its way through her parted lips.

She gave a startled movement, but, afraid he would stop, apologised immediately. 'I'm sorry,' she whispered quickly.

'I'm going too fast for you.' He blamed himself.

For answer she placed her lips over his and tasted his mouth with her tongue. She heard his groan of pleasure, and was thrilled anew. It seemed right to tell him that she loved him, but shyness held her back.

Then Jonah was creating all manner of new sensations in her when one caressing hand moved from her back to take slow caressing hold of her firm swollen breast. She jerked back, but he understood that too. 'It's all right,' he soothed.

But she was shy of his intimate touch, and leaned into him, and he took his hand from her breast and held her quietly to him for long moments. 'Have we proved that I don't have any kind of hang-up?' she asked.

'Do you want me?' he asked, and helped her out by adding, 'In case you haven't realised it, I confess, my dear, that I want you.'

Again she so nearly told him that she loved him, but bit it back—her love was something he had just not asked for. 'I feel I'm stumbling about in the dark,' she confessed.

'Shall we stop?'

'I didn't say I wasn't enjoying it,' she replied, and he laughed a joyous kind of laugh.

'What a delight you are,' he breathed.

It wasn't a declaration of love, but to hear him say she was a delight was music to her ears. 'I want to touch you,' she admitted shyly. But was nervous when, without more ado, he removed his robe, tossing it to one side. She swallowed hard, her eyes glued to his chest, her peripheral vision taking in long naked legs and some kind of undergarment.

'I want to touch you too,' he said softly, and moments later his mouth was over hers while his hands moved to capture both her breasts. And, while her desire for him made her feel breathless, he tenderly moulded her breasts, his fingers moving to tease the hardened tips, while Lydie gripped his naked shoulders tightly. Then all at once he was calling a halt. 'Oh, Lydie, Lydie,' he said hoarsely, his fingers reluctantly pulling away from her breasts. She felt his firm grip as he took hold of her upper arms, and was on fire for him when, as though struggling to find an even tone, Jonah said, 'If we don't stop now, we're going to be in deep trouble.'

But he had awakened feelings in her that had been dormant, and, 'I don't want you to stop!' she cried. That was before modesty belatedly galloped in. 'I shouldn't say things like that, should I?' she asked, a little self-consciously.

'Oh, my dear,' he murmured. 'If we don't stop, I'm going to have to see you without this tantalising piece of equipment,' he said, touching the material of her nightdress.

'Oh!' she gasped, and knew she was not as immodest as she had a moment ago thought. The idea of sitting there without a stitch on was something she was not quite ready for.

'And worse,' he went on, trying to inject a little humour into what was a very heat-filled time of sharing, 'there's a great risk you might catch a glimpse of me without mine.'

Lydie went hot all over. 'Truly a fate worse than death,' she attempted.

'Oh, sweetheart!' he groaned, and they kissed again, and clung to each other until abruptly Jonah broke from her and turned and reached for his robe. Only when it was safely about him did he turn to look at her. 'All right with you if I go now?'

'The alternative?' she asked.

'You don't need to ask,' Jonah told her, his wonderful blue eyes looking warmly into hers. 'But, since I can safely say we've become more committed this weekend than I intended in our non-committed pre-marriage time together, I think perhaps I should go.'

He went then, but when, later, both of them showered and dressed, they met in the kitchen, there was no awkwardness at the heady moments they had shared together.

Though, while Lydie was feeling slightly amazed that he could so matter-of-factly make coffee, toast and conversation as though nothing untoward had taken place between them, she discovered a short while later that he was not feeling so matter-of-fact as she believed.

'Let's go out,' he suggested.

'I thought you wanted a leisurely morning,' she reminded him.

He paused, and, eyeing her wryly, he replied, 'I did, but that was before your response in our lovemaking threatened to push me over the edge.'

Lydie stared at him, her heart soon thundering again.

'Are you saying what I think you're saying?' she asked. And, confused to know if he was meaning that if they stayed confined to the house he might make more love with her, 'I wish I knew more about this lovemaking business,' she mumbled.

Jonah looked solemnly at her. 'All in good time, Lydie,' he promised. 'All in good time.' And she went pink, which seemed to delight him, and they went out for a drive for him to acquaint her more with the area and to collect the Sunday papers.

Perhaps because she knew that there was every chance that when they said goodbye she would not see him again until she stood beside him in church, Lydie found she had no appetite for lunch. Jonah did not appear to eat a great deal either, she observed, but she rather thought that was because his mind was more on the business he had to return to London for than the fact that he would not see her again for almost two whole weeks.

He came into the house with her when they reached Beamhurst Court and said hello to her parents. And, while her mother went into raptures to her about just the 'right' hat she had bought on Saturday, Lydie saw that Jonah and her father had wandered over to the other side of the room and seemed to be having a very satisfactory conversation. She saw them shake hands—and her heart sank—Jonah must be planning to leave at any moment.

They ambled back to her and her mother, and although Lydie hadn't a clue what they had been talking about, she saw they seemed the best of friends. Which meant all in all everyone was getting on famously. But Jonah was on the point of leaving, and she didn't want him to go. She might not see him again for two long weeks, and already her heart was aching.

'Jonah has business he has to attend to,' she announced—rather starkly, it seemed to her.

'You won't stay to dinner?' Hilary Pearson invited, and

Lydie felt cheered that her mother was at last showing Jonah the warmer side of her nature.

Jonah charmingly declined, said goodbye to her mother, shook hands with her father again, and, when Lydie was ready to run up to her room and stay there until she saw him again, 'Coming to see me out, Lydie?' he asked.

They left her parents in the drawing room, and as they walked out to his car all Lydie could think was, Don't go, don't go. To counter the feeling, the fear that those words might actually spill out, 'Have a good trip,' she smilingly bade him as they halted at his car.

Jonah turned and looked down into her wide green eyes. 'Remember what I said. Any problems, anything at all, ring Eileen Edwards and she'll get a message to me.'

'I'll remember,' Lydie replied, and, just to show that she wasn't the smallest bit bothered that she might not see him again until she married him, 'Don't do anything I wouldn't do.'

'Which is guaranteed to curtail my—er—life.' Lydie laughed. The missing word there was 'sexual', as in 'sexual life'. 'You're even more beautiful when your face lights up in laughter,' Jonah told her.

'For that you may kiss me goodbye,' she allowed loftily.

Jonah reached for her, held her in his arms and looked long into her eyes. 'Did you think I wasn't going to?' he asked, but as his head came down, he did not require an answer. Their lips met, and with her heart thundering that familiar beat Lydie had the hardest work in the world not to throw her arms around him. She wanted to beg him to take her with him—but theirs was not a love match, and he would think her soft in the head.

He said not a word when he let her go. Just looked at her for a long silent moment or two. Then he was getting into his car and driving away.

Lydie walked back into the house, tears in her eyes. She loved him so much—and there were a whole thirteen days to be got through until she saw him again.

Lydie hoped each day to see or hear from Jonah, but heard not a word for over a week. It was a busy week, and she was glad it was so because her time with Jonah at Yourk House was starting to feel like light years away. Had they really kissed and caressed the way they had? Was she doing the right thing in marrying him the way she was? What alternative did she have? She recalled her father, his face happy and smiling when talking to a relative over the phone. She did not, she knew then, have any alternative. Her father was back to being the man he had been—and did not seem to have a care in the world.

The next week slowly dragged into being, and, after Saturday, her wedding day coming ever nearer, it was on Tuesday that Lydie packed up some of her clothes ready to take to Yourk House. She packed another couple of cases with clothes she thought she might need on honeymoon. They were spending Saturday night at Yourk House prior to jetting off to their honeymoon island on Sunday.

On Wednesday, with four days to go before her wedding, Lydie started to get nervous and began to experience grave doubts. When she received a phone call from Jonah, Lydie felt she would have been quite happy if he had called to cancel the whole thing.

'Where are you?' she asked tautly.

'Sweden.'

'When are you coming back?'

'You sound uptight, Lydie?'

'I'm sorry. I know ours isn't the normal head over heels thing—' well, not on his side anyhow '—but I think I'm just about in the worst stages of bridal nerves. We'll be all right, won't we, Jonah?' she asked him anxiously.

'Oh, my word, you are suffering.'

'I wish you were here,' she replied, totally without thinking. And, as she died a thousand deaths to have said such a thing, she quickly added, 'I've loads and loads of luggage to take over to Yourk House. You know,' she hurried on, 'my on-holiday clothes, and—um—stuff I'll need when I get back.'

'I should have thought of that,' Jonah replied. 'Mrs Allen will be there tomorrow if you've time to go over. I'll give her a call and tell her to give you a spare key—she always keeps several spares.'

'I—um…' Grief, she was feeling tongue-tied with the man—and she was marrying him in three days' time!

'We'll be all right, Lydie, I promise you,' Jonah came in to reassure her when she got stuck for words.

She felt wretched. 'I'll—um—see you on Saturday, then,' she said, and there seemed little else to say. She said a quick, 'Goodbye,' and put down the phone. Oh, heavens! She was going to be his wife in three days' time—she only hoped her nerves held out until then.

CHAPTER EIGHT

BY SATURDAY, while still in a state of nerves, Lydie knew that above all else she wanted to marry Jonah. She had no idea how they would fare together, but she would do her best to make her marriage to him work.

She was awake early; her mother was already up and doing. To Lydie's tremendous surprise, when if it had dawned on her at all that she would have breakfast in bed, she'd have thought their housekeeper would be delegated to bring it to her, Hilary Pearson herself came in carrying a breakfast tray.

Coping with her surprise, Lydie began, 'You shouldn't...'

'Yes, I should,' her mother contradicted. 'This is your special day, and my mother brought me my breakfast in bed on the day I married your father.'

'W—' Lydie broke off. 'Thank you,' she accepted gratefully.

'How do you feel?'

'I'm not sure yet,' Lydie confessed, adding truthfully, 'But inclined to think I should pinch myself to check I'm awake and it's all real.'

'Which is perfectly natural.' Her mother smiled, and to Lydie's astonishment went on to say, 'I'm sorry if you've had reason to think from time to time that I've been in training for The Most Miserable Old Trout Of The Year, but this has been a most difficult time for your father and me.'

'It must have been truly awful at times,' Lydie sympathised.

'Our—difficulties—came close to wrecking our marriage,' her mother admitted, but smiled cheerfully when she went on, 'But, thanks to Jonah, we've come through.'

'You're referring to that cheque he gave me?'

'That was our darkest moment. I'm extremely grateful to him, Lydie.' She smiled again. 'Even if I haven't always managed to show it. He has no idea of the headaches he caused when he gave me just six weeks to get everything ready for today.'

'You've worked very hard,' Lydie stated. 'And I do thank you.'

'I don't need your thanks; it's what I'm here for.' Hilary Pearson beamed. 'Though I will say some of it has been a nightmare. Now, eat your breakfast and don't hurry to come downstairs—the house is packed with your cousins and aunts. Make the most of your peace and quiet,' she advised.

Her mother left her to go and check out the breakfast room, ready to organise anyone who, in her opinion, needed organising. She really had worked hard, Lydie reflected, and knew that, while perhaps her mother's sometimes acid tongue might occasionally grate on her, she loved her mother and her hard-working mother loved her.

With nothing but the best good enough, Lydie had protested fiercely about the cost of her wedding. Where was the money coming from? she had wanted to know. The last time she'd made her objections felt she had been told she was being a perfect pain and sharply requested not to interfere again. From then on Lydie had tried not to wince at the next 'must have' her mother had thought of.

Her marriage to Jonah was taking place at two that afternoon, and, while Lydie tried to keep to her room, she might just as well had joined all her relatives downstairs, for she had a constant stream of visitors.

Donna, the only attendant who had not stayed overnight, arrived at noon. Nick and their children were with her, but Donna was the only one of them her mother allowed upstairs.

'Your dress is gorgeous, absolutely gorgeous!' Donna

exclaimed, on seeing it hanging on the outside of the wardrobe. It was a dress of empire design, the bust embroidered with silks and pearls, with folds of the soft jersey silk material falling straight from beneath the bust to hem. It had short sleeves and a modest rounded neckline that would reveal just the merest hint of cleavage. With it Lydie would wear the pearls her parents had given her for her twenty-first birthday, and the whole ensemble would be completed with a full-length veil kept in place by the family diamond and pearl tiara borrowed from her father's sister. The tiara was passed down the female line and would one day be passed down to Lydie's cousin Emilia.

Lydie had bathed when she had got up, but at twelve-thirty she decided to shower prior to getting ready. If it was supposed to be a tranquil time for her—it was not. Apart from the fact that one or other of her cousins had arrived yesterday without some essential to complete their toilet, and charged in to borrow a brush, a comb, a hairdryer, Lydie had started to be swamped by her nerves.

She couldn't wait to see Jonah, but heartily wished this day were over. Nerves were well and truly getting to her. She had long since overcome that dreadful shyness of adolescence but, with all these people about, it seemed to have returned with a vengeance. She wished she had never agreed to a large wedding—though, recalling the way her mother had gone into action, did not think she'd had very much choice. Lydie was glad when everyone went to get dressed.

She seated herself before her dressing table mirror. Solemn green eyes stared back at her. In a little over an hour she would become Mrs Jonah Marriott—she felt all trembly inside at the thought.

At one-fifteen her four attendants came to her room. 'How do we look?' the beautiful Kitty asked, giving a little twirl in her empire line dress of midnight-blue.

'Beautiful,' Lydie answered. 'You all do.'

'Now you, Lydie,' said Donna, and as chief attendant

and matron of honour she firmly pushed the others out. Lydie, her night-dark hair looped into a crown on the top of her head, and with the small amount of make-up she wore in place, was ready to slip on her dress. All that remained was to place her veil and tiara around the crown of her hair.

Donna seemed stuck for words when, having helped Lydie, she stood back to look at her. 'Will I do?' Lydie asked.

'Oh, Lydie, you look sensational!' Donna exclaimed, and looked quite weepy.

As did Hilary Pearson when she came into the room a minute later—the mail which had been forgotten about earlier forgotten again when, seeing her daughter in her bridal finery, she dropped the post down on Lydie's dressing table, and, 'Oh, darling,' she cried, 'what I picture you look!'

'So do you,' Lydie said lightly—that or have the whole three of them in tears. But her mother, in heels higher than normal for her and a wonderful frothy hat, did look superb.

Her mother stepped towards her, looking as though she might give her a hug, but, as if fearing to spoil or crease her dress, stepped back again. 'Right,' she said, adopting a bracing tone, 'it's time the bridesmaids were on their way to church,' and, ushering Donna out in front of her, she went to get them organised.

Lydie looked at herself in the full-length mirror when they had gone. Would Jonah think her a sensational picture? Remembering the stunning blonde, Freya, Lydie rather thought he was used to sensational.

But she did not want to dwell on thought of his past 'friends'; her stomach was churning enough without that. Lydie found a distraction in the mail her mother had brought in. There was an array of wedding cards, which she would open later, but there was also one letter. It was from a firm of solicitors.

Lydie checked that it was addressed to her and decided she had time to open it—and did. And almost collapsed in shock. The solicitors were executors for Alice Mary Gough, and Lydie, it appeared, was her aunt's sole beneficiary. By her will, Miss Gough had left her the house known as No. 2 Oak Tree Road, in the village of Penleigh Corbett. 'We have obtained the keys from the local authority, to whom they were inadvertently delivered, and shall be pleased if you will call and sign for them.'

Lydie read the letter through twice and, her eyes misting over, she had just slid the letter back into its envelope and placed it back on her dressing table when her parents came into her room.

Her parents spoke both together. Her father to say, 'Oh, my baby girl, how lovely you are!'

Her mother said, 'I'm going now,' and, catching sight of her daughter's misty eyes, 'Oh, please don't cry, Lydie, you'll start me off.' She then swallowed noisily and turned abruptly to her husband. 'I shall expect you to leave in exactly twelve minutes' time, Wilmot.'

'Yes, dear,' he answered sweetly.

'And don't laugh at me!' she commanded.

'No, dear,' he said, and, relieving the tension, they all three laughed.

Left alone with her father, though, Lydie just had to question, 'I thought Aunt Alice rented her house from the council?'

The perfect father, he didn't turn a hair, but took her question as the sort of question brides normally ask when they are trying to concentrate on something else to take their mind off the nerves they are enduring. 'She did,' he replied. 'For years and years. In fact she'd been a tenant for so long, paid rent for so long, that when—under some government scheme—she had the chance to buy it from the council she could have bought it for some ridiculously low price. She never had any money, as you know, but I did offer to lend her all she needed. She wouldn't take it, of course.'

'You didn't lend her the money?'

'It was only a trifling sum, but she was too proud to take it. Said, quite snootily, that she didn't care to be beholden to your mother. She was a stubborn old bat—lost a property that must be worth something in the region of a hundred and fifty thousand at today's prices.' He glanced at his watch. 'We'll have to go in a few minutes. Now, don't worry,' he went on cheerfully, 'I wouldn't let you go to Jonah if I wasn't fully convinced he'll do right by you.'

They went down the staircase with Lydie starting to real-ise that her great-aunt must have managed to scrape to-gether the money to buy her house—and, typically Great-Aunt Alice, had kept her business to herself. Lydie did not want her house, she would much rather that her great-aunt would be in church to see her married that day.

Mrs Ross, who was keeping a sharp eye on the caterers, came to see her before she left her home for the last time as a single woman. But the housekeeper's eyes filled with tears when she saw her, and all she was able to say, before she handed Lydie her bouquet from the hall table, was a choked, 'I know you'll be very happy.'

Lydie thanked her. The bouquet of pink and white lis-ianthus was gorgeous, and worth the battle. She left her home to the sound of church bells, but on the short ride to the church Lydie, beset by nerves, could only think of Jonah waiting for her. She would make him a good wife, she *would*, she vowed—and then, out of nowhere, she was assaulted by the most torturous realisation that—she should not be marrying him!

And it wasn't just nerves. Her reason for marrying him, apart from her deep love for him that he knew nothing about, was because he had given her a cheque for fifty-five thousand pounds that she could not pay back. For her fa-ther, who had been hurting like the blazes that there was no way he could pay an outsider that money, she was mar-rying Jonah in order that he should be an insider.

Thoughts were rioting around in her head at a tangent. Jonah hated to be cheated. He was marrying her—yes, because he had decided it was time for him to marry—but, on thinking about it then, in her het-up state, she was sure a lot of that decision stemmed from having witnessed for himself the near broken man her father had been! A man then nothing like the buoyant man her father was today. Jonah had the highest respect for her father—but would Jonah have any respect for her when he knew that, thanks to her legacy from her great-aunt, he need not marry at all? His intended bride could pay him back. She could sell the property and return that fifty-five thousand pounds to him. Lydie gasped in shock as the realisation hit her that to marry Jonah would be—*to cheat him*!

'You're very pale,' her father said in concern as they arrived at the church. 'Are you all right, Lydie?'

She should tell him. Tell him that the wedding was off. 'Fine,' she murmured faintly, her head in turmoil as they walked up the path to where her attendants were waiting in the sunshine.

All before she had been able to marshal any coherent thought, her bridesmaids were falling in behind her. And while Lydie, nerves grabbing her by the throat, was reeling from her thoughts, in the next instant so the organist changed from the Handel he had been playing to Wagner's 'Bridal March' from 'Lohengrin' and the congregation rose to its feet.

I'll talk to the vicar. Lydie's thoughts raced in panic. I'll whisper to him that I need to speak to my fiancé in private. I'll... She saw Jonah up ahead, tall and straight in his morning suit, and suddenly she couldn't think of anything but that she loved him so heartbreakingly much and wanted so to marry him, to be his wife.

Swiftly she looked from him to her left, where her mother, her brother and his new wife were standing. Her mother would kill her if she cancelled now. After all her labours, her hair-tearing, her mother would probably never speak to her again if now, at the very last minute, with everyone there to witness it, she called the wedding off.

Lydie looked to the front again, and she and her father arrived next to Jonah and his best man, his brother Rupert. Lydie's thoughts were in total disarray when she felt that Jonah was looking at her. She turned her head to look at him—he smiled at her—and quite simply she loved him so much that what she should do and what she did were poles apart. She married him.

It was as if in a dream that Donna relieved her of her bouquet, that her father gave her away, and all Lydie was conscious of was of Jonah. Her voice was husky; his voice was firm, unhesitating as they exchanged their vows. Their eyes met, and she felt like melting at the warm encouragement in his superb blue eyes—as if he was very aware of the dreadful shyness that had chosen that day of all days to roar in and trounce her.

His touch on her shaking hand was magical, tender, as he placed his ring on her marriage finger—and they were declared man and wife. Shortly afterwards, the marriage register signed, witnessed, and all formalities completed, the organist was breaking out into 'The Wedding March' from Mendelssohn's *A Midsummer Night's Dream*. And, with her hand through Jonah's arm, they were soon heading the procession back up the aisle and going out into the sunlight, the bell ringers again busy.

They stood together at the church steps, people milling around, photographers, professional and amateur beavering away. Jonah bent to her. 'I know you've heard all the compliments, but out of this world doesn't begin to cover how indescribably lovely you look, Lydie.'

'Thank you,' she murmured. But by then her brain had started to wake up, and the enormity of what she had just done began to thunder in. *She had cheated him!* Oh, my… She should tell him. She saw her mother—beaming.

'You're still shaking,' Jonah bent to say quietly. 'We'll be…'

'Jonah, I…' There were people everywhere, friends, family, everyone smiling, everyone in first-class humour.

'Gone shy Lydie?' he teased, perhaps to help her feel a little less strung up when, having interrupted him, she had nothing more to add. She couldn't answer. He'd hate her when she told him. And tell him she would have to.

Though in the following hours, although they were together the whole time, there was not the smallest chance of any kind of a private conversation. And Lydie's nerves stretched and frayed.

She had stood with him to greet the guests. Had introduced people to him he had not previously met; he had done likewise. Charlie Hillier came and kissed her cheek and she introduced him to her new husband. Jonah weighed Charlie up in two seconds' flat, and was charming to him. Then Jonah was introducing someone called Catherine—and as Lydie shook hands with her she could not be jealous because she trusted Jonah not to allow her to shake hands on this day with any of his old flames.

And all the while that was what was getting to her—she could trust Jonah but, by cheating him, he could not trust her!

They sat down to a meal that was quite splendid; her mother would not have countenanced anything else. Then the speeches began. First Rupert made a humorous speech—Catherine, seated next to him, turned out to be his latest in a long line of girlfriends. Then Lydie's father made a wonderful speech where he let everyone know that if he'd had to personally choose a husband for his dear daughter he would not have done better than to have made the choice she had made. Then Jonah was on his feet, his speech short but sounding sincere when he said that he would want for nothing more than to be married to Lydie.

Had that been true Lydie felt she would have fainted away on the spot from the sheer joy of it. But as spontaneous applause broke out, and her mother and Jonah's mother, and even Kitty, seemed quite moist-eyed, Lydie knew that it was not true.

In fact she started to think that all of it was a sham, and

she was heartily glad when the time came that she could disappear up to her room to change. She needed to be by herself. Though in actual fact she had time only to read through again the letter from her great-aunt's solicitors and to slip it inside her handbag—oh, why had it had to arrive today?—before her cousins and Donna were in her room to help her change. Lydie was quite able to change without assistance, and could have done without company just then, but tradition was tradition, she supposed.

'Are you feeling all right, Lydie?' Donna asked under cover of the three cousins hooting with laughter at some tale of Gaynor's. 'You seem quiet, if you know what I mean.'

'I'm absolutely fine,' Lydie answered. 'It's been a bit of a long day, though, hasn't it?'

'You should be home by eight, nine o'clock at the latest. And you'll have two whole months on your island in which to recuperate.' Donna smiled.

From where Lydie was viewing it, she would be very surprised if, after she had told Jonah what she had to tell him, they would be going anywhere. Forget the honeymoon.

Though, with their goodbyes seeming to take for ever, Lydie started to think they would be lucky if they reached Yourk House by nine that evening, let alone eight. And by the time she was at last alone with Jonah, she was feeling so uptight she didn't think she would be able to say a word to him. Yet she must. Before this day was out he had to be told—that his wife was a cheat!

'Alone at last!' Jonah commented as he swung his long sleek car out past the gates of Beamhurst Court.

Tell him! Lydie opened her mouth—and closed it again. 'Jonah...' she tried, but her voice sounded all kind of cracked and strangled in her ears and she could find nothing to add.

Jonah glanced at her and smiled, one hand leaving the steering wheel briefly to take her hand in a reassuring squeeze. 'Try to relax, Lydie,' he said kindly. And, his smile deepening, 'You know I don't bite.'

Oh, heavens, he thought she was nervous with him. That on this, her bridal night, she was tense and starting to get worried. But it wasn't that—she longed to be in his arms, ached for his kisses. She had not seen him for almost two long weeks. Almost two long weeks since she had last been in his arms, had last been held by him, held and... She blanked her thoughts off and closed her eyes, and was tormented all the way to Yourk House. She wanted to be his wife. But that word 'cheat' rattled around and around in her head. Cheating. Was that any way to start to build a marriage?

'Tired?' Jonah asked as they pulled up at Yourk House.

Lydie guessed he could be forgiven for thinking that. Her replies to any conversation he had attempted had been monosyllabic to say the least. She found refuge in the answer she had given Donna earlier.

'It's been a—a bit of a long day,' she replied, and as Jonah got out of the car and came round to the passenger side she quickly stepped out—in consequence bumping into him.

She would have turned away, but the hands that came out to steady her continued to hold on to her. Lydie looked up into a pair of fantastic, understanding blue eyes.

'Stop worrying. I'm not a monster.' He gave her a small shake. 'We don't have to seal our marriage tonight. We've got two whole months in which to intimately get to know each other.' He smiled encouragingly. 'There's no rush.'

She stared at him, all thoughts of how she had cheated him gone temporarily from her mind. 'You—don't want to make love to me?'

He laughed. It was wonderful to see. 'Oh, Lydie,' he said softly, 'have you got a lot to learn.' And, so that she did not misinterpret his reply, 'I want you, quite desperately, but I want more desperately that everything is right for you.'

Lydie looked at him, startled. But before she could begin to assess what, if anything, he meant by that last bit, he had picked her up in his arms and was carrying her over to the front door of Yourk House.

'Traditional, I believe,' he murmured, unlocked the door, and carried his bride over the threshold of her new home.

He did not set her down until they were in the drawing room. And by then Lydie's thoughts and emotions were all over the place. Her heart was racing just to be so close to him. Don't tell him, urged the part of her that wanted so badly to stay with him. Why tell him? If that letter from those solicitors hadn't come today she would have been married to him for two whole months before either of them knew anything about it. By then they would have grown to know each other intimately. Perhaps by then Jonah, her husband, would have begun to care for her a little. Who knew? Don't tell him.

He lowered her to the floor, and she stood with him in the circle of his loose hold. 'Mrs Ross will have left us some supper,' he began.

But Lydie was shaking her head. She was starting to get confused. Food would choke her. 'I'm—not hungry,' she said quickly, her voice sounding all kind of staccato even to her ears.

'You've had a busy day,' Jonah answered, 'chatting to all our guests with never a minute to yourself. Would you like to go to bed?' he asked. And, when she went to jerk out of his hold, 'Shh,' he quieted her, but kept her there in his arms. 'You're trembling,' he murmured, and smiled re-assuringly as he tried to ease the new moments of being alone at the start of their married journey together. 'We'll share a bed, but until you feel comfortable having me there next to you we'll just lie together.'

'Oh, Jonah!' she cried, emotional tears welling up inside as she coped with a feeling of being stunned that he should be so considerate, so thoughtful. 'You're so kind.'

He looked at her, his mouth curving wryly. 'Does that

entitle me to kiss my bride?' She stared at him, her heart going wild within her. And, when she was too choked to speak, Jonah appeared to take that as an indication that she had no objection. Because a moment later he was drawing her that little bit nearer and his head was coming down— and his lips were claiming hers.

It was a gentle kiss, a tender kiss, and when he pulled back they just stood staring into each other's eyes. What he was reading in hers she had no idea. Certainly there was no objection there to his kiss. And, as he drew her that little bit nearer still, Lydie did not have any objection to make when he kissed her again.

Of their own volition her arms went around him, and suddenly she was on the receiving end of a kiss that made her legs wilt. 'My wife,' he murmured against her mouth, and as she responded their bodies came close, and they kissed and moulded to each other.

She loved him so, and her lips parted voluntarily to allow the tip of his tongue to enter. She pressed to him and felt a fire scorch through her when he moved his hands to her hips and he pulled her yet closer to his wanting body.

And her body was wanting too. 'My wife', he had called her. She was his wife. Joy started to break in her. But as the words 'My wife' throbbed through her, and passion between them mounted, so that part of her that was essentially honest chose just that moment to rocket in and bombard her.

Wife! She had no right to be his wife. She felt his hands on her skin beneath the short jacket of her suit. Felt the bliss as he caressed her silken skin. He kissed her again, ardently, his hands caressing her back, her bra a barrier to that caressing. He unclasped her bra, his hands travelling freely, deliciously, over her soft smooth back while his tongue penetrated that little bit further. His mouth was still over hers, creating mayhem to her senses when his palms moved round to her ribcage. She felt his warmth and seemed not to be breathing at all when his loitering hands inched their way up under her bra. Then in breath-holding moments his hands caressed their way ever upwards until both her firm breasts were in his hold. Again he kissed her, and as his fingers made a nonsense of all coherent thought in her he stroked and moulded in exquisite torment around the hardened peaks of her breasts that welcomed and wanted more. Instinctively she pressed into him, hearing his small sound of wanting; it was how she felt too.

He kissed her again, and his mouth was still over hers when his reluctant fingers left her breast, and with that hand caressing the side of her face he looked deep into her eyes, and softly breathed, 'I think we'll be more comfortable upstairs, don't you?' He bent, as if to pick her up in his arms and carry her to their marriage bed.

Her sharp, *'No!'* stopped him, though she hardly knew from where that protest had come. He was her husband and she wanted to be his wife.

Arrested by her protest, he stared at her, as well he might—she had been giving him very affirmative signals. 'No?' he echoed.

'I—c-can't,' she stuttered, and knew that she could not. She loved him too much to cheat him. If she said nothing, she would be his wife—their marriage consummated. It was what she wanted. She wanted to be part of him, of so much, to share her body with him, to share his body. But—no! It could not be. It had to stop. With her heart aching she turned her back to him and did up her bra, and, her throbbing, wanting breasts once more confined, she straightened her jacket and turned to him. He was looking nowhere but at her, a thoughtful expression on his face.

'Okay,' he said calmly after a second or two, 'let's go back five minutes. I'll apologise for what's just happened if you want me to, but you're a very desirable woman, Lydie—you'll have to forgive that my antennae read it wrong. So we'll go upstairs—but perhaps you'd better sleep alone tonight after all.'

'Oh, Jonah. It's not—' She broke off, shyness belatedly

arriving so that she could not tell him that it was not that she did not want to follow where he lead in their lovemaking, but that it was not right that she should. 'I can't...' she said helplessly.

'You don't have to tonight. I've already said...'

'I can't—*ever*,' she butted in, because she had to.

'Ever?' He looked puzzled, and as if he was trying to work out what was going on here.

'Never,' she replied chokily.

'Oh, Lydie,' he sympathised. 'Your nerves are shot. Don't worry, after a night's rest, everything will—'

'Our marriage will have to be annulled!' she butted in quickly, while she could still find the strength.

'*Annulled?*' Oh, heavens, she could see that Jonah did not care at all for this development. Though his tone was controlled when he quietly asked, 'You don't think I might have a little something to contribute to that decision?'

'You don't understand,' Lydie said desperately, keeping her distance from him—she still felt all of a tremble from his kisses and needed all the strength she could find. Though she rather thought, knowing his strong aversion to being cheated, that he would help her on her way when she told him what she had to tell him.

'You're right there. I don't understand,' he replied.

'I—I cheated you,' Lydie confessed, her heart falling into her shoes when she saw him frown—he did not take kindly to hear he had been cheated, she could tell. She hurried on, 'I have the money—or will have. The fifty-five thousand! I knew it just before I left for the church,' she admitted breathlessly. And, as she had to, 'I should never have married you,' she owned shakily.

What she expected once that stark confession was out in the air, Lydie was not sure. Probably that, hating that anyone should attempt to cheat him, Jonah would send her back to Beamhurst Court without delay. That, she having cheated him, would be got rid of *tout de suite*. Their marriage annulled before the ink on their wedding certificate was set.

What she had not expected was that Jonah would be remotely interested in knowing more than that she had cheated him. But, to her consternation, he fixed her with a stern look and, 'You've just said you should never have married me,' he took up toughly. And, looking directly into her anxious green eyes, he as toughly added, 'Then perhaps, my dear, you'll have the courtesy to explain exactly why you did?'

Lydie stared at him, numbed. She wasn't ready for this. She need not have married him for her father's sake; she had known that before she had reached him at the altar. It therefore followed that she had married him solely because she loved him and had wanted to marry him more than she had wanted anything in her life. But there was no way she was going to tell him that. Though, with Jonah standing there watching, waiting, everything about him was telling her that she was going nowhere until she had given him an explanation—but what explanation could she possibly give?

CHAPTER NINE

LYDIE had still not answered him when Jonah, his expression telling her he was insistent on having that answer, sifted through what she had said and, to her great alarm, bluntly asked, 'Why marry me at all, Lydie, when you knew that you did not have to?'

'It was too l-late,' she stammered, and, clutching at straws, 'My mother would have murdered me had I called everything off at the last moment.'

'You've stood up to your mother before when you felt strongly enough about something,' he reminded her, and dissected in an instant what she had said. His face darkening, he came back to challenge, 'You're saying you cheated me, but didn't feel strongly enough, guilty enough about it, to risk your mother's displeasure and not marry me?'

'It wasn't... I... Oh...' She was floundering and knew it. 'I d-didn't get, read, the letter from Aunt Alice's lawyers until a short while before I was due to leave the house for the church.'

'Your great-aunt left you some money?'

'She left me her house. I didn't even know Aunt Alice owned it, but she must have. Her lawyers...'

'So you married me, despite knowing that once that house is sold—I take it you aren't intending to live in it?' he inserted, sounding hostile, 'you'll have sufficient funds to be out of my debt?'

Lydie nodded. 'From what my father said—'

'You've discussed this with your father?' he cut in sceptically.

'No! Only to say I thought Aunt Alice rented her house.

He doesn't know about the letter. He said that Aunt Alice had the chance to purchase her house very cheaply some years ago and that, had she done so, it would be worth about a hundred and fifty thousand pounds today.' Lydie swallowed on a dry throat, and went tremulously on. 'Once I've repaid my debt to you, there should be sufficient over to pay the caterers and any outstanding items from t-today.'

Jonah heard what she had to say and, his eyes on her, he seemed to silently deliberate. He took a pace away and half turned from her, his mind occupied. But then, as if he had reached a decision, he turned back to her, and, his eyes steady on hers, he quietly let fall, 'I think you'll find, Lydie, that all accounts—apart from yours and mine—have been settled.'

Wordlessly Lydie stared at him, questions rushing to her lips. All accounts—apart from theirs? What did that mean? She shelved that question, pride giving her a nasty time as she asked, appalled, 'You didn't pay for my wedding? You didn't ask for all bills to be sent to you?' And, feeling mortified with embarrassment, 'My father didn't allow you to finance today's—'

'Would he?' Jonah interrupted. And, not waiting to hear her reply, stated firmly, 'He would not.' Jonah paused, and after a moment quietly informed her, 'Trust me, your father can well afford to settle for today's function without it hurting too much.'

Lydie didn't believe it. 'The last I heard was that he was broke. My mother called me a pain because I've worried so much about today's expense.' And, feeling hostile herself, even though she knew that she was the one in the wrong here, 'Now you're telling me I need not have worried at all? I don't believe it!' she snapped.

'Why should you believe it?' Jonah agreed. But, his hostility fading suddenly, 'Come and sit down,' he suggested, indicating one of the sofas, 'and I'll explain…'

'There's nothing for you to explain.' Lydie cut him off agitatedly. She had an idea that he might decide to share that sofa with her—and she had been closer to him than was good for her not so long ago. 'I cheated you. You'll want an annulment, and that's all there is to it.'

Jonah looked at her for long, long moments, then, with his glance fixed on hers, his tone perfectly audible, 'Correction, Lydie,' he clearly said, '*I* cheated you. I married you because I wanted to. And there is *no way* this marriage is going to be annulled.'

Her insides started to churn more fiercely. She knew he had wanted to marry, that he had decided it was time he married. But her? 'You could have married just about anybody, it didn't necessarily have to be me.' She spoke her thoughts out loud. And what had he just said about him cheating her? It was she who had cheated him! 'I must be more tired than I thought. None of this is making sense.'

'Would you like to go to bed? We can have this discussion when we get to the island tomorrow.'

'You still want to go on our honeymoon?' she asked, her eyes widening in surprise.

'Have you forgotten so soon? I told you when I asked for your promise to marry me that divorce is not an option. The same goes for an annulment.'

Suddenly her legs felt as if they were about to give way. To sit down seemed a good idea. By the sound of it, even though she had confessed to having cheated him, Jonah still wanted to stay married to her.

'I think I'll…' she mumbled, and went over to the sofa. Jonah surprised her by taking a chair close by—opposite her. Realising that she had no chance of hiding her expression from him, Lydie lowered her gaze as she apologised. 'I'm sorry I married you when as soon as Aunt Alice's house is sold I shall be able to repay that loan.'

'And I'm sorry you feel you have to repay it,' Jonah answered. 'But, if it will make you feel better, I have to tell you that the fifty-five thousand was repaid, with the accumulated interest your father insisted upon, a couple of weeks ago.'

Her head shot up. 'Repaid!' Her brain wasn't taking this in. 'Who repaid it?' she asked. And, as her intelligence started to go into action, 'Are you saying that—I needn't have married you?' She wasn't sure she did not go pale; she felt pale. 'You said...' She struggled to recall what exactly he had said. 'You said y-you had cheated me. Is that what you meant? That you had cheated *me* into marrying *you*?' That couldn't be. She had cheated him! 'Would you explain? I didn't think I'd drunk too much champagne, but I'm not coping with this at all well. Who repaid you that money? My father doesn't have any, and...' She stopped, feeling totally perplexed.

That feeling wasn't helped much when all at once Jonah left his seat and came over and took a seat on the sofa next to her. 'Poor love,' he murmured, and, catching a hold of her hands in his, 'This moment has come far sooner than I'd anticipated,' he continued. 'But perhaps it's as well that we start our marriage with certain matters out of the way.'

'You're still insisting that we stay married?' she asked, a touch shakily.

'It's the only way,' he replied, which told her precisely nothing.

'I can pay you—or will be able to pay...'

'Your father has already done so.'

'My father doesn't have any money!'

'He does now.'

'How?' Lydie questioned. 'Only a couple of months ago he was in deep despair that he'd sold everything he could possibly sell. Where did he get the money?'

Jonah was half turned to her. Lydie, pulling her hands from his hold, half turned to look at him, her eyes pleading for answers. 'Your father,' Jonah began, 'has sold a half of Beamhurst Court.'

Shocked to hear such a thing, Lydie stared at him in utter astonishment. 'He wouldn't!' she exclaimed. 'My mother wouldn't allow him!'

'She did,' Jonah stated calmly.

And Lydie just sat stunned. Jonah sounded as though he knew it for the truth. Half a dozen questions jostled for precedence in her head. Her father had sold half of Beamhurst Court? Unbelievable! Her mother had sanctioned it? Impossible! And how was Jonah so much in the know, Lydie wondered, when she, the daughter of the house, had been totally in the dark about it? And... Abruptly then, though, a whole new question burst in on her intelligence.

'You said that fifty-five thousand pounds was repaid to you a couple of weeks ago?'

'That's right,' Jonah agreed—but seemed to be already anticipating her next question.

He showed no surprise anyhow when, quite a bit startled, she had to admit, Lydie slowly questioned, 'Then, if that money was repaid, my father no longer in your debt—why did I marry you? You let me marry you,' she went on, feeling winded, 'when there was absolutely no need whatsoever for me to marry you.'

'I'm afraid there was. Apart from other considerations,' Jonah commented, 'you had told your father that I'd some proposition to put to him.'

'You told him you were going to ask me to marry you.' She reminded him of what he had said.

'That was part of it.'

'Part? But not all?'

Jonah shook his head. 'It had to be part, for the rest of it to follow,' he explained, but when Lydie looked totally mystified he revealed a little more detail. 'At the same time of telling me how you'd told your father I'd a proposition to put to him, you also told me how he had been prepared to sell Beamhurst Court. You mentioned too that your brother wasn't remotely interested in the property.'

By then her brain was working overtime. 'You found a buyer for my father? Someone interested in purchasing only a half of the property?' How on earth would that work? She couldn't see her mother sharing her home with anyone!

Lydie's puzzled eyes were fixed on nowhere but Jonah's wonderful blue eyes, when, quietly, he revealed, 'I am the buyer, Lydie.'

Her eyes went saucer-wide. 'You're the buyer?' she echoed faintly.

'While you and I will live here at Yourk House, as we planned, Beamhurst Court is now in the joint names of you and your father,' Jonah replied. And while she stared at him, thunderstruck by that astounding statement, 'I know how you love the place,' he added. 'I bought a half of it for you, Lydie.'

She stared at Jonah witlessly. 'You—bought it—for me?' Her voice was barely above a whisper. 'You...' It must have cost him a small fortune! 'You...' she tried again. 'My father...' It was no good. As what he had said started to sink in, she was so totally stunned she did not seem able to frame another sentence.

Looking at her, seeing how dumbstruck she was, Jonah took pity on her and began to elucidate. 'You'll remember, the day of your great-aunt's funeral, your father and I went to his study?'

'You said you'd gone to tell him that you wanted to marry me. You said that our being married would make you a family member, an insider, so my father wouldn't feel too badly about...' The small quirk on Jonah's superb mouth made her hesitate.

He smiled encouragingly, but corrected, 'Insider, nothing! Son-in-law or no, your father would never rest until he paid that money back. I *knew* that. He *knew* that. You, Lydie, thinking with your love for him and not your mind, were emotionally blinded by a sign that he might be returning to his old self, and *missed knowing* that.'

'But...' She broke off, a dawning realisation hitting her that it was just as Jonah had said—her father had started to brighten up and she hadn't looked further than to see him take a new lease on life, than to go along with whatever

Jonah told her. 'Have I been incredibly naïve?' she asked, still feeling more than a mite shaken.

'No father could have a better daughter,' Jonah answered softly, and disclosed, 'Once I was in the study with him that day, I told him that I would very much like to marry his daughter. He at once gave me his blessing, and I then put the proposition you had suggested to him that I intended to.'

'But you didn't have a proposition.'

'Your father is well aware of your attachment to Beamhurst. I put it to him that I would very much like to have your name on the deeds as my wedding gift to you.'

'Oh, Jonah!' she whispered, unable to hold it back. But she grew suddenly terrified that he would see how his incredibly generous gesture had hit at the heart of her. From somewhere, she knew not where, she somehow managed to find some stiffening to her wilting backbone, and questioned, 'And my father, he agreed—just like that?'

'He said he would think about it, but I could see he was at once very taken with the idea. Anyhow, by the time you and I came back from our walk...'

'When you asked for my promise to marry you,' Lydie put in, her head starting to spin.

'Where you gave me your promise,' Jonah agreed. 'By that time your father had it all worked out. He suggested he and I return to his study to discuss my proposition in more in-depth detail.' Lydie remembered clearly. She had seen them heading for the study when she'd been on her way upstairs to change. 'Wilmot had by then seen the advantages: he would have money to settle what he considered his debt to me and have money at his disposal. Before we could get the property professionally valued and everything legally drawn up, though, he wanted me to understand that, should he sell, your brother would ultimately inherit his half. Also, he felt your mother would insist on an assurance, that should Oliver at some future date change his mind about wanting Beamhurst Court, you would sell your half to him. I agreed on your behalf on the assurance that, at some very much future date, we—you and I—would have the first option to purchase, should Oliver wish to sell.'

She was spellbound that all this had gone one. 'And—my father consented?'

Jonah nodded. 'The deal was completed a fortnight ago—naturally in the utmost secrecy. I told your father I wanted to surprise you on our honeymoon with a copy of the deeds showing Lydie Marriott as joint owner.' Lydie Marriott. How wonderful that sounded. 'Wilmot felt he had to tell your mother, but he was certain, once she knew all details, that she would raise no objection and would, as was essential, keep our secret. So all in all,' Jonah ended, 'your father was again happy. Your mother, with money available to see you married in respectable fashion, was happy. And you, Lydie—' he smiled at her '—I'd like very much for you to be happy—but, I'm sorry, that does not include an annulment.'

Lydie knew that she wanted to stay married to him, but, while she did love Beamhurst, she just could not get over the fact that he had bought a half of it—for her!

'It's too much!' she exclaimed. 'You've solved all of our problems but—what about you? What do you get?'

'Oh, my dear,' Jonah answered softly. 'While it pleases me tremendously to see that look of strain gone from the face of a man I admire so much, what I have, this day, is you.'

Lydie stared at him. He was rather marvelous, this man she had married. And she knew that what he was actually saying was that, having decided to marry, he had this day got himself a wife. But—was that good enough?

'Is it—all right to marry when—love isn't there?' she asked, and, not wanting him to see how much it mattered to her, she looked away from him, her eyes giving her wedding band serious study in the lengthening tense kind of silence that followed.

Then she was at once wishing that she had never uttered a word about love. For as the tension, the silence stretched, she knew for certain that Jonah had never thought about love in any of this. She so desperately wished he would say something—the taut silence was getting to her.

Though when, after long moments of considering what she had said, Jonah did break the silence, he caused her to be totally panic stricken when he stated, quite clearly, 'But love is there.'

As soon as his words hit her ears Lydie was on her feet. She leapt from the sofa, her emotions in complete chaos. And had taken several rushed steps across the room before she was aware of it. But, halting, turning to see that Jonah was on his feet too, she stared at him absolutely stupefied.

'You know I love you?' she gasped, horrified, and saw him freeze in his tracks—shaken rigid.

'What—did you say?' he clipped, his tone all kind of shocked, as if he could not believe his hearing.

'Nothing!' she denied, faster than the speed of light. 'I didn't say anything.'

But he wasn't having that, though still seemed too stunned to move. 'You said you love me,' he reminded her, when she needed not the smallest reminding. And, shaking his head as if dazed, 'I refuse to start off this marriage with lies, Lydie Marriott. Tell me the truth. Do you have feelings for me?'

She shook her head. Anybody would think it was important. 'It doesn't matter,' she answered, making a poor showing of the off-hand tone she had been hoping for.

'Of course it matters!' he retorted. A few yards separated them but neither of them was moving an inch, she as frozen now as him.

'W-why?' Oh, why had she said what she had? It was blatantly obvious now that Jonah had had no idea of her love for him.

'Why? Because...' He hesitated, paused, and, as if he had just come to a decision, his head came up a proud fraction as he said, 'I married you today, Lydie, purely because it was what I wanted to do.'

'For my father's sake,' she butted in. 'You married me because my father…'

'My decision to marry you had nothing at all to do with your father or anyone else.' Jonah set her straight. 'I married you for the reason I stated at our wedding reception, because—for weeks now—I've wanted nothing more than to be married to you.'

'Because you felt it was time for you to be married. That's what you said.'

'Oh, Lydie, Lydie, I have to tell you now that I discovered you are not the only one who can lie their head off,' he confessed, causing her to stare at him. But her eyes grew yet wider when he added, 'I am not lying now—nor will I ever lie to you again—when I tell you that I married you for no other reason than that I want, and need, to be with you for the rest of my life.'

Her breath caught in her throat. 'Y-you married me—for m-me?' she questioned with what breath she had left.

'I married you solely for you,' he confirmed. 'I married you, my dear, dear Lydie, because I one day woke up to the fact that I had fallen quite, quite hopelessly in love with you.'

Lydie stared at him in stunned amazement, a kind of roaring going on in her ears. 'You didn't!' she denied. And, remembering how sensitive he was with her sometimes, 'You're only saying that so I shan't feel I have made such a complete fool of myself.'

But already Jonah was shaking his head. 'No more lies, Lydie, from either of us.' She still didn't believe him. 'Come here,' he said. 'Meet me halfway. Let me hold you in my arms and convince you.' He took a step towards her; she took a panicking step back. He halted.

'Convince me from there!' she exclaimed. If he took her in his arms again she would be lost, would be deaf to anything but that which she wanted to hear.

Jonah smiled, as if he knew something of what she was going through. 'I'm feeling not a little emotionally shattered myself,' he admitted, every bit as if her statement that she loved him had knocked him sideways. 'Shall we at least sit down?'

It seemed the sensible thing to do, and just then Lydie felt very much in need of something sensible to latch on to. She went and sat in the chair he had occupied earlier.

She had expected he would use the sofa but he made her heart beats start to jump around again when he took hold of another chair and drew it up close, opposite hers.

They were almost touching knee to knee when Jonah, his eyes on her face, asked, 'Am I allowed to say how very beautiful you are, and how for me a day without you is a day without the sun?'

Oh, Jonah! If she hadn't been sitting down Lydie would not have given much for her chances of not collapsing into a chair. She strove to be sensible.

'This is you convincing me that you didn't say you l... what you said, purely from some kind of sensitivity because of w-what I said?'

'You said you loved me, Lydie,' he reminded her gently.

'Don't!' she moaned.

'Don't be embarrassed, my darling. While I'm still having the greatest trouble taking it in, in actually believing that it can possibly be true, I want you to believe that I love you so very much that at times it has been like a physical pain.'

Lydie stared at him, her green eyes huge. She knew that feeling. 'But—you never said. Never so much as hinted...'

'How could I? I was terrified of frightening you off.'

'You were terrified...' She found that hard to believe, and guessed her feeling of disbelief must have shown.

'I've sound reasons,' he cut in, 'which I suppose stemmed initially from having you as an extremely shy but charming sixteen-year-old imbedded somewhere in my mind.'

'I was still sixteen in your mind?' she queried, intrigued in spite of her shaky feelings inside.

'Only to start with. You were beautiful then. In the seven years since you have blossomed to be even more beautiful than my imaginings.'

'You'd thought of me—since then?'

'Off and on. I made a return trip to your home three years ago—to give your father the money I owed him. I'd hoped to see you, but you weren't around.'

'You wanted to see how I'd turned out?'

'Something like that, though I never actually put it into words. Anyhow, there I am, ten weeks ago, returning to the office from doing some negotiating overseas, to have my PA tell me that a Lydie Pearson was anxious to contact me.' He paused, and then owned, 'When at last I did see you, I found you quite captivating, my Lydie.'

Captivating? His? The whole of her felt weak. 'I wasn't very pleasant to you,' she commented, trying desperately hard to keep both feet on the ground.

'You thought I'd reneged on the debt I owed your father,' he reminded her gently. 'Somewhat to my own surprise, when it's usually my business head that rules me, I found I was reaching for my chequebook. As you know, I hold your father in high regard, and told myself I was writing that cheque because he had given me financial help when I asked for it. I knew full well that he was too honourable to ask for my financial help unless he could see a way of repaying it. But even while, as you rightly said, I was conning you into paying that cheque into the bank without delay, I was not thinking of being repaid—my head was full only of you.'

Lydie blinked. 'You mean, you—er—were attracted to me?'

'Oh, Lydie, I wasn't yet ready to admit some woman had started to tie me up in knots,' he answered, his lips quirking.

'I did that?'

'As I said, I wasn't admitting it. Though I have to say it came as a bit of a jolt to see you at the theatre with your friend Charlie. I didn't like it.'

Lydie searched the depths of his fantastic blue eyes. His gaze did not falter. Could he really love her? She was too stewed up by all that had happened and was happening to know. She decided to stick to fact, as she knew it. 'You said for me to come to your office the following Monday,' she remembered, but the way Jonah was looking at her, tenderly—dared she hope lovingly?—was making such a nonsense of her she could barely remember why she had gone to see him. 'I came to see you,' she struggled through, 'to discuss how I should repay that money.'

'And I found myself in a state of upheaval.'

'Upheaval?'

He smiled at her surprise. 'I wasn't bothered about the money. You were the one making an issue of it. But perhaps I could use that to my advantage.'

Lydie was stumped. 'Advantage?' She could not help repeating him again.

'I knew then that I wanted to see you again. Perhaps it was the last throes of my long-schooled wary bachelor faculty at work, perhaps it was because I knew that you were different—call it what you will—but, while I didn't want to deprive myself of your company, I decided that I didn't want any involvement. To see you at your brother's wedding seemed to me a good way to see you again while at the same time making our meeting less one-to-one personal.'

She was staggered. 'That's why you wanted that wedding invite!' She stared at him in amazement. 'But,' she began to recall, 'the very next day, after Oliver's wedding, when I came to see you at your apartment, you were suggesting that I come here to Yourk House and spend the weekend with you!'

'Why wouldn't I? You'd just told me you'd previously stayed overnight with your friend Charlie! I didn't care at all for the thought you might be spending the next Saturday night in some man's bed. I know, I know, you were never lovers, but I didn't know that then and, while I wasn't admitting to feeling a tinge green whenever I thought of you and him, dammit, I was as jealous as hell.'

Lydie was fairly reeling. Jonah, jealous of Charlie? 'You told me to dump him.'

But the next moment Jonah had taken her hands and was drawing her to her feet. 'Lydie, I can't take much more of this. I know I probably haven't convinced you yet, but I love you so much, and if you love me only half as much, you'll let me hold you.'

She stood with him. 'You want to hold me?'

'I need to hold you, my darling,' he murmured.

It only required one small step towards him. Lydie drew a shaky breath—then took that small step. And the next she knew, she was in his arms, held up against him in a gentle tender hold.

Jonah held her like that for many long wonderful minutes as barriers they had both erected came tumbling down. But at last he pulled back, so that he could see her face, and look into her eyes.

'Love me half as much, sweet Lydie?' he needed to know.

She felt shy suddenly, but he loved her. She knew then that he would not lie to her about that. 'M-more than that,' she whispered shakily.

'My darling,' he breathed, and tenderly kissed her. Joyous loving seconds passed. 'Say it,' he pulled back to request. 'Say it again.'

'What?' she asked huskily.

'You said, "You know I love you?" That's seared into my brain, into my heart, and I shall never forget it—I'm still getting over the almighty shock to hear you say what I have so craved to hear. May I not hear it again?'

Shyly, she smiled at him. 'I love you so, Jonah Marriott.' She pushed through an unexpected barrier of reserve to tell him, and, when he held her up close to him once more, 'I feared so that you might see—and there I went, blurting it out.'

'I'm so glad you did,' he murmured against her ear.

Lydie pulled back this time. 'Would you have told me, if I hadn't slipped up?'

Jonah placed a tender kiss on her upturned face and, looking adoringly into her shining green eyes, 'I was hoping we would grow closer on our honeymoon, hoping I could earn a little of your love,' he owned.

'You have it all,' she whispered, and was soundly kissed in exultation.

She had no idea they had moved until she found she was seated on a sofa with Jonah, one of his arms around her, one hand holding her hand.

'Oh, sweet, sweet Lydie, how you brighten up my day.'

'Do I?'

'Did I not tell you?' Lydie shook her head. 'I've wanted to, so many times. Little love, since knowing you again I've come to know that I only come alive inside when you are there.'

What a wonderful thing to say. 'I love you so,' she said softly, spontaneously.

Jonah beamed her the most sensational smile. 'That's all I've longed to hear.'

'Truly?' she asked breathlessly.

'Truly,' he answered. 'I've ached so.'

'Me too,' she confessed. 'When did you know?'

'That I was in love with you?' The answer was in her eyes, and he smiled gently, and quietly began, 'It was that Friday that your dear great-aunt died. You were supposed to be coming here for the weekend. I'd had business not far away from Beamhurst Court and, while I wasn't fully ready to acknowledge it, I couldn't wait to see you. All I had to do was make a small detour and I could enjoy seeing you sooner. Respecting your wish that I kept away from your home, I waited, about to ring on my car phone to find out if you were still home. But suddenly what do I see but you flying along—in totally the wrong direction.'

'You were furious,' she recalled.

'I was outraged,' he agreed. 'I have never in my life felt so churned up.'

'Because I was going in the wrong direction?' she teased gently, loving that she was able to do so.

'Because when I caught up with you, you said you weren't coming to Yourk House, and I saw your overnight bag in the back of your car. You were obviously spending the weekend with someone—someone who wasn't me.'

'You thought...'

'I thought you were going to spend *our* weekend with some other man.'

'Charlie?' she asked faintly.

'None other. I have never, ever been so crazed with jealousy. It hit me so hard! I was jealous and, I knew then, hopelessly in love.'

'Oh, Jonah!' she sighed softly. And, as she thought of that day, 'I knew that same night, at the hospital, that I was in love with you.'

'Sweet darling,' he breathed, and held her close, and kissed her tenderly, and held her close again.

'That was weeks ago! All these weeks and neither of us knew!'

'I was afraid to tell you how it was with me,' Jonah owned, looking deep into her eyes.

'Afraid?' she prompted gently, and Jonah settled her into his arms, her head against his shoulder.

'I'd kissed you, the day after your great-aunt had died, and you'd pushed me away.' Lydie remembered; it had been a wonderful kiss. 'And I knew then that I was going to have to take it very slowly with you.'

'That kiss turned my legs to water,' Lydie confided, and, when Jonah pulled back his head in disbelief and looked into her face, 'I wanted to kiss you back,' she further confided.

'So you pushed me away?'

'I had to—I was drowning—and, well—um—you weren't the only one to become acquainted with the demon jealousy.'

'You were jealous?' He looked incredulous—but delighted.

Lydie smiled self-consciously. 'I couldn't help thinking that you'd probably have your arms around some other woman that very night.'

Jonah smiled into her face. 'What a joy you are,' he said softly, and kissed her. 'I'm going to have to stop doing that,' he said a moment later. 'Your tempting lips are wrecking my sanity. Love me?'

'So much.'

'Oh, my love.'

'All these weeks...'

'We've loved, and not known,' he ended for her. 'And there was I, impatient, yet fearful you might marry someone else before I could get you to agree to marry me. As I saw it then, I had to act, and act fast.'

'You told my father that you wanted to marry me.'

'It was the truth.'

'Oh, Jonah!' She sighed. If she was dreaming, she never wanted to wake up. 'But—you didn't feel you could tell me—um—how you felt?'

'How could I, my darling? You hadn't shown the smallest sign of caring for me. Hell, I'd kissed you—you'd pushed me away. Then there was Charlie ever-present.'

'Charlie?'

Jonah smiled. 'Nerves were getting to me—any man who looked at you was a threat. I wanted you. To my mind there wasn't time for me to come courting. You were proud; that fifty-five thousand stood between us. What was the point of my trying to date you? That fifty-five thousand would always be there.' Lydie stared at him in amazement. All this had gone through his head! 'To tell it how it was,

Lydie,' he continued, 'I was running scared that someone else would get you.'

'Oh Jonah,' she whispered.

Gently he placed a kiss on the corner of her mouth, pausing to gaze at her beautiful face before going on, 'I wasn't sure you would swallow that line about your father preferring to owe money to someone inside the family...'

'But you tried anyway—and it worked.'

He grinned. 'It worked. But I knew, when you tried to find an "out" to say no, that it was too soon to tell you of the depth of my feelings for you. You said it would be cheating to marry me if you could find the money to pay me back, but I couldn't tell you that I was cheating you by not telling you of the proposition I had just put to your father. And if I needed more evidence that you weren't thrilled about marrying me, then I didn't need to look further than when, while accept me you did, you made no bones about telling me you didn't want my kisses.'

'Oh, Jonah, did I hurt you?'

He smiled. 'It started to get better.' And, when she looked at him questioningly, 'About a fortnight ago?' he hinted.

She stared at him a second or two longer, then went a delicate shade of pink. 'When we came here so I could get away from our two mothers sending me potty.'

'It was a wonderful weekend. While I'd been working all hours, afraid to find time to see you more than briefly in case I blurted out how much I cared for you, I at the same time became desperate to see you, to spend some time with you.'

'It was the same for me,' Lydie confessed. 'I couldn't wait for that Friday.'

'Little love!' He kissed her because he just had to. 'It was a perfect weekend. Up until then you had shown all too plainly that you didn't even want me to kiss you.'

'We did kiss, didn't we?' she softly reminisced.

'Oh, we did,' he agreed, his eyes on her lovely mouth.

'It was wonderful. Though I'd still no intention—with our wedding so close—of blowing it all by telling you of my feelings.' He paused, then added, 'And when I rang you from Sweden on Wednesday, and you coolly suggested that ours wasn't the normal head-over-heels thing, I was glad I hadn't—even if I did feel a bit defeated.'

'Defeated?'

'Defeated, and not knowing where in blazes I was. For me, my darling, it was, and is, a head-over-heels thing. But there you are, dropping me down one moment and the next raising my hopes again. Making my heart lift by telling me ''I wish you were here'', only to crush my hopes by as good as telling me the only reason you wanted me there was because of the amount of luggage you had to transport.'

Lydie looked at him, stars shining in her eyes. It seemed incredible to her that anything she said should have such an effect on him. 'I meant it about wishing you were there, with me,' she confessed. 'The words just slipped out, and I had to hurriedly use the amount of my luggage as a cover in case you thought I was coming over all—um—personal.'

His smile broke through, and, as though that word 'personal' was some kind of a signal, Jonah stood up, taking Lydie with him. And, looking adoringly down at her, he then gently kissed her. 'It's been a long day, dear wife,' he said softly, and, picking her up in his arms, 'Unless you've any strong objection, I suggest it's time for bed.'

A delicate pink began to flush her skin, but she smiled as she shyly answered, 'I've no objection at all, dear husband.'

Looking down into her face, Jonah laughed softly in delight. And, his head coming nearer, 'Don't worry about a thing, sweet love,' he breathed against her mouth, 'I shall be with you.'

He carried her to the stairs, kissed her again, lovingly, lingeringly, and together they ascended.

An Accidental Engagement

JESSICA STEELE

CHAPTER ONE

SHE stirred in her sleep. She felt troubled, and her eyelids fluttered. She tried to recall what she was troubled about, but could not remember. She opened her eyes and lay there quietly, for a moment or two at relative peace with her world.

That peace was not to last. Suddenly her eyes widened—not only could she not remember what it was that troubled her, she could not remember anything! Could not remember anything at all. Everything was a complete blank!

Striving hard to keep a lid on her feeling of panic, she fought to remember something, even the tiniest detail, but there was nothing there. She could not even remember her own name!

She looked around her, but the pink walls of the room were alien to her; she did not recognise them. Involuntarily she cried out and tried to sit up—and discovered she barely had the strength to raise her head from her pillow.

But she was not alone. Alerted by her cry, a plump woman in a nurse's uniform came swiftly over to her bed. 'You're back with us, I see,' she said softly, calmly.

The young woman in the bed did not feel calm. 'Who are...? Where am...? I don't know where I am, who I am,' she whispered, her voice a panicking thread of sound.

The nurse was efficient and in no time a doctor was there in the room with them. After that, time passed for the young woman in a confusing semi-vacuum of visitors in white coats, of questions and tests, of medication and sedatives and a twilight world of drifting in and out of sleep.

Nurses attended to her healing cuts and bruises, but she

5

made no progress in remembering who she was. She had lost her memory.

On different occasions she surfaced to find one or other of two expensively suited males in her room. They made frequent calls to her bedside. One was tall and comfortably built. He was somewhere in his mid-forties, and she seemed to vaguely realise that he was a consultant of some sort. From time to time he would arrive and shine a light in her eyes and while asking her questions would converse easily with her. Though what he made of her answers she could not tell. More often than not, whether it was because of whatever was wrong with her or because of the strong medication that was administered, she invariably floated off to sleep mid-conversation.

Her other frequent male visitor was about ten years younger than the other man. That man was about thirty-five or thirty-six, was equally tall, but was trimmer, fitter-looking. But he did not ask questions. Instead he would come and sit by her bedside and would sometimes quietly chat to her or sit silently by her bed. She went to sleep on him too.

Days passed without her being aware of anything very much. They called her Claire; she supposed somebody must know her and had told them who she was. She had blurred recall of moments of panic, moments of near hysteria, before some injection or other would float her away to calmer waters. She had a hazy recollection of being transferred from one ward to another, and then of being moved from there to another hospital entirely—but while she was in a sea of new faces and nurses she did not recognise the consultant and the other man were still constant visitors.

Then one morning she awakened and for the first time did not so soon drift away again. This time she stayed awake. While she still had no memory, and her head still felt a little muzzy, she felt stronger and, with relief, as if she was ready to join the land of the living.

'Where am I?' she asked the pretty nurse who at that moment came in to check on her.

'Roselands.' The nurse answered straight away. And, obviously aware that that piece of information meant nothing to her, 'It's a private clinic. You were transferred here two days ago—a sure sign you're on the mend.'

'My name's Claire?'

'Claire Farley,' the nurse replied without hesitation, clearly knowing all that there was to know about her patient.

'What happened to me? How…?'

'You were in a road traffic accident. You're badly bruised and were in a coma for a short while, but you've come through and have nothing life-threatening wrong with you. You've had a few stitches in your right thigh—all out now—and cuts and grazes to your right arm which didn't require stitches, and some muscle trauma, but otherwise,' the nurse added with a comforting smile, 'no bones broken.'

'Is my head all right?' Claire asked, feeling panic rising but finding she had a little more control than she'd had previously and managing to hold her panic down. 'I can't remember…'

'Your head's fine,' the nurse hurriedly assured her. 'If there's a test around we know about, you've had it. You've been X-rayed, scanned and, given that the whole of you received one almighty jolt when you went flying through the air, I can promise you, you've been left with no permanent damage.'

'But I can't remember who I am.' A hint of panic had started to creep into her tones.

'Try to relax,' the nurse soothed. 'I'm Beth Orchard, by the way. As I've mentioned, you were in a coma for a brief while, and your poor head has decided it wants a rest. Now, the sooner you can start to relax, the sooner your memory will return.' From where Claire was viewing it, she seemed to have been having one enormous long rest just lately. 'Now, is there anything I can get for you?'

Claire looked around the room. There was the most beautiful flower arrangement in one corner of the room, and another small posy on her bedside table, plus a basket of fruit. 'I seem to have everything,' she replied, and wanted to ask more questions, but somehow, even in her highly anxious state, did not seem to have any energy.

Beth Orchard went away, and Claire began to experience emotions of hysteria starting to rise—everything was a blank, a brick wall—and she just could not get through it. She pushed and pushed, but there was nothing there.

'Claire Farley,' she said out loud, fighting for calm, but the name sounded alien on her tongue.

Just when panic was on the rise again, however, the door opened and the consultant she seemed to know as Dr Phipps entered. Though, since he was a consultant surgeon, she hazily recalled the nursing staff respectfully addressed him as Mr Phipps. 'How's the head?' he enquired, coming to the bed and casting a professional eye over her.

'Everything's black. There's no light. Nothing there,' she replied, telling him that which was the more important to her.

'You need rest,' he said confidently.

'So Nurse Orchard said.'

'Try your best not to worry,' Mr Phipps suggested.

'How long? How long will it be before I get my memory back?' Claire asked anxiously, and, more essentially, '*Will* I get it back?'

'It could return any time at all now,' he replied. 'If it's purely a case of a knock on your head, your memory might come trotting back within the next day or week or two. Just rest and...'

'If?' Claire questioned, discovering she had an intelligence of a sort that wanted to know more. 'Is that an implication that there might be more to my condition than a knock on the head?'

He hesitated briefly, but gave her the straight answer she

required. 'Sometimes when a person has endured some kind
of enormous emotional stress, to an extent that the person
just cannot take any more, the brain decides enough is
enough, and for a while decides to block everything out.'

'Do you think that may have happened to me?'

'It is possible for the two to come together—the bang on
the head and the overloaded emotional trauma—but, from
eyewitness accounts of you having an argument with a moving vehicle, I believe at this stage that your accident is the
culprit.'

Claire accepted that. She had no choice. Mr Phipps was
a clever man, and she trusted him. 'My family?' she asked.
'They know I'm here?' He did not answer. 'I do have a
family? Perhaps I don't?'

'When I said you were to rest, I meant it.' He smiled.
'Let that poor brain of yours take it easy for a while.'

She felt exhausted suddenly, as if any fight she had in her
had just been flattened. 'All right,' she agreed, and closed
her eyes.

She had no idea how long she slept, but awoke to find
that she was alone. She was feeling anxious and disturbed
again, and terribly lethargic too. She looked down at her
right hand resting on top of the bedcover and noticed, quite
incidentally, that while the fingers on that hand were slender, and actually quite narrow and dainty, her nails must
have grown while she was in hospital—they could definitely
do with a trim.

Hope began to fill her that her memory might soon come
back, because, somehow, she just knew that as a general
rule she did not care for her nails to be overlong.

She took her left hand from beneath the covers to inspect
the nails on that hand—and went rocketing out from her
feeling of lethargy when, with disbelieving amazement, she
saw she was wearing the most beautiful diamond solitaire
on her engagement finger. She was engaged! Engaged to be
married!

Who to? Not that dark-haired man, the other tall one? She dimly remembered that he had been sitting by her bed yesterday—or had it been the day before?

She started to panic again and looked feverishly around for a bell so she might ring for a nurse. Before she could do so, though, she managed to gain a modicum of control, sufficient anyway for her to realise that the nursing staff must have plenty of better things to do than rush in to pat her hand and say There, there.

What could anyone do that wasn't being done already? Panic began to rise again that she couldn't remember being engaged. Could remember nothing. Suppose she never regained her memory?

Just when she was having a hard time repressing a fresh urge to ring the bell anyway, she heard someone at the door of her room. A second later that someone came in. Any relief she might have felt, however, that she might have company which might ease her panic, quickly evaporated when she saw that the person who had entered was the tall, dark-haired man whom she thought she might be engaged to.

'Am I that scary?' he asked, over at her bed in a couple of strides, causing her to realise she must have been looking extremely alarmed. He smiled then, and she began to feel a touch better.

'Am I—am I engaged to you?' she asked.

He went over to bring a chair nearer to her bed and sat down beside her. 'It was I who put that ring on your finger,' he answered gently.

She stared at him. Surely to be engaged to him must mean that she loved him, and yet looking at him she felt nothing— except relief that he hadn't staked his claim by kissing her in greeting. 'I don't know your name,' she told him. He had steady grey eyes—she did not seem able to stop looking at him.

'Tye,' he supplied, and, with a most superb grin, 'Allow me to introduce myself. Tyerus Kershaw at your service.'

She found she was smiling. 'I think I could like you,' she said, quite without thinking—and swiftly realised, Oh, the poor man. It was her love he wanted, not her liking. 'I'm sorry,' she apologised quickly. 'I don't seem to know very much. Though...' She hesitated.

'You've remembered something?' Suddenly he was looking very serious, stern almost.

She shook her head. 'I noticed my hands for the first time today. My nails need cutting. I've a feeling, in fact I'm sure, I don't normally have them this long. I—' She broke off as she all at once realised something else. 'I don't know what I look like!' she said on a gasp. And, looking at him earnestly, 'Am I plain?' she asked hurriedly.

His mouth curved upwards. 'You are beautiful,' he assured her. 'Quite beautiful.'

'Are you just saying that because you're engaged to me and beauty is in the eye of the beholder?' She did not wait for him to reply this time, finding instead that she urgently needed to know what she looked like. 'Is there a mirror anywhere?'

For answer he left his chair and went and opened the door to the small adjoining bathroom. 'Your consultant tells me he wants you to sit out of bed for a short while this afternoon,' he announced. And, coming back to her, while she was taking on board that he must have seen Mr Phipps very recently, Tye leaned down, pulled back the covers and, taking care not to hurt her bruised body, gently collected her in his arms. 'We'll do a trial run,' he said conspiratorially.

To feel through the thinness of her nightdress his strong all-male arms so securely about her caused warm colour to flare to her cheeks. She was thankful that she seemed decently enough clad, and was never more grateful that her bedwear, being an expensive-looking silk and lace affair, was not the open-up-the-back hospital issue.

Her blush had barely subsided, however, when she found that the stranger she was engaged to had carried her into the bathroom and had turned so she should see herself in the mirror above the wash basin.

'You—said—beautiful,' she commented slowly, studying the creamy complexioned blue-eyed blonde who stared solemnly back at her.

'As well as enduring cuts, abrasions and heavily bruised muscle, your whole body has been in trauma—and that's leaving aside your poor head,' Tye answered. 'You are beautiful now and you'll be absolutely stunning when you have more of your natural colour back.'

She looked from her image and into his face. More of her natural colour? Was he saying he was aware of her blush earlier? He had a nice mouth, she observed—and looked hastily away. It seemed impossible that she had exchanged kisses with this sophisticated man, this man who, probably without him even being aware of it, wore an air of knowing exactly what he wanted from life and how to get it. Yet she was engaged to him, so they must have kissed, had probably made love. Warm colour surged to her face again at that thought.

She pushed nervous fingers through her blonde hair. 'I want to go back to bed!' she said abruptly. She felt shy, shaky, and all at once not a little weepy.

He looked down at her and, she knew, must be noticing her fiery cheeks. 'Just take it easy,' he bade her kindly when without more ado he carried her from the bathroom and without fuss popped her back into her bed. 'Everything is all haywire for you at the moment, but it will get better, I promise,' he assured her as he tucked the bedclothes in around her.

'Have I always felt shy with you?' she asked, and, feeling another wave of panic start to attack, 'I don't even know that—if I was ever shy with you!' she exclaimed. 'Shouldn't I feel comfortable with you?'

'Why should you? At this stage in your recovery I must seem a perfect stranger to you.'

Claire found a smile then. 'Thank you for being so understanding.'

He smiled back. 'You're lovely,' he said, and she suddenly discovered that she *was* feeling comfortable with him.

She yawned delicately. 'I don't seem to be able to keep my eyes open for longer than ten minutes at a time,' she apologised.

'On that big hint,' he teased, 'I'll go back to my office and get some work done.'

He went. He went without kissing her goodbye, or even giving her a peck on the cheek. She was grateful to him for that. He *was* a perfect stranger to her, and she had enough going on inside emotionally without feeling his nice warm mouth against her skin.

She realised then that Tye Kershaw disturbed her more than somewhat. That was to say that from lying there in her bed with nothing very much going on in her head, after ten minutes spent with him she had gone from shy to tense and nervous, and from there to comfortable. She could still recall the feel of his strong arms about her. She had blushed twice—had she always blushed so easily?

She recalled the features of the young woman in the mirror: wide blue eyes, dainty nose and a pleasant mouth. She looked to be somewhere in her early twenties. She must ask Tye... She fell asleep.

She awoke with her thoughts disjointed. Tye had been going back to his office. He had obviously taken time out to come and visit her. She had no idea what work he did. She must ask him. How had he known she was in hospital? She supposed she must have failed to turn up for some date with him. Perhaps she had been close to the appointed place, and he had heard of the accident and had come looking for her. Tye...

Tye went out of her head when a nurse brought her the

shoulder bag that had been found at the scene of the accident. It was of good quality, but as Claire examined the contents, a lipstick, a compact, a purse, she saw nothing that triggered any memory.

Over the following week she made rapid progress in her recovery. So that Mr Phipps, whose visits were less frequent now, was talking of discharging her. She was so much better, she knew that, but she still had some way to go before she regained her full strength. While her memory of events prior to waking up in hospital was as blank as ever, and though she was starting to fidget about being hospital bound, the thought of leaving panicked her.

Which meant that with part of her she could not wait to leave the clinic, while another part of her dreaded the thought of departing from that which had become secure to her.

Tye came to see her most days, but not always since his work involved him travelling about the country and occasionally staying out of London overnight.

Up until then she had not known where in England she was, and only then realised she must be in London. It was Tye who filled in a few other blanks. But—and she gathered it was so as not to confuse her by telling her everything at once—there was still a very great deal that she did not know.

She had asked him about his work, and he had been quite open about that. 'I'm an independent business analyst,' he had replied. His company was called Kershaw Research and Analysis, and from the little he had told her she was able to glean that he had a team of first-class troubleshooters working for him. She had also gathered that his company was in constant demand by businesses that needed their top-class analytical skills to delve into why and where the problem of pending failure or collapse threatened and lay.

Claire would have liked to know more, but Tye seemed to think he had told her enough. So she had asked him what work she did. He had told her she was between jobs at the moment, and somehow, when meaning to press him on what work did she normally do anyway, he had gone on to another subject.

'How did we meet?' was another of the questions she had asked, to which she had not received a very full answer. Though she understood the reason for that. Apparently their romance had been one of those love-at-first-sight romances. But perhaps aware, or maybe even following some kind of instruction from Mr Phipps, of trying not to strain her emotionally, Tye had steered the conversation elsewhere.

And in truth she could not say she was sorry. It did not exactly embarrass her to think of the loving relationship she must have had with Tye, but, recalling yet again his strong arms holding her that time, she could not deny she felt quite emotionally muddled up inside when she thought of it.

She waited on Sunday, expecting all day that Tye would pay her a visit, but when eight o'clock that evening arrived and he had still not come she knew that he would not be coming. And she wanted him to come.

She realised that being his own boss meant that he worked all sorts of hours, weekends too. Perhaps he was working outside of London somewhere and still had work to do. Which was a pity. She was on the point of being discharged from the clinic and had not the slightest idea of where she lived. Nor, she had discovered, did any of the nursing staff know where she lived. Or, if they did know, no one was telling.

She had been sitting out of bed for quite some while, but as her anxiety began to mount, she decided to get back into bed. She was very stiff in places—her muscles would recover in due time, she had been assured—but while admittedly not breaking any speed records, her body ached as she made it into bed and sat there pondering. What did she do now?

She had asked Tye about her family and he had replied

that her parents were travelling, touring somewhere in North America. He had thought—if she was in agreement, and since her memory loss was not life-threatening—that he would not try and contact them and break the holiday they had looked forward to for so long.

Since she would not know them even if they were located and did rush back, Claire was in complete agreement. She surmised she must be an only child. What did bother her now, though, was the thought that she could not possibly occupy a bed at the clinic for much longer; it would be the height of selfishness if someone more needy were waiting for a bed. But nor did she fancy leaving the clinic, where a nurse or cleaner or someone would bustle in every hour or so, to go home to an empty house and stare blankly at the walls all day.

That was if she lived in a house. For all she knew she might have a small flat somewhere, a bedsit, even. Her feelings of anxiety went up another notch. Then suddenly, just when she felt desperate for someone to talk to, the door opened—and Tye came in.

'Oh, I'm so pleased to see you!' she cried, and, embarrassed that she was all at once feeling quite tearful, looked away from him.

'Hey, what's this?' he asked lightly, and, coming quickly over to her, he perched on the edge of her bed and placed an arm about her shoulders. Then he placed his other hand to the side of her face and made her look at him. 'What's wrong?' he asked gently—and at his tone, his touch, she went all marshmallowy inside.

She swallowed, desperate not to cry. 'Mr Phipps says, given that I shall have to come back for a check-over, that I'm almost ready to leave here.'

Tye Kershaw studied her face for some silent seconds. What he was trying to read in her eyes she had no idea, but she was totally unprepared for his quiet, 'Like—tomorrow.'

'L... tomorrow?' She quickly caught on. 'I can go home tomorrow? You've seen Mr Phipps?'

'I managed to have a few words with him on the phone,' Tye answered, and smiled a smile she was beginning to love when he added, 'So what worries you about that to cause those big, beautiful, astonishingly blue eyes to shine so unhappily?'

'I don't know where I live!' she mumbled helplessly.

'Oh, my dear,' he crooned, his arm tightening soothingly across her shoulders.

'Where *do* I live?' she asked urgently. 'Nobody seems able to tell me.' She looked at him expectantly, and he seemed about to speak but hesitated. And all at once Claire suddenly thought she knew the reason for his hesitation; thought she understood. 'I live with you,' she said. 'We live together, don't we?' And, as the implication of that abruptly rocketed into her head, so scarlet colour flared in her face. 'Do I—sleep with you?' she asked croakily.

'Shh...' Tye hushed her, and, as if to make their relationship less personal, he took his arm from about her shoulders and moved away from the bed. His expression was hidden for a few seconds while he took up the visitor's chair and brought it over to the bed. Then, perhaps so she should not have to strain to look up at him, he casually lowered his length on to it and, looking across, sent her a calm, encouraging smile. 'You are making excellent progress,' he said. 'But you're a long, long way from being fit enough to share a bed with anyone. And apart from that,' he added, his smile becoming a most fascinating grin, 'I have given Mr Phipps my most solemn undertaking that, even should you beg me to make love to you when I take you home, I will not.' She laughed then. It was a good sound, her laughter. She felt as if it was a long time since she had laughed out loud, or inwardly either.

'Your laughter is as lovely as your voice,' Tye remarked lightly, his eyes on her face, and it was almost as if he had never heard her laugh before—she supposed it *had* been a long time.

She forgot that when something he had just said came back to her, and in that instant she became serious. 'You said you were taking me home? Where?' she asked quickly. 'Where is home? Here—in London?'

He shook his head. 'A village in Hertfordshire,' he answered. 'Mr Phipps believes you should have rest and quiet, peace to fully recover. He thinks you'll rest much better there than in my London apartment.'

'You have two homes?' she questioned, having formed the opinion that Mr Phipps would prefer her to receive information slowly, but wanting to know everything at once.

'I recently inherited Grove House from my grandmother,' Tye responded.

'Have I been there before?'

He shook his head. 'It will be a new beginning for you,' he replied. 'You know no one there and no one will know you.' He gave her an encouraging look. 'So you won't have to worry about whether or not to say hello to someone you pass in the street.'

She hadn't thought of that. Although, since she was only recently on her feet, she doubted she could walk a hundred yards without collapsing. To take a walk outside had not featured largely in her thoughts.

'Your grandmother died?' she asked, some quirky side of her brain hopping on to that thought.

'She died a few months ago.'

'I'm sorry.' Claire suddenly felt she had been insensitive to ask the question. 'Did I know your grandmother?'

'You never met her,' he replied, adding encouragingly, 'You'll like Shipton Ash; I'm sure of it.'

'That's where Grove House is?'

'It's only a small village. A shop, a pub, and a few other properties scattered about.'

'I'll live there on my own?' she asked, while not wanting

to live with Tye as though she were his wife starting to feel a little worried about leaving the clinic, with no memory, to spend each day and night in some strange house by herself.

'I'll be there as much as I can,' Tye promised her. And, at her quick nervous look, 'Don't worry, you'll have your own room. And when I'm not there Jane Harris, my grandmother's former housekeeper-cum-nurse will come and stay with you.'

Claire's eyes widened slightly. 'You've arranged all this? While I've been—idling here, you've been busy arranging all this for my welfare?'

'I've led a pretty selfish life,' Tye informed her. 'Indulge me.'

'I don't believe you have a selfish bone in your body,' she denied. 'Your visits to me have been constant...' Her voice trailed away. Was that what you did when you loved someone—looked after their welfare, smoothed their path when things got a touch rocky? 'Do you love me?' she asked abruptly, and, quickly after that thought, 'Do I love you?' she asked.

Grey eyes stared into her deeply blue ones. Unexpectedly her heart had started to pound at the thought that this extremely attractive and sophisticated man might be about to tell her that he loved her, but he did nothing of the kind, but said instead, 'I think for the time being you and I should just be friends, and nothing more than that.'

'Oh,' she murmured. And, with either her pride or her intelligence at work, 'You'd like your engagement ring back?' She went to remove it from her finger, but Tye stretched out a hand and placed it over her hands, staying her movements.

'That's not what I'm suggesting at all!' he stated. 'What I'm saying is that for the time being, until you are fully well, our engagement becomes a platonic affair.'

'A platonic engagement,' she echoed, more to get over

the tingling kind of sensation the touch of his warm hand over hers was causing. But, when she did think of what he was saying, 'I like it,' she said, and Tye let go of her hand and stood up.

'I'll leave you to get some rest,' he commented. 'You've an exhausting day in front of you tomorrow.'

'Clothes!' she exclaimed, having a last-minute panic; she didn't really want to make the journey to Grove House in her nightwear.

'All arranged,' he assured her. 'Get some rest,' he repeated, and left her.

Claire was awake for ages after he had gone. She looked at her engagement ring. Platonic engagement. The two words brought a smile to her face. He was nice, her platonic fiancé. She felt she liked him, and would have done so even if she had not known him prior to losing her memory.

Mr Phipps had said her memory would return any day now. She wished it would hurry up. Not only on her own account, but Tye's too, she realised. She wanted to know more of him as well. Wanted to remember about him and their relationship. What they did, where they went, what they talked about. She wanted to recall their favourite places, their favourite restaurant.

She again thought of the feel of his strong arms around her that day she had wanted to know what she looked like— and wanted to remember their more intimate moments together. She was pretty sure, Tye being such a virile-looking man and everything—not to mention that she had lived with him—that they must have been lovers. And yet she had no memory of sharing herself with him. And Tye? He seemed in no hurry to share so much as a kiss with her. All of which made him a rather superb platonic fiancé. For the first time since her accident she went to sleep with a smile playing about her mouth.

It had gone two the next afternoon before she saw Tye again. He had to work, she knew that, and she tried to be patient, but while a percentage of her felt hesitant and even a touch reluctant to leave the security of Roselands clinic, there was a greater part of her that wanted to make that journey to Grove House. Perhaps once she was on the outside of hospital life, living a normal kind of existence, her memory would come rushing back.

Tye arrived carrying a suitcase—the contents of which, as well as some expensive-looking underwear, included jeans, trousers and tops. All of which appeared to be new. Perhaps he had packed only the newest additions to her wardrobe.

'I couldn't have been wearing any of this when I was brought into hospital!' she commented slowly. It seemed to her that if her body had taken such an assault that she'd been unconscious for days, some of what she had been wearing at the time must have suffered some snag or tear at the very least.

'Apart from your shoes, you weren't,' Tye agreed. 'Not to dwell on the subject too much, you were completely out of it, making it impossible for you to tell anyone if you hurt more in one place than another. Rather than do more damage in getting you out of your clothes, the solution was to cut your clothes from you so the doctors could quickly trace the source of the blood and assess the extent of your injuries.'

'Everyone put in a lot of effort for me, didn't they?' she said gratefully.

And was grateful again, to Tye this time, that, when he must have seen her at some time totally without her clothes, and might even have helped her out of them occasionally for all she knew, he said, 'I'll get a nurse to help you get changed.'

It was Beth Orchard who came and helped her to dress, and, having thought she would need very little assistance, Claire was amazed at how weak she felt and how much help she needed.

'Lying in bed will do that for you,' Beth Orchard said cheerfully, even though Claire had sat out of bed daily and for progressively longer periods.

Claire thanked everyone for their splendid care and, holding on to Tye's arm, she left the clinic. It was a mild October day, and it was wonderful to be out in the air, a light wind fanning her face and hair.

Tye walked slowly. She was glad that he did. Incredibly, she felt exhausted by the time they reached his long sleek Jaguar. 'In you get,' he said lightly, without fuss helping her into the passenger seat.

It was a joy to be out, to be a human being as opposed to a patient. She wanted to savour everything, and looked about her as they left the car park hoping that perhaps something, any little thing, might trigger off some spark of memory.

But, look around as she did, she saw nothing that spurred a memory, and slowly her eyelids began to grow heavy and she fell asleep. She woke up once, glanced at the man by her side; he glanced back, they smiled at each other—and she went to sleep again.

She awakened just in time to see a sign saying Shipton Ash. 'We're there!' she exclaimed, and unexpectedly started to feel worried. 'Will Jane Harris be there?' she asked anxiously.

If Tye noticed her suddenly anxious state he gave no indication, but replied calmly, 'I hope so. I could murder a cup of tea.'

Claire felt instantly better again. 'I'm sorry,' she apologised, perfectly aware that, while he was quite capable of making his own tea, he was doing his best to ease for her this time of leaving the security of the clinic. Perhaps Mr Phipps had warned she might feel a trifle agitated from time to time.

Abruptly then she forgot all about how she was feeling, for Tye was stopping the car and was getting out to open a pair of high and wide iron gates. Astonished, having for no particular reason supposed Grove House to be a small cottage kind of a house, she saw at the end of an avenue of beautiful trees that lined the drive the most elegant building that could have been quite appropriately named manor house.

She opened her mouth to say as much as Tye got back into the car. But as she looked from him down the long tree-lined drive, suddenly, without warning, and as if from far off, she heard herself say, 'My mother loved trees. She—' Claire broke off, turning sharply to Tye, switching her gaze away from the trees to him, her mouth falling open in shock.

Immediately his hands came out and he caught a firm hold of her upper arms. 'You're all right,' he assured her quietly, calmly. Then questioned, 'You've remembered—?'

'Only that!' she cut in, feeling totally shaken. Then, urgently, her eyes growing wide, 'I said that my mother loved trees. *Loved!*' she emphasised. 'You said my parents were on holiday in—' She broke off, her breath catching. 'Is my mother dead?' she asked faintly. 'Is she?' she asked urgently. 'Tye, please tell me.'

CHAPTER TWO

TYE looked into her troubled blue eyes, his expression controlled. 'Let's get you inside the house,' he said after a moment, and started the car's motor.

Her head had begun to ache. She subsided back into her seat. She had no idea where that memory had sprung from, but it was there, as fact—her mother *had* loved trees.

Jane Harris must have been on the lookout for them because she had the front door of Grove House open as they drew up outside. She was a well-covered woman in her late fifties who beamed a smile and stood back as Tye, with an arm around Claire, helped her into the wide hall.

He introduced them, adding, 'The journey has been a bit much for Claire. I'll take her straight up.'

'Your rooms are all ready for you,' Jane Harris replied. 'Shall I bring some tea?'

'Would you, Jane?' he accepted, and, turning to Claire, commented, 'You're never going to make those stairs under your own steam,' then, as if she weighed nothing, he picked her up in his arms and made for the wide and elegant staircase.

'I can walk!' she protested, but owned she did feel a mite exhausted.

Once more held against his chest as—effortlessly, it seemed—he carried her to one of the upstairs room, Claire tried to dispel the unsettling feeling that something was wrong—something was very, very wrong.

In the room Tye set her down on the bed, moving her so that she was sitting leaning against the pillows with her feet on the bed. But even as he was straightening up she was asking, 'Tell me about my mother, Tye?'

24

He looked into her distressed eyes and was silent for a second or two, and then, 'The truth is, little one,' he answered, 'I don't know anything about your mother.'

'You never met her?'

'I never did.'

'But... But you said my parents were on hol—' She broke off, her intelligence at work. 'Did you and Mr Phipps think it better I should think my parents were on holiday rather than I should know my mother was dead?' she asked.

'He didn't want you to be concerned about absolutely anything,' Tye replied. 'And, quite honestly, I think you've coped with more than enough for one day. I'll get your case, and Jane can help you into bed.'

'What if I remember something else?' Claire asked, starting to panic suddenly.

'I'm not going far, only out to the car,' he assured her, and had not been gone for more than a minute when Jane Harris arrived with a tray of tea.

Claire took to Jane Harris, who asked her to call her by her first name, and they were sipping tea when Tye returned with the case he had brought to the clinic.

'I'll leave you to it,' he said. 'I'll—'

'You're not leaving...' Claire cut in hurriedly, and, feeling slightly shamefaced that he had become her anchor and that she should feel so panicky at the thought of him going '...yet,' she added.

He smiled. 'I've nothing pressing to get back to London for.'

Jane unpacked her case when he had gone, and helped her into bed. When her eyelids started to droop, Jane went quietly away and left her to rest.

But Claire could not rest; her head would not let her. She knew that her mother had had a feeling for trees, and that her mother was dead. Those two scraps of knowledge spun round and around in her brain. So that by the time Jane brought her an early-evening meal Claire was feeling close to being spent of all energy.

When Jane had gone, from innate good manners Claire attempted to eat as much of the casserole Jane had been good enough to prepare as she could. But Claire had scant appetite. She started to fret that she was putting everyone to a lot of bother.

She contemplated getting out of bed and carrying her used dishes downstairs, and was just pondering the possibility of the tray and her shaky self arriving in the kitchen in one piece when Jane returned.

'Not hungry?' she enquired, as with a professional glance at Claire's slight figure Jane picked up the bed tray. 'I can see I shall have my work cut out trying to put a few pounds on you,' she added lightly.

'I'm sorry,' Claire apologised, aware that for all she curved in the right places, and was not lacking in the bosom department, still the same she was on the thin side of slender. 'The casserole was delicious.' She thanked the woman who could add first-rate cook to her list of other skills.

'I'll just take your tray downstairs and tidy up a bit, then I'll be off.' She smiled warmly. 'Now, is there anything you need before I go?'

'You're not staying the night?' Claire asked in a flash of alarm.

'Mr Kershaw will be here,' Jane quickly assured her, and was all sympathy as she straightened the bedcovers and soothed, 'Try not to worry. It's only natural you should suffer pangs of insecurity from time to time. But—' her tone brightened '—between us we'll get you right.'

Claire survived her small attack of panic, and found a smile. 'You're a nurse as well as a four-star cook,' she remarked.

'Fully trained nurse and a muddle-along cook,' Jane laughed.

'You didn't care for nursing?'

'Loved it,' Jane replied. 'Until my back went. But I was lucky,' she went on cheerfully. 'Just when I knew I was going to have to look for an alternative occupation I heard old Mrs Kershaw needed a housekeeper—knowledge of nursing an advantage. She wasn't ill then, but frail, and with an ulcer that took for ever to heal.' She paused to give a chubby grin. 'And, as usual, I'm talking too much.'

Why, when she had done little that day, she should suddenly feel tired again was a mystery to Claire, but no sooner had Jane gone than she seemed unable to keep her eyes open.

She awoke with a start to find a tall man bending over her bed—and, as an almighty fear shrieked through her, '*Go away!*' she screamed in fear. 'Don't you dare come in here!' she yelled, rocketing upright, using what strength she had to leap horrified out of bed.

The man pulled back from the bed and made as if to come after her, but he stopped, frozen in his tracks when he saw the look of absolute horror on her face. 'My dear, it's...'

And suddenly, hearing him speak, seeing his face clearly now that he was no longer bending over her, so she recognised Tye, her fiancé. She drew a long shuddering gasp of breath, realising that his face must have been in shadow until she had moved. 'Oh, Tye,' she cried, thoroughly ashamed. 'I didn't know it was you.' With that, her legs weak, she dropped heavily on to the edge of the bed, her face ashen.

With the trauma of the moment over, Tye came round to her side of the bed and, seating himself next to her, took her into his arms. 'You're all right, sweetheart,' he said gently. 'I'm here. Nothing's going to harm you.'

She drew another fractured breath. 'Did someone harm me? Some man?' she asked, raising her head to look at him, her eyes troubled.

Tye studied her for long moments, 'I don't know,' he answered, his eyes not leaving her face.

'Mr Phipps said my loss of memory might be the result of my accident, but that sometimes a memory loss occurs if someone is trying to blot out something emotional. It can sometimes be both.'

'So I believe,' Tye replied.

'He told you the same?'

'I wanted to know all there was to know.'

Claire expected that he did. Tye was that sort of man. She gave a shaky sigh, was all at once aware that she was trembling, and realised that Tye must be aware of it too, for he held her quietly against him for some while.

Then slowly, as she began to recover from whatever unknown demons were in her past, Claire suddenly became conscious of the scantiness of her attire. Her nightdress was blue this time, bringing out the lovely deep blue colour of her eyes. One strap had fallen down her arm, and as she pulled back from Tye she saw that the silk material left very little to the imagination. She shivered unexpectedly.

'You're cold,' Tye said, smiling at her as he drew back, his eyes scanning over her. She glanced down, following his brief tour of her person, and went scarlet as she observed the swell of her breasts with the hardened peaks clearly outlined by the thinness of the material.

'I'm sorry,' she said for no reason, and their eyes met.

'Well, at least you're a better colour,' Tye teased, and she thought she knew why she had loved him. 'Just in case you're heading for a bit of shock—not to mention that it's nearly midnight,' he went on, his teasing manner falling away, 'I think we'll get you back into bed.'

In no time she was in bed, with Tye sitting in a chair next to her. He stayed with her for quite some while, conversing on various subjects, but mindful that she had no memory.

He commented lightly on Jane's delicious casserole, and Claire replied that the good thing about casseroles was that you could prepare them and then forget about them—a boon on a busy day.

'How did I know that?' she exclaimed as soon as the words were out. 'Was I some sort of a cook?'

'You never were just a pretty face,' Tye answered easily. And, looking at her, and plainly judging that she was not going to go into shock, 'Will you be all right if I leave you?' he asked.

'Of course,' she answered without hesitation.

'I'm just along the landing if you need me,' he informed her. 'I'll leave my door open. Give me a shout if—'

'Oh, Tye!' she exclaimed helplessly, and guessed then that, apart from her feeling of horror earlier, Jane must have told him of her feelings of alarm and insecurity at the thought of being alone that night. 'I'm sorry to be such a nuisance. You must be wanting to get back to London...'

'Now, why would I want to do that when my best girl's here?' he cut in lightly. Was she his best girl? It made her feel a little more secure to think so, she had to admit. 'Don't forget, I'm just along the landing,' he said, and was heading out of the room when she stopped him.

'Tye!' she called. He halted, turning, and from nowhere she found herself blurting out, 'Tye, would you kiss me?'

'I...'

'Sorry!' she swiftly exclaimed, then added, 'I seem to be for ever apologising,' and explained, 'It's just that I've forgotten what your kisses are like, and...'

'You're a glutton for punishment,' he drawled, and, with an exaggerated sigh that made her laugh, came back to the bed. 'You promise not to have your wicked way with me?' he questioned mock-toughly.

'You have my word, sir,' she said, and Tye bent down to her. A moment later his lips touched hers and she was on the receiving end of a warm but chaste kiss.

'All right?' Tye asked as he drew back, his eyes searching hers, almost as if he suspected some man might have attacked her and she wanted to heal—whatever the unknown scars—with a kiss from someone she trusted.

While it was true that her heart was racing to beat the band, and that she was experiencing the almost uncontrollable urge to throw her arms around Tye and beg for another, perhaps less chaste kiss, Claire felt just then that she had never felt so right inside.

'Absolutely,' she answered, feeling strangely light-headed from the touch of his lips on her. 'Goodnight, Tye.'

He looked down at her approvingly. 'Sleep tight,' he bade her, and went quietly from her room.

She did sleep tight. But, perhaps because she had slept quite soundly before midnight, she was awake very early. Awake and suddenly feeling better than she had been feeling in a long while. Her body had more or less healed, her head was taking a little longer—so why was she lying in bed?

It was still early, still dark outside, but Claire was suddenly certain that she had led a very busy life. It seemed to go totally against something in her to lie there idle when she should be up and about and doing something.

There appeared to be nothing very much that she could do, though, and she was aware that she was still regaining her strength. But, was she to lie there for the next couple of hours, waiting for Jane to perhaps arrive and bring her a cup of tea?

Claire thought of Tye, who was 'just along the landing', and wondered how long it was since anyone had brought him a cup of tea in bed. Then she realised that perhaps, before her accident, she had made him tea and taken it to his bedside. Perhaps they had made love…

She drew her thoughts hastily away from such subjects, even as her cheeks grew hot as she recalled his superb mouth over hers last night.

As if to escape such thoughts, she got out of bed and decided it was time to make more of an effort. So far she had not been allowed to take a bath without someone accompanying her. She would start by taking a bath on her own.

She was already acquainted with the adjoining bathroom, but was astounded to find how little strength she had. Even the simple procedure of bending over the bath, securing the plug and turning on the taps caused her to need to sit on the bathroom stool while she waited for the bath to fill.

Five minutes later, however, she lay resting in the water and was starting to feel extremely proud of herself. Gone were the days of someone escorting her while she bathed. She had managed on her own—she would not have to wait for Jane to arrive.

She soaped herself, noticing that she still had traces of bruising in places. She realised then just how astonishingly lucky she had been not to break any bones when the accident had happened. Even now—and she owned she had lost all sense of time but it must be weeks later—her body was still feeling a little creaky in places. She rinsed the lovely perfumed lather away and, feeling tired again, rested in the water, letting her thoughts drift.

She thought about her mother and wondered about her father. Had her mother died recently or a long, long time ago? Had her parents been devoted to each other? Or maybe they had been divorced and... It was no good; her head was beginning to ache again. There was a barrier there and it just seemed impossible to get through it.

Claire went on to think about the way she had reacted when she had awoken last night and found Tye bending over her—probably checking to see if she was asleep. Oh, the poor man. He had been so good—and she had screamed at him for his trouble.

Had some man attacked her? She abruptly turned away from the question. She did not want to know, and for once she was glad to have no memory.

But demons seemed to be all at once tormenting her, and hurriedly, with more speed than thought, she leapt out of the bath—only to find that instead of landing on her feet she had landed in a heap on the floor.

For a moment she was too shaken to try to get up. But as she started to get herself back together again she was staggered to discover that a stitched, grazed and badly bruised body, plus some days spent comatose and more days of just lying in bed, had left her feeling shatteringly debilitated! She hurt when she tried to move too. But a few minutes later she used what energy she could find to pick herself up and make it to the bathroom stool.

Seconds, perhaps minutes, ticked by when all she was capable of doing was just sitting there. She felt battered, bruised and utterly exhausted, and was more concerned just then with finding some strength from somewhere than with the fact that she needed to dry herself.

Then someone knocked on the bathroom door. Oh, thank goodness. Jane. Claire's spirits lifted. Only it wasn't Jane. It was Tye's voice that came through the wood panelling. 'I'm not too happy about you taking a bath on your own,' he called, and Claire, with a start, realised he must have heard the water running in the plumbing system.

'I'm certainly not inviting you to join me!' she called back sharply, finding that she did not care to be discovered naked, and that, while the rest of her seemed to be incapacitated, there was nothing wrong with her tongue.

'I'm concerned in case you have a dizzy bout!' Tye returned shortly.

She did not care for his tone. 'I'm not the dizzy type!' replied she who had not a clue as to what type she was.

'You...' he began toughly, but checked, and then, more evenly, reminded her, 'You've been ill.'

'I shall feel a whole lot better when you've gone!' she retorted, and knew she was far from being herself. She was cranky, pathetically weak—and he who had been nothing but good to her did not deserve her spleen. She could only imagine that it could not be part of her normal way of life to sit naked, having a conversation with someone on the other side of a door, and that some kind of confused modesty was pushing her. 'Are you still there?' she asked, less sharply, starting to feel ashamed of herself.

'I'll stay here while you get out,' he replied.

'I am out,' she answered, and was suddenly feeling totally used up and miserable.

'Are you all right?' he asked, when seconds had passed and there were no sounds of movement.

'Of course,' she replied. 'I...' She went to stand—and was appalled that her legs felt all wobbly. 'Is—is Jane around?' she asked, trying to sound casual but with weak tears coming to her eyes.

Those tears did not fall; they were stifled by the shock she felt to hear Tye open the bathroom door. She stared at him in a stunned moment of nothing happening. Then, as she glimpsed him take in her seated and damp naked body, so she bent forward, as if hoping to hide from his view the nakedness of her breasts.

But she had no need to worry on that score, she soon saw, for in one glance Tye seemed to take in the whole situation. And while she was still cowering there, stunned, he had grabbed up a warm fluffy towel from the heated towel rail and, draping it across her shoulders, tucked it around her.

She immediately started to feel a shade better. 'Is Jane coming today?' she asked, with no clear reason other than that, oddly, weak tears were again pressing.

'You're going to have to put up with me until later today,' he replied, and instructed, 'Sit tight. I'll be back in a minute.' True to his word, having left her only to go and collect an armful of more fluffy towels, he was back. 'Imagine I'm your best bloke,' he said, and before she could blink he had whisked one damp towel away from her and had wrapped her in a dry one. Before she knew it he was hoisting her up in his arms and was carrying her into the other room.

'I feel such a fool,' she sniffed, tears smarting again.

'You wouldn't dream of crying on me, I hope?'

'What sort of a girl do you think I am?' she rallied.

'A very lovely one,' he answered, placing her down on the edge of the bed. 'A very lovely one who's doing the very best she can in a world where everything must be completely confusing.'

'Oh, Tye!' she cried. 'I'm sorry I was so cranky earlier. I was so nasty and you are so good. I c-can't believe I have so little energy.'

'Your system has suffered one gigantic shock—nobody expects you to jump up and start doing aerobics,' he calmed her, and through the over-large towel that encased her he began to rub her dry. When that towel was damp, without the smallest fuss he whipped it from her and wrapped her in a fresh one. 'Feel snug?' he enquired. She nodded, feeling suddenly extremely tired and sleepy. 'Into bed, then,' he instructed matter of factly and, perhaps never intending her to move by herself, he lifted her, still wrapped in the dry towel, and put her into bed.

She looked up at him, and tired though she was she had to smile. 'You're a bit special, aren't you?' she mumbled, and closed her eyes.

She was already half asleep, but drifted off certain she heard him say softly, 'You're a bit special yourself, sweetheart.'

She awoke feeling hot and a little confused. The towel Tye had wrapped around her had loosened, and for a moment, as it began to come back to her why she was lying in bed naked, she could not remember where her nightdress was.

Her confused world soon righted itself when she realised it must still be in the bathroom. But she did not want to sit around in her nightdress all day. She was never going to regain her strength by just sitting around.

Her thoughts of getting out of bed, if only to sit out, as

she had at the clinic, were interrupted when someone, as if thinking she might still be asleep, tapped lightly on her door.

'Come in!' she called, and felt embarrassed when Tye accepted her invitation. She had a feeling that the only reason he had knocked on her door at all was to forewarn her. Quite obviously he had no wish to invite a repetition of her screaming at him, should she awake to find him bending over her, as she had last night. 'What time is it?' she asked to cover her embarrassment, while at the same time she struggled to free herself of the over-large towel and sit up.

'A little after ten,' he answered. 'You don't—?'

'Shouldn't you be at your office?' she butted in, looking up at his handsome face and feeling guilty that she was keeping him from his work.

'That's one of the perks of being your own boss,' Tye replied, coming and taking a seat on the edge of her bed. 'I can take a day off whenever I like.'

She found him quite charming. 'But your work will suffer!' she protested.

'No, it won't,' he denied, his eyes searching her face, assessing for himself if she had recovered from her earlier attempt to overdo her strength. 'I've set up office in an annexe next to my grandmother's library.'

Claire stared at him wordlessly for some seconds. He had previously told her that his grandmother had died a few months ago, but the fact that Tye still referred to the library in the house he had inherited as his 'grandmother's library' seemed to state that he still thought of the house as being his grandmother's.

In a moment of impulsive sympathy, knowing somehow that Tye had been extremely fond of his grandmother, Claire leaned forward to touch him. Then, as the bedclothes fell away from her, so she went crimson.

'Oh!' she wailed, frantically grabbing at the covers to hide her partially revealed breasts. 'Oh!' she cried again, but felt better for being covered up—given that her shoulders were exposed. 'Does everybody lose their modesty when they start to get used to people in white coats coming in to check on their progress?'

Tye smiled a friendly smile. 'You haven't lost your modesty, or even mislaid it,' he promised. 'I swear I never knew anyone to blush so prettily,' he teased. 'Or,' he added, 'so frequently.' She was still a shade pink and he, it appeared, was determined to tease her out of her discomfiture when he enquired, 'Now, what do you propose attempting for your next adventure?'

She knew he was referring to her last adventure being her attempt to get from bed, to bath and back to bed again unaided. 'I'm sorry.' She felt she owed him that. 'I would never have tried the bath had I—'

'What?' he interrupted aghast. 'You'd do me out of my rescue?'

She wasn't sure about his teasing—she could feel herself going pink again. 'Did I always blush—even before we became lovers?' she asked abruptly, and blushed again at the very thought of being lovers with him.

Tye looked as if her question had almost stumped him. Then he grinned, a heart-turning grin. 'You were ever a delight,' he said, and added briskly, 'Mr Phipps is of the opinion you should take things easy this morning and perhaps walk up and down the landing for ten minutes or so this afternoon.'

'I've done nothing but take it easy for…' Claire began to protest when suddenly something, perhaps her intelligence stirring, struck her. 'You haven't been in touch with Mr Phipps since we arrived here yesterday?'

'Why wouldn't I?' Tye asked, his expression serious. 'I had intended to anyway, when you remembered or seemed to know that your mother had a soft spot for trees. When it was obvious last night that you fear something in connection with some man or other, I felt we should have professional guidance.'

She sighed. 'I don't want to be this much trouble.'

'Good!' Tye was straight back to teasing. 'That means you're going to obey my every instruction?'

'In your dreams!' she laughed—and loved it when he laughed too. 'I think I'll get up now,' she said.

'I'd better get you something to wear.'

'I'll get dressed,' she decided.

'I thought you might,' he answered mildly, and went from the bed to root in the drawers of the chest and selected several articles of underwear that Jane had put away when she had unpacked for her. From the built-in wardrobes Tye extracted trousers and a shirt. Then he approached the bed, and Claire would swear that there was the very devil alight in his eyes when, dropping the trousers and shirt down on the bottom of the bed, he came towards her with a bra and a pair of lacy briefs. 'I'll help you,' he offered, his eyes *definitely* alive with mischief.

'I haven't lost *that* much modesty!' she erupted.

Tye gave an exaggerated sigh. 'Then I'd better go and get you some breakfast.' And he left her to take as much time as she needed in which to dress herself.

She stared at the door after he had gone, and knew that there was a great mass of information about herself which she did not know. She looked down at the beautiful engagement ring on her finger and realised that, while she might not have the smallest recall that she loved the man, what she did know was that Tye Kershaw was a man whom she most certainly liked very much.

Because she was still stiff and tender in places, as well as her movements not being as swift as she felt surely they must have been before her accident, it took her some while to get dressed. But she felt better for the effort, better for being dressed and out of bed. She was not going to return to bed in a hurry.

Breakfast was more of a brunch. 'You're trying to fatten

me up!' she accused Tye when he carried in a tray of bacon, eggs, baked beans and crisply fried bread.

'You have a marathon to run this afternoon,' he reminded her. 'Eat hearty.'

It was around three when Tye next came to her room. 'I can manage the landing on my own!' she protested, having already walked about her room a good deal—admittedly with rests in between.

'I know you can,' he replied, but didn't budge.

'I'm keeping you from your work!'

'It's all on computer—I can do it tonight,' he replied easily.

'Have I much computer experience?' she asked, her spirits suddenly plummeting that she didn't even know that much.

'Hasn't everybody?' he answered lightly. And, plainly not expecting a reply, 'Come on, Claire, time for a canter.'

Up and down the long landing they went, and for her it *was* a marathon. Not that there was anything hurried about their stroll, with Tye slowing her down when, aware he had work he must want to be getting on with, she went to move from stroll to cruise.

'Was it something I said?' he enquired, slowing her down by the simple expedient of placing a hand on her arm.

'I'll regain my strength more quickly if I push myself just that little bit,' she argued.

'Perhaps,' he conceded, determined, it seemed, not to argue. 'But—' he smiled down at her '—not today.' Looking up at him, Claire prepared to argue anyway. Then found that Tye had given her something else to think about when he went on to promise, 'If you make steady progress, we could try taking a walk outside by the end of the week.'

She instantly fell into step with him. The way she was feeling right then she knew she would be hard put to make it halfway up the long, long drive. 'It's Tuesday today?' she documented, all days having blurred into one at the clinic.

'It is,' he confirmed.

'Does Friday count as the start of the weekend?'

Tye gave her a smile that warmed her heart. 'If you behave yourself,' he agreed.

Claire was ready to attempt another length of the landing and back again, but had to admit that she was not too put out when he decided she had done enough for one day.

They parted at the door of her room and she went in, deciding to take her ease in the window seat. It was from there that she saw Jane arrive in her car, and not long afterwards the ex-nurse came to her room with a tray of sandwiches and a pot of tea. 'Just a little something to keep you going until dinner,' Jane explained—when Claire was still feeling full from brunch.

'It's a conspiracy!' she exclaimed, and Jane laughed.

'I think you probably lost a pound or two while you were in hospital,' she opined. 'Is there anything I can tempt you with for dinner?'

'You're staying on for a few hours?'

'I'm enjoying myself,' Jane replied. 'I'll be back around nine tomorrow morning, by the way. If you can stay in bed that long, I'll be here as soon as I've walked my neighbour's dog. He—my neighbour—isn't so good on his feet these days.'

Jane stayed chatting for a brief while, and after she had gone Claire rather surmised that Tye had soon had a word with Jane on the possibility of her being around at bathtime tomorrow morning.

Quite when, having transferred herself to a padded bedroom chair, her spirits began to take a nosedive, Claire could not be sure. She had been thinking along the lines of Tye's goodness, borne out by the fact that, engaged as they were, he was making not the smallest demand on her. His patience was quite astonishing, she realised, when she considered that, as intimate as they must have been in the past—as intimate as they had been now in that he had seen her in various stages of undress—he was bothering to call in Jane to help with her bath. Claire felt hot all over when it came to her that for all she could remember they might well have bathed together!

And that was the trouble. She could not remember. Push to remember though she might, there was nothing there but a huge blank blackness. She pushed and pushed—but nothing. It was all very well for everyone to say relax, her memory would come back. But it wouldn't; so how could she relax?

She began to feel on edge, anxiety gnawing at her. She got up out of her chair. She couldn't take it—this blankness, this isolation of body and mind. She went to the door, not knowing where she was going but feeling she would go mad if she did not get out from there.

Out on the landing, she strove to keep her breathing even. She was having a bit of a panic attack, that was all. She needed something else to occupy her mind. Trying to dig for memories that just weren't there was driving her crazy.

Claire found something else to occupy her mind when she decided to negotiate what suddenly seemed like a mile-long staircase. She took her time, with part of her impatient and urging, For goodness' sake, you seem more like a hundred than twenty… Twenty-what? She didn't even know how old she was!

Feeling desperate all of a sudden, it was only by an effort of sheer will that she did not slump down on the stairs and burst into tears of utter desolation, frustration and fear.

She *made* herself go on. *Made* herself go down, a step at a time. So, OK, her body *had* felt as though it had been flattened by some ton weight, but she was sure she did not ache nearly so much today as she had yesterday. Positive, that was the way forward. Stay positive.

She owned she felt close to collapse when she reached the last three stairs. She gripped the beautiful wood banister and was determined, given a little respite, that she was going to make it the rest of the way.

Being sure she had not made any noise in her descent, she was startled to suddenly see that Tye had just come out from one of the doors along the hall.

'What the…?' he began, and, his face like thunder, came striding towards her, his arms reaching for her as he halted at the bottom of the stairs. But, after her mammoth journey, she wasn't having that.

'No!' she yelled, and, ignoring his thunderous expression, 'I want to do it myself,' she said stubbornly.

Tye stared angrily at her, his grey assessing eyes looking hard into her deeply blue ones. There was a wealth of exasperation in his expression, but his arms did drop to his sides, and he did take a step back.

Feeling that her legs were going to give way at any moment, Claire bent her head and drew on all her reserves of strength. She peppered that strength with a helping of bravado, and, hoping he was too busy watching her feet to notice that her knuckles on the hand holding the banister were white, she negotiated the rest of the stairs.

Only when she had made it to the hall floor and was standing beside him did she look up. After such black despair, adrenalin was pumping away in her—adrenalin at her achievement. She was not sure it wasn't a hint of admiration she had glimpsed in his eyes. But, ready to drop though she might be, she had made those stairs on her own!

'Now?' Tye enquired dryly, and she knew he was asking was she ready now to accept his assistance? The alternative, she was fairly certain, was to fall flat on her face in front of him.

'Now,' she accepted, and from such a void of dark-filled hopelessness she gave a triumphant laugh as Tye bent and picked her up in his arms.

He carried her into the drawing room and deposited her

gently onto a sofa. Then, standing back, he asked, 'What am I going to do with you?'

'Don't be cross with me,' she begged. 'I was…' She stopped. He had enough to do without listening to her woes.

But, 'You were?' he insisted.

'I needed to get out of my room. Events w-were crowding in on me,' she answered, her voice on the shaky side. 'That is,' she continued after a gulp of breath, 'non-events were getting the better of me. I tried to remember something, anything, but…' her voice started to fade '…but there's nothing there.'

'Oh, my dear,' Tye murmured, sitting down beside her. 'I feel helpless to help—other than to tell you that Mr Phipps believes there's a good chance your memory is starting to stir.'

'I wish it would hurry up.'

'Hopefully it will.' Tye changed the subject. 'You were splendid with those stairs. What, I wonder, are you going to do for an encore?'

He was teasing, and she thought she could love him. 'Swing from the chandeliers?' she replied, but felt dreadful suddenly for keeping him from his work. 'Is it all right if I just sit here for a little while?' she asked.

'The change of scene will do you good.'

'But only if you go back to work,' she bargained.

'Slave-driver! Am I glad I don't work for you!' She grinned, and saw his eyes on her mouth. Then he was asking, 'Are you going to be all right if I leave you for a while?'

'Of course. I'm over whatever it was.'

He gave her hand a light squeeze and stood up. 'If you put your feet up on the sofa and rest for a while, there's a fair chance you'll be allowed to stay down for dinner.'

Without another word she took off her shoes and stretched out on the sofa. She closed her eyes, waited a moment, and then opened one eye. Tye was still there, watching her. But just before he walked away she saw his mouth pick up at the corners.

Dinner, for the most part, was a pleasant meal. Claire made it to the dining room under her own power, and enjoyed sitting at a dining table for what she realised was the first time that she could remember.

Since, however, Tye seemed to know very little about her family, and because she felt a need to absorb some knowledge of his, she asked, 'You've probably already told me, but would you tell me again about your family? Have I met any of them?'

'You're acquainted with Miles, my stepbrother, but not Paulette, his exuberant wife,' Tye replied.

'Your parents?' Claire prompted, when it seemed he had nothing to add.

'My mother left home when I was a toddler. I hardly know her.'

'Did—did your grandmother bring you up?' Claire asked, thinking it sad that he should have so little to do with his mother, but supposing, since she had gained an impression that he'd been close to his grandmother, that that lady had played a large part in his life after his mother's departure.

'I lived with her during the week. My father wanted me with him at weekends. When he remarried he insisted I live permanently with him and my stepmother.'

'The arrangement was successful?'

'Very. Anita is a little older than my father, and has a son ten years older than me. But she couldn't have been kinder had I been her son too.'

'You all got on well?'

'Extremely.'

'How lovely.' Claire smiled, not doubting that there had been trauma in Tye's life, but feeling happy that in the end everything had worked out so well. 'You were happy all round, including at your grandmother?' she remarked.

'Well, I wouldn't exactly say that.'

'You wouldn't?'

'Family skeletons,' he confided with a conspiratorial quirk to his mouth. 'Grandmother did not exactly take to Anita.'

'Ah!' Claire murmured, suspecting the fact that Anita had taken over guardianship of the senior Mrs Kershaw's charge might have had something to do with it. But, not wanting to pry into what might be a sensitive issue, particularly sensitive with the death of his grandmother so recent, Claire changed direction to ask, since Tye had just told her he had a stepbrother, 'Do you have any brothers or half-brothers? A sister per...?' She gasped, the question lost, shock taking her, her colour draining, her world spinning.

'What?' Swiftly Tye had left his seat and was standing over her. 'What is it?' He drew up a chair close to her and came and sat next to her, bending so he could see into her face.

'I'm all right,' Claire gasped, her world starting to right itself, but not so much that she wasn't glad to hang on to his forearm as quickly she asked, 'Tye—do I have a sister?'

Her eyes searched his; she needed to know. But he was taking his time answering. And it was not an answer, but a question when he replied, 'Why do you ask?'

'I think I have,' she said, and explained, 'I was about to ask you if you had a sister when suddenly I had this picture in my head of two girls—one was older, the other—I think it was me—was about five years old. We were on a beach somewhere. I'd fallen and cut my foot,' she went on shakily. 'The older girl was looking after me. Tye,' Claire said on a hoarse gasp, 'I have an old scar on my foot!'

'I noticed it,' he replied carefully. 'You had a couple of stitches in it at one time.'

She stared at him, her eyes wide. 'Do I have a sister?' she insisted. 'Do I belong to someone?' she cried.

'Oh, little sweetheart,' Tye murmured, catching hold of her hands. 'Of course you belong to someone!' And, his eyes on her pleading expression, 'You belong to me.'

CHAPTER THREE

'OH, TYE,' Claire cried helplessly. While it was an unimaginable comfort to hear him say that she belonged to him, she still desperately needed to have her question answered. 'Do I have a sister?' she pleaded. 'I need to know.'

Tye stared into her strained expression. 'I don't know,' he answered after some moments. 'I just don't know if you have a sister.'

'I never mentioned having a sister to you?' she insisted, her eyes searching his serious-eyed look.

'You never did,' he replied.

She found that odd. 'Perhaps,' she pondered slowly, her intelligence looking for an answer, 'perhaps there was some kind of family rift. Perhaps that's why I never spoke much of my family to you?'

'Could be,' he murmured, but a hint of a smile was pushing through the seriousness of his expression. 'But the good news is that your memory appears to be rousing.'

Her lovely blue eyes were huge in her pale face. 'I wish it would get a move on,' she replied, her voice barely above a whisper. And, feeling closer to tears than ever, she knew only that, despite her earlier eagerness to be out of her room, back in her room was where she wanted to be. 'I think I'll go—to bed,' she stated jerkily.

She saw him glance to her half-eaten meal, and liked him some more that he did not suggest she stay and finish it but accepted that her appetite had totally disappeared a few minutes ago. And she was so grateful to him for that, that when he said, 'Come on, then, love, let's get you back to bed,' and bent to take her in his arms, she did not resist. In any event, as Tye carried her across the hall, to her eyes the

45

stairs looked toweringly high, and she had grave doubts that she would have managed them on her own.

They were at the door of her room when guilt smote her. Guilt that she could have been a better house guest that day than she had been. True, she and Tye were romantic partners, so from that point of view she supposed his home was her home—and that meant she was not a guest—but equally true she had been a bit less than gracious that day. In fact she had been exceedingly crabby when he had come to the bathroom door early that morning.

'I'm going to behave tomorrow,' she announced as he carried her into her room and placed her down on the bed.

Tye stared down at her. 'Don't go making rash promises,' he instructed dryly. She laughed. She enjoyed his humour. 'Want me to stay around?' he asked.

Oh, she did. Suddenly she knew that she did not want him to go. She knew that she liked him, and felt safer somehow when he was near, safer when she could see him. Then she remembered how she had kept him from his work that day, and how he had said that it was all on computer and that he could work that evening.

'Not at all,' she answered. And, feeling that was a bit blunt after his goodness, 'I'll be fine, honestly.'

Tye studied her for some seconds before accepting her answer. Then, 'Get into bed when you're ready,' he advised. 'I'll look in again before you settle down for the night.'

Claire sat in a chair for quite some while after he had gone. She thought of him, his goodness, his patience, and felt it was no wonder at all that she had fallen in love with him. The evidence that he had been in love with her was there in the ring she wore on her engagement finger. Had, however, being the operative word. Did Tye still love her?

He had never said so. Would not, in fact, have even kissed her had she not asked him to. She recalled his chaste kiss. It had hardly been a lover's kiss. Yet, who was she to complain? She was so mixed up in her head she did not know that she could cope with a stronger emotional involvement with him.

And, yet again remembering his chaste kiss, remembering how she had felt at the time, there was a part of her that seemed to want a warmer embrace from him. Uneasy with her thoughts, she abruptly got up from her chair. Too abruptly—the room spun.

Clutching hold of the bed-end to steady herself, she felt a tidal wave of frustration descend and threaten to swamp her. Instinctively she knew that she was unused to being ill and, that being so, she was finding it irksome in the extreme that she was so sapped of strength that she could not even jerk out of a chair without the risk of falling over.

She found a fresh nightdress and made her way to the bathroom, determined she was going to clean her teeth and get washed and changed without assistance.

A half-hour later she was back in bed, feeling very proud of herself and determining that, having floundered about somewhere near rock-bottom, she was now going to leave all that behind her. She was going to get better. She *was* going to recover her memory. She... There was a knock at her door. A smile came involuntarily to her mouth.

'Not asleep yet?' Tye enquired.

It was ridiculous to be so pleased to see him. She lowered her eyes. 'I've slept enough just lately to last until Christmas,' she replied.

'All part of the healing process,' he commented lightly, coming to stand by the bed and looking down at her. 'Have you all you need?'

She wished he would take a seat, perhaps stay a little while. But clearly Tye had finished his work and was minded to get to his bed. 'Yes, thank you,' she answered politely.

'You've taken your medication?'

She hadn't. 'I've decided not to take any more,' she owned.

Tye eyed her seriously. 'I see,' he remarked, and, while she sat in her bed and looked solemnly back at him, 'You've got a stubborn look about you,' he observed.

She felt stubborn, and did not want to be talked out of her decision. 'It's how I feel,' she admitted.

'Are you going to let me into your logic?' he enquired, not pressuring her at all over her decision but taking a seat on the side of her bed, seeming to have all the time in the world to sit and listen.

She began to feel bad about that. He'd had a busy day and must want to get to his bed. But, when she knew that the quickest way for him to get there would be for her to either say she did not want to talk about it or change her mind and take the wretched medication anyway, she discovered that her stubbornness would not let go.

'My head aches barely at all now.' She found she was explaining the logic of her thoughts. 'And if the other tablet is some sort of tranquilliser to stop me getting in a stew at the brick wall of nothingness I keep crashing into, then it seems to me that if I don't take that tablet I shall be much more alert to catch hold of—and keep hold of—any stray strand of a memory when it floats by.'

Stern grey eyes contemplated her at some length, then, as she looked at him, suddenly she saw his mouth begin to turn up at the corners. He stretched out a hand to take a hold of her hand, lying on top of the coverlet, and he smiled.

'What you've just said sounds perfectly reasonable to me,' he concurred. 'Though...'

His smile seemed oddly to make her spine without stiffening, and the feel of his hand holding hers was more comforting than she would ever have imagined. 'Though?' she questioned, finding she had to swallow before she could speak.

'Though it's a bit late to ring Mr Phipps and ask if he agrees with us.'

Her eyes widened and she stared at Tye in amazement.

He would ring Mr Phipps? She did not doubt that Tye had his home phone number. 'There's no need to disturb him!' she exclaimed hurriedly. 'He—'

'He *is* the expert,' Tye cut in calmly. 'The expert who, as well as being the one to prescribe your medication, has expressed the view that with a little rest and relaxation and in its own good time there is every chance your memory will come tripping back. Which leaves me wondering if, before we start running the risk of undoing all the good work he began with his excellent care and attention, should we not, out of courtesy to him if nothing else, chat it over with him first?'

Tye had asked her to let him into her logic, but something in his reasoning seemed to make her logic a non-starter. Added to which, the way he had referred to them as 'we', as if every decision made was a joint decision, seemed to weaken her. 'I…' She attempted to argue anyway, only to find that that 'we' was still getting in the way of any argument she might find.

'You're trying too hard,' Tye suggested gently, and his very tone, not forceful, but kind and understanding, weakened her further.

'You—needn't ring Mr Phipps,' she gave in.

Tye lightly squeezed her hand and let it go. Casting a glance to her bedside table, checking that she had a glass and some water, he got to his feet. 'I'll leave you to it,' he said, and was over by the door when he advised, 'Jane will be here early tomorrow.'

Claire stared at him unsmiling, but as it hit her that what he was really saying was that she must wait for her bath until Jane arrived, Claire very deliberately stuck her tongue out at him.

What was it with the man? She had expected he might be a touch offended. But, no, not a bit of it! His head went back a few degrees—and he laughed. 'Goodnight,' he said—and left her with a fast-beating heart.

She swallowed her medication and almost immediately went to sleep. But her sleep was tormented and she awoke in the early hours in a troubled frame of mind. Demons, unknown demons, seemed to be chasing her. It was still dark outside. She sat up and hurried to switch on her bedside lamp. Light illuminated the room, but a heavy sort of darkness was oppressing her.

Her breath caught in fear, but fear of what she had no idea. Tye! She thought of Tye in his room along the landing and was half out of her bed before she had a chance to think about what she was doing. 'I'll leave my door open—give me a shout if…' he had said.

From somewhere, however, she managed just then to find a stray strand of control, and got back into bed again. And as more control arrived she began to feel more than a mite ashamed of herself. Poor Tye, he had enough to contend with, trying to do his work while at the same time having to care for her while she floundered in an abyss of wanting to know so much but remembering nothing.

She left the light on while she strove to find some calm to go with that control. And a few minutes later realised she was again wondering if Tye still cared for her. He cared for her physical wellbeing, that was without question. Her mental wellbeing too, as far as he was able, given the result of her accident. But did he care for her emotionally?

That question puzzled her for quite some time. While it was true he had suggested that they keep their engagement platonic until she was fully well, she kept remembering that the only time he had kissed her was when she had asked him to. Perhaps he had gone off her? He had shown not the smallest sign of desiring her and, let's face it, to her knowledge he was used to seeing her in various stages of undress. That was to say he had seen her mainly with only her one layer of clothing: namely her flimsy nightdress, half on her shoulders half off. And once, only yesterday morning, he had seen her naked and it had made no difference. True she had bent forward to hide her breasts and the front of her, but he had sharp eyes, and she didn't doubt he had caught glimpses of her that she would prefer that he had not.

But had he desired her? Had he blazes! Not that she wanted him to, of course. But not for a moment had he shown the smallest sign of panting to, as he would have put it, have his wicked way with her.

She was starting to think that perhaps Tye might have sated any desire he had for her when they had previously been living together when she suddenly recalled how he had grinned when he had said he had given Mr Phipps his solemn undertaking that he would not make love to her—even should she beg him to.

Well, she was glad about that, even if she did feel a touch miffed that the man she was engaged to could so easily keep a lid on his emotions where she was concerned.

She fell to wondering when, if ever, she would be 'fully well'. And as she stared into a void of nothingness, so a black cloud of despair started to oppress her. Did she have a sister? And, if her mother were dead, where was her father? Surely she must have some family out there somewhere. Did nobody care about her? And who was this man lurking in that darkness, this man she seemed so afraid of that she had been totally panic-stricken when she had awakened to find Tye bending over her?

How long she stayed awake she had no idea, but eventually she found calm enough to dare to close her eyes.

In consequence of that wakeful time, she was fast asleep when Tye knocked on her bedroom door. She awakened to see him coming in carrying a tray bearing a cup of tea. She struggled to sit up.

Nothing was lost on him, however. 'Bad night?' he enquired evenly, his glance taking in the mauve shadows under her eyes.

'N...' she began to deny, but realised she was wasting her breath when Tye's glance went to the still switched-on bedside lamp, evidence in itself that she had felt the need to light part of the dark hours. But she had had enough of dark despair, so set her mind to having a happier day today, and giving Tye nothing whatsoever to be concerned about. 'I'm truly going to be on my best behaviour today,' she promised brightly.

'I don't like the sound of that. Should I start to worry?' he asked wryly.

'Not at all. You can go to work and forget I ever existed.'

'I doubt you'll be that easy to free from my thoughts. But, bearing in mind you didn't eat much of your dinner last night, are you going to eat a good breakfast today?'

She wasn't hungry. 'Er...' She was about to say she wasn't interested in food, and then realised that was hardly the way to give him nothing to be concerned about. 'I'm starving,' she lied—which fooled him not one iota.

He gave her a rueful look. 'Drink your tea and then go back to sleep,' he instructed, and left her.

In other words, Stay in bed until Jane is here. Claire obediently sipped her tea, but did not go back to sleep. She would have liked to take another shot at having a bath unaided, but could not easily forget yesterday's performance.

She was, however, feeling stronger today than yesterday, she decided, and was in the window seat watching for Jane's car on the drive when she saw her pull up at the gates, get out and open them, and then come chugging down the drive.

It was bath first, then breakfast in her room, but this was definitely the day Claire intended to stop being treated like an invalid. So, OK, there were parts of her that still ached somewhat, but enough was enough.

She had thought that Tye would make tracks for London as soon as Jane arrived. But according to Jane, who came to collect her breakfast tray and tidy around, he had been deeply involved in work in the library annexe just now when she had taken him a cup of coffee.

Claire had not thought she knew what love was, but wondered, when her heart lifted to know that Tye was still home, if it did so from the feeling of love she must have known for him before her accident, or was it just that she felt so much more secure when he was there?

She decided not to ferret at it but to just accept matters as they were. She had other things to be doing, and they did not include staying in her room all day.

That being so, but bearing in mind she was not yet up to her full strength, silently, so as not to disturb Tye, she very slowly made her way down the stairs.

She rested for a brief while at the bottom, then, being careful not to make the smallest noise, she followed her instinct and went looking for the kitchen.

She knew she was headed in the right direction when at the end of a long passageway she heard faint sounds of someone obviously busy. She opened one door—it was a breakfast room. But two doors down revealed a large and airy kitchen, and Jane.

Who stared at her in astonishment. 'Wh…?' she began.

Claire grinned. 'I thought it about time I made some sort of effort.'

'You're not fully w—' Jane halted, and changed it to, 'I was just going to make you some coffee.'

Claire rested in the kitchen while they both had coffee, and found the retired nurse very easy to get along with. Then Claire asked if she could help in any way, insisting that she needed some kind of occupational therapy.

She felt briefly happy to be busy when Jane allowed her to sit at the kitchen table and peel some potatoes for the evening meal. But that done, and no other chores in the offing, she told Jane she would like to take a walk outside.

'I'll come with you,' Jane responded instantly.

'Do you mind if I go on my own? I sort of—need to.' Claire apologised, and realised, had she not known before, that Jane must have been a special kind of caring nurse, for she understood immediately and insisted only that she must wear a coat.

Because it pleased Jane that she did so, Claire borrowed her over-large topcoat, but, for all Claire felt keen to seek new adventures, she was well aware she would not be going far. The length of the drive still seemed to be a dreadfully long walk away.

It was so good to be out, though. She breathed in the crisp October air and looked about her, marvelling that at the onset of winter the rosebeds still hosted a profusion of flowering roses.

She became quite fascinated. At home... She gave a little gasp. At home—what? She felt defeated as she recognised she had been on the brink of another memory—but it had escaped her. Feeling flattened for a moment, she felt in need of support, and went to lean against a wall of the house.

Morning sunlight warmed her, but, push though she might, the memory that had begun with 'At home...' would not come through. Her home was with Tye. Normally they lived in his London apartment. Did he have a garden there? Were there roses...? Did...? It was useless—nothing was coming through.

Her head started to ache. She moved away from the wall and, as if hoping that perhaps a closer inspection might conjure up that defiantly elusive memory, she walked over the lawn to one of the rosebeds.

She was lost for minutes as she stood looking, gently touching and bending to sample the fragrance which might perhaps kick-start that memory. But, no matter how hard she tried, the memory just would not come.

Disappointed, she turned about and was halfway to the path when she looked up. Her breath caught again, but this time in surprise. There at one of the lovely Georgian windows stood Tye. How long he had been standing there watching her she had no idea.

He opened the window. 'Like the coat!' he called.

She looked down at the all-enveloping garment. 'Well, you can't have it!' she replied smartly and, when she had never felt less like smiling, discovered as she went back into the house that she had a wide smile on her face.

Jane was preparing sandwiches and a salad for lunch when Claire entered the kitchen. 'Mr Kershaw only wanted something light, but if you'd like some soup or something on toast it would be no trouble,' Jane tempted her willingly, refusing her offer of help.

'A sandwich will be fine,' Claire replied, and, her assistance not required, she left the kitchen. She promised herself she would get back up the stairs under her own steam that afternoon, but for now she went to the drawing room.

Out of nowhere dark despair was suddenly there again, and she went to the window to stare out. Would she ever get her memory back? She tried hard to be patient, but it was not easy.

She was still staring unseeing out of the window when Jane brought her lunch in on a tray. 'You shouldn't have!' Claire protested. 'I could have come and collected that.'

'It's no bother,' Jane assured her sunnily. 'I've just taken Mr Kershaw's lunch to the library.' From that Claire realised that Tye would probably work through lunch. 'If there's nothing you need me for, I'll pop back home for an hour or two,' Jane added, tacking on that she would return to see to dinner and anything else, and departing.

Claire waved to her when she went by the drawing room window, but had not moved when the sound of the drawing room door opening made her turn round. Tye stood there, tall, grey-eyed and friendly.

'What have I done to you that you prefer to eat your lunch alone?' he asked, his glance taking in her untouched lunch tray.

'I thought you'd be working.'

His answer was to come and take up her tray. 'I'll show you the library,' he offered.

She went with him purely because she was pleased to see him.

The library was larger than she had imagined, lined wall to wall, its shelves almost up to the high ceiling, with books ancient and new. 'Wow!' she exclaimed. 'You said library, but this is something else.'

'My grandfather was something of a collector,' Tye replied, and, placing her tray down on a round, highly polished antique table, he showed her the next-door room. It was the room he had called the library annexe but which now, with its computer, laptop and about every other piece of modern technology, looked more the last word in an up-to-date office than anything.

His own meal tray was on a side table, and he collected it and placed it beside hers on the table in the library. He drew out a chair, inviting her to take a seat. When she was seated he took a chair next to her and selected a sandwich.

'So, given that I'm fairly certain you descended those stairs without help, and probably have plans to make a solo return, how's the best behaviour plan going?' he enquired.

She enjoyed his light humour; he had the ability to temporarily lift her feelings of desolation. Then she remembered her other solo trip, that one over to the rosebed, and she urgently asked, 'Do we have roses at your—our—other address? Our home in London?'

'You've remembered something?' he asked, his look alert.

She shook her head. 'I was on the brink… Out by the roses… There was something there, but it had gone before I could catch it.' She sighed, finding it terribly difficult to be bright. 'I really, really think I should stop taking those tablets,' she said a degree mulishly.

'You're assuming they are tranquillisers. They may not be,' he hinted. 'How's the head?'

She had a thundering headache if he really must know. She helped herself to a sandwich she had no particular inerest in, took a neat bite without tasting it, and told him, 'Jane makes a fantastic sandwich.'

Claire glanced at him then, and saw a sensitive kind of look in his eyes. 'You'll get there,' he promised quietly.

She stared into those sensitive eyes, and found she was blurting out that which had occupied many of her thoughts. 'Do you still care for me, Tye?' Feeling herself going a trifle pink, she looked from him. 'I mean, I know you are caring for me, none better, but—can you still love me?' She wished, heartily wished, when an age passed without him answering, that she had not said anything. 'I'm sorry,' she mumbled. 'I've embarrassed you.'

'No, you haven't,' he denied, and to prove it he placed an arm about her shoulders, gave her a brief hug. A light-humoured note was back in his voice when he said, 'And as for loving you, my dear—who could fail to love you?' He took his arm away. 'Now, eat your sandwich!' he ordered bossily—and she laughed.

All in all, Claire reflected, as she lay in her bed that night, given that her headache had seen her having to resort to taking her medication, it had been rather a splendid day. True, she had endured many a dark moment in pursuit of that reluctant memory, but she had made the stairs, up and down, on her own—twice. She had, as common sense, her headache and instructions from Tye had decreed, returned to her room to lie down for an hour or so during the afternoon, but by evening her headache had cleared and she had joined Tye downstairs for dinner.

Tye had been a superb dinner companion, conversing on all and everything save her accident, her family and her lack of memory. He had been so thoughtful too—deliberately, she realised, never once referring to any of the things they had done together. She owned she would not have minded if he had perhaps tried to remind her of some outing or other they had shared. It might well have triggered some memory or other. But today had been Best Behaviour Day, and, since he was so interesting to listen to, she'd been on her best behaviour to go along with anything he decided upon.

He had walked back up the stairs with her, in no hurry when, while going as fast as she could, she realised it must have been torturously slow for him.

Claire settled down to sleep, recalling how they had said goodnight at her door and she had gone into her room, washed and changed into her night things—and had taken her prescribed medication. Sleep put an end to her pleasant reverie.

She awakened with a start about four hours later when the gremlins of the previous pre-dawn morning returned to storm in and assault her. She awoke afraid and troubled, and almost knocked over her bedside lamp in her anxiety to find the light switch.

She was awake for a long, long while as she did battle to control the nightmare in her head. As a result, she awoke again at eight to find a cup of tea going cold by her bedside, indicating that Tye had already been into her room.

He returned again shortly before nine and her heart seemed to somersault in her body. He was immaculately suited, good-looking and sophisticated with it, and was clearly not intending to stay home that day. For a moment she panicked. She did not want him to go.

'Was it something I did?' she asked.

He looked indulgently down at her. 'I'll hang on for Jane, then I'll be off.'

'Will you be home tonight?' she asked, pushing anxious fingers through her tousled blonde hair, try as she might, unable to keep the stress she felt out of her voice. Tye was her anchor—she would be floating about in a sea of nothingness without him.

'I may be late, but I'll be back,' he promised, and she immediately felt guilty again.

'You don't have to,' she assured him quickly, starting to

feel dreadful. 'I don't want you rushing back here if your business is more than you can complete in one day!'

'And what if I *want* to come back here?' he asked indulgently.

'Am I being a pain?'

'Considering what has happened to you, I think you're being very brave,' he answered seriously. And, while she did not think she was being very brave at all, 'You've nothing to worry about,' he assured her. 'Jane won't leave you on your own.'

Claire felt a shade awkward that Jane was going to have to give up her day to keep her company, and she wanted to tell Tye that she would be all right on her own. But her experience of those early-morning gremlins had badly rocked her.

'Well, have a lovely day,' she said brightly. She smiled cheerfully up at him, and thought for one nebulous moment that Tye was going to bend down and kiss her.

Her heart did a crazy flutter at the infinitesimal movement he made towards her, only for it to steady when he seemed to check, then smiled. 'Be good,' he bade her, and strode from her room.

She stayed staring after him for some time, knowing then, if she had not known before, that he was fully aware of her feelings of insecurity. She supposed that feelings of insecurity were probably all part and parcel of starting a new life—as of a few weeks ago when she had awakened in hospital with absolutely no memory of her past or of who she was. Perhaps it was all part of that insecurity that she did not relish the idea of being in the house by herself, of being alone for hours on end, when that dreadful despairing feeling of hitting that brick wall of nothingness would assault her again.

She watched from the window as Tye drove away in his car. And wanted him back with her. But he had work to go

to, and she was being selfish, and he thought her brave—
and she wished that she were.

When Jane came upstairs to be near while she had her
bath, Claire determined that she was going to be truly brave
from now on.

So that when just after lunch Jane let slip that she had
not walked her neighbour's dog that day, Claire, renewing
her 'truly brave from now on' determination, suggested, 'If
you want to take him for a walk now, I'll be fine on my
own.'

'Oh, I couldn't possibly,' Jane responded.

'Of course you could,' Claire countered with a smile, but
did not find it easy to persuade Jane. Eventually, however,
with Jane insisting she take down her mobile phone number
just in case she wanted company, Jane drove off.

Left on her own for the first time, Claire tried to keep her
mind clear of gremlins and concentrated her thoughts on
anything but her need to know all and everything that had
been wiped from her mind. Black despair was forever hovering, but it had been easier to cope with somehow when
someone else was in the room.

She said her name out loud. 'Claire Farley.' She did not
feel like Claire Farley, but then, for that matter, she did not
feel like anyone else either.

She was in the drawing room when the phone rang. It
made her jump. She was alone. There was no one else there
to answer it. What if it was a business call for Tye? She
realised she had no choice but to take the call.

'Hello?' she said.

'What sort of a day are you having?' It was Tye's voice.
Her heart lifted.

Please come home. 'Quiet, relaxing and restful.' She told
him that which she thought he would like to hear. How
wonderful of him to ring!

'You're getting on all right with Jane?'

'Absolutely,' she replied, and suddenly realised that he

had probably only rung to speak to Jane anyway. 'Did you want to have a word with her?' she asked, finding she had hit another blank spot when she tried to think up some excuse for Jane not being there.

'I rang to speak with you,' he answered pleasantly, which pleased her on two counts: she wasn't going to have to lie— no way was she going to tell him Jane was not there—and Tye had rung to speak to her.

'Did you want anything in particular?'

There was a pause, but she was sure there was a smile in his voice when he did answer. 'Can't a man ring to speak to his platonic fiancée without an inquest?'

She could not keep from smiling. 'I'm glad you did. Ring, I mean.'

'Good,' he replied. 'You're behaving yourself again today?'

'My behaviour is impeccable,' she answered.

She realised the phone call was over when he stated, 'I'll see you some time tonight.'

She did not want him to go. 'Bye,' she said. It seemed a pride thing that she said it first.

'Bye,' he replied. She thought he added, 'my darling,' but guessed she must have misheard. He had, after all, not a minute ago reminded her that their engagement was, for the time being, a platonic affair, and a softly spoken 'my darling' just didn't fit in with that.

She stayed in the drawing room reflecting how extremely glad she felt that Tye had taken the time out of his busy day to ring to say hello. Then she suddenly became aware that she was playing with the ring on her engagement finger. It felt comfortable there, as if it belonged there. She smiled.

By the time night had fallen, however, her smile had long departed. Dark clouds were descending. She knew that she was not doing herself the least bit of good by pushing and pushing for some kind of memory of her past, but she just did not seem able to stop. She needed to know—and there was nothing there.

Out of courtesy to Jane, who had decided not to stay the night but would not leave until Tye came home, Claire tried to hide the despair she felt. When, though, shortly after an early dinner, Jane reminded her that she was still in a state of convalescence and added that this was the longest she had been out of bed without a rest, Claire was grateful for the suggestion that she had an early night.

In her room, she wondered what time Tye would be home. Again she found her fingers on her engagement ring. He had said he would return home that night, but she felt so agitated suddenly that she wanted him home now. Somehow everything seemed better when he was there.

Another hour ticked by, and her feeling of agitation had grown and started to mingle with feelings of utter despair. Knowing she just could not stay alone in her room another minute longer, she was about to leave her bed to go downstairs to find Jane when all at once she heard the sound of a car. Tye was home!

Instantly, just knowing he was near, she began to feel less fraught. She wanted to see him, but started to wonder if, after his long day, he would come in to see her. Jane would tell him that the day had gone without mishap, so he would have no need to come and check on her.

Claire heard the sound of Jane's car starting up, and knew she was making tracks for her own home. Claire felt so grateful to her. She did not know how she would have got through the day without Jane. While it was certain that Tye without doubt was rewarding Jane handsomely, it all the same had been an awfully long day for Jane.

Claire made up her mind she would be more in control in future. The next time Tye had an early-morning start she would insist that there was absolutely no need for her to have someone with her. Although with nothing in her head but blankness she had to face that she might never recover her memory! She tried not to panic at that thought, but knew that she could not go through the rest of her life with someone for ever in attendance.

Claire decided then, since no matter how hard or how desperately she pushed and prodded for some kind of memory—for any kind of memory—with nothing coming through, that she was straight away going to be more positive than she had been. Then there was a light tap on her door—and Tye appeared.

A smile instantly beamed to her face. 'I didn't think you would pop in!' she exclaimed, her relief, her pleasure evident.

'And what sort of a fiancé would that make me?' he asked lightly, coming over to the bed and looking down at her. 'How did your day go?'

'I wanted to ask *you* that!'

'The day went well,' he replied, paused for a moment, and then added, 'Jane tells me she left you on your own for a short time while she took her neighbour's dog for a walk.'

'I insisted. But I wasn't going to tell you.'

'We can't have secrets.'

'I don't know *any*!' Claire responded frustratedly. But immediately apologised. 'I'm sorry. After your long day you don't need me to get all stroppy.' She smiled at him and confided, 'I've decided that from now on I'm going to be more positive. More—'

'You're doing very well as you are,' Tye cut in firmly, reminding her, 'It's barely a month since you went sailing through the air. Both your body and your head need time to mend. You mustn't rush these things.' She supposed she must have looked a little bleak, for, as though believing he had been a little severe in his lecture, Tye smiled encouragingly. 'Sleep now,' he said, and bade her goodnight.

'So, I'll be positive,' she determined when he had gone, and, ignoring the demons that had a tendency to wait until dark to come and trounce her, she bravely switched off her bedside lamp. She instantly wanted to switch it on again—but would not.

Eventually she fell asleep, but only for that sleep to be again tormented by demons—giant, faceless demons. She choked on a sob and woke up—woke up in absolute terror. Her mouth was dry, her breathing laboured, and she was far too panic-stricken to remember how she was going to be more positive in future.

In that awful darkness the thought that she might never recover her memory was just more than she could take.

Groping frantically for the light switch, she sat up. Light flooded the room—but by then she was in such a ferment it was of little help. She did not seem able to think straight. What was she doing there? Who was she? Where were her family?

Tye should know. But Tye did not seem to know—not very much anyway. Once more she found herself on a merry-go-round of pushing and pushing at the night-black shutters of nothingness. Her head ached, throbbed. Despite her medication her head felt as though it was splitting in two. She seemed to sense that there was a memory—some memory—that was near—yet she just could not pull it through that dense mass of pitch blackness.

Along with her panic came fear. She felt lost and alone. Felt too as if her head was going to explode as she tried desperately to break through that dark solitude of emptiness. Tried until she was totally both mentally and physically exhausted. And still nothing would come.

She attempted to lie down, to calm down, but the moment she closed her eyes, even with the light on, a crushing weight of dark wretchedness closed in on her. She jerked upright, scared and so alone. Frightened, but of what she knew not.

Terror gnawed at her, chased her, and all she knew then was that she could not take any more of this blank, black nothingness. Without further thought she shot out of bed.

She needed Tye. Everything was all right when he was there.

Tye had said he would leave his bedroom door open. She felt so in need of having someone to hold on to then that, as she flew to her bedroom door, she knew that if his bedroom door was not open she was prepared to open every door on that landing until she found him.

But that proved unnecessary. In the light streaming behind her from her own room she could see that a door two doors down was ajar. Claire was not thinking but was acting solely on instinct when she hurtled into that room, crying out 'Tye!' as she went.

Afterwards she supposed that he must be the kind of man who slept with half an ear on the listen, for even as she rocketed into his room he was sitting up in bed and putting on the light.

'Tye!' She cried his name again, and went flying over to him. She guessed her face must be showing her agony of mind because as, heedless of the strain she was placing on her healing muscles, she dashed to him, so he opened his arms and gathered her to him.

'It's all right. You're all right. I'm here,' he soothed, his arms round her, holding her to him, stroking her hair. 'Bad dream?'

'I think I'm going mad,' she whispered fearfully.

'No, you're not,' he comforted her. 'You're safe. You're doing fine,' he encouraged.

But her terrors were not so easily forgotten. 'Can I sleep with you?' she asked, her voice a thread of shaken sound.

'I...' He seemed to hesitate—until he looked into her ashen and afraid face. Assessing the situation in that one look, he hesitated no longer. 'Climb aboard,' he invited gently, and as he pulled back the covers so she should get in, so he eased himself away and to the edge of the bed. 'Close your eyes while I get something on,' he instructed, and only then did she notice what she had been too traumatised to notice before—that she had been comforted against his bare chest.

He was gone only for a few seconds and, as his broad chest was still bare, she vaguely gathered that he must sleep naked and had left his bed merely to don a pair of undershorts.

'Come here,' he said softly, joining her under the covers. Without hesitation she moved to him, and he took her into the secure haven of his arms. Gently then he eased her to lie down, tucking her head into his shoulder and tenderly stroking the side of her face. 'Try to sleep,' he suggested softly.

A dry kind of sob left her. 'I'm sorry,' she apologised.

'Poor lamb,' he breathed.

'There were demons and gremlins and...and...' She couldn't go on; she was shaking.

'I've got you now. Try to relax,' he murmured.

'You won't make me go?' She supposed she meant back to her room.

'I won't make you go,' he promised. 'Just lie quietly. I'm here.'

'You won't put the light out?' she begged on an urgent whisper.

'I won't.'

'Hold me. You'll hold me?'

'I'll hold you, little love,' he gave his word.

'And you won't let me go?'

'I'll never let you go,' he promised.

CHAPTER FOUR

SHE stirred in her sleep. She felt warm, safe and secure. More secure than she could ever remember. That feeling was not to last! She drowsily moved her legs—and met other legs! Her eyes flew open. She saw that the bedside lamp had been left on, but took more heed of the great strident alarm bells that were suddenly clamouring—she was not in bed alone!

Hard-muscled strong male arms were around her, holding her close! She swallowed hard, and then it was that she knew why she felt so snug and warm: her back was against a naked male chest, and all at once his skin was burning through the thin material of her nightdress. With everything within her in one tumultuous uproar, she on that instant jerked out of the man's hold.

He was at once awake, and as she, her body protesting at such rapid movement, leapt from the bed, so he, immediately alert and watching her, was getting out of bed his side and reaching for his robe.

'Who are you?' she exclaimed, shock making her voice throaty. She knew then that up until a month ago she had never lain eyes on the man.

'You don't remember?' he questioned, his tone quiet, his eyes concerned. He looked as though he would come over to her, but did not.

'My head's alive with memories!' she exclaimed.

'Your memory has returned?' he asked, and again appeared about to come to her to comfort and reassure her, but again stayed where he was. 'You don't remember me?'

'I do. Yes, I do,' she answered.

She started to come out of her shock and looked at him—

his short robe revealing so much of his all-masculine legs, part of his broad chest showing through the opening of the garment. But that was when she became overwhelmingly aware of what she must look like standing there facing him. Suddenly she was horrifyingly conscious that the expensive nightdress she wore was next door to transparent.

Burning colour surged to her face and she swiftly brought her arms in front of her. 'Oh!' she cried in anguish, but was spared further embarrassment when Tye, awake to her action, glanced to her crimson face and took charge.

'Go back to your room,' he instructed calmly. 'You remember where it is?' he asked, a frown creasing his forehead as though he was considering that with the return of her past memory she might have lost more recent memory. She nodded, important other matters starting to crowd in. 'Go and get into bed. I'll join you—that is, I'll come and see you—in a very few minutes.'

She did not waste a second. She wanted to see him. Questions were going off like fireworks in her head, shooting in all directions. But just then it seemed important that she get some clothes on. With her head reeling, she went quickly—perhaps too quickly.

Whatever, on reaching her room she found that with her head being bombarded, memories flashing in and flashing out, being overridden by other memories, by sad thoughts, she had no mind or energy to look for fresh clothes. In any case, she now knew that she never dressed without showering first.

That thought lightened her mood. That thought triggered off the wonderful realisation that, yes, she definitely had her memory back.

Her emotions began to be mixed. While she was starting to feel exhilarated that she could recall such a small thing as showering every morning, she also began to fear that her memory might swiftly go again. She was striving hard not to panic at that thought when she heard Tye coming along the landing.

Conscious again of her flimsy covering, and with no time now to get dressed, she hastily got into bed—just as her fiancé came into the room. Fiancé? Her memory was a blank on that one. She stared solemnly at him when, now clad in shirt and trousers, the tall man came over to the bed and stood looking down at her.

'What's my name?' he asked her, his expression equally solemn.

'Tye,' she answered huskily. 'Tyerus Kershaw at my service.'

His mouth quirked upward at that. 'You've awakened with a sense of humour,' he remarked softly, remembering as she obviously did that that was how he had introduced himself to her at Roselands clinic. 'And what's your name?' he probed.

She had no trouble with that one. 'Larch Burton,' she told him.

'Your memory is returning?'

'Most of it, I think. Who's Claire Farley?' The question seemed inconsequential as soon as she had asked it.

'You were in Farley Ward, and someone thought Claire suited you,' Tye answered, and went on with what she supposed must be relevant to him from his point of view. 'You remember the accident?'

She tried hard to think, but had no recollection whatsoever of any accident. She shook her head, and, feeling a touch panicky, 'Will my memory go again?' she asked urgently.

'I shouldn't think so,' he replied straight away. 'But, until he can get here, Mr Phipps wants you to rest quietly.'

'You've been in touch with Mr Phipps?' she exclaimed, amazed.

'He's on his way.'

'From London?' she gasped, feeling utterly astonished.

'He lives about ten miles away.'

'You must have got him from his bed!'

'He's a doctor—he's used to it.' Tye smiled at her. 'I'll get you a drink of something…'

She didn't want that. 'Don't go!' she cried, adding rather desperately, 'In case I lose my memory again, I live in a village called Warren End; it's near High Wycombe in Buckinghamshire.'

'You don't live in London?' Tye asked, coming to take a seat on the side of her bed.

She shook her head, moving her legs to give him extra room. 'That's where I was when the accident happened, wasn't it?'

He nodded. 'Do you remember why you were in London?'

'I…' That was a question she did not want to answer. It brought back memories of a kind she did not want to remember. 'No,' she said stubbornly.

If Tye suspected there was more to it than that he gave no sign, but changed tack to question, as though the question was more important, 'Are you married? Some married women prefer to not wear a wedding ring.'

'Not married,' she answered, which prompted the memory that she was wearing this man's engagement ring. 'Why—?' she began, but he was cutting in with another of his important questions.

'Do you live with some man? Have you any special man-friend?'

'I live with my sister—and her husband,' she mumbled. 'Why am I wearing your engagement ring? We can't be engaged or you wouldn't have had to ask me about other men in my life.'

'My, you have woken up sharp,' Tye commented lightly, but said seriously, 'I shouldn't be questioning you like this. Shall we leave it until after Miles has seen you?'

'Miles?' she queried, questions in respect of their engagement sent temporarily to the back of her mind.

'Miles Phipps,' Tye answered. 'My stepbrother.'

'Mr Phipps is…?' Larch guessed that this was her day for surprises. 'Why—?'

'You're going to get me into serious trouble,' Tye broke in. 'I'm supposed to be keeping you calm.' He smiled encouragingly. 'We'll talk later. But for now you should be resting while we wait for Miles to arrive.'

From where she was viewing it, Larch could not see any reason why Tye should have called his stepbrother to chase over to Shipton Ash to see her. 'But…' she started to protest, but anything further she might have asked died in her throat at Tye's stern look.

'Do you trust me?' he asked bluntly.

She did not like his tone. 'How could I not?' she exclaimed belligerently. 'I've just spent half a night in your bed—to no avail!'

He laughed, and she found she loved his laugh. It immediately sent away her sudden sour mood. 'You'd have died on the spot had I tried anything,' he taunted, and reminded her, 'You know full well that I gave my word to Miles that I wouldn't lay a sexual finger on you.'

Larch realised she had gone a shade pink, but discovered she was not one to back down in a hurry. 'Always the bridesmaid!' she sighed, but smiled. 'All of which makes you rather a nice person.'

'Oh, to wear such rose-tinted spectacles,' he said. 'How are you feeling now?'

'More in control than I was, but still excited that my memory—or most of it—seems to have come back.' A look of pleasure appeared on her face. 'I *do* have a sister. Her name is Hazel, and she is a lovely person, and—'

'And nothing,' Tye cut in. 'Either you're going to keep quiet and rest, or I'm going to have to leave you.'

Larch stared at him, her heart starting to flutter a little.

'I'll be good,' she promised. 'Only there are so many questions…'

'I know,' he agreed, but got to his feet saying, 'Perhaps it would be a courtesy, considering I've roused Miles from his bed, if I went and opened the gates for him. You'll be all right?'

'Of course,' she answered, but the moment he had gone found she could not sit still in bed. She found her wrap and went to sit in the window seat.

From there she saw Tye emerge and head up the drive. It was only just starting to get light, and as Tye approached the iron gates, so she saw car headlights appear. Tye opened the gates and got into the passenger seat. Never one to waste time, she guessed he was filling his stepbrother in as they drove down to the house.

She returned to bed, hoping with all her heart that Tye left out that bit where she had fled from her room in the middle of the night and had hurled herself into bed with him. Had she *really* done that? In the cold light of day it seemed incredible that she had done any such thing.

She was sitting up in bed, the covers up to her chin, when Tye brought his stepbrother into the room. 'I hear you don't care for the name we gave you,' was Miles Phipps's cheerful greeting.

'I'll put some coffee on,' Tye stated, and tactfully left them.

In all, Miles Phipps was with her for around twenty minutes, but Larch rather thought he had seen, heard and taken in all that he needed to in the first five minutes of his visit.

He was an exceedingly clever man and spent the rest of his visit in what might have appeared to be casual chat but from which, from her responses, she realised, he was probably able to confirm his assessment.

She realised too that he was more Miles Phipps, step-brother to Tye, that morning, than Mr Phipps, eminent consultant, when he put away his bedside manner, suggested she call him Miles, and asked how she found life at Grove House.

'I've been extremely well looked after,' she replied.

'You're looking far better than you did,' he observed. 'When Tye proposed that you should come here, I thought the tranquillity and peace might aid your recovery,' he revealed.

'It's lovely here,' she agreed.

'You know that I would not have sanctioned you coming with Tye were I not aware that he is a man of the most unimpeachable integrity?'

'I know he is.' She smiled, and hoped she did not look as pink as she felt as she recalled how she had gone to his room and asked if she could sleep with him. The only finger he had lain on her had been in a touch of comfort.

Miles Phipps got ready to leave. 'Any missing pieces of memory will most likely filter back during the next few days,' he advised. 'And when the first rush of adrenalin at knowing you are back to being Larch Burton again begins to fade, it's possible you may start to feel a little low. I don't foresee any major problems,' he assured her. 'Though I'd still like to check on you again—say, in about a month's time. Meanwhile, if you have any worries, please don't hesitate to contact me.'

She thanked him so much, and felt quite a fraud when he had gone that Tye had roused him from his bed on her account. But she supposed she must still be feeling a little euphoric in that her thoughts were almost immediately chasing away, hither and thither.

Guessing that Tye would not see his stepbrother on his way without the coffee he had spoken of, Larch decided she had time to take a quick shower and get dressed. She felt much stronger now than she had felt even two short days ago, but was not yet ready to risk taking another bath without Jane being around.

Larch was collecting fresh underwear together when it suddenly struck her that no wonder all of her clothes looked new. They *were* new! Had never been worn. Oh, heavens! She had assumed, accepted, that because Tye had said they lived together he had packed only her newest things that day he had brought her case into the clinic. But he had not only brought them, he had *bought* them—paid for them. Purchased them because she had never lived with him, and the only clothes she'd had were those she had been wearing and which had been cut from her at the hospital!

Larch was in the shower when the low point Miles Phipps had spoken of came, sooner than she had expected. Suddenly it hit her that, since she had not lived in London with Tye, since she was absolutely nothing to him, and in fact must have been a total stranger to him, she had no right at all to be here at Grove House!

She had no idea what the engagement ring on her finger was all about, but what she did know was that she had no business to be here, accepting his hospitality. It was at once plain to her then that soon—today, obviously—she was going to have to leave.

She did not want to go. She wanted to stay here with Tye. She... Abruptly she blanked that thought and hurriedly stepped from the shower.

She was drying her left foot when she noticed that neat scar again. A smile came to her serious mouth. She knew what that scar was all about now. Her smile faded as she recalled her parents. Long before her mother's illness their parents had taken her and Hazel for a seaside holiday. That holiday had included a hospital visit when Larch had cut her foot on some broken glass some careless person had left lying about on the beach. Hazel had been upset and had half carried her back to their parents.

Larch was in her room, dressed and ready to face what had to be faced, when Tye tapped on her door and came in. As he must have observed she was showered and dressed, so Larch saw that he must have showered too, for he was now clean-shaven.

'I thought you might have been up to mischief,' he commented dryly on her decision not to wait for bathtime aid. 'I've made some fresh coffee. Would you like it here or downstairs?'

They obviously had to talk. Just as she obviously had to return his ring to him. 'Downstairs,' she opted, but found she had used up quite a lot of physical steam, and that when it came to going down the stairs she had little energy to hurry.

Tye did not offer to carry her, and for that she was grateful. He kept slow pace with her, enquiring as they went, 'Things settling down a little?'

'I'm getting over the initial shock, and so thankful to have my memory back,' she replied.

Tye escorted her to the drawing room and left her briefly while he collected coffee from the kitchen. When he returned he waited until she was seated on a sofa, a low table in front of her, before he handed her a cup of coffee and took a chair on the other side of the table.

'I—um—I'll leave, of course,' Larch found she was blurting out. 'It's very kind...'

'Leave?' Tye seemed most surprised, and placed his coffee cup and saucer down on the table. 'Oh, I don't know that I can allow that,' he informed her nicely.

'You can't allow?' Perhaps because she did not want to go, Larch had to push herself to aggressiveness. 'You can't stop me!'

She stared belligerently into steady grey eyes that clearly stated that stop her he would, if he wanted to. But when she was fully expecting a load of hostility from him—and she would hardly blame him after the way he had taken her in and seen to her every need—he calmly picked up his coffee again. 'I know this can't have been the most pleasant few days of your life,' he remarked, 'but I truly don't think you are physically fit enough yet to go anywhere.' Stubbornly she would not answer, and he went on, 'Has it really been so awful for you here?'

She immediately capitulated. 'Oh, Tye, you know it's not you or your lovely home. Just as you know I've had some dreadful dark moments here, you must know how well I've been looked after. And I appreciate that, I really do. It's just that I have no right to be here. No right to disrupt your household, to disrupt your work, to—' She broke off and found she was staring down at her left hand, staring at the wonderful engagement ring. Feeling for some odd reason the utmost reluctance, she slowly drew the ring from her finger. 'I have no idea why I've been wearing this, but I know now that I have absolutely no right to wear it.' She stretched a hand out and placed the ring down on the table between them. Her engagement finger felt lost without it. 'There are still a few gaps in my memory, but we never were engaged, were we?'

Tye was quiet for a few seconds before, making no move to pick up the ring, he replied, 'No, we never were.'

'And I'm positive I would have remembered had we ever lived together,' she went on, and, her face suddenly flaming, 'I can't believe that I actually came to your room last night and asked if I could sleep with you,' she gabbled in an embarrassed rush.

'Don't think about it. You were having a torrid time in that unrelenting dark void,' Tye said, and he smiled as he tacked on, 'I was fully aware that you had no designs on my person.' She gave a sigh—he had such a devastating smile.

Swiftly she bucked her ideas up. 'I'm getting away from the point; there's so much going on in my head,' she explained, 'I don't know which bit to tackle first.'

'Let me help,' he offered, and she immediately began to feel selfish.

'You've done more than enough for me,' she replied.

'I've interrupted your work for long enough. You must be
wanting to get to your office and...'

'I'm not going to London today.'

'You're not?'

'Not.' That teasing expression she knew so well came to
his face. 'You've forgotten,' he accused. 'We were going to
tackle a walk outside today.' Oh, Tye. Just then she could
not think of one tiny reason why she would want to leave.
'But let's get some priorities sorted here. The hospital contacted the police with your description in case anyone
should report you missing—your details will have been cir-
culated. So far no one has come forward looking for you.
But now you've remembered you lived with your sister and
her husband, perhaps we should phone them to let them
know you're safe.' His expression suggested that he did not
know why they should bother if her sister could not stir
herself to report her missing. But he had referred to getting
priorities dealt with first.

'Hazel has been away for some weeks...' Larch paused
to do a few simple calculations '...but she's due back
home—er—tonight, I think. She's on an extensive working-
while-training study course in Denmark. Hazel's an accoun-
tant with a firm of auditors who are expanding over there,'
Larch explained. She was proud of her sister who, with a
natural aptitude and through sheer hard work, was doing so
well in her career.

'Your sister furthers her European knowledge at weekends too?' Tye enquired.

Larch wasn't sure that she did not resent his inference
that Hazel either stayed in Denmark at weekends or cared
not, when she returned to spend weekends at home in
England, that Larch was not there.

'Hazel rang—' Larch broke off, nausea taking her as she
remembered.

'What's wrong?'

'Nothing,' she quickly denied, and could only suppose

that her feelings of revulsion had shown in her face. Hurriedly she got herself together, and explained, 'Hazel rang—it must have been the day I went to London.' Larch knew full well it had been that day—that fateful day of her accident. She hadn't spoken to Hazel—Neville had. 'Hazel rang to say she had a seminar to attend the next day, Saturday, and also had an endless backlog of studying to catch up on. She wanted to know if we would mind if she didn't come home that weekend.' Neville had minded—my stars, how he'd minded! He had tried to take his frustration out on her. 'Anyhow,' Larch continued, trying to wipe the terrible scene that had followed from her mind, 'Hazel must have decided to stay on in Denmark until all her work and studying is complete. But...' Suddenly it dawned on Larch that if Hazel *had* been home in the last month then there must be some very special reason why she had not reported her missing. 'W-would you mind if I rang home—just in case Hazel's there?'

Without a word Tye went and brought the telephone over to her. Larch's home number came readily to her and she dialled, hoping that Hazel was not there. She could not bear the thought that her dear sister might have spent the best part of a month going hairless with worry about her. If Hazel was not already home, then, Larch thought, just in case her sister arrived home first today, she would leave a message on the answer-phone to say she herself would be home at some time that day.

The ringing out tone stopped. But, to Larch's disquiet, it was not Hazel who answered the phone but Neville, Hazel's husband. Larch overcame her aversion to speaking to the man to enquire, 'Is Hazel there?'

'Well, well,' Neville sneered, evidently recognising her voice, 'if it isn't my errant employee.' And, his tone changing, 'Don't bother coming back—you're fired!' he said nastily.

As if she would want to work for him again! Though,

while wanting to thank him for that good news, Larch had more important things on her mind. 'Will you give Hazel a message for me?'

'If I ever see her again! She seems to have taken root in Denmark. All in the good name of advancement!' he added spitefully.

'Hazel hasn't been home since—?'

'Not since you decamped to go and stay with your mother's godmother, leaving me and my office high and dry in the process!'

She was not interested in his office; he exploited his staff mercilessly, and, given she was not at all sure how she could explain to Hazel why she had left her job, Larch was very pleased she did not have to go back to work for him.

'She's phoned, though?'

'Once! And then only to ask for Ellen Styles's phone number—apparently your godmother is ex-directory. What a pity I couldn't find my wife's address book,' he said sarcastically, causing Larch to know he had not bothered to look for it. 'I take it Hazel hasn't managed to phone you?'

Larch had known that matters between Hazel and her husband were going through a bad phase, but it sounded as though they had deteriorated dramatically. Hazel had thought him wonderful once, and probably, beneath their present disharmony, still did.

'Would you give Hazel a message if she gets home before me today…?' Larch began.

'Tell her yourself! She's not coming home until Tuesday!' Neville Dawson retorted, and slammed down the phone—and Larch started to panic. That was until Tye's voice broke in on her thoughts, causing her to have to fight to get herself more of one piece.

'Your sister's not home?' he enquired evenly.

'She's not coming back until Tuesday,' Larch said without thinking.

'You lived in your sister's home with them, I think you said?'

Larch had not actually said that, but the fact that half the house belonged to her, she and Hazel having inherited it jointly from their parents, was hardly an issue, Larch felt. 'Just the three of us,' she agreed, but got herself together to tell Tye, 'I must have told Neville—Hazel's husband—that I was going to stay with my mother's godmother for a while. There are a few blank spaces in my memory,' she explained, wishing she could forget Neville Dawson's assault on her and never, ever remember it again. 'But the fact that my accident happened in London seems to suggest I was on my way to spend some time with my honorary aunt Ellen.' Larch had no memory at all of catching a train to London. But another memory flashed in. 'Aunt Ellen insisted at my mother's funeral that I go and stay with her whenever things got too much for me.'

'Your mother *is* dead?' Tye probed gently.

'Both my parents,' Larch answered.

'Oh, my dear,' Tye murmured, and, as if he could not help it, he came to the sofa where she was and, taking hold of her hands, sat down beside her. 'How old are you?' he asked, as though thinking she was young to have suffered such a loss.

'Twenty-three,' she replied, but felt weepy suddenly and needed to not think of her parents just then. 'As Aunt Ellen obviously hasn't been in touch with Neville, I can only suppose I either intended to ring her when I got to London or rang her and she wasn't in—it's all a blank,' she ended lamely. 'I remember leaving my house, and—'

'And now you're offending me by suggesting you want to leave mine,' Tye got in smartly.

'Offending...' She was appalled. 'Tye, I don't want to offend you! You must know that I don't!' she exclaimed swiftly. 'But you're not responsible for me—nobody is, for that matter. But—'

'Tell me,' Tye cut in, 'does your sister's husband work?'

Larch had no idea what tack Tye was on now, but saw no reason not to answer. 'Yes, he does.'

'From home?'

'No, he has an office. I don't know what he was doing at home today. Perhaps he forgot something and went home for it. He has a manufacturing company in…'

'So if I took you home today you'd be in the house by yourself during the day, with no one there to look after you?'

'I…' Oh, heavens! It only then dawned on her that, with Hazel in Denmark until Tuesday, there would be no one else in the house but her and her ghastly brother-in-law. She felt sick at just the thought, and wasn't sure she had not lost some of her colour, but felt honour-bound to point out, 'N-Neville doesn't normally work at the weekends. He'll probably be there tomorrow and Sunday.'

'But not for the rest of today or Monday and Tuesday?' Tye paused, then said, 'It's not on, is it, Larch? Truly now,' he pressed when she did not answer. 'Look at you,' he went on. 'You're looking drained now. Are you going to undo all Miles's good work? The work of the nurses, not forgetting Jane, who have all worked hard to make you well again? There will be no one at your home to make you so much as a cup of tea.'

While Larch was perfectly certain she was quite able to make a cup of tea for herself, she was just as certain that Neville would let her starve before he thought of making a meal. 'I'll be fine,' she protested.

'You're intent on going?'

Without Hazel there, Larch had the greatest aversion to entering again that house she had run from in such panic. The only alternative was to go and stay with Aunt Ellen—which, Larch felt, suddenly feeling as drained as Tye had suggested she looked, was hardly fair. To go and park her convalescing self on the frail elderly lady… 'I can't impose on your hospitality any longer,' Larch stated stubbornly.

'So, for the sake of your obstinate pride you'd go?'

'But—why would you want me to stay? Until a month ago you'd never set eyes on me. We are not engaged—I have no hold on you.'

'Yes, you have!' he retorted.

Her heart was suddenly thundering. 'I have?' she asked faintly.

He bent to pick up the engagement ring, his expression hidden, and she watched while he slipped the ring into his pocket. Then he looked at her and said, 'I've grown to like you, to like having you here,' going on logically, 'You have no one at your home, while here you have Jane, and you have me.' His handsome mouth picked up at the corners. 'And my grandmother would have loved you to stay.'

Larch smiled at that, and could feel herself weakening. It wasn't right to impose on his hospitality, and she knew that it was not. But Tye had said that he liked her and that he liked having her there at Grove House. Bleakly she thought of the alternative: going back to spend the weekend alone in the same house as her odious brother-in-law. Oh, she couldn't. She just couldn't!

Solemnly she looked into the steady grey eyes that were silently watching her. 'Say you will?' he urged gently.

She opened her mouth to tell him no. 'Tye…' She hesitated—and found she was asking, 'M-may I stay until Tuesday?'

He smiled that devastating smile. 'I'll make us some breakfast,' he said.

According to Tye, she needed time and space in which to adjust to having recovered her memory. With that in mind, after breakfast he suggested that she return to the drawing room and rest on a sofa for a while.

Whether these instructions came from him or from his stepbrother, she had no idea, but while it was true that her head was abuzz, she felt she had rested more than enough. She was about to say as much when it came to her that Tye probably had work in the library annexe that he would not mind getting on with.

'You want to go and get on with some work, don't you?' she asked.

He looked as though he would deny any such suggestion. But, as if reading her mind, 'I can spend time with you if you prefer,' he replied.

That did it. 'I'll be in the drawing room if you need me,' she stated—and loved it when he laughed.

Tye occupied quite a lot of her thoughts that morning. At other times, though, she was remembering happy times, sad times, and times that she would far rather forget. She supposed it was only natural that that last encounter with her awful brother-in-law should be the most dominant memory.

Up until the age of fifteen, her childhood had been little short of idyllic. Then her mother had fallen ill—the prognosis had shattered their world. Within a year her mother had been confined to a wheelchair. By that time Hazel had been doing extremely well in her career and, while it had been unthinkable that their mother be looked after by strangers, it had been equally unthinkable, for all Hazel had tried to insist, that she give up her career to take care of their mother and their home.

The obvious solution had been for Larch to take over. 'You'll have your chance later,' her distracted father had promised when at sixteen Larch had willingly left school. She had not wanted to think about later—her mother had been given two years' life expectancy.

As it happened, her mother had lived for another seven years. Larch wondered if she would have died then had not their father been involved in an accident that had killed him.

Having expected that their mother would die first, it had been a tremendous shock when nine months ago they had attended their father's funeral. A month later, their mother had given up her struggle.

Larch was bereft. So too was Hazel. Hazel no longer lived at home, having met and married Neville Dawson. But Hazel had come home to stay with Larch for a few days after their mother's funeral and, more business-minded than Larch, had taken on the task of looking into the family's financial affairs.

It was Hazel who had found their father's will and sorted out any complications involved in him leaving everything to their mother, but in the event that she predeceased him everything was to be split equally between their two daughters.

As Larch had known in advance, Hazel was scrupulously honest and fair, insisting that she read everything and understood everything. What Larch had not known until Hazel confessed was that Neville Dawson's business was in trouble and that it needed a cash injection.

'Neville's suggested that we sell this place,' Hazel had gone on. 'But, apart from the fact I wouldn't dream of foisting such a decision on you at this present time, it's going to take an age for Mum and Dad's estate to be sorted out. Which means we won't be able to sell anyway. What I have suggested, having looked at it from all angles, is that Neville and I sell our apartment and—only if you're agreeable, of course—we move in with you. What do you think?'

'I'd love it!' Larch jumped at the suggestion. She felt terribly adrift without her parents, and was hurting inside from losing them. To have Hazel home would be a joy. Larch had had very little to do with Neville, so did not know him too well. She assumed, because Hazel was such a very nice person, that he would be very nice too. Wrong!

Their apartment was in a much sought-after area, and it sold quickly. Hazel, perhaps realising how bereft her younger sister felt, arranged to move in straight away. Then she turned her attention on to Larch personally. 'When the estate is settled you'll have enough money to enable you to train for a career of some sort. Is there anything in particular you would like to do?' she asked.

Although having done very well in her school exams seven years ago, all Larch's recent experience had been in attending her mother and home-making. 'I'm sure I'd like to do something, but Mum and Dad—' She broke off to get her feelings in check. 'It was so sudden—I can't seem to think about the future.'

And that was when Hazel told her that Neville was always looking for office staff, and how did she feel about doing a temporary stint in one of his offices to see if an office atmosphere suited her?

Larch was willing to try anything, and at once started work. She quickly absorbed the job content, but in no time she was discovering first-hand why Neville Dawson had such a high turnover of staff. The man was a slave-driver!

At first she was glad to be busy. Busy enough to be able to push sad thoughts of her parents to the back of her mind for short spaces of time. But she was not sleeping well. There was no respite at work, and when the person who had given her work instructions one day exploded at the pressure and walked out—and was not replaced—Larch found she was doing the work of two people.

She began to feel stressed, and wanted to leave the company, but around that time Hazel came home with the exciting news that she had been singled out for huge advancement, which included a three-month stint working, training and studying in Denmark. By then Larch had become aware that her sister's marriage was not all the sweetness and light she had allowed them to believe that it was. Larch had no wish to be a cause of further friction between husband and wife by leaving his company. And by then she was certain, knowing more of her sister's husband, that he would go on and endlessly on about the chance he had given her and look at the thanks he had received. Larch kept quiet and her temporary job became permanent.

Then, in the week that Hazel flew to Denmark, another member of staff walked out, and more work was piled on to Larch. She could not cope. She started taking work home. She worked late and slept little, and began to feel utterly worn out. She did not know for how much longer she could take it.

Matters came to a head a couple of weeks later. It was that Friday she raced out of her home, heading, she rather thought, for Aunt Ellen's home in London. That whole week had been particularly stressful for Larch. And on Friday there had been no let-up. She had taken work home, knowing that Neville Dawson was very much anti the Burton sisters for some reason, but she was feeling glad that Hazel would be arriving home for the weekend later that night.

Larch made Neville the meal he was expecting and then shut herself away in her bedroom. She had only just started on the work she had brought home to complete when she thought she heard the telephone ringing. She was half off her seat when, knowing that Neville would answer it, she sat back down again. The way he had begun to look at her sometimes was starting to make her skin crawl, and she did not wish to have more contact with him than she had to.

Then suddenly her bedroom door was violently thrust open. She jumped out of her chair in surprise, and was horrified when Neville charged in, his eyes bulging as he spewed out the result of Hazel's telephone call. Furiously he mouthed out why Hazel was not coming home that weekend—and weren't they lucky they probably wouldn't see her again until she had finished her work in Denmark? And wasn't *he* lucky too that he had been the one to answer the phone? It had not been him her sister had wanted to speak to but *her*!

With each word he grew more and more incensed, and Larch began to feel alarmed at the expression on his face when he came closer and closer, belching out his tirade. But she began to feel quite terrified when, threateningly near, he caught a hold of her by her shoulders and began mouthing words that indicated if he could not have Hazel her sister would make an ideal substitute. With that he yanked her up against him, his mouth clamping on hers making her want to heave, his weight forcing her on to her bed.

Three times she scrabbled off the bed, and three times he forced her back again. Furiously she fought him and somehow—she had no recollection of how—she got free of him on her fourth attempt. She had no memory of picking up her shoulder bag, but since it had been with her at the accident she knew that she must have. What she did remember was her flight down the stairs, the rattle of the front door as she slammed it behind her. She recalled falling over in her haste to get away, recalled barely stopping to get up but racing as she got to her feet, and then running, running, running... And then—nothing until she had woken up in a London hospital.

A shudder went through her, and so engulfed was she in that terrible memory of Neville Dawson attempting to force himself on her that she had no idea that the drawing room door had been quietly opened. Not until, 'My dear!' Tye exclaimed, 'What is it?' and came quickly over to her.

Her breath caught, and she could only imagine that the horror of that memory must have shown in her face. 'Nothing,' she at once disclaimed. Aside from loyalty to Hazel, Larch felt totally incapable of sharing that memory with anyone.

Tye was not prepared to be put off, it seemed, as he probed, 'You remembered something very dreadful?'

'Not all memories are happy memories,' she answered obstinately, and, having had enough of being cosseted, even if she wasn't back to her full fitness by some way yet, 'If you're very good I'll make you a sandwich for lunch,' she offered.

From his lofty height he studied her. But when she had a distinct feeling that Tye was not the sort to veer from finding out that which he wanted to know, possibly because he was judging that this day might be proving stressful enough for her, he did not press her to tell him the very dreadful matter she had remembered.

'Jane's coming in to fix dinner and a snack lunch. If *you're* very good we'll take a walk up the drive.'

Larch was on her feet in no time, and went from the drawing room and into the hall with him to see that he had been upstairs to collect a heavy sweater.

'It's cold out,' he said, handing the bulky sweater to her from the newel post.

'For me?'

'You'll look stunning,' he promised, and grinned, and her heart seemed to tilt. 'Hang on to my arm,' Tye instructed as they left the house and went by the rosebeds.

She found she had a contrary streak and did not want to hang on to his arm. Was it contrary, though, or was she suddenly shy of hanging on to him? Grief, woman—you've *slept* with the man!

'At home, my father used to love his roses,' she said in a rush, then took a calming breath and put her hand through the crook of Tye's arm. Funnily enough, she found it felt comfortable there.

'How long ago did you lose him?' Tye asked.

'Nine months ago—ten months ago now, it would be,' she replied, realising her hospitalisation had taken care of one month. It seemed to her then that perhaps it was about time that she opened up a little about herself. Tye, after all, need not have taken her in and looked after her so splendidly. She could not bear to think how she would have coped had she been left to her own devices on her discharge from the hospital, where she would have gone, how she would have fared. 'My mother was terminally ill,' Larch volunteered. 'W-we never expected to lose my father first.'

'Your mother died recently?'

'A month after my father.'

Tye's hand came to her hand in a touch of sympathy. 'You lived with your parents?'

She nodded, feeling a little choked, but overcame the moment to tell him, 'It was a pretty ghastly time afterwards, so Hazel suggested I did a temporary job in her husband's company while I made up my mind what I wanted to train for. A bit old to start training, I know.'

Tye quickly sorted through what she had so far said. 'You'd previously stayed home to care for your mother?' he asked.

'I treasure that time of being with her,' she answered quietly, then coughed on a husky throat and charged, 'You didn't know I was working for my brother-in-law when you told me I was "between jobs" when I asked you?'

He neatly ignored the charge. 'You're not going back to your temporary job.' It seemed more of a statement than a question.

'No,' she answered.

'Have you decided what you want to train for?' he asked, halting just short of the gates at the end of the drive.

'Not yet. But I have discovered I'm pretty quick with figures, so perhaps I'll follow Hazel into accountancy. I'm quite nifty on the computer too, by the way,' she informed him, her eyes twinkling.

He looked down at her, and perhaps recalled how two days ago she had asked if she had much computer experience. 'This is far enough for today,' he decided, turning about. 'How are you feeling?'

'Wonderful!' she replied, and smiled a sunny smile.

They returned to the house and the question that had been burning on her tongue was there again—how had that engagement ring got onto her finger? But she was suddenly again conscious of what Tye had done for her, and in consequence how very much she had intruded on his work. And she became afraid of intruding further.

'Thank you for the loan of the sweater,' she thanked him politely.

'Hang on to it; you might want to slip out from time to time,' he suggested.

'See you later,' she said nicely, not wanting to delay him any longer. Though she was conscious of him standing watching her as she headed for the drawing room.

When Jane arrived and learned that Larch had her memory back, it transpired that, because of the possibility of her memory returning when Tye was not there, he had briefed Jane on the exact position of their relationship.

'This is great!' Jane beamed, and could not help but give Larch an impulsive hug even as she warned, 'Now, you mustn't go getting over-excited. You still need to take things easy.'

Having been used to being busy, it was starting to get to Larch that she had done nothing for ages. A sure sign, she realised, that she was improving by the hour. But she had bigger concerns than her present enforced idleness. Apart from having to tell Hazel that she was not going to go back to working for her husband, how was she going to tell Hazel that she wanted to move out and get a place of her own?

The idea of having to return to her lovely home where Neville Dawson now lived was nauseating to her. She did not want to do it. With Hazel getting on so well in her job, being promoted to the more expanding European side of the business, there was every likelihood of her frequently working away from home.

The thought of staying in her home alone with Neville Dawson was something Larch could just not take. Yet, since he was her sister's husband, and Hazel loved him, there was absolutely no way she could tell Hazel of his assault on her.

Tye worked through his lunch and Larch had a snack with Jane in the kitchen. Jane allowed her to help with the dish-

washing afterwards, but, taking a close look at her, suggested, 'If you're hoping to stay down for dinner tonight, it
might be an idea to take a rest this afternoon.' Larch thought
it about time she ceased her redundant lifestyle, but before
she could offer to help out a little Jane was going on, 'Mrs
Lewis from the village is coming up to do a spot of cleaning,' and Larch realised that she might be in the way.

'I'll see to my room,' she told Jane, and went upstairs,
her head again filled with flashing past memories of her life
at home.

Then all at once, as she sat in what was now her favourite
window seat, she found she was remembering snatches of
her life after she had run, terrified, away from her home.
Remembering—and questioning.

Clearly now she could remember Tye sitting quietly by
her in the hospital, quietly watching and quietly talking to
her. She remembered how quietly vigilant he had been. And
yet—he didn't even know her!

Why, when she was a stranger to him, had he said that
they lived together at his London home? Larch puzzled over
that for some minutes, before suddenly realising that Tye
had never actually said that they lived together. It had been
she who had said, 'We live together, don't we?' Oh, grief,
she remembered now. She had followed that up with, 'Do
I sleep with you?' Oh, the poor man—he must have been
embarrassed to death!

Larch stayed in her room physically resting, but with her
head chasing one thought after another. She had lost her
memory in an accident and had assumed Tye must have
heard of the accident and come looking for her. But it hadn't
been like that, because Tye hadn't even known her then. So
how, if she hadn't been able to tell them, had they found
her fiancé?

They had taken it as gospel that Tye was her fiancé—so
how had that come about? She had no idea. What she did
know, however, was that when she had run in fear from her

home that Friday she had not been wearing an engagement ring. Yet when she had awakened to the world in hospital, some time later, there was definitely a ring on her finger.

It was time, she rather thought, that she started to ask a few pertinent questions.

CHAPTER FIVE

LARCH felt she would never be out of Tye's debt when, early that evening, she donned a white shirt and black trousers that he had purchased for her.

'Did you go and buy these personally for me?' she asked Tye when she joined him in the drawing room.

'Of course,' he answered briefly, but was more interested in how she was than in any fashion statement she might be making. 'You were supposed to rest this afternoon,' he accused, as though to suggest that she had not.

'I did!' she protested. 'Physically, anyway. My brain's been dormant for so long it's no wonder it has some catching up to do.'

'You haven't remembered anything to upset you?'

'Not at all!' she answered smartly—perhaps too smartly. Tye did not appear convinced.

'As you know, Miles mentioned the cause of your amnesia might not be solely on account of your accident.'

'Oh?' she answered, just as if she did *not* know.

'There was a possibility you were suffering some trauma you were trying to blot out,' Tye persisted. She did not want to lie to him but how could she tell him how distraught she had been, not only on her own account, but that her brother-in-law should have betrayed her dear sister in such a despicable way? 'Losing your parents the way you have is a tragedy on its own, Larch,' Tye pressed when she made no answer. 'Did something else traumatic happen to you that you needed to blot out?'

'I—er—told you I was good at figures. I found I was doing the work of two people. I suppose it could have become more than I could cope with. It worried me.'

'Your brother-in-law took advantage of your family loyalty?'

You could say that. 'I honestly don't want to discuss it,' Larch replied dejectedly. 'That makes me sound mean, after your goodness to me, but—'

'Forget it!' Tye cut in. 'I'm attempting to aid your recovery, not make you unhappy. Let's go and eat.'

Larch went with him to the dining room. She took her place at the table, feeling fairly certain that Tye—whom she knew had not forgotten the way she had yelled at him when she had woken up to find him bending over her—was aware that there was some happening in her recent past that she wanted to keep dead and buried.

How could she tell him? It sounded so—tacky. Again she thought of the way she had gone and got into bed with Tye. Heavens above, what a difference in two men! Tye so trustworthy. Neville so awful—and her poor sister was married to him. She couldn't go back home to live; she couldn't— she just could not.

'Don't dwell on it, Larch!' Tye sharply interrupted her thoughts. Proof enough, should proof be needed, that he knew that it was not just pressure of work that had pushed her to that welcoming vacuum of memory loss.

'This suet pie is delicious,' she answered, and smiled.

'Jane will have us both as fat as otters,' Tye replied, his mouth quirking nicely upwards.

'Are otters fat?'

'I've no idea,' he answered, and Larch just burst out laughing.

'And they said the Hatter was mad!'

Tye's eyes were on her laughter-lit mouth. 'So, tell me about the men in your life?' he suggested.

'Men?' Her laughter had gone.

'Boyfriends.'

She relaxed. 'Who had time for boyfriends? I was working every—' She stopped suddenly, realising she had an opening here that she did not intend to waste. 'And anyhow, what would I be doing with a boyfriend when…?' She left the question there and changed tack to ask, her expression serious, 'How did I come to be wearing your engagement ring, Tye?' It was only then, though, that it came to her that he could not have purchased the ring especially for her. 'I'm sorry,' she immediately apologised as she guessed that the ring had probably been previously worn by his ex-fiancée. 'If it's painful…'

Tye leaned back in his chair, his eyes on her sensitive face. 'I suppose it's inevitably painful when someone you care for dies.'

Her breath caught. 'Oh, Tye,' she replied huskily. 'Your fiancée died?'

He shook his head. 'I was never engaged.'

Larch studied him solemnly. 'So how did I come to be wearing that ring? Where did it come from if—?'

'Let me explain,' Tye cut in, and began, 'I lived here at Grove House for quite some while as a child, and stayed here often in my growing years. I was a more frequent visitor when my grandmother became frail and housebound. But even in her frailty my grandmother was staunchly anti her two daughters-in-law—my father's first and second wives,' he inserted. 'That being so, when my grandmother died and I realised that at some time someone was going to have to personally go through her belongings, I knew I'd have to be the one to do it.'

'You couldn't possibly ask one of them to do it. Your grandmother would have hated that.'

'How well you understand,' he said, but went on, 'I did think of asking Paulette, my stepsister-in-law, but somehow that didn't seem right either. Anyhow, one has certain duties, and…'

'You're far more sensitive than you want anyone to know,' Larch interrupted gently.

'Shut up,' he replied, but the quirk at the corners of his

mouth took any sting from his words. 'I came across the ring in my grandmother's bedside drawer. It was her engagement ring—I knew I would never have need of it.'

'You think it unlikely that you'll ever marry?'

He looked from her to cut into his meal, then gave a shrug as he replied, 'Highly unlikely, I'd have said. I haven't reached thirty-six without having a few—encounters...' She'd like to bet that 'a few' was an understatement... 'but I have never felt so much enamoured that I'd want to ask any woman to be my wife.' He swerved from that particular subject to go on, 'Bearing in mind my grandmother's antipathy for her daughters-in-law, it wouldn't have felt right to have passed the ring on to one of them. I decided that Paulette might like to have it.'

'Miles Phipps's wife?'

Tye nodded. 'I didn't have time then to drive from here over to Miles's place, so I slipped the ring into my pocket with the idea of stopping by the hospital where he mainly works and handing it over for him to have it enlarged for Paulette. My grandmother had incredibly slender, delicate fingers,' he explained. 'With both Miles and I so busy, it's easier to meet in London than elsewhere.'

'You went to the hospital where I was first taken?'

'That's right. I knew from experience that any appointed time I make to see Miles stands a fair chance of not happening because of some emergency or other, so I went to the hospital when I thought he was about to come off duty.' Tye glanced across at her. 'He *was* held up—you were the emergency that came in before we'd had the chance to more than greet each other.'

'You were there, at the hospital, when I was brought in?'

'Poor love, you were out cold.'

'Oh,' she murmured, and thought he looked a touch disquieted as he remembered. Ridiculous! She pulled herself together. 'So...?'

'So, with Miles obviously busy, I made myself scarce and decided I could just as well see Miles the next day.'

'You came to the hospital again the next day?'

'And again Miles was busy with a patient. I decided to save myself another journey and wait a short while to see if he would be free. While I was hanging around I saw the nurse who'd been with you the previous evening and asked after the young lady who'd been brought in. She said where you were, and that they'd probably let me see you if I went up to Intensive Care.' He shrugged. 'It didn't look as if I'd be seeing Miles for ten minutes or so...'

'So you came to see me?'

'You were still unconscious—in a coma.'

'You came again, after that occasion, to see me?'

'It seemed mean not to. Everybody else in that hospital was having hordes of visitors. Poor Larch—or Claire, as you were shortly to be—there was no one visiting you.'

'It was very kind of you to bother.' She thanked him.

'I told you, I'd led a selfish life.' He grinned. 'My grandmother was prodding me in the back.'

'Did she also prod you to put that engagement ring on my finger?' Larch asked with a smile.

'Ah, that,' Tye replied. 'A new nurse, one I hadn't seen before, had just come on duty that day. You were still in a coma, with no sign of coming out of it. I was sitting beside you, looking at you and hoping that you would soon wake up, when I happened to glance at your delicate hands. It was then that I realised I had only ever seen such beautifully long narrow fingers once before. My grandmother's.'

'Really?' Larch queried, taking a look at fingers she had never given any great thought to.

'Don't ask me why—perhaps for something to do—there wasn't a lot going on—and I still hadn't managed to pass the ring over to Miles, though I'd still got it with me—before I knew it I'd taken it from my pocket and tried it on your engagement finger. To be honest, I was staring at it, slightly incredulous at what I'd done, when it dawned on me that the ring was a perfect fit.'

Larch smiled, picturing the scene. 'Did I get to go to the ball?'

'You got to make me more amazed when, after lying there lifeless for a couple of days, perhaps because of the unaccustomed feel of the ring around your finger, you suddenly started to show signs of life.'

'How? Wh…?'

'There am I, feeling slightly foolish, I admit, when you do no more than curl your hand into a dainty loose ball.'

'I alarmed you?'

'Not at all. It was the first sign that you might be waking from your unconscious state. I got the nurse over to you fast. The next time I paid you a visit you'd been moved to a different part of the hospital.'

'Was I awake then?'

'You were in a kind of twilight world for a short while,' he replied. 'No bones broken but a body that was in pain and in need of healing.'

She supposed that 'twilight world' was about right. She had probably been sedated into the bargain. 'Why didn't you take your ring back?' she asked. 'There must have been an opportunity.'

'There was,' he agreed. 'Only by then the ward you'd been transferred to was guarded by fierce dragons. Said dragons transformed into little angels when one of them, aware of your engagement ring, took me for your fiancé. After that I was allowed to visit you without restriction.'

'Why would you want to? Visit me, I mean? You didn't know—'

He shrugged, and cut in, 'I passed the hospital most every day—it wasn't such a great effort.' His mouth quirked. 'Besides, you'd got my ring.'

She felt her lips tweak too. 'You could have taken it any time.'

'Like I said, while you were still being carefully moni-
ored, as your fiancé, I got to see you whenever I cared to.'

She wanted to ask him why he would care to, but that
would make it seem as if he really did have a personal
nterest in her, and she suddenly felt shy to presume so
much. 'You let me think I was engaged to you,' she re-
:alled. 'I can remember asking you if I was engaged to you,
and you...'

'I let you believe that you were.'

Her heart hurried up its beat. 'Why?' she just had to ask.

'You'd only recently come to an awareness that you had
no memory. You were scared, understandably so. You were
alone, vulnerable. You needed something solid, some constant in your life.'

She clearly remembered her feelings of panic. That lost
and alone feeling. He was so right. 'That was kind of you,'
she murmured. Was it any wonder that she was in love with
him? She stifled a gasp as the suddenness of that knowledge
struck, and pulled herself sharply together. She would be
drooling over him any minute now, and he must not know.
'But—why...? I mean...' She struggled to find the right
words. 'That constant, yes, I needed that, and I do so thank
you for it. But to extend your kindness, to put yourself out
to the extent that you brought me here to Grove House. Fed
and clothed me!' Suddenly she was feeling overwhelmingly
discomfited.

'You're blushing, you're feeling awkward, and there's absolutely no need,' Tye stated sternly.

'Apart from anything else I've intruded on your personal
life!' she blurted out, feeling hotter than ever.

'No, you haven't. I hadn't, nor do I have, anything in any
way pressing in my personal life. Besides which, while I
haven't yet fully decided what I want to do with Grove
House, by being here we're able to keep the place aired and
lived in.'

'I'll go home tomorrow,' she stated, as in all fairness she

felt that she must. Oh, my word—his expression was suddenly as black as thunder.

'We've been through all this!' Tye rapped sharply, clearly a man who did not care to repeat himself. 'There's no one at your home to look after you. And if you think I'm going to allow you to undo all the good work that has been done in getting you this far in your recovery, then…' He gave her a harsh look, and she didn't like it at all.

'Then I can think again?'

'Exactly!' he said heavily.

And she did not want him angry with her—she found it too upsetting. 'Are you going to give me a hand with the dishes?'

She thought his lips twitched at her swift change of subject. 'Jane will…'

'I'm not leaving these for Jane to do in the morning,' Larch told him decisively. He might have got his own way in that she would not be asking him to drive her to her Buckinghamshire home tomorrow, but by no chance was she going to leave a pile of dirty dishes in the sink when she went to bed that night.

As things turned out, while Larch did not ask Tye to drive her anywhere the next day, drive with him she did. It was his suggestion when he asked, 'Coming for a drive?' that the stimulus of seeing something other than the inside of the house would do her good.

She wanted to jump at the idea, but love and a feeling that she had already encroached too much on his time made her hold back. 'You don't have to…' was as far as she got.

'Would I if I didn't want to?' he questioned, and, throwing in a killer, 'Am I not entitled to see something other than the four walls of an office either?'

'Oh, well, if you put it like that. Can I borrow your sweater?'

He laughed, and she loved him all over again, and, having kept his sweater, went to her room to collect it. She had no idea of when she had fallen in love with Tye. It was just there.

It was a joy being out with him. Sometimes they chatted; sometimes they didn't. Proof that she wasn't yet back to being her old self was there, though, in the fact that on two occasions she found her eyes were closing and she was drifting off into a light sleep.

They had lunch out and arrived back at the house around three that afternoon, having motored all around—but nowhere near Buckinghamshire. 'I really, really enjoyed that.' Larch thanked him.

'So did I,' he answered, and, with her eyes shining, she found it incredible that such a simple statement could make her feel so happy. She went to her room to rest, as he had instructed. Though more from her point of view so he should have his own space.

Larch felt she had progressed physically in leaps and bounds that weekend. She felt so much better than she had, and in fact barely ached at all. And only then, thinking of how she had been, did she fully appreciate the punishment her body had taken.

Her headaches were almost a thing of the past too, and it was so good to have her memory back, for all her thoughts seemed to begin mainly from the time she had become acquainted with Tye. He seemed to be the centre of her universe. She understood now, of course, why he had never referred to any of the things they had done together, why he had not referred to her family. The simple reason being that, until he had come across her in hospital, they had never *done* anything together, had never been anywhere together. They had, in fact, been perfect strangers to each other.

When Larch was not thinking of Tye, her thoughts went to her sister. Which inevitably brought to her mind that vile memory of Hazel's husband.

Larch wished she could confide in Hazel as she had always done in the past. But this was one occasion when the last person she could confide in was Hazel. It would destroy her to know what the man she loved had attempted.

Now, more than ever, did Larch *not* want to return to her old home. But where else was there for her to go? Initially, anyhow. She would have to move out, but what on earth was she going to tell Hazel?

Larch was up early when Tuesday morning came around. She could not settle to try to go to sleep again. With her head spinning, having tried half the night to think up some way to tell her beloved sister that day that she was leaving the home they owned, Larch left her room and made her way down to the kitchen.

She set the kettle to boil, knowing it was impossible for her to stay in the house she had been born and brought up in. Yet what could she say that would be acceptable to Hazel? The truth would crucify her! But to stay, not knowing how soon or how often Hazel might go away again, leaving her alone in the house with that man, was more than Larch could contemplate.

She poured boiling water into the teapot with her spirits somewhere down around her feet. She would dearly love to see Hazel again, but oh, how she did not want to leave Grove House—and Tye.

It started to worry Larch that since Tye knew she would be returning to her home that day he might offer to drive her. Her stomach heaved at the thought that she might arrive before Hazel. Neville might be there; she might be alone in the house with him!

'You're up and...' At the sound of Tye's voice Larch spun round. So deep in her thoughts, in her revulsion, had she been that she hadn't heard him come in. But Tye was staring at her. 'You're ashen!' he exclaimed, and coming over to her he caught hold of her arm and guided her to a chair. 'Did I scare you?' he asked, taking a chair next to her, his eyes searching her face.

'It's not you,' she answered chokily, totally without thinking.

'Who, then?' he questioned, and appeared determined to have an answer. She shook her head—how could she tell him? But this time it seemed he was not prepared to let her get away with it. '*Some* man scared you, though, didn't he?' he pressed.

'Don't...' she whispered. 'Tye, don't.'

Gently he took her hands in his. 'I think it's too late for "don't", wouldn't you agree?'

She tried to deny it, but with his grey eyes steady on hers she found it difficult. 'It—it isn't only me,' she replied at last, only vaguely aware that she was in her night attire, while Tye appeared to be wearing a short robe and nothing else.

'This man who attacked you—he attacked somebody else?' Tye insisted.

'No!' she exclaimed. 'It was just me...' Her voice trailed off. 'How did you...? I didn't say I'd been attacked!'

'You didn't have to! Something has had a very profound effect on you. It caused you to be terrified that night I came to check on you and you woke up unable to immediately recognise me.'

'It's all right,' Larch told him hurriedly, hoping he would accept that and leave it there. No chance!

'Whatever happened is still haunting you, Larch,' Tye said quietly. 'And I would be failing in my care of you if—'

'Oh, Tye,' she butted in unhappily. 'Your care of me has been excellent. But I cannot allow you to—'

'You cannot stop me,' he cut in pleasantly. 'Now, as I see it, we have three options.'

'No, we don't.'

'One,' he went on, as if she had not spoken, 'we get outside help—I can ring Miles and ask him which professional body would be the best for you to see.'

'I don't want—'

'Two, you can tell me what happened to you that has you drifting off into unpleasant thoughts too frequently since you regained your memory four days ago.'

'Do I do that? Drift off?'

'You do. Quite plainly something is tormenting you. Three…' He paused, then, looking deeply into her lovely blue eyes, 'Or three, I shall have to tell your sister my suspicions and…'

'You can't!' Larch exploded. 'You *can't* tell Hazel!' she repeated feverishly, rocketing off her chair, too panic-stricken suddenly to be able to sit still.

But Tye was on his feet too, reaching for her, drawing her to him in a hold of comfort. 'Shh…' He quieted her, his left arm holding her close, his right hand gently stroking her blonde hair.

Oddly, when she had been feeling so alarmed, after about a minute of being gently held by him Larch began to feel calmer. 'It's so—tacky,' she whispered into his shoulder.

'Who was it?' Tye asked quietly against her ear. She could not tell him. 'Someone you knew?' She swallowed and clutched on to his arm. 'Your—sister's husband?' Tye, perhaps recalling she had told him she hadn't time to have boyfriends, made another guess. Larch's gasp of breath told him that his guess was accurate.

She pulled out of his hold and went back to the chair she had rocketed from. 'Perhaps it was my fault,' she suggested disconsolately.

'A classic victim reaction!' Tye stated sharply, resuming his seat and bending towards her. 'Trust me, Larch, whatever happened, I know that you are completely blameless.'

Any sharpness in his tone was negated for Larch by *his* absolute trust in *her*. 'What I meant was that, had I not been so both emotionally exhausted from Hazel and I losing our parents and mentally worn out from trying to keep on top of my workload, I might have had something left over to be able to deal better with the situation when…' She did not want to think about it, but in all honesty wondered if she could have handled it better had she not been so tired when confronted by the lecherous madman Neville Dawson had become. But, remembering how it had been, she suddenly knew that there was nothing she could have done to change anything.

'Situation?' Tye probed, not allowing her to go away from him.

'Hazel phoned—that Friday,' Larch began. Tye had guessed anyway. And tacky, sordid, as it was, she now saw little point in holding it in any longer. Nor, now that she knew of her love for Tye and knew implicitly that she could confide in him, did it seem as disloyal to Hazel as it once would have. So Larch went on. 'She wanted to speak to me, so Neville said. He was furious about it. Anyhow, I was upstairs in my bedroom, doing some office paperwork, when—when he burst in and—and...' Her voice faded away until she became aware that Tye had taken a hold of her hands again in a hold that seemed to give her courage, and she felt more able to continue. 'Anyhow, Hazel had rung to say she wouldn't be home that weekend, and Neville was in a rage. He came crashing into my room without knocking, grabbed me...' It was all so vividly there as she relived it, all so real that she could hardly breathe, but she made herself go on. 'He forced me onto the bed...' Her voice dried, and as her face started to crumple, 'I was t-terrified,' she cried, her voice fracturing.

'Oh, my dear,' Tye mourned, holding her hands tightly, and there was something in his voice that seemed so much as if he was suffering as much as she was suffering that Larch found the strength to try and make things better.

'I eventually managed to somehow get free—before he could carry out his intention,' she said in a rush. 'I don't remember stopping for anything. I just shot out of the house. I must have grabbed up my bag as I went. I had it with me

anyway in hospital—when, although I didn't appreciate i
then, I mercifully couldn't remember anything.'

If she had not known before of Tye's wonderful sensitivity, she knew it then when he tenderly raised one of her
hands to his lips and placed a most beautiful healing kiss
on the back of it.

And quietly he documented, 'Aided by that traffic accident, your exhausted physical, mental and emotional self
was shut down by nature until you were rested enough to
cope again.' He gave the hands he held a small shake, and
then asked, 'You feel better able to cope now?'

'Oh, yes,' she answered, and with more confidence than
she felt. 'Naturally I shall move out from there as soon as
I can.'

'You intend to leave your brother-in-law's house?' Tye
enquired, sounding as though he thoroughly approved of the
idea.

'It was never his house,' Larch answered. 'Our parents
left it to Hazel and me.'

'That man has no right there?'

'Well, he is my sister's husband,' Larch pointed out.
'Anyhow, as soon as I can think up some sound reason to
give Hazel for wanting to move out, I'll go.'

'You don't intend to tell her the truth?' Tye questioned
sharply.

'Good heavens, no! I *know* that the man she married is
not worthy of her, but Hazel doesn't know it. Sometimes
they're a bit scratchy with each other, but she loves him
very much. It would destroy her if she heard so much as a
whisper of what he is capable of.'

Tye was silent for some long moments, and then commented, 'I don't think you're as strong yet as you like to
believe you are.' Adding, 'It could be quite some while,
Larch, before you're fit enough to live on your own.'

The same thought had occurred to her. 'I'm getting
stronger, day by day,' she answered with a smile.

'And what will you do, while still living with your sister, should your brother-in-law come after you again?' Tye wanted to know.

She wished he had not asked—that same horrendous thought was something else that had plagued her. 'I'll be all right while Hazel's there.'

'And when she isn't?' He was starting to sound a shade difficult. 'What about when she's at her place of work, or in Denmark again, or when her husband returns home during the day—as he did last Friday?' Tye reminded her, unnecessarily, as if determined to bring all her fears out into the open and deal with them.

'I'll be able... And anyway, I'm sure he won't try anything like that again,' she answered, wondering which one of them she was trying to convince. Then, changing the subject completely, 'Would you like a cup of tea?' she asked brightly, getting up and going over to the teapot.

Tye came and stood by her as she poured out two cups. Astonishingly he had let her get away with her non-answer. And she realised that he must be accepting that soon she would no longer be his responsibility—not that she ever had been.

Though let her get away with it he had, as she handed him his cup and saucer so blue eyes met grey, and all at once she was not at all certain about the hard glint that had suddenly appeared in his eyes. It worried her.

'I—er—think I'll take my tea back to bed,' she said, and as quickly as she could she went from the kitchen and back up to her room.

When Larch next went down the stairs it was to find that Jane had just arrived, as had the cleaning lady she had spoken of.

Jane introduced Mrs Lewis, who had worked at Grove House before and was familiar with the lay of the house, and as she went off to start work Larch hid her feelings behind a smile as her spirits took an instant dive. If Jane was here there was every chance that Tye would shortly be leaving for his London office. Perhaps he had already left. Perhaps he would not be home until late tonight.

Larch held down a knot of raw emotion at the thought that she might never see him again. She knew her sister well enough to know that Hazel would not hesitate to come and collect her the instant she knew that she had been in hospital.

'I've a dental appointment this afternoon,' Jane was explaining as she busied herself about the kitchen. 'I thought I'd make a casserole for this evening. All it will need then will be for either you or Mr Kershaw to switch the oven on to heat it through.' Larch felt too dispirited to mention that she would not be there that evening to partake of anything Jane had cooked. But her heart lifted instantly when Jane went on, 'First things first. I'll just make Mr Kershaw a cup of coffee, then I'll—'

Tye was still here! 'I'll do it!' Larch at once volunteered.

'I...' Jane seemed about to protest but perhaps thought it might be a bit of therapy of some sort, and smiled instead.

Larch guessed that Tye was busy at work in the library annexe, but once the coffee was made she began to feel unaccountably shy of taking it in to him. She recalled how, only a few hours ago, he had held her gently in his arms prior to her revealing all the awfulness of her brother-in-law's base actions against her and his wife.

Thinking of Neville Dawson made her shudder. She couldn't go back; she could not. But where else could she go? She pushed all such worries from her. Soon she would part from Tye; she wanted this day, her short time with him, to be harmonious. She wanted good memories—she would face Neville Dawson when she had to.

With Tye uppermost in her thoughts, she placed the coffee on a tray and carried it from the kitchen, along the hall and to the library. Tye was busy at work, and her heart fluttered at just seeing him.

'Don't get up,' she said, but it was too late. He was already on his feet and coming to take the tray from her.

'You didn't have to...' he began.

'I know,' Larch answered. 'Jane would have brought it, but I'm used to being busy. Well,' she qualified, 'before I came here and started to lead a life of utter idleness.'

She turned and was about to go when Tye suddenly stopped her dead in her tracks. 'We can change all that,' he informed her. She turned, looking at him, a question in her look.

'We—can?' she queried slowly.

'I have a job for you.'

Her wide eyes widened. Did he...? Was he...? 'You're offering me a job in your London office?' she asked, the idea having immediate appeal, if only so she would not totally deprive herself of seeing him again.

'I don't think you're ready to return to a full-time job,' Tye confused her by saying, but began to clear some of her confusion by explaining, 'Until Miles gives you the "all clear" to start work again, I thought perhaps next week or the week after—when you feel up to it—you might like to do an hour or so a day cataloguing my grandfather's book collection onto the computer.'

Larch stared at him, her heart drumming in her ears at the wonderful chance Tye was offering her. 'You mean,' she began very carefully, 'that I should stay here while I did the work?'

'It seems more sensible than you trying to find accommodation hereabouts and making your way here daily,' he replied casually—too casually for Larch, who had an enquiring mind. 'Until you have your full strength back you'd be creased by the walk down the drive every morning before you started work,' he added, still in that same casual take-it-or-leave-it tone.

Her pride, which had been well and truly dented because she'd had no other option but to accept so much from him, all at once erupted in full force. 'Some of those books look extremely valuable.' She stood facing him to charge. 'I can't see someone who loved books so much failing to have them already meticulously catalogued.'

'You're right, of course,' Tye agreed mildly. 'But, since I haven't been able to find such a catalogue, now seemed as good a time as any to have them brought up to date and computerised. You're quite nifty with a computer, I believe.'

'Oh, Tye.' She had to laugh to have her words bounced back at her. 'But—working just an hour or so a day it would take me simply ages to have all these books recorded!'

'Did I say there was a time limit?'

She shook her head. 'I can't.'

'Can't what?' He looked determined, and as if he just did not recognise the word 'can't'.

'I can't work for you. I have to go home—today.'

'You'd go back to that house, to that man who is ultimately responsible for you lying in hospital half dead?'

Larch did not know about 'half dead'. Although perhaps being lifeless in a coma came close. She shook her head and, the conversation over, took a step back as she explained, 'You have done so much for me already, Tye. I just cannot take advantage of you any longer.' Oh, she wanted to stay, wanted to catalogue those books, wanted to catalogue them for as long as it took—even if it took for ever. 'You've been so good, so kind, but you must see that—that I can't impose on your kindness any longer. I'll—'

'Nonsense!' Tye cut in shortly—and that annoyed her. 'Your place is here, where you can be looked after!' he rapped.

'I'm not a parcel to be looked after!' she flew, hardly knowing where such temper came from—she'd never used to have much of a temper before. But then she had never been in love before, and was afraid she would give in and stay when pride and everything else decreed that she go.

'You'd prefer to go where that apology for a man can get his lecherous hands on you the moment your sister is out of the way?'

Tye looked tough, talked tough, and Larch, who had never seen him like this, started to feel she might be losing a battle here. 'I have to go! Hazel will come for me as soon as I contact her, and—'

'Good!' Tye chopped her off. And, while Larch stood looking at him, wondering what that 'good' had been all about, he totally shattered her by adding, 'I should like to meet your sister.'

'W-why?' Larch stammered, starting to grow wary; that tough look about Tye was beginning to get to her.

And a moment later she knew she was right to be wary when Tye coolly stated, 'I think it's more than high time someone told her of the criminally licentious antics her husband gets up to when she's not there.'

Larch's mouth fell open. 'You—wouldn't!' she gasped faintly.

Tough was not the word for it, when, 'Try me!' Tye retorted harshly, 'just try me!' Larch stared at him utterly horrified—she knew he was not joking!

CHAPTER SIX

SECONDS ticked by as Larch stared at Tye in wordless stupefaction. 'You...' she gasped when she had her breath back—and was suddenly outraged. 'I told you what I did in complete confidence!' she erupted hotly.

'So sue me!' He was unrepentant.

'You wouldn't. You wouldn't truly tell Hazel?' Her fury had faded a little, a hint of trying to reason with him in her tones.

Tye was unyielding. 'Oh, I would,' he replied, everything about him saying she had better believe it.

'But...' Again she was furious. 'You'd ruin my sister's marriage because...?'

'Your sister *has* a marriage?' he cut in aggressively, and Larch could see that there was just no arguing with the man.

'I can't take any more from you, Tye.' She tried another tack. 'I have to go home. You've done so much for me...'

'So here's your chance to repay me.'

She stared at him mulishly. 'It isn't a proper job,' she challenged. 'You've invented it to—' She broke off again. 'Why would you invent a job? For my pride? To save my pride?' She searched for a reason. 'Why would you? You've done more than enough. If you hadn't happened to be calling on Miles at the hospital that day I was brought in you would never have known me.'

'It was because I was at the hospital, because I saw you when you were rushed in, because I've witnessed the battle you've had since, that I can't have you sliding backwards. You've made excellent progress in the week you've been here. I have absolutely no intention of letting you go back

112

to where that man can prey on you and your emotions and so impede your recovery to full health.'

'But…' She was weakening; she knew that she was. The thought of just seeing Neville Dawson again sickened her.

'But nothing,' Tye said, but his tone had softened. 'Tell me, are you unhappy here?'

'Oh, Tye, you know I'm not.'

He looked pleased with her answer, but was not letting up when he suggested, 'Just look at it logically. You were going to find alternative accommodation from your home anyhow. This way you don't have to wait until you're physically up to all that involves—flat-hunting, moving in, keeping house. On your own admission you're used to being busy—that tells me you're either going to be looking for another job, or taking steps towards that career training you spoke of. Here, believe me—' he glanced around the shelves '—these books really do need to be computer-catalogued.'

'I might make a mess of it,' she attempted.

'I don't believe that for a moment,' he denied, his charm starting to sink her.

'Hazel's not going to like it.'

'Let me talk to her,' Tye suggested.

'I'm keeping you two a mile apart!' Larch exclaimed, not likely to give him a chance to breathe a word of the confidences she had shared with him. He grinned. He could afford to. He knew he had won, as did she. 'When do I start?' she asked. Might as well admit defeat.

He accepted victory with a kind look. 'We'll see how you feel next week.'

Larch made up her mind that by next Monday she would be fully fit.

She left him to drink his coffee and, in her endeavour to get 'fully fit', went out of the house and took a walk alone up to the very end of the long drive. She found, for all her pride not to be a burden to Tye, that she was smiling.

She was not smiling when at five that late afternoon she

began to feel anxious about what she would say to Hazel when she phoned her. She knew what she was *not* going to say to her. In fact Neville Dawson's name was not going to pass her lips if she could help it. Because her sister had always looked out for her, Larch could not see her mildly accepting that she'd had a bit of an accident, was better, but was staying on in the home of the man who had taken it upon himself to give her shelter, without asking some very forthright questions.

It was just after six when Tye came and joined Larch in the drawing room. 'You're looking a little strained,' he observed, coming over to where she was seated on one of the sofas.

Did the man miss nothing? 'I'm rehearsing what to say to my sister when I speak to her.'

'You think she'll be back now?'

'I think there's a good chance.'

His answer was to go and bring the phone over to her. 'Ring her,' he suggested. 'You'll feel better once it's done.'

She hesitated. 'I need help here. What shall I say?'

'Since you seem determined to not tell her the truth, stick as close to the truth as you can,' he advised.

Larch thought he might leave her to it. But, whether or not he had an idea she would stay dithering if he went she did not know, but stay he did. She dialled—and all her rehearsed phrases fell apart when she heard the anxiety in her sister's voice.

'Where are you?' Hazel demanded the moment she knew who it was.

'I'm all right,' Larch quickly assured her.

'I can hear that! Where are you? Aunt Ellen was completely mystified when I rang ten minutes ago and asked to speak to you. She said she hasn't seen a glimpse of you in the weeks it's been since Neville says you walked out on your job. This isn't like you, Larch. What's been happening. I was just about to ring the police and report you missing!'

'I'm sorry you've been worried.'

'I only got in fifteen minutes ago. Neville never said a word about you quitting your job until now—just that you'd gone to stay with Aunt Ellen for a while.'

'I intended to go and stay with Aunt Ellen, I think.' Oh, help, she was useless at subterfuge; she hadn't meant to add those last two words.

As suspected, Hazel missed little. 'You *think*?' she queried. 'Don't you know?'

'I—um—had a bit of an accident,' Larch had to confess, but added quickly, 'I'm fine now, honestly. I—'

'You had an *accident*!' Hazel sounded winded. 'What sort of an accident?'

'I—er—got hit by a car. I'm sorry,' Larch apologised, knowing Hazel was still suffering—their father had been killed in a car accident at the beginning of the year. 'I'm out of hospital now, and—'

'Oh, my... You've been in hosp... Where are you? I'm coming straight away!'

'I'm not in High Wycombe. I'm in a village called Shipton Ash. It's in Hertfordshire.'

'Hertfordshire!' Hazel exclaimed, then got herself together. 'You'd better give me the full address... Have you had surgery? Why didn't you contact Neville? I would have come home straight away. Did you break—?'

'No, no,' Larch assured her. 'Not a break in sight.' Larch did not think it would make Hazel feel any better if she told her she had lost her memory for a short while. 'And I wouldn't have wanted you to leave your work to come back.' Larch hoped that would do for an explanation of why she had not contacted Neville in all this time to tell him of her accident. 'Er—there's no need for you to drive all this way. I mean, if you've only just got in from Denmark...'

'I'm coming to bring you home!' Hazel announced, no two ways about it.

Oh, grief. Larch started to panic. Tye would tell Hazel

exactly why he did not want her to go back to her home in Warren End; Larch knew that he would.

'I'm—er—not ready to—er—come home yet,' Larch said as quickly as she could.

'You're in some kind of cottage hospital, convalescent home?' Hazel asked faintly. 'Just how badly are you hurt?'

'I told you, I'm fine now. Just—um—taking things gently for a little while.'

'I'll come and see for myself,' Hazel determined, as perhaps Larch had known that she would.

'You must be tired.'

'I'm still coming.'

'Er—could you—bring some of my clothes, do you think?'

'Where are you?'

'The house is called Grove House,' Larch supplied.

'What sort of house is it?'

Larch knew she meant was it some kind of medical establishment. 'It's just an ordinary house,' Larch replied, feeling herself go pink—it was a vast house. Her eyes caught Tye's glance on her. He smiled encouragingly.

'Who owns it?'

Oh, grief, Hazel! Tye was sitting there listening and Hazel was like a terrier, but then Larch supposed she had known that too. 'It's owned by a Mr Tyerus Kershaw. He's been—'

'Tyerus Kershaw of Kershaw Research and Analysis?'

'You know him?' Larch asked in surprise.

'Not personally. He's as straight as a die, though. He at once called in our top auditors on one occasion when a section of the firm he was looking into started to smell a touch less than fragrant. You say you're staying in his house? Is he there?'

'Yes.'

'I'd better have a word with him.'

'There's no need,' Larch replied rapidly, and was greatly relieved when Hazel, for the moment, accepted that.

'You're sure you're all right?'

'Absolutely.'

'Stay that way 'til I get there.'

Larch slowly put down the phone. Then she looked up at Tye. 'Hazel knows of you. You once called in her firm, Berry and Thacker.' Tye did not say anything. 'She said you're as straight as a die, and wanted to have a word with you.'

'But you didn't want her to?'

'Not until I've got your word that you won't breathe a whisper to her about what I told you—about her husband.'

Tye looked back at her, his expression serious. 'Let me put it this way,' he said after a while. 'I promise not to shatter your sister's illusions about the man she married, if you promise never again to live under the same roof as him.'

'That's blackmail!'

'It's any name you choose, Larch,' Tye answered, and, his tone stern, 'I have *your* word that you do not intend to let your sister persuade you to go back with her?'

'I don't appear to have any choice.'

'True,' he replied, and smiled. 'One of us should go and check if there's sufficient of Jane's casserole to feed three. Or...' he paused '...will she come accompanied?' Larch paled at the thought that her sister might ask her husband to come with her. 'Don't worry, I shall be here,' Tye quickly assured her—proof there, if proof be needed, that by no chance was Larch ready to go back to her former home. They both knew it too.

As it turned out Hazel, when she arrived, did not appear to have much of an appetite. 'Oh, Larch!' she cried when Larch opened the door to her. Hazel came forward, giving her a big hug then standing back to look into her rested face. 'If anything, you're looking better than when I last saw you,' she commented. 'What's been happening to you?' she wanted to know.

'Come in and meet Tye,' Larch replied, and turned to the

man who was standing in the hall watching the two. She introduced them, overwhelmingly grateful that Hazel had come alone.

Over the next hour, Larch explained all that had happened after the accident. And Hazel was able to see that it was not so much that Larch had walked out on her job, but that she had not remembered having a job. Larch was grateful to Tye that he allowed her sister to believe that her temporary amnesia had stemmed solely from the car accident and had had nothing whatsoever to do with any emotional crisis she had been going through.

And while at first Hazel was very much alarmed that her younger sister had lain in bed not knowing who the dickens she was, with all the trauma that accompanied that realisation, Hazel gradually came to terms with it.

Yet for Larch, who knew Hazel well, it seemed that Hazel appeared strangely distracted somehow. Watching her, Larch did not think it was solely on her account that every so often Hazel would fleetingly appear to have her thoughts elsewhere.

'Is anything the matter, Hazel?' she asked after some minutes of observing her pushing her food around her plate.

'With me? Not a thing,' Hazel answered brightly. 'When I drove here I was determined you must come home with me,' she admitted. 'But you seem to be making good progress. And—' She broke off, looking a tinge worried.

'I'd like Larch to stay here, if you wouldn't mind,' Tye cut in.

Hazel looked instantly relieved. 'Are you sure?' she asked. 'The thing is, now that I can see Larch is doing so well, I should really go away again. It would mean I won't be around to check she isn't overdoing things. I know, given half a chance, Larch would be thinking of sprucing up the house for Christmas. And, with rest and quiet recommended, it might be better for her to stay here for a little while longer.'

'Larch knows she is more than welcome,' Tye replied urbanely.

Larch, while a touch surprised that Hazel was not insisting she go back with her, was not sure that she cared too much for being spoken of as if she was not there. She opted to follow the trend. 'Tye has offered me a job, cataloguing his library,' she told Hazel.

'I know you like to work, but take things steadily,' Hazel advised. 'When do you see your consultant again?' She was by then acquainted with the fact that Larch's consultant was none other than her host's stepbrother.

'I'm in frequent touch with Miles,' Tye cut in. 'He thinks Larch needs to have a few more weeks' rest before he'll be ready to discharge her as fully fit.'

There seemed little more to discuss and, after going to the car and collecting the case she had packed, Hazel stayed only long enough to take a note of the telephone number of Grove House so she could keep in contact. When she had driven away, Larch decided to go to bed.

'Tired?' Tye enquired.

'A bit,' she admitted.

'It's been a long day for you.'

'Thank you for not telling Hazel.'

'Go to bed,' he said. 'I'll bring your case up.'

It seemed to Larch that after that night she made great strides in regaining her former health. Her body stopped aching, and by the end of that week she was more marching up to the end of the drive than taking a leisurely stroll.

She realised that Tye must have seen her striding out, possibly from a window, at some time. Because on Sunday afternoon, when she was in the throes of thinking she might explore beyond the gates at the end of the drive, he came and found her and suggested they might take a short walk.

'You've been reading my mind,' she accepted, and loved him to pieces when, after changing into a reefer jacket and trousers her sister had brought, Larch strolled with Tye around the tiny village.

It was a pretty village, and she knew that she would not at all mind living there permanently. She abruptly brought her mind away from such thoughts. Whatever she did, she must not start to get too familiar with that idea. Soon, she knew, she was going to have to part from Tye. She did not want to. Heaven alone knew that she did not want to. She wanted to be close by him for ever.

She was sorry when, all too soon, Tye guided her to a turning that would bring them back to Grove House. Just being out with him was a joy. It seemed incredible that just a simple walk around the village should give her so much pleasure. Though, as she was well aware, the key words there were 'with him'.

'I enjoyed that,' she told him honestly as they entered the house.

He stood observing her. 'It's brought a touch of colour to your cheeks,' he commented with some satisfaction, and, as if he just could not help himself, he bent and touched his lips to hers.

Larch did not know who was the more startled. Her heart was fairly thundering. 'I...' she murmured on a stray found breath.

Tye abruptly took a step back. 'Forgive me,' he apologised at once. 'I didn't mean to do that. Um—we're going to have to blame it on your lovely colour.'

She had somehow known, without him saying so, that he had not meant to kiss her. Perhaps he was embarrassed that he had. She wanted to help him. 'Think nothing of it,' she said lightly.

'You'd better go and rest,' Tye said shortly—and strode away.

Larch saw little of him in the week that followed. If he had been deliberately avoiding her he could not have been more successful. He had worked from home on Monday, spending long hours in the library annexe, where the phone seemed to ring constantly. He had stayed away overnight on Tuesday and, despite Larch's protest, arranged for Jane to come and sleep overnight.

'I shall be fine on my own!' Larch had tried to argue.

He would have none of it. 'It's all arranged,' he answered shortly, and had business elsewhere of more importance, it seemed. Larch glared at his departing back.

'It seems unfair you have to be uprooted!' Larch remarked to Jane as they sat watching television on Tuesday evening.

'I enjoy coming here,' Jane protested. 'I've been like a fish out of water since old Mrs Kershaw died. Coming here gives me something to do, an aim.'

Hazel was back in Denmark, but telephoned without fail every evening. Larch wanted to confide in her about her love for Tye, but found that she could not. It was much too private.

The love she had for him began to create an ache in her heart when she saw little of him on Wednesday and Thursday. He came home around eight on Friday but seemed so brusque that her pride started to rear up.

That same pride began to soar out of control when, having held back dinner hoping he would arrive some time that night, conversation over the meal was sparse. When, dinner over, she began to clear the table only for him to snarl, 'Leave that!' her pride and anger went roaring into orbit.

'I didn't ask to stay here, remember!' she exploded, and, tears spurting to her eyes, she slammed the dishes back down on the table and shot from the dining room.

She did not make it as far as the bottom of the beautiful staircase before Tye caught up with her. Caught up with her and took a hold of her arms, turning her to face him. Serious grey eyes searched into shining blue ones.

'Don't cry,' he said, a kind of a hoarse note there in his voice. 'Please don't cry.'

'I won't—if you stop being such a complete pig!' she retorted pithily, but immediately started to feel ashamed. Clearly, tough though he could be at times, Larch realised that Tye could not bear to see a woman in tears. Suddenly she folded completely. 'I'm sorry,' she apologised. 'You've had a busy day; you don't need this.'

His answer was to give her a gentle smile and then, as though he could not help it, 'Aw, come here,' he said, and took her in his arms.

It was bliss, pure and simple, to be hugged by him, to be held up against him, but she dared not relax. She loved him and he must never know, but would know if she held on to him as she so sorely wanted to. She pulled back and Tye immediately let her go. 'I never used to be like this—argumentative, snappy,' she said, taking a small step backwards, denying her need to take a big step forwards. 'Do you think that blow to my head released some kind of cross-tempered streak?' She did not expect him to answer, knowing herself that her suddenly new mixed-up temperament stemmed solely from falling heart and soul in love with him and, as a result, being hyper-hyper-sensitive to the smallest hurt, real or imagined, from him.

'You're in recovery, Larch,' he answered seriously. 'Your world had started to cave in before your accident. You're doing well,' he said, and added, 'And I'm a brute.'

She wanted to deny any such thing, but, as ever, was sensitive that she might unthinkingly somehow reveal her true feelings for him. So she grinned cheekily instead, and told him, 'At last we agree on something.' And when, after a small taken aback moment, he laughed, she stepped forward and, totally because she could not help it, stretched up and kissed him. She was at once staggered and quite appalled at her lack of control. Good grief, what had got into her? 'Quits,' she cried, and, hoping with all she had that he would think she was paying him back for kissing her last

Sunday, she turned hurriedly about and went quickly up to her room.

The weekend was no exception to Hazel telephoning her. 'I'm still in Denmark,' she said when she rang on Sunday.

'There's no need to ring every day,' Larch assured her, 'I'm fine.'

'I know,' Hazel replied, and Larch knew she would call her just the same.

She knew how lucky she was to have a sister like Hazel. Briefly Larch thought of her sister's husband, of his betrayal of her dear sister, and felt so badly that she should tell her— but knew that she never would. Hazel loved him, she deserved better, but what good would it do to cause her pain?

Tye started out for London so early on Monday morning that Larch was only out of bed in time to see the rear lights of his car as he went up the drive. He appeared to have made Grove House his present home, but she had no idea for how much longer that would continue before his London home would once again become his main address. All Larch hoped, as she came away from the window and went to shower, was that he would be coming home to Grove House that night.

For her part, she was feeling so well now that she knew another day spent in enforced idleness would send her potty. There was a restless energy in her as she went down the stairs that would not allow her to settle quietly to read or take a walk. And with Mrs Lewis there to do the housework, and Jane refusing to allow her to do anything major in the kitchen, Larch went and got herself some breakfast. She knew that today would see her making a start on that mammoth task of recording the books in the library onto the computer.

By nine-thirty she had the computer ready for action. What seemed like five minutes later, but which turned out to be eleven o'clock, Jane came looking for her.

'So this is where you've got to!'

'I'm having a splendid time,' Larch replied. She had no clue how one went about cataloguing a library of books, but had worked out a very clear and precise system she was happy with.

Jane smiled at her enthusiasm. 'I'll bring you some coffee. Unless you want a break?'

Larch would have been happy to work while she had her coffee. But quite a number of the books she was handling were old and valuable. She would never forgive herself if she spilt so much as a tiny drop of coffee on one of them.

After her coffee she returned to the library and worked solidly until one, when Jane again appeared and advised a break for a sandwich, and in her opinion a rest that afternoon.

While admitting, but only to herself, that she did feel just a tinge fatigued, Larch felt she had spent sufficient time resting and opted to take a walk. 'I'll come with you,' Jane volunteered.

It was the start of a wonderful week as far as Larch was concerned. Hazel phoned early every evening from Denmark and sounded less distracted than she had, which pleased Larch.

Tye came home every evening and seemed pleased to see her. She had mentioned that she had spent an hour or so borrowing his computer but, having been instructed not to do too much, agreed that she would not. She was more interested in his work, and was thrilled when he selected some of the lighter moments to share with her.

By Friday, however, it was beginning to chip away at Larch that, since she was feeling so well now, she had no possible excuse to linger on at Grove House. Those same thoughts preoccupied her when, after being called away by Jane to have her lunch, Larch returned to the library to put away a collection of books she had left on the library table. She was perched on a fascinating set of steps on wheels, replacing the books she had taken down, her thoughts a mixture. She was in the middle of thinking that this job which she felt certain Tye had invented purely to save her pride did not go anywhere near to repaying him for all his kindness to her, when, as she was dwelling on his many kindnesses, the library door suddenly opened. And Tye stood there—looking anything but kind!

'What the devil do you think you're doing?' he charged furiously.

'You're early! I didn't expect you back yet,' she answered innocently.

'Obviously!' he snarled, and, striding over to where she was perched, 'Come down from there at once!' he demanded.

'I'm only…'

'Now!' he barked.

What had she done, for heaven's sake? 'Since you ask so nicely,' she dared bravely, but blanched when his hands came to the steps and he looked angry enough to physically yank her down. 'I'm coming, I'm coming!' she cried, followed by a wobbly kind of, 'Oh-er-wo…' when, with a couple of books in one arm, she found coming down one-handed was not so easy as coming down empty-handed—and she started to slip.

The books went sailing through the air and Tye made a grab for her—about all he could do when it became all too apparent that to do nothing would leave her crashing head-first onto the table. From being flightless to in flight, to safe and secure all in one second, took her breath. But Tye's speedy grip on her was awkward, and her feet were dangling in the air when she began to slide downwards in his hold.

Somehow, probably more in his haste to catch her than to bother where he caught her, his hands were beneath her light sweater. She continued to slip, but as she was sliding down so his grip was sliding up, and from trying to hang on to her ribcage suddenly Larch became aware that Tye had his hands on her breasts. She was momentarily stunned to feel his hands firmly cupping her breasts, and just stared speechlessly at him.

Then all manner of emotions were breaking in her, and in the next moment she had gone a furious red. 'Take your hands off me!' she yelled.

Before she could blink Tye let go of her and her feet abruptly hit the floor. He did not move, other than to take his hands from beneath her sweater, but stayed close and endeavoured to calm her. 'You've got nothing to—'

'Don't you dare touch me!' she hurled at him.

'My dear, I...' Tye tried again. But as swiftly as her panic had arrived, so it as swiftly disappeared, and she could not apologise fast enough.

'Oh, Tye, I'm so sorry!' she apologised, almost tripping over her words in her rush, memory flooding in of just how much she could trust him. This man would never harm her. For heaven's sake, had she so soon forgotten that night when everything had become too much for her and the way she had climbed into his bed? He had held her close through the rest of that night, for her comfort, not his. Sex had just not come into it. 'I'm sorry,' she repeated rapidly, 'so sorry. I don't know what came over me.'

Tye stared at her, up close but no longer touching her. He was studying her, and looked slightly worried. 'Has what happened to you made you afraid of men?' he questioned. He seemed then to lose some of his colour. 'Are you afraid of me?' he asked, and seemed very much shaken at the very thought.

'No—no, of course not. Not you.' She felt it was urgent that he should know. 'I trust you implicitly,' she stated quickly. He did not look totally convinced. 'Honestly, Tye,' she went on, 'I don't know what was in my head to make me panic.' And she tried hard to explain. 'I suppose there might have been a stray thread of memory of Neville Dawson and what he tried to...in there somewhere. But you're nothing like him.'

'I'm glad to hear it,' Tye answered, but he was still watching her, and appeared to be still wondering if she had been permanently damaged by her brother-in-law's assault on her.

'And I suppose—well, to be absolutely truthful, I—er—I'm not familiar with—er—' She broke off. She didn't want Tye stern like this, worried like this, so she continued, 'With men being familiar with my person, either accidentally or on purpose. I—um—suppose it was a bit of a shock.'

Tye's stern expression did not let up. 'You're—totally inexperienced?' he questioned slowly.

She could feel her hot colour returning, but mumbled, 'Yes,' and, feeling awkward suddenly, 'Can I have a hug?' she asked.

And, at that proof of her absolute trust in him, the stern and worried look went from Tye. He put his arms around her and she laid her head against his chest and never wanted to be anywhere else. She felt she had come home.

'All right?' Tye asked after some moments, and although he appeared in no hurry to let her go, Larch took it that what he was saying was that his hug of comfort was over.

She drew back. 'Absolutely,' she said, and his arms fell to his sides.

Strangely, Tye did not step away, but stayed close, and, looking into her eyes, seemed to want to assure her that she was safe with him. 'You do know that I would never take advantage of your innocence?' he asked seriously.

But Larch did not want him back to being stern and worried again. 'Never?' she asked with an impish smile. And, wanting to make him smile, 'Not even if I begged you?' she asked wickedly.

He did not smile. What he did, after a stunned moment of just looking at her, was to burst out laughing. 'That tongue of yours will get you into serious trouble one of these days,' he warned.

Then, as they looked at each other, all at once neither of

them was laughing. They just stood there, staring into each other's eyes. Then, while still looking into her eyes, Tye bent his head and started to come close. They both had all the time in the world to change their minds, but Larch wanted Tye to kiss her, and she could only suppose, when his lips met hers, that he wanted to kiss her too.

Her heartbeats raced as his arms came about her again, only this time to draw her closer to him not in a hug of comfort but in a warm embrace.

Their kiss, though not passionate, was wonderful as far as Larch was concerned. In fact everything was wonderful—being up this close to Tye, being held so firmly in his superb masculine arms. And she wanted more.

Their kiss came to an end and Tye drew back, but she wasn't moving. 'You're a devil for punishment,' he murmured, and his head came down again.

Oh, Tye, I love you so much, she wanted to tell him, but of course could not, so eagerly gave him her lips again, adoring him. And when he drew her yet closer to him and his kiss deepened, she discovered a need to be even closer to him. She pressed herself to him, and an instant later felt his response, and knew that as she had started to feel a physical need for him, so he had an answering physical need for her.

They seemed to mutually pull apart then. She from shyness at this new world she was dipping her toes into, and Tye to give her an askew look as he gently scolded, 'Allow me to tell you, Miss Burton, that you have the power to put a severe strain on a man's resolve.'

Severe strain or no, it did not prevent him from taking his arms from around her, and Larch knew that there would be no more kissing. But those moments shared with him had been little short of magical. So magical that she could hardly speak.

She did manage to find one word, though. 'Good,' she answered, and even managed to find a grin when, not trusting herself not to beg him to take her in his arms again, she turned from him and sailed dreamily out from the library.

CHAPTER SEVEN

LARCH felt she had never been so truly mixed up as she was in the weekend that followed. 'Let's go for a drive,' Tye suggested on Saturday morning. So in love with him was she, she would have agreed had he suggested they had a go at bungee-jumping. So long as she was with him, nothing else mattered.

Again and again she relived those kisses they had shared. His mouth was stupendous—his mouth on hers spine-melting. He made no attempt over the weekend to kiss her again, however, much as she would have welcomed his kisses, but nor did he pretend it had not happened. Even if he did not actually mention those 'close up and personal' moments, he did, during that drive, refer to his coming home early the previous day.

'I'd asked Jane on my way in how you'd been and she said you'd spent the morning happily busy in the library.' Larch's heart picked up a joyful beat. Did Tye often ask Jane questions about her welfare? Did he care? Of course he doesn't, her saner self scoffed, not in the way you want him to care.

'Jane told you that was where I was?' Larch asked, turning her head to look at him as he watched the road up in front.

'Where you *still* were.'

Uh-oh! 'I'm in trouble, aren't I?'

'You were not supposed to be working even *half* a day! Our agreement was for an hour or so.'

'Was that why you were so furious?'

'That and the fact that I thought you'd have more sense than to go shinning up ladders.'

130

Larch could feel her newly awakened argumentative streak begin to strain at the leash. But she wanted to enjoy her time with him—she was not going to think about a time when she would no longer be with him. 'I don't want to fight with you, Tye,' she said quietly.

He turned his head to look at her. 'Does that mean you're going to obey my every instruction?' he asked, his mouth starting to pick up at the corners.

'Of course,' she lied.

And at her blatant lie he laughed. Though he sobered to say, 'Promise me you won't go leaping about on ladders unless either Jane or I are in the library with you.'

Larch thought the idea a touch restricting, given that it would be physically impossible to reach some of the top library shelves without some sort of a ladder. But she still did not want to argue, so instead—reasonably, she thought—she asked, 'Why?'

'Because Miles hasn't given you the "all clear" yet. For all we know you could be up ladder and start to feel dizzy. It happens to people who haven't had a head injury. You don't want to hit your head again, do you?'

Recalling that awful desolate time when she'd had no idea who she was, remembering the black panic of despair she had sometimes experienced, Larch had no wish whatsoever to experience it ever again. She most definitely did not want to risk another bang on the head.

'OK—I'll be good,' she promised. 'Do you think I should ring Miles and ask him when he thinks I might be ready to see him? It can't be much longer now.'

'It isn't. You're seeing him at three next Friday.'

'Three on Friday!' she repeating, feeling slightly winded.

'At Roselands outpatients' clinic,' Tye confirmed.

'How long have you known?' she asked, feeling a little startled for all she had said it could not be much longer now before she saw Miles for a final time.

'A few days,' Tye replied.

'You didn't think to tell me?'

'I would have remembered by Friday,' he said, his tone off-hand.

He made it sound as if he had temporarily forgotten, but she had an idea that there was very little he had ever 'temporarily' forgotten.

Though she was to wonder at her own ability to temporarily forget that appointment when, back at Grove House, Hazel rang in the early evening and Larch forgot entirely to tell her sister of her appointment.

Although that could have been put down to the fact that Hazel was still in Denmark when she rang, and not at home where Larch had expected she would be. 'Will you be in Denmark for very much longer?' she asked. Even while wanting to be pronounced fully fit by Miles on Friday, she knew that as soon as he discharged her she really would have to do something about leaving Grove House, about leaving Tye. 'I mean,' she added quickly, unable to take thinking of leaving, 'will you be coming home soon?'

'You're all right?' Hazel asked quickly.

'Of course I am,' Larch told her brightly, and came away from the phone knowing that she was far from all right. Oh, how could she possibly leave? Yet, after Friday, she would have no excuse to stay!

Larch did not sleep well that night, but by morning she had decided that she was not going to think of a time when she would be apart from Tye. That time would come all too soon.

Tye had work he wanted to complete that day, but did find time to tell her to put a jacket on. 'Come for a walk round the village,' he suggested.

She stored up more memories. Standing with Tye on a tiny footbridge. Tye placing an arm about her shoulders while he turned her to draw her attention to a most magnificent red-berry-bearing hollybush. She stood quietly in the shelter of his arm, and although they stayed like that for a while, as though he had forgotten his arm was holding her, he all too soon remembered and removed it.

She had not felt cold before, but she felt cold then. Cold and bleak. The hollybush reminded her that next month would see the arrival of December. She would be back home for Christmas. She did not look forward to it. Home was not home any more. Where would Tye be?

He left for his office very early again on Monday. But when Larch went to start work in the library her heart lifted. The stack of books that had been reposing on the highest shelves had been taken down and were now on the large library table. She felt a glow of love for him. Tye had done that for her.

He returned home just before seven and her spirits lifted just to see him. They had finished dinner when, Jane having gone home, Larch insisted she was quite well enough to wash a few dishes and not leave them for Jane or Mrs Lewis in the morning. For once he allowed that she probably was strong enough, but in turn insisted, 'I'll come and give you a hand.'

'You don't have to!' she protested. 'I'm sure you've got a briefcase full of stuff you'd prefer to be getting on with.'

'You refuse to let me explore my domestic side?'

Larch gave him a speaking look. 'There's no arguing with you,' she retorted sniffily—secretly loving the domesticity of it when he helped her carry their used dishes to the kitchen and he dried while she washed. They were moments to store, to hold, to keep.

They were chatting in a companionable way that warmed her heart when Tye revealed that he would be going away on Wednesday for a few days.

'Oh,' she murmured. Some input was called for from her, but any lifted spirits at once plummeted that by the look of it she would not see him for at least two whole days! Her chilled feelings turned to dread. How on earth was she going to feel when, as must soon happen, she would never see him again?

'You'll be all right,' Tye assured her, perhaps taking that 'oh' for apprehension at the thought of being in the large house all by herself. 'I've already spoken with Jane. She'll be here from Wednesday morning until I get back.'

'There's no need for…'

'I think there is,' he contradicted before she could finish. 'You've come a long, long way from when I saw you first. Aside from the bumps and bruises you collected, the stiffness and pain you endured while your body healed, I know it hasn't been easy for you. A good part of the time it must have been totally nightmarish. But you're almost there now.' He smiled at her. 'Indulge me, Larch,' he requested with charm enough to sink a battle cruiser. 'Let Jane sleep in, then after Friday—' He broke off to smile again before going on, 'I'm probably going to regret this, but, subject to Miles discharging you from his "follow-up" list, I'll allow you to do anything at all you may wish.'

Larch had to smile back at him. 'I might keep you to that,' she answered lightly, adding as casually as she was able, 'Any idea when you'll be back?'

'If you're worrying about your clinic appointment, I'll be back to take you to Roselands.'

'You don't have to,' her pride reared up to state. 'I can—'

'No, you can't. I'll be here by about midday on Friday,' he promised.

'You're cutting your work short because of me,' she accused, feeling dreadful suddenly that through her his work had been disrupted, causing him to catch up evenings and weekends.

'Will you stop feeling guilty?' he requested good-humouredly. 'I promise you my work is not suffering, nor has it suffered in any way. In fact,' he went on, 'my business has gone from strength to strength.'

'But…'

'But nothing. I'll be here to take you to see Miles,' he reiterated firmly.

She was still feeling guilty, but rather than argue with him, this man she loved, said 'If you're sure—'

'I'm sure,' he cut in, and was looking steadily at her when he added quietly, 'I'm looking forward to it.'

Before she had a chance to analyse that remark, or to wonder or indeed decide if there was anything to analyse, the kitchen phone rang and Tye walked over to answer it. 'Larch is here,' he said, and asked a pleasant, 'How are you?' before turning to hold out the phone to Larch. 'It's your sister.'

'Hello, Hazel,' Larch greeted her brightly, and they chatted about matters inconsequential for a few minutes, until Larch asked, 'You're still in Denmark?'

'I'm coming home this weekend,' Hazel replied. 'I—' She broke off. 'It doesn't matter. I'll tell you when I see you,' she said.

'Sounds important?'

'Stop fishing,' Hazel laughed.

'You've another promotion and…?'

'So tell me what you've been doing.' Hazel refused to be drawn. 'You're keeping well? You haven't…?'

'I'm fine,' Larch assured her. 'Actually, I'm going for my final check-over on Friday.'

'Don't count your chickens.'

'Now who's the mother hen?' They both laughed, and ended the call—Hazel, Larch presumed, to do some more studying.

'Your sister has a promotion?' Tye asked as Larch replaced the phone.

Nothing like blatantly listening in. Though, since he was in the same room, Larch realised that there was not very much else he could do. 'It sounds very much as though she has,' Larch replied. 'Hazel works hard enough. She has something to tell me, anyhow, but refuses to tell me until she comes home this weekend.'

In her bed that night when, as was usual now, Larch relived every moment shared that evening with Tye, she recalled his 'I'm looking forward to it' comment. Did he mean he was looking forward to Friday when Miles would pronounce her as fit as a flea so Tye could say, Goodbye, it's been nice knowing you?

She paled at the thought that Tye could not wait to be rid of her. Then she recalled how he had insisted that she stay at Grove House until she was well again, and she began to feel a touch better. But that was only until she realised that she *was* well again now—so what was she hanging around for?

Love, she was on to realising, after going through yet another gut-tearing gamut of emotions, played the very devil with one's instincts, one's sensitivity. In fact love, her love for Tye, was making her doubt her own shadow. She would be a nervous wreck if she kept this up.

Larch finally fell asleep, but only after she had firmly decided that she was not going to look under the stones of everything Tye said. While she supposed it was true that he seldom said anything he did not mean, she would drive herself scatty if she started to dissect every throwaway utterance he ever made. From now on, she determined, she would take all and everything he said at face value. Therefore 'I'm looking forward to it' meant just that. He was looking forward to taking her to the clinic on Friday because... Oh, stop it. You're doing it again. Stop it.

For all the doubts that had plagued her during the dark hours, Larch was in the window seat in her room early the next morning to watch Tye's car disappear up the drive. Face value, she reminded herself as she stood under the shower.

She had breakfast and started work in the library, smiling to see yesterday's books had miraculously sailed back up to their appointed shelves, and that there was a fresh stack of books now reposing on the library table.

It was just before twelve when Larch left the computer to return another batch of books to the library table and heard a car come roaring up the drive. Jane never drove like that! Larch glanced out of the window to see an expensive-looking car pull up at the front door. Moving to the side of the window, Larch continued to watch as an elegant and well-dressed woman of about forty left the car and approached the front door.

With the recovery of her memory it was no longer important for someone to be in the house with her at all times. Consequently, while Jane was on hand a lot of the time, more now as cook—a job she revelled in—than anything, she was not expected for a while.

The doorbell rang. Larch had no idea who the caller was, but saw no reason not to answer it. She went from the library and along the hall, and had just reached the front door when the bell rang again.

'Ah!' the woman exclaimed as Larch pulled back the stout oak door. 'You *are* in!' She smiled a friendly smile, but, when Larch did not invite her over the threshold, 'I'm Tye's sister-in-law,' she introduced herself.

'Paulette?' Larch pulled the name from her memory bank, and the attractive older woman seemed exceedingly pleased.

'You've heard of me!' she trilled. 'I know I'm too late for coffee and too early for lunch, but when my husband let slip that Tye had a live-in lover, I got over here as fast as I could.'

Larch's jaw dropped in astonishment. This woman thought she and Tye... Larch did not know which to do first—put the woman straight on that score before they went any further, or to invite her in. 'Come in,' she invited, deciding that this was not a discussion she wanted to have on the doorstep. 'Would you like coffee?' she asked.

'No, no. Thank you all the same. My, this house hasn't

changed much. Not that I came here all that often.' She laughed suddenly. 'Well, not after old lady Kershaw suggested one time that if I did have to ''rattle on'', as she put it, would I please do it elsewhere as I was giving her a migraine. My heavens, she could be blunt—and that was without bothering to put her mind to it,' she added with another laugh.

By that time they had reached the drawing room and Larch stood back to let her guest, whom she realised, in the manner of things, had more right there than herself, precede her into the room.

'Take a seat,' Larch invited pleasantly, and, taking a seat across from her, waited only until Paulette Phipps was seated before she at once began to set her straight. Or, at least, attempted to. 'I don't know what Miles told you—'

'You've met him?' Paulette interrupted.

'Yes, but...'

'Now, isn't that typical! You'd think I was an agent for Spies Incorporated the little my beloved tells me! Just because I—positively years ago—happened to mention to a friend a very minor matter, so minor as to be insignificant, about one of his patients, he now tells me absolutely nothing! It's such a trial,' she said, then laughed an infectious kind of laugh as she added, 'Thanks be that there's so much other stuff to gossip about.'

'Which—' Larch attempted to get in—then wondered if she must have a very quiet voice because Paulette did not appear to have heard her.

'Miles arranged to have today off—unless of course some emergency crops up, which of course it will. He was operating until four this morning, so didn't get up until nearly eleven.' She 'rattled' enthusiastically away, going on with amazing breath control since she did not appear to take another breath, 'I wanted to go to a place in town for lunch, but Miles said he just wanted to potter about and relax. Well, you know how it is. I wanted to be up and doing and he, poor sweetie, wanted to stay home to unwind. So, purely to give him some time to himself, while at the same time not being too far away—we spend so little time together as it is,' she threw in, not laughing, but beaming, 'I said I'd find something else to do.'

Larch, who up until then had led a reasonably quiet life, was finding her visitor's personality a touch swamping. She had a feeling she should try and stop this friendly but gabbling woman from revealing anything further. She doubted Paulette would be so open if she knew that Larch's relationship with her stepbrother-in-law was not as she imagined. Or would she? Larch was suddenly unsure. Though she was determined she would set her straight about her relationship with Tye any second now.

'I know your husband works very hard,' she attempted, as a prelude to telling her just how she knew that and then going on to the reason why she was, for the moment, residing at Grove House.

'Tell me about it!' Paulette took up. 'Anyhow, where was I? Oh, yes.' Again she did not pause for breath. 'So there was I, thinking to make myself scarce, but not too scarce— I idolise the man,' she said with another of her laughs. 'So I told Miles, You potter, darling. I think I'll go and take a look at Grove House. I mean, with Tye always so busy, it could have been a positive age since anyone had been to take a look—squatters could have moved in or anything. Until Tye decides what he's going to do with the place somebody has to keep an eye on it. But imagine my surprise when Miles said I mustn't come anywhere near Grove House. Naturally I wanted to know why!'

'Naturally,' Larch responded faintly.

'Well, you can imagine my surprise that, when pushed, Miles told me I must stay away because Tye had a house guest. House guest? I ask you! As soon as I knew Tye's guest was female I had to come over. I mean, I just never thought I'd live to see the day that Tye took one of his lady-loves to *actually* live with him. He's always been far too wily for that.'

Larch again opened her mouth to tell Paulette Phipps the precise reason why she was Tye's house guest. But to her own surprise heard herself query, 'Wily?'

Paulette gave her a lovely smile, as though to soften her words, but when she started off, 'Forgive me, my dear,' Larch knew she was not going to like what she was going to hear. Nor did she, when Paulette went on, 'But I just never thought Tye would ever put himself in the position where, when the first flush had faded, he might find himself with a problem—depending on her clingability, of course—when he wanted to live—er—unencumbered, as it were. Of course, now that I've seen you I can see that—' A telephone rang; it was Paulette's mobile. 'Excuse me,' she said, and took her phone from her bag.

'Yes,' she said, and, 'Yes,' again. A beaming smile and, 'I'd adore to! Are you sure you don't want to…? All right, darling.' She checked her watch. 'I'll be with you in twenty minutes. What? No, of course not! I wouldn't dream of going anywhere near Grove House.' She ended her call, put her phone away and stood up. 'My husband knows me too well. I bet he thinks I'm on my way here and that by dangling the carrot of the lunch I wanted at my favourite restaurant he thinks I'll forget all about Tye's mistress.' She was already making for the door.

Larch felt a panicky urgency to speedily tell her the true facts. But her visitor was obviously in a rush to go and have lunch with the husband she idolised.

'Do you know, I don't even know your name?' she said as they went hurrying along the hall.

'Larch. Larch Burton,' Larch supplied. 'Paulette…' she began as they reached the front door.

'I'm sorry it was such a short visit. Perhaps we'll do lunch one day?'

'I…'

'Meantime I must fly!' Paulette was through the door and about to get in to her car when she called over its roof to a stunned Larch, 'What's the betting my conscience will get the better of me and before the year's out I confess to that man of mine that I didn't have to go anywhere near Grove House because I was actually there when he rang?' Again Paulette laughed. 'Bye, Larch,' she said, and—foot down, with a roar of the engine—she was gone.

Larch went to the library but was too shattered, too shaken by Paulette's visit, to be able to concentrate on computer work. She still had not resumed when Jane popped her head round the door to enquire if she fancied chicken pie for dinner that evening. 'Are you all right?' Jane asked. 'You look…'

'I'm fine.' Larch quickly got herself together. 'Paulette Phipps called,' she mentioned.

'Ah!' Jane exclaimed, as if that totally explained why she should look so shaken. Life at Grove House had so far been serene and peaceful.

Ah, indeed! A few minutes later, alone once more, Larch went over again everything Tye's stepsister-in-law had said. The thing was that Larch felt she could quite get to like Paulette Phipps. She was open and she was friendly—but Larch could quite understand why Miles told his garrulous wife so little. What she knew, she shared. What she did not know she assumed, and shared that too.

With the words 'mistress' and 'clingability' bouncing around in her head, Larch found it impossible to fully concentrate on what she was doing. She was glad to abandon the library and go and have a sandwich with Jane.

They decided to go for a walk that afternoon, but Larch could not outpace her thoughts, and returned from their walk in mental torment. Was she clinging? Worse, because Tye was good and kind, was she making it impossible for him to say that she was well enough to go?

She went up to her room, her insides churning as doubts

and 'mistress' and 'clingability' continued to bombard her.
Demons of doubt had her in their grip, pursued her so that
in the end she knew she was going to have to leave. She
was not, and never had been, Tye's responsibility. Nor did
she wish to be. But—where would she go?

Needing to be busy, but feeling too discomposed to settle
to anything very much, she returned downstairs. She peeled
and cleaned vegetables for the evening meal and told Jane
she could quite well cope with it if she had any plans for
the evening.

'Well, if you're sure? There's a meeting of the Christmas
bazaar committee tonight. I wouldn't mind checking a few
things over before then,' Jane accepted.

Jane was far from Larch's thoughts when at half past six
she heard Tye's car on the drive. She felt that she probably
ought to mention to him that Miles's wife had called, but
she was feeling too bruised to want to start a conversation—
the subject being, what the loquacious Paulette had spoken
of. Anyhow, since Paulette clearly was not thinking of men-
tioning her visit to her husband just yet, Tye was not likely
to hear of it for quite some while. Bleakly, Larch knew that
when that time came she would be long gone.

'Good day?' she asked Tye when he came and found her
in the kitchen. She looked over to him, her heart turning
cartwheels just to see him.

'Can't complain. How about you?' he asked pleasantly,
standing there, briefcase in hand, his eyes on her face.

'The usual,' she lied. 'I told Jane I would see to the meal.
What time would you like dinner?' she asked, her tone perhaps a little off-hand in her attempt to counter any suggestion that she might be thought to be 'clinging'.

Tye looked at her for a silent moment or two. 'When it's
ready,' he answered, and went from the kitchen—she presumed to shower and freshen up.

Larch tried hard to appear natural when later she and Tye
were having dinner. But each time some naturally thought

comment would pop into her head she found she was pausing to question it—did that comment sound clinging, or was
that the sort of comment a mistress would make?—and the
comment never got uttered.

Why it should surprise her that Tye, as observant as ever,
should notice that something was slightly amiss she could
not have said. But she was taken out of her unhappy
thoughts when later, as they stood in the kitchen attending
to the used dishes, he quietly asked, 'What's wrong, Larch?'

'Nothing,' she answered quickly.

He did not believe her, and, putting down the drying
cloth, he caught hold of her by the shoulders and turned her
to face him. 'You're not worrying about Friday?'

You could say that, she supposed, knowing for certain
that on Friday she would be leaving Grove House and never
coming back—yet still had no earthly idea where she would
go. 'Good heavens, no,' she replied. 'I shall pass any test
Miles cares to give me with flying colours!'

Tye smiled encouragingly. 'That's the spirit,' he said,
adding, 'If you're very good I'll take you for a celebratory
dinner afterwards.'

Oh, Tye, don't do this to me! She could think of nothing
she would rather do than go out to dinner with him. But he
was being kind again, and he deserved better than to have
some woman latch on and cling to him.

'I'll be so good you wouldn't believe,' she answered,
hoping he would not go to any trouble booking a table. She
would not be there.

Together they finished the dishes, and her heart ached at
such wonderful domesticity. She found she was glancing at
the kitchen clock, almost as if counting the hours until she
must part from him.

'Hazel's late,' Tye commented, following her glance.

'I expect she's tied up with something,' Larch replied
lightly. Though he was right; her sister had usually phoned
by this time.

Larch went with him to the drawing room. She knew that she never ever wanted to part from him, but full well knew that he would be going away tomorrow and the next time she would see him would be Friday, when he came to Grove House to take her to keep her appointment at Roselands clinic. Her emotions started to get out of hand. Mistress, clinging, leaving, never to see him again—all chased each other round in her head. When would she tell him that she would not be coming back to Grove House on Friday? When…?

Abruptly she got out of her chair. She could not take it. 'I think I'll go to bed!' she said jerkily.

'Larch! What is it?'

'I shouldn't think Hazel is going to ring now,' Larch said, speaking quickly, heading for the door.

Before she could get there, though, Tye had somehow managed to get to the door first. He halted her, staring down into her agitated beautiful blue eyes. 'Something's troubling you?' he questioned.

'Not at all!'

'You're sure you're not worrying about the outcome when you see Miles on Friday?'

'Certain. Honestly!' she replied. It was what happened after that, after she parted from Tye, that worried her. How would she cope with not seeing him? 'I'm not worrying about a thing!' she promised, forcing a cheerful note.

He was not convinced. 'You have a headache?' he questioned, not budging an inch from blocking her way out of the door.

'I'm fine. Absolutely. Perhaps just a bit tired,' she lied. Tye studied her for perhaps another ten seconds more, then stood aside and opened the door for her. 'Goodnight,' she said quickly, and slipped through the doorway. She did not look round, would not look round, but she sensed he was still in the doorway as she went swiftly up to her room.

She was not tired and did not want to go to bed. That

was to say, she was not physically tired, but she was oh, so weary of the same spirit-defeating thoughts that tossed around and around in her head.

Eventually she went and showered and got into a nightdress, telling herself she had known anyway that she would soon be leaving. It was just that after Paulette's visit that day the knowledge that she could no longer stay had become set in concrete.

Mistress. Clinging. Had she clung so much that Tye was unable to prise her away? That sinking thought battered at her again and again. As did the knowledge batter her that she had truly spited herself, in that by taking herself off to bed she had done away with any chance to see him again before Friday. She could hardly intrude on his early morning tomorrow, when he would be busy getting ready to go to his office.

Friday! She did not want to think about Friday. Oh, she wasn't worried about seeing Miles. She felt so well now it was a foregone conclusion that he would discharge her from his list. But—what was she going to tell Tye? Would he be relieved? Probably—totally, came back the unwanted answer.

A dry kind of sob took her, and Larch forced herself to concentrate on matters practical. As yet she had no idea what reason she was going to give Hazel for not returning to their old home. Larch knew, now that she was no longer exhausted by her workload and was strong again, that she was just not going to live again under the same roof as Neville Dawson.

Which meant that early tomorrow morning she must get on the phone and start trying to find a bedsit somewhere. It need not necessarily be in High Wycombe, she realised. Since she was set on leaving home, she could live anywhere. Hazel would be a problem; Larch knew that. Given that she had been the one to stay home and look after their mother, it had not prevented Hazel from looking out for her younger sister. It was going to be difficult.

And the most difficult part would be in saying a permanent goodbye to Tye. But, with that hated word 'clinging' refusing to stay out of her head, there was no other way.

Larch was sitting in the window seat in her nightdress and light wrap, her thoughts taken up solely with the man she would next see on Friday but never again after that, when to her surprise he knocked on her bedroom door and after a few seconds came in.

Tye looked serious, and she left the window seat with an idea that she was in trouble over something. He had shed his jacket, but whether he had been working or on his way to bed she did not know. What she did know, as he quietly closed the door and came over to where she was standing, was that he wanted a word with her, obviously over some matter that would not wait until Friday.

He stopped when he was about a yard away from her where, even in the shaded lamp of her bedside light, he could see her expression. 'What…?' she began.

'Exactly!' he said. 'What?' Larch stared at him, realising he looked more kind of coaxing than angry. 'What did Paulette say that upset you?'

'You know she was here today?' Larch exclaimed.

'*You* didn't tell me,' he replied. 'Why not, Larch?'

'It—er…' She had been about to lie and say it had slipped her mind, that she had forgotten his stepsister-in-law's visit. But Tye would not swallow that. Paulette was like a whirlwind—blow in, devastate the area—in this case Larch's peace of mind—and, like a whirlwind, blow out again. Nobody would ever forget Paulette! 'Has she just phoned about something?' Larch asked instead, reasoning that since Tye had not known about Paulette's visit at dinner, and since he had not been outside the house since, he must have heard over the phone.

'Miles rang.' Tye corrected her impression it was Paulette who had made the call.

'Hmm,' Larch mumbled, realising that Paulette had come clean about her visit sooner than anticipated. 'Paulette was only here for a brief while...'

'But in that brief while she managed to upset you?'

'Not at all,' Larch denied. 'I found her a very likeable person.'

'She is,' Tye agreed. 'Deep down she is quite a warm and generous woman. Unfortunately, she's a lady whose portion of tact has been substituted by an Olympian-sized ability to constantly put her foot in it.' Larch felt her lips twitch. She noticed there was a hint of a smile on his superb mouth too. 'So tell me, what particular piece of prime tactlessness did Paulette blithely floor you with today?'

'It wasn't that bad!' Larch felt she should deny it, but realised too late that she had just admitted Paulette had floored her with something.

'So?'

Tye was waiting, his smile not making it. And, while Larch had not the smallest intention of giving him a verbatim report, since he did not look likely to budge until she had told him something, she haltingly revealed, 'Paulette assumed that I—that I was—your—mistress.'

'Oh, Larch,' Tye murmured softly. 'I'm sorry. I never...'

'It's not your fault. Apparently Miles doesn't discuss his patients with her, but he inadvertently let her know you had a guest here.'

'Paulette put two and two together and made her usual dozen.'

'I did try to tell her, but—'

'But you couldn't manage to get a word in,' Tye interrupted, as though he knew exactly how it had been. 'I should have thought to warn you just in case she called—people have been known to dive into hedges when they see her coming,' he inserted, bringing a smile to Larch's mouth. 'It just never occurred to me that she would, as Miles put it just now, think to keep an eye on the place. I'll ring her tomorrow and put her right.'

'You don't…'

'Yes, I do,' he contradicted, and Larch warmed to him— then her smile faded, her sensitivity playing nonsense games with her again. Quite plainly Tye did not want anyone believing he was her lover. 'What have I said?' he asked, his eyes reading her every expression.

'Nothing,' Larch lied. 'I just hope you have better luck than I did.'

'Well, I know I'll have to be quick,' he agreed. And there was a teasing note there when he went on, 'Dear Paulette once had a go at scuba-diving—but had to give it up when she found she just couldn't keep her mouth shut under water long enough to—'

Larch burst into spontaneous laughter before he finished. 'You've just made that up!' she accused.

His mouth curved upwards, and she realised he was purposely trying to make her feel happier. He proved it when he said, 'That's better,' and, suddenly taking a step nearer, he reached for her and gathered her in his arms in a hug of comfort.

Larch knew he meant only to comfort her, to sort of make up for all the worried turmoil she had been in ever since Paulette's visit. But feeling his warmth through his shirt, his body so close, Larch all at once started to lose all perspective. All she knew as Tye held her was that after Friday… But she did not want to think about Friday. Did not want to think… Her arms went around his waist, and as he held her, so she held him.

After a few soul-soothing moments she felt him move, as though to stand away from her. But she did not want that. She held on to him. 'My dear,' he said, in a strangled kind of way.

She looked up. Stood in the circle of his arms and looked

up, not backing away. She looked at his mouth, that wonderful mouth, and wanted him to kiss her. She raised her eyes to his, saw his glance flick to her lips—and guessed when his head started to come down that Tye wanted to kiss her too.

He did kiss her. It was a gentle kiss, but a warm kiss too. He pulled back, but his arms were still around her. 'I should let you go,' he murmured.

'No, you shouldn't,' she answered with a shy smile, and loved it when Tye appeared to need no further invitation than that.

Gently he laid his mouth over hers again, and it was wonderful. Her heart raced, and as the pressure of his mouth over hers suddenly started to increase, so he began to draw her closer to him. Willingly, she went.

'You're beautiful,' he murmured against her ear.

Oh, Tye, I love you so much. She held him closer, stretching up to kiss him, feeling his hands on her through the thin covering of her nightwear. Oh, Tye, Tye. She wanted to call his name as he parted her lips with his own, a thrill of pure delight shooting through her when she felt the tip of his tongue on her lips.

'Oh, Tye,' she cried involuntarily.

His answer was to pull back again, as though to check all was well with her. Her answer was to reach up, to kiss him, and to touch his lips with the tip of her tongue.

His response was all she could have hoped for. His arms tightened about her, and then he was kissing her in a way she had never imagined, thrilling her anew as his hands caressed over her back, drawing her yet closer to him.

He held her in the firm hold of one arm while one hand caressed tenderly to the front of her. She made a small swallowing sound when gently he captured one of her breasts. He heard it. 'Are you all right with this?' he asked throatily, sensitive fingers sending her mindless as he teased and tor-

mented the hard peak of her breast. 'Do you want me to
stop? Say now,' he demanded, his tone urgent.

'Don't stop! Don't stop,' she cried, and was glad when
his mouth triumphantly claimed hers again, because she had
so very nearly added just how much she loved him.

She had thought their kisses could not get much more
passionate, but knew she had a lot to learn when the next
time he kissed her he aroused such a vortex of feeling in
her.

She felt her thin wrap fall to the floor and cared not; she
was a willing pupil. He bent and traced feather-light kisses
over her shoulders, moving the fine straps aside from first
one shoulder and then the other. She felt her nightdress start
to slip down and away from her, and experienced a belated
moment of modesty, so clutched at it, holding it to her.

A modesty she forgot a minute later when she knew an
urgent desire to touch his skin. She freed her arms from her
straps and began to unbutton his shirt. 'Am I being forward?' she asked shyly, and he laughed in delight.

'We have been introduced,' he assured her softly, and
undid the rest of the buttons himself.

He had a most magnificent chest, she observed a few
seconds later, her heart drumming in her ears, his shirt now
reposing on the floor. She wanted to kiss his dark hair-
bestrewn, hard-muscled broad chest. And did. 'Oh, Tye,'
she murmured in awe, and just had to taste his nipple.

'Fair's fair,' he breathed as she raised her head, and he
bent to first kiss her lips and trace tender kisses over her
throat and shoulders, then he moved the material of her
nightdress down and took the peak of her left breast inside
his moist mouth.

She was in a no man's land of wanting, pressing against
him, his mouth doing mindless things to her. At which point
her nightdress started to slip, and quickly fell to the floor.
'Tye!' Larch exclaimed faintly, and knew he had picked up

the faint note of panic when he took his lips, his tongue, from her breast and raised his head.

'I'm frightening you?' he queried tenderly.

'No!' she denied. 'No, not at all. It's just…'

And she loved him when he smiled a gentle smile and understood. 'This is all so new to you, isn't it, my darling? And I'm going too fast.'

'It's—it's wonderful—really,' she protested softly.

But he had taken a small step back—small, but far enough that when he glanced down he was able to see her body in its entire nakedness. 'Oh, my dear, dear, Larch. You are exquisite,' he breathed. Then he glanced up to her face— and saw it was aflame with colour. He stared into her eyes, then a dull tide of colour came up under his skin too. 'I'd— better go,' he said, his voice all kind of thick in his throat.

Go! She could not have that. In the next second Larch had covered the small space between them, thrilling anew as her naked breasts touched his bare skin. She pressed closer, her breasts firm against his chest.

'Kiss me!' she whispered, and heard him groan—then his mouth was against hers, one arm around her waist, a hand cupping her buttock, sending her into raptures as he pulled her against him.

She knew then how desperately he wanted her. And it was wonderful, because she wanted him too, quite as desperately. Again he began to part her lips with his, and she clung on to him, mindless of all and anything but the enchanted world that he was taking her to.

Then all at once Tye was breaking that kiss. 'No!' She heard that faint strangled sound, and incredibly he was pulling away from her, his hands coming to her upper arms, gripping her as if he needed some strength, as if he needed something to hold on to. Iron bands clamped on to her, held her from him as he tried not to look down at her delicious breasts, and the sweet curve of her belly, and the magnet of her thighs. 'No!' he said again, and as if trying to convince himself he shook his head. 'No. I'm sorry,' he added on a kind of despairing sound, his hands falling away from her.

And while, open-mouthed, stunned and disbelieving, Larch followed him with her eyes, Tye, not waiting for anything, certainly not pausing for so much as a split second to pick up his shirt, went striding from her room.

CHAPTER EIGHT

IT WAS a long night. By morning Larch knew one thing without fear of contradiction, and that was that Tye—no matter how much his body might have desired her body—had no time for clinging women.

And, remembering just how clinging she had been, Larch wished herself a thousand miles away from Grove House. She recalled how all Tye had meant to do at the start was to give her an unsexual kind of hug because he'd known she was upset. He had even tried to get away, and what had she done? She had only clung onto him, that was all!

She groaned in mortification. 'I should let you go,' he had said. 'No, you shouldn't,' she had replied. Larch buried her head under the bedcovers as though trying to hide from the determined knife-stabbing onslaught of her memories. She was glad she was not going to have to see him until Friday. The way she was feeling—Friday would be too soon.

Unable to rest, Larch sat up and, needing something to cheer her, switched on her bedside lamp. She had two whole days to get herself back together again before she saw Tye. She had an idea that two days would not be nearly enough.

But she did not have even that much time. Because just then there was a knock on her door and, totally unexpectedly, dressed in a business suit and plainly on his way out, possibly to keep some business appointment, Tye came in.

Her heart went into overdrive, and as she recalled the way she had last night stood naked in front of him scorching hot colour burned her skin. Tye came over to her bed, his eyes on her riotous blush, and, looking down at her, 'Hate me?' he asked softly.

And she wished that he hadn't, because it was another instance of why she loved him so much. She was at fault—and he was taking the blame! 'I shall need notice of that question.' She somehow managed a prim note, but found a smile so he should know she was not so much affected.

Tye perched on the edge of her bed and took a hold of her hand. 'I'm not going to apologise,' he said, his grey eyes fixed on hers.

Apologise? Suddenly it came to Larch what he was talking about. He meant did she hate him for making love to her, making her want him so, but only to walk out on her? 'One of us had to be sensible,' she mumbled, but could feel herself going red again.

'Oh, Larch,' Tye said gently. 'Don't be embarrassed. These things happen. But I've more experience—I shouldn't have let it happen.'

How could he blame himself? She had been the one to cling on to him, not the other way around! 'Well, don't let it happen again,' she said severely, and they both laughed, then stilled—and her heart thundered when she thought from the look in his eyes that he was going to kiss her again.

But he did not. He just gave the hand he was holding a squeeze. 'Be good,' he instructed, and, standing, added, 'I'll see you on Friday,' and was gone.

Weak tears sprang to her eyes. He had not been going to kiss her, nor would he ever again. And she loved him, and she would soon be leaving, and she would never see him again—and she couldn't bear it.

Larch showered and dressed with her head filled with thoughts of Tye, with thoughts of how, on Friday, she would leave Grove House for the last time. She would have to tell Tye she was not coming back—though he would know that when he saw her suitcase.

She made her bed and tidied her room—and came near to tears again when she picked up his shirt, the one she had helped to unbutton last night. She held it against her cheek for countless seconds while she strove for control.

Going downstairs, she made a pot of tea and tried to instil in herself some sense of purpose, some kind of energy. Hadn't she decided to spend that morning phoning round to find a bedsit she could move into come Friday? She had little idea of her expected finances, Hazel would be dealing with all that, but, apart from the pittance Neville Dawson had paid her, she had a small amount in her savings account. She would have enough to afford some modest hotel for a week or two if she were unable to find rented accommodation straight away.

Perhaps she would find somewhere in the Hertfordshire area? She was just scolding herself for the thought, for wanting to stay in the same county where Grove House was situated, when someone rang the front doorbell.

Hoping against hope that the caller was not Paulette Phipps—Larch did not think she was up to Paulette's lively chatter that morning; it was only a little after eight, for goodness' sake!—Larch reached the door with Tye in her head again, realising that he might well decide to sell Grove House, so should she opt for Hertfordshire that would rule out any faint possibility of ever accidentally bumping into him anyway.

She pulled open the stout front door and was dumbfounded to see her sister standing there. 'Hazel!' she exclaimed. 'I thought you were in Denmark.' And in the following ten minutes she had something other than Tye to focus on.

'I came home last night,' Hazel replied.

'Come in. Have you had breakfast?'

Hazel shook her head and stepped over the threshold. 'Tye's not here, I suppose?' she asked as they went along the hall towards the kitchen, as if she expected any businessman would be up and on his way to his office by this time.

'He's away on business for a few days,' Larch replied.

In the kitchen she set the kettle to boil and turned to hear Hazel blurt out in a rush, 'I needed to see you urgently. It wouldn't wait.'

'Something's the matter?'

'Not now,' Hazel replied. 'Things have been a little, well, murderous, I suppose you could say. But everything's more or less fine now.' Then quite out of the blue she dropped her bombshell. 'Neville and I are getting divorced,' she said.

'Y...?' Larch stared at her sister in astonishment, trying to take in what she thought she had just heard. 'You're...?'

'I've thrown Neville out!' Hazel announced.

'You've thrown...'

'Well, not physically, and it's going to cost me financially—he refused to go otherwise—but he's gone—went last night, and...' she paused '...you'll be pleased to learn he's not coming back.'

'*I'll* be pleased to learn?' Larch questioned faintly.

'You'll be delighted, or should be,' Hazel said. 'You don't have to pretend any more, love. And—neither do I.'

By then both of them were sitting down and had forgotten all about coffee, tea or breakfast. 'I thought you were—um—head over heels in love with him?' Larch gasped, coping with shock.

'I was one time, but that was so long ago I can barely remember.'

'But...'

Hazel smiled. 'Oh, I know I gave the impression that everything was all right in the Dawson camp. But with Mother so poorly, you looking after her, and Dad little short of demented at the thought of losing her, there was no way I was going to bring my troubles home.'

'Oh, Hazel, has it been so bad?'

'In a word—foul. Not to begin with,' she amended. 'At the beginning we were like two turtledoves. Then the philandering started. At first I couldn't believe it. I was all set to walk out then. But he asked forgiveness and said it would never happen again. I, like a fool, believed him.'

'It did happen again?' Larch asked, starting to get her breath back.

Hazel nodded. 'I don't suppose I heard of every occasion. But in the end it stopped hurting, and I realised I was out of love with him.'

Larch was still feeling staggered, but was trying to keep up with what Hazel was saying. 'But you didn't leave him?'

'He became something of a habit, and at the same time I started to get promoted higher and higher with Berry and Thacker. Besides, leaving him would have meant telling you and our parents, and I reckoned you'd all got enough on your collective plate to be going on with.'

'So you said nothing. You didn't even hint how bad things were.'

Hazel smiled wryly. 'They got worse. About the time Dad died, Neville's secretary came to the apartment and said she was pregnant. No need to guess who the father was. She had an abortion when Neville didn't want to know. But it was kind of the last straw. I knew then that I wanted to finish it. Then Mum died, and while you and I were dealing with our sadness and loss Neville revealed to me the giant hole his business was in.'

'You helped him out by selling the apartment.'

'To be honest, my first inclination was to let him sink. But he'd got a workforce dependent on him.'

'So you sold your lovely apartment and came home to live,' Larch supplied.

'Oh, love, I would never have done that had I known,' Hazel mourned, and looked so pained Larch knew she was truly hurting inside.

'Known?' she queried. 'Known what?'

Hazel gave a sorrowful shake of her head. 'What was I thinking of?' she muttered, clearly blaming herself. 'I knew Neville was not to be trusted with women, but it just didn't occur to me that he'd try out his "charms" on my baby sister.'

'You know about that!' Larch exclaimed, taken totally aback.

'I didn't—not until last night.'

'Does—does that have anything to do with why you're home? I thought you were staying in Denmark until the weekend.'

'I was. Until I rang Neville at his office yesterday. He's taken to sloping off in the evenings and at the weekend, so I rang to ask him to be around on Saturday, telling him that I wanted to have a serious talk with him.'

'He told you yesterday that he had—um—made a pass at me?' Larch asked hesitantly.

'To start with, no. To start with he seemed to guess what I wanted to talk to him about at the weekend. He went all bolshie, but said enough to make me certain that there was no way I was going to wait until the weekend to confront him. I went straight away to see Rune—Rune Pedersen, my head of department in Denmark,' she inserted with a hurried kind of breath. 'Rune arranged for me to catch the first available flight. I got in around the same time as Neville, and straight away told him I wanted a divorce.'

'I don't want you to break your marriage through anything connected with me!' Larch put in quickly.

'I'm not!' Hazel answered just as quickly, and, while Larch was wondering why Hazel suddenly appeared to be a little flushed, she went on to confess, 'Actually, I've—um—met someone else.'

'Hazel!' Larch gasped in astonishment.

'I know. Can you believe it? I never expected it, never thought I would ever fall in love again. But Rune…'

'It's Rune—your head of department in Denmark?'

'It is,' Hazel admitted. 'He's been so supportive. He's been through a divorce himself, so he's aware of the trauma

you endure before you know without a single doubt that
your marriage is over.'

'You know that now?' Larch asked gently.

'I fancy I've known it for a long while. Though at first,
when Rune and I were initially attracted to each other, and
I confessed what a sham my marriage was, I was still
plagued with indecision about what I should do. I knew I
should have phoned you more often, but I didn't want to
risk having to speak to Neville. Nor did I want to come
home at the weekends to spend time with him either, and
blindly—I see that now—I thought you'd be okay during
those weekends I was away in Denmark.'

This, Larch realised, explained why Hazel had appeared
a little distracted when she had last seen her. 'You knew,
when you went back to Denmark three weeks ago, that
you'd be asking Neville for a divorce,' Larch probed gently.

'I imagine I did. I knew for certain anyway, when I got
back and saw Rune again. I knew I didn't want to give up
the sort of peace of mind I'd found with him. Though I have
to say that peace of mind had been badly shattered prior to
my going back when I learned about your accident. But
when I'd rushed here and Tye said something about your
consultant wanting you to have rest and quiet, I realised that,
with hostilities between me and Neville about to turn into
open warfare, it might be better if I kept you away from
that rancorous atmosphere. Better for you if you stayed here
until I'd got it all sorted. Tye seemed OK about it.'

'He's been extremely kind,' Larch replied quietly.

'It's a pity he's not here. Perhaps I'll have a chance to
speak to him on the phone. I should have liked to thank
him in person for the way he has so splendidly put himself
out for you.'

'I—er...' Larch tried, dread starting to enter her heart as,
shaken to the core, she realised what lay behind her sister's
words.

'Shall I come and help you pack?' Hazel asked, confirming the worst.

'I'm—leaving here?' Larch questioned, her voice little more than a whisper even as she tried to hide just how completely devastated she suddenly felt.

'Oh, love, there's no need for you to worry,' Hazel said quickly, totally misinterpreting the reluctance to leave to be heard in Larch's voice. 'I told you, Neville is no longer back home. He moved out last night. I'll have to take out a mortgage on my share of the house to pay him off, but it will be worth it. When I think of him making a play for you, the...'

'He told you about it?'

'At first, no. When I rang from Denmark yesterday, to tell him I'd something to discuss this weekend, I also told him that I was hoping to have you back home by then.' This was news to Larch, but she realised that Hazel would have been thinking along the lines that once she had been pronounced fit by Miles Phipps on Friday there would no longer be any need for her to remain at Grove House. 'I told Neville that I didn't want you to be involved in any unpleasantness, and that I wanted our conversation to be away from the house. Anyhow, he must have suspected I intended to ask for a divorce, and he got nasty and determined he wasn't going to make it easy for me. He started by saying that you weren't the goody-goody I thought you were. That the real reason you were no longer working for him was because he'd sacked you after you'd gone to our bedroom one night and propositioned him.'

Larch was appalled. 'He said that!'

'Don't worry. I know him and you too well to believe that,' Hazel assured her. 'He's incapable of rejecting that sort of proposition. But I straight away began to fear that something had happened. Which, when I turned what he had said on its head, could mean only that *he* had come to your room one night and that *he* had propositioned you. I came home at once.'

'I'm sorry,' Larch apologised.

'Don't be.' Hazel smiled. 'I'd already made up my mind to end things between him and me, but had I not done so that would have clinched it. Up until then I was having pangs of guilt that I was in love with Rune and not my husband. But the moment Neville eventually admitted—and only then because he knew I would ask you if he didn't—that he'd angrily come to your room and—a polite word for it—attempted to seduce you, ice entered my heart. So—' she smiled suddenly '—ready to go?'

'I...' Larch hesitated. Even then, even when she knew that it was the answer—she would not even have to go and find herself a bedsit, but could go home—she hesitated.

'Don't you want to come home?' Hazel teased, seeing her hesitation. Then she realised what might be the reason for it. 'You think Tye will be offended when he comes back and finds you have left without saying a word?'

And that was when Larch bucked her ideas up. Only a short while ago Hazel had referred to how Tye had 'put himself out' for her. And Larch knew that he had, very much so. Were it not for her he would be residing in his London home and going about his normal social occupations.

'I'll write him a note,' Larch said with a smile, a knife twisting in her at the thought of him resuming his normal social occupations—a jealous knife. 'Jane will be here shortly. Can we wait until Jane gets here?'

'Of course we can.'

'You're not rushing back to Denmark?'

'No need,' Hazel replied, smiling. 'I've a few days' leave of absence. It was late by the time Neville left last night, too late for me to ring you, but Rune was waiting for my call. He's coming to England for the weekend.'

It took Larch an age to write her letter to Tye. She did

not want to leave, and felt she was bleeding inside. But with her sister now at home, and her brother-in-law not, from whichever way Larch looked at it she did not appear to have even the remotest excuse for staying. Eventually she wrote:

Dear Tye,

Hazel paid me an unexpected visit this morning—I thought she was still in Denmark. More unexpectedly, she called to say that she is divorcing Neville Dawson and that he has left our home. Which means I can now return there without cause for anxiety. Naturally I cannot leave without first thanking you so much for bringing me to Grove House and, with Jane, giving me such super care. I'm afraid I wasn't always an easy guest.

She still blushed when she thought of the way she had gone to his room that dreadful night and climbed into his bed—he must privately have been having forty fits.

But I honestly don't know what I would have done without you.

My warmest thanks, Larch.

She was not satisfied with what she had written, but knew that she could spend the whole morning in trying to compose something that showed him her gratitude but hid her love, and she still would not be satisfied. She went to his bedroom to leave her note, and felt tears close again when she glanced to the bed and flooding back came the memory of how she had awakened with Tye's arms around her. She recalled again those waking moments when she had felt safe and so secure. Everything had seemed so right then—everything so wrong now.

Jane, when she arrived, was surprised at the news that she was leaving, and gave her a warm hug. 'Thank you for...' Larch began.

'It was my pleasure.' Jane beamed, and came to wave them off.

Larch had always been the best of friends with her sister, but as she drove them home Larch was glad that Hazel had too much on her mind to want to talk very much.

With her thoughts mainly with Tye, Larch somehow got through the next twenty-four hours.

'Are you all right, Larch?' Hazel asked at one stage on Thursday. 'You're very quiet.'

'So are you,' Larch replied lightly.

'That's a point.' Hazel laughed. 'Does it show—that my thoughts are somewhere the other side of the North Sea?'

Larch smiled. 'Only a little,' she replied.

'You'll like him,' Hazel said. 'Rune,' she added, just in case there was any doubt about whom she was referring to. 'As it happens, you having your medical check-up in a London clinic will work out very well. We can go on from there to the airport to collect Rune tomorrow.'

'I—er—was thinking of cancelling my appointment,' Larch stated, wanting to see Miles, when he might mention Tye, while at the same time not wanting to hear him mention Tye's name in case he caught her at an unguarded moment and she somehow revealed her inner feelings. Larch owned she was feeling exceedingly vulnerable just then.

'No way!' her sister objected, but softened her words with a smile when she went on, 'When I think of how you nursed and cared for our mother, *and* kept the home going, then I think it's more than high time somebody looked after you.'

Somebody had looked after her, looked after her unbelievably well. Oh, Tye. 'But I'm fine now,' she said quickly. 'There's no need...'

'I don't think you fully realise just how traumatised you've been!' Hazel butted in firmly. 'Apart from your accident, you were still rocking from Mum and Dad, and that was before Neville came on to you. From what I've discovered, Miles Phipps has a first-class reputation. Keep your appointment. To please me, if nothing else?' she asked. 'I promise, once he says you're completely fit, we'll put everything behind us and we'll both start off afresh.'

Oh, that it was so simple. Larch wanted to look forward and not back, but it just wasn't that easy! How could she think of the future when Tye dominated almost her every thought? She did not want to dwell on the past, but time and again she remembered things he had said, things they had done together.

Just a simple walk with him had been magical. Driving through the countryside with Tye at the wheel so wonderful. 'You belong to me' he had told her once—oh, how she wished that were true and not said just from kindness because, back then, she'd had no one to belong to.

With a void in her heart, an ache for Tye, regret in her every step that she had ever left Grove House, Friday at last dragged its way into being. Larch knew that to leave Grove House had been her only option, for goodness' sake. Pride demanded that she did not become a burden to Tye and outstay her welcome, but pride did not make her feel any the less heartsore.

He would return home that morning, and she felt guilty that, but for her, he would probably have stayed where he was, working somewhere.

After an early lunch, Hazel appeared anxious to be on their way to the clinic. In love herself, Larch fully appreciated that her sister was probably counting the minutes until she saw Rune again. But, having started out early, they were way too early at the clinic for Larch's appointment.

With neither of them wanting to bother with refreshments, they waited in the car until nearer her appointment time, which gave Larch an opportunity to discuss something she had been mulling over in an attempt to stop thinking of Tye every other minute.

'I've been thinking, Hazel,' she began.

'Dangerous territory,' Hazel quipped, plainly feeling on top of the world.

'The thing is, I can't imagine that you'll want to stay permanently living at home if Rune is living in Denmark.'

Hazel was silent for a second or two, but, looking over to her, confessed, 'I was going to save this conversation until after you'd seen Miles Phipps today, but since you've brought it up—I've decided to apply for a transfer to Denmark. That doesn't—'

'It's the obvious thing to do,' Larch butted in. 'What I've thought,' she went on, 'is that since I shan't want to live in that big house on my own, we could sell it and—'

'Are you serious?' Hazel interrupted in surprise.

Larch nodded. 'I'm not sure what training I want to do yet, but if the college I choose is out of the area, then I could buy a small flat with my half, and—'

'You're not suggesting this purely so I won't have to go into debt to pay Neville off?' Hazel took her turn, in the way sisters have, to butt in.

That too had figured in Larch's thoughts. It seemed criminal to her that when Neville had been such an awful husband Hazel was going to have to go into debt for a huge mortgage before she could find happiness in her new beginnings.

'It just isn't logical for me to stay in that big house on my own,' Larch answered. 'I wouldn't want to.'

'You could come to Denmark and live with Rune and me,' Hazel suggested at once.

'I'll come and see you as often as I can,' Larch replied, and would not be persuaded to make her proposed visits any more permanent than that.

What she wanted—really, really wanted—was to live where Tye lived, be it Grove House or his London address. She sighed hopelessly, then, when she saw Hazel glance swiftly to her, she beamed a smile.

'Let's go and see if Miles is running early,' she suggested.

They found that in actual fact he was running late. 'I'm terribly sorry, Mr Phipps had to deal with an urgent emergency. He's running about three quarters of an hour behind time,' the woman on the desk apologised.

Larch was all for cancelling her appointment, but Hazel would not hear of it. 'We'll wait,' she said firmly.

'But it might make you late getting to the airport!' Larch reminded her.

Hazel did look a shade pulled two ways, but insisted, 'We'll wait.'

The three quarters of an hour delay proved to be out by fifteen minutes, and it had gone four by the time a nurse came and took Larch in to see Miles Phipps. 'Larch,' he greeted her pleasantly. 'You're looking so much better. Come and tell me how you've been.'

For all he was by then running well over an hour late, he appeared in no hurry whatsoever. And it was a full half an hour later that he completed every one of his very detailed tests. Then he shook her by the hand.

'You've made a splendid recovery,' he pronounced. And he smiled a lovely warm smile as he charmingly added, 'Regrettably, it will not be necessary for me to see you again.'

Larch smiled back. He had not mentioned Tye, this man who was her last link with the man she loved. She did not mention Tye either. 'Goodbye,' she said, and thanked Miles, and went from his office knowing that, having just been discharged as his patient, having been declared fit, she should be in high spirits—when in actual fact her spirits were somewhere down on the floor.

She wanted Tye. She wanted him to be there. She wanted to be able to tell him that his stepbrother had just deleted her name from his clinic list. That, fit once more, her case papers would now be filed permanently away.

Oh, Tye. She loved him so, and by now he had probably read her note, and was no doubt very much relieved that, by leaving, she had saved him the chore of driving her to Roselands clinic today.

She swallowed hard, then raised her head a fraction before turning the corner and going into the waiting room where, some thirty minutes or so ago, she had left Hazel.

There were several people in the various chairs in the waiting room. But Hazel was not amongst them. Realising that, with time going on, Hazel was most likely in the car park with the car engine running, Larch picked up speed and went hurrying towards the outer swing doors.

But only to almost cannon in to a tall, dark-haired man who was about to come in. 'S...' she began to apologise. But as she looked up, so her apology never made it. 'T-Tye!' she stammered, scarlet colour flooding her face, her heart at once thundering.

'Hello, Larch,' he replied calmly, and, placing a hand on her arm, he helped her free of the door and to the outside. And there, as nice as you please, he bent and placed a light kiss on her cheek, and, looking down at her, stood back to ask, 'What have you got to tell me?'

CHAPTER NINE

'WHAT are you doing here?' Larch gasped, and, still flushed from the emotion of seeing him again, not to mention his unexpected kiss, felt herself going red again as the answer to that question came rushing at her. 'Of course—you've come to see Miles. He's running late. He...' She stopped. She was gabbling—and Tye still had a hold of her arm. 'I left you a note,' she said, and felt hot all over at the inadequacy of that remark. 'Hazel's in the car park,' she added, and determined that henceforth she would shut up.

But, 'She isn't,' Tye replied evenly.

'She isn't?'

'We said hello. I was able to explain, that running late or not, Miles would still insist on giving you a very detailed final check. Your sister seemed a little anxious to be at the airport,' Tye informed her blandly. 'Apparently she has a date with a very special Dane.' Larch stared at him wordlessly—Hazel had confided in him about Rune Pedersen? But Larch's surprises were not yet over when Tye followed up with, 'Hazel knew she could trust me when I suggested if she wanted to go that I would give you a lift home.'

Larch's mouth fell open. 'Oh, I couldn't let you!' she exclaimed quickly.

'Why couldn't you?'

She was momentarily stumped. 'Because...well, you've already done so much for me. And—and Warren End is miles out of your way.' Larch got herself more together. 'I can get a train and—'

'And put me in your sister's bad books for ever?' he cut in.

Larch looked at him, and loved him, and because she

168

loved him and had missed him so much she could not hold out any longer. She gave in, and went with him to the car park. She knew she was being greedy, but she could not resist this unthought chance to spend a little more time with the man who held her heart. Involuntarily her hand went to the cheek he had kissed, and she was entranced for a moment. That kiss of greeting had seemed almost as if, pleased to see her, he could not hold back on the impulse.

Rats, said her saner self, and as they reached his car and he opened the passenger door for her she knew she was going to have to guard against such weird thoughts. 'Er— Hazel would have waited,' Larch felt a need to say when Tye came round and got in beside her.

'Without question she would,' he agreed, and paused for a second or two, then added evenly, 'As a matter of fact, though, I rather wanted to have a word or two with you.'

Larch turned to look at him. 'What about?' she asked, but he was busy switching on the ignition and did not appear to have heard. And, since he seemed to be concentrating on getting his long sleek car out of the overcrowded car park without mishap, she did not repeat her question.

The traffic was heavy, and rather than distract him in any small way she stayed silent while he negotiated the route. She was unfamiliar with London streets, but when some ten minutes later she began anticipating that Tye would shortly be making for the motorway, she was a little surprised when he drove into the forecourt of a very imposing-looking apartment block.

She looked questioningly at him. 'I need to stop and pick something up,' he said by way of explanation.

'You—is this where you live?'

'Come up,' he invited. 'I shouldn't be too long, but then again…' He left the words in the air and, having been prepared to wait for him in the car, she picked up a hint there that he might be delayed—perhaps taking an unexpected phone call or something—and could do no other than give in to the sudden urge to see inside his apartment. She could not expect to see him after today, she knew, but it would be a bonus to be able to imagine him inside his apartment. Perhaps relaxing, unwinding after a busy day. Maybe reading his newspaper…

'All right,' she agreed, and went with him into the smart building, and into the lift with him up to the top floor.

He showed her into his high-ceilinged, elegant, uncluttered drawing room. There were a couple of oil paintings on one wall, a couple of sofas, a couple of well-padded chairs, low tables—she was glad she had seen the room.

'Have a seat,' Tye invited, seeming in no hurry at all to collect what he had come for. Larch went to the nearest seat, a sofa, and for no reason all at once felt a degree nervous. She did not know why. She would trust Tye with her life. Perhaps it was that small sense of tension that was in the air. 'Would you like some tea?' he asked nicely, proof if she needed it that he had no immediate hurry.

Larch relaxed a little, and even smiled at Tye, realising that he must be aware that, for all there was a small restaurant at the clinic, that she had been hanging around for ages that afternoon without refreshment.

'Let me make it,' she volunteered, grateful for any chance to spend a few more minutes with him. 'You've been working and—'

'I took the day off,' Tye interrupted.

'Oh!' That took her a little aback. 'You've—um—been busy, though, I expect.'

'You could say that,' he replied, and to her surprise, instead of heading to either the kitchen or to go and collect what they were there for, he came and took a chair close by. 'I worked until the early hours this morning,' he said.

'Oh,' she murmured again, and as her brain slowly woke up she began to associate the word 'work' with something else he had said. 'You said you wanted to have a word or two with me,' she remembered, and her heart suddenly started to race—was he going to offer her a job after all? Oh, for the chance to see him occasionally when he was at his office...

'That's true,' he agreed, but paused for long moments, strangely as though choosing his words very carefully. Then he said, 'I was surprised to read your note on Wednesday.'

She hadn't expected that, and pushed her shining blonde hair back from her face in a nervous kind of gesture. 'You read...' Her voice dried. 'On Wednesday? You went back to Grove House on Wednesday?' Her lovely blue eyes widened. 'I didn't think you were going back there until today?'

'That was my original intention,' he accepted, his grey eyes steady on her, watching, taking in, reading. Swiftly she lowered her eyes. But hurriedly raised them to stare in disbelief when he continued, 'But when nobody seemed to be around when several times I rang Grove House, I thought I had better contact Jane Harris.'

'Oh, Tye. Jane told you I'd gone with Hazel. But...' Larch hesitated. 'You didn't leave your work because of me? Of course you didn't,' she contradicted, at once feeling foolish.

Though she felt more speechless than foolish when he confirmed, 'I did.' She stared wordlessly at him, and he went on, 'I couldn't believe you had gone—just like that.'

'You—read the note I left, you said.'

Tye gave an impatient movement, and then half terrified her by saying shortly, 'I thought there was more between us than some polite little letter.'

He knows! He knows I'm in love with him! Larch looked swiftly away from him, realising that the tension she had felt earlier came solely from her, and her fear that he might see the love she had for him.

'You didn't get to see M-Miles today?' she said, rapidly changing the subject, ready then to latch on to anything other than her and Tye and what was between them. Without a doubt he was referring to the way she had clung on to him on Tuesday night.

'I didn't need to see Miles.'

'Oh,' she murmured, unsure what to make of that. Surely, had Miles not been running so late with his outpatients clinic, Tye would have waited around to discuss whatever it was he had gone to the clinic to see him about. 'You'll be glad to know I was discharged as perfectly fit today,' she offered brightly.

'I know,' Tye replied. And that caused her to look at him again.

'You know?' she questioned. And, her brain on the meddle again, 'How do you know? Even Hazel doesn't know y—'

'At the risk of Miles being thought unethical—though I have to say there is a great deal he and I would do for each other—Miles rang my mobile, where I was stationed at Roselands entrance, the second you left his office.'

Larch stared at Tye open-mouthed. 'You...' She tried again. 'You arranged with him that he should ring you...'

'You obviously didn't want me to come with you today.'

'Oh, Tye. It wasn't like that!' she protested. Had she, by leaving the way she had, hurt his feelings? Surely not! But her brain, that always had sought to know more, was on the search again. 'You weren't there to—at the clinic—to see Miles?' she asked slowly. 'But...' her heartbeats were suddenly thundering '...but to see me?'

He did not deny it. 'I knew you'd be there.'

He had been there purposely to see her! Her hand went nervously to her hair again. 'How?' she asked, a dozen and one things starting to chase around in her head. 'How did you know I'd be there? I didn't want to go,' she admitted. 'I was all for cancelling my appointment with Miles.'

'Your sister would never allow you to miss your appointment,' Tye remarked confidently.

Larch looked at him sitting there, leaning slightly forward, his eyes on nowhere but her. How dear he was to her. But this would never do! Somehow she found a cheery note. 'Well, I'd better start making tracks for Warren End!' she said. She would have got to her feet then, only so smoothly, and without apparent haste, before she could do more than collect her bag from the side of her, Tye had left his chair and was all at once sitting next to her.

Then, while she was feeling pink, red, all colours, he had taken a hold of her right hand and was preventing her from going anywhere. 'We haven't had our—discussion yet,' he said calmly.

She wished she could feel as calm. 'D-discussion?' she stammered. And, managing to get herself a little under control, 'This is the word or two you wanted to have with me?'

'I never intended our talk to be all one-way,' he replied, his tone a tinge warmer, she rather thought, though she would not be surprised if she had that wrong. With Tye sitting so near, it seemed to be closing down her thinking capability.

'W-what's the subject?' she queried, somehow thinking it would be better if she hadn't asked, but her curiosity choosing that moment to want to have its twopenny worth.

Tye looked at her, his grip on her hand firming—every bit as if he was the one feeling tense and not her. 'Us,' he very clearly said.

Had she been free there was every chance she would have bolted. But her right hand was held firmly in his grip and it did not look as if he was going to allow her to bolt anywhere in a hurry. 'Us?' she echoed faintly. And, because he was good and kind, and because she had no option, 'Oh, Tye, there is no us,' she said. She thought he went a little pale, but she wasn't taking heed of her imagination just then. Tye had been so wonderful to her, but she was nothing to him. 'I know I was a bit clingy on Tuesday night.' She went red, 'Well, a lot clingy, actually, when we—you know. But you don't have to be kind to me and—'

'Who the hell's being kind?' he cut in, startling her by his sudden aggressiveness.

'You've seen—' She broke off with a catch of breath. Oh, my stars, she had so nearly told him that she loved him!

'I've seen quite a lot.' He took over when she abruptly ran out of words. 'I've seen you ill, scared, brave, proud. I've seen *you* kind, and I have wanted to do all I could for you...'

'Tye, you did!' she exclaimed urgently. 'I've put you to so much trouble.'

'No, you haven't,' he denied.

But she was not having that. 'When I think of how I got into your bed that night—' she began for starters, but was again interrupted by him.

'Something you would never dream of doing had I not given you the impression that we lived together and that you were no stranger to my bed,' Tye cut in, his aggression suddenly gone.

Larch looked at him, glad he wasn't angry with her any more; she did not want him angry with her. 'Can we be friends?' she asked.

'I'd like that,' he answered, and, while that pleased her, she thought she had better go now. But when she again went to gather up her bag prior to leaving, 'Not yet,' Tye said quietly.

'I don't want—' she began, above all not wanting him to know that she was hopelessly in love with him.

But he was again cutting in. 'And what about what I want?' he asked quietly.

And Larch dropped her bag and turned and looked into his steady grey eyes. Were it in her power she would give him anything in the world he wanted. 'What is it you want?' she asked—and was stunned by his reply.

Though first he took a long drawn breath, and then, his other hand coming to take a hold of her left hand, he looked deeply into her eyes. 'You,' he said. 'I want you, Larch.'

Wordlessly, barely breathing, she stared at him. Her brain seemed to have seized up. 'You don't,' she denied huskily.

'I do.' His look was unflinching.

'But, but...' She took a steadying breath. 'But on Tuesday, when we...' She faltered again. 'You could have... You know I would have—um—made love with you. Only you didn't want to.'

His amazement was obvious. 'Are you mad?' he asked incredulously. 'Didn't want to! Ye gods, I was desperate for you!'

'Desperate? You—were?'

'You *must* have known I—' He broke off. 'Oh, my dear,' he said softly, 'You had no idea in your innocence of what it took me to break away from you that night.'

She stared at him, feeling slightly stunned. 'I th-thought I'd been too clinging,' she said faintly.

'Clinging? You?'

'Paulette said something about—'

'Oh, Larch,' Tye cut in. 'Much as I am very fond of my stepsister-in-law, would you now, and in the future, take most of what she babbles on about with the proverbial grain of salt?'

Now *and* in the future! Larch was starting to grow confused, so decided to concentrate solely on what Tye was saying—subject: us. 'But...' She was about to argue, then changed it to, 'I wasn't clinging? I thought I was. You said you should let me go, only I wouldn't let you.'

'I haven't forgotten. In fact—' his look was deadly serious '—in fact,' he continued, 'thinking about the way you were with me had me awake most of that night.'

'Because—you wanted to make love with me?' she asked, feeling not a little fog-bound.

'That, of course,' he agreed. 'But more particularly I spent many wakeful night hours wanting to believe, yet being afraid to believe, that you were perhaps just a little...'

he paused '…in love with me…' His grip on her hands was firm when she would have jerked out of his hold.

'Well, of course I'm fond of you,' she said hurriedly, borrowing his word for his feelings for his stepsister-in-law in a panicky rush of defence. 'Who wouldn't have grown fond of you in the circumstances?'

She thought that he again briefly lost some of his colour, but she was inwardly panicking too wildly to know anything for sure but that she should never have been so weak as to have got into his car. Greed, that was what it had been. She had greedily given in to her need to spend more time with him.

But Tye was shaking his head. 'No,' he said.

'No?' she echoed, her throat more than a touch dry.

'It has to be more than that.'

Fondness, did he mean? 'I'm sorry,' she apologised, hoping he would think she was sorry she could not be a little in love with him.

His eyes were fixed on her as he studied her, and she began to feel nervous again. It was as though he was trying to see into her very soul. And she could not have that. Though when she would have said something, said anything to break the silence, Tye shook his head. 'No,' he said again. 'I have spent more time than you can know over these last few days dissecting every word, every look, every nuance that has passed between us.' He gave her hands a small shake. 'I can't believe—'

'I don't want this conversation!' Larch cut in bluntly, inwardly drowning in panic.

But his study of her was unrelenting. Then all at once a hint of a smile tugged at the corners of his mouth. 'I'm scaring you?' he asked, every bit as though he had just discerned exactly what she was scared about—his guessing at so much as the tiniest bit of love she had for him.

'I think I'll go home now,' she stated shortly. Only found,

when his hands came to her arms, that she was going nowhere until he was ready.

'Don't be alarmed. There's nothing to be afraid of,' Tye
promised her soothingly.

She wished she could believe that, but since she could
not get away without some undignified push and shove, she
did the only thing possible. 'I'm not interested in your lies!'
She went into the attack.

'Lies!' He seemed surprised.

'You wanted to make love to me but, as desperate as you
were, you calmly walked away that night.'

'*Calmly!* My recollection of it is that I bolted while I still
could.'

'A likely tale!' she jibed, though clearly recalled that he
had left his shirt behind, he had been in such a hurry to go.

That hint of a smile was coming to the corners of his
mouth again, every bit as if he had just seen through her
attack and had recognised it for what it was—an attempt to
put him off. 'You're not going to make this easy for me,
are you, sweetheart?' he questioned gently.

She almost softened on the spot at his tone, never mind
the bone-melting 'sweetheart'. 'You're blaming all this on
me—and I hardly know what all this *is*,' she burst out chokily. 'Other than it's all to do with you wanting me, but
denying your need. I...'

'How could I do anything other?' he asked.

And that made her cross. 'There you are, confusing me
again!' she exclaimed. 'I'd rather have answers than questions—if you don't mind.'

'You shall have anything it's in my power to give you,'
Tye replied, and she wished her imagination would behave,
because she distinctly thought she saw a certain kind of
tenderness in his eyes.

'That sounds promising!' How she managed to answer so
snappily, when what she wanted to do was to throw herself

at him and ask him to hold her, she did not know. But what he said next almost had her in a state of total collapse.

For he smiled, and then he tenderly, definitely tenderly, said, 'Forgive me if I'm going about this all the wrong way, but you have wound your way into my heart, Larch Burton, and it has rather messed up my previous, prior to knowing you, totally logical way of thinking.'

Absolutely thunderstruck, she stared at him. 'Er—well, maybe I will st-stay a little bit longer,' she conceded with what voice she could find. And was glad she was sitting down when he leaned forward and placed a light kiss on the corner of her mouth.

That was when her voice went completely, and, feeling all of a tremble, all she was capable of was just to sit there and stare at him. Had he *really* said that she had wound her way into his heart?

'You really are the most beautiful delight to me,' Tye said softly, and kissed the other corner of her mouth before pulling back. 'You're distracting me again,' he charged, then seemed to get himself more together, muttering, 'Logical order,' and, while she was still looking a touch staggered at him, he began, 'So there was I, at the hospital to see Miles, when you were wheeled in.'

'This is going back to…'

'To when I first saw you, beautiful, broken and bloodied, but not as broken as I at first thought. Poor love, you did look in a state. Then, when I promise you I seldom do anything without considered thought, I find that under the pretext of going to the hospital to see Miles I'm going to the hospital to check on your progress.'

'You came more than once.'

'I became a regular visitor. As we both know, your only visitor.'

'You still came to visit me—even when I came out of the coma,' Larch said, her heart racing, seeming to stop, start, and race on again.

Tye grinned self-deprecatingly. 'I naturally told myself I was only going to see you so I should get my grandmother's ring back.' His grin faded. 'Then we realised you had lost your memory, and such a feeling of wanting to keep you safe came over me that, when you asked, "Am I engaged to you?", looking so lost and alone—you had no one—I just wanted you to have someone. There was simply no way I could tell you no. There was no way either,' he added, 'that, while I admit I didn't quite trust what was happening to me, I was going to let you leave the clinic to adjust to a life with no memory with anyone but me.'

'Oh, Tye,' she whispered. He didn't trust what was happening to him? What? What was it that he did not trust? She was impatient suddenly to learn. But so far her confusion had cleared, and she did not want it to return, so thought perhaps she had better let things go at the pace he set.

'When Miles agreed I might take you to the peace and quiet of Grove House, I said I would keep in close touch with him.'

'You rang him…?'

'Constantly,' Tye replied. 'I almost got him out of bed that night when things were at their very darkest for you and you came flying into my room. While it was continually in my head that for all I knew you might be married or be in some serious relationship, I had to quickly decide whether to try and calm you myself or ring Miles and wait for him to arrive. Your need seemed more urgent than to wait. I gave in to my need to cradle you better. I thought I had made the right decision when at last you started to relax and finally fell asleep.'

'And when I woke up my memory was back,' she supplied.

'Your memory had returned, and before I knew it you were talking of how you'd disrupted my household, disrupted my work,' he reminded her, but was gripping her firmly when he added, 'And I didn't feel it appropriate at that time to mention just how much you had disrupted—me.'

Larch blinked, her eyes widening. 'Er…' was as far as she could manage. 'Um—how do you mean?' She got a little farther.

'For one,' he began without hesitation, 'you seemed to be forever talking of leaving.'

'Forever?' she challenged mildly.

'I was sensitive on the subject,' he said with a grin. 'You said you had no hold on me, but, my dear, you had.' And, while her heart started to furiously race again, 'A hold on my heart,' he said softly.

'Oh, Tye,' Larch whispered shakily, and didn't feel any less shaky when he placed a tender kiss on her lovely mouth.

'What's a man to do?' he asked. 'You're there in my head the whole time, yet you're talking of leaving.'

'You found me a job putting those books on the computer,' she reminded him, having to latch on to something factual while she coped with the fact that Tye had said she had a hold on his heart.

'Which you at first declined.'

'Until you blackmailed me into staying.'

'I certainly wasn't going to allow you to return to your brother-in-law's orbit,' Tye said forthrightly. But he was gentle when he asked, 'You have me where you want me, Larch Burton, so what are you going to do about it?'

She smiled; she loved him so. And he had actually said she had a hold on his heart. She had heard him say it. 'I'm not terribly sure,' she answered, and loved him enough to dare to confess, 'I have—er—grown to be quite—er—um—care for you.'

'Care?' he took up, his eyes on hers. 'Care as in, it's burning a hole in your gut? That kind of caring?'

Her lips parted in surprise. 'You—know the feeling?'

'It's a feeling I live with,' he answered, and added those two magical words, 'for you.'

'Oh, Tye,' she murmured tremulously, and was drawn suddenly into the circle of his arm.

Her heart was beating so she could hardly breathe. And when Tye looked deeply into her lovely blue eyes and said, 'I love you, my darling,' she felt on the point of collapse. He loved her! He loved her. Had he actually said those three wonderful words? He bent and kissed her. She did not resist and, perhaps heartened that she did not, Tye pulled back and asked, 'Can you tell me now if it's possible you love me a little?'

'You know,' she answered shyly.

He shook his head. 'Trust me. I need to hear it. Need to hear you say it.'

She looked at him, her heart in her eyes. 'Little is such a puny word.' Shyly, she added, 'Tye, I love you with all of my heart.'

Larch was not conscious of time passing when in the next five minutes he held her close, kissed her, still holding her close. Then it seemed he just had to look into her face. Look into her face and kiss and hold her again. And Larch, such joy in her heart that Tye loved her in return, held him and returned his kisses, marvelling at his love for her, and that she no longer had to hide her love for him.

But it was Tye, finally leaning back to let daylight between them, who commented, 'I can hardly believe this. I've been half off my head about you, and here you are...'

'Have you? Been half off your head?' she whispered, totally enthralled.

'You have no idea.'

Her smile beamed. Was this really, really happening? 'When...? Why...?'

'When did I start loving you? Why? Where do I start?' He paused to kiss her and to cradle her lovingly against him. 'It began with my heart giving a leap the very first time I laid eyes on you. It could be—and was, I assured myself—totally because I was unused to seeing road traffic accident victims at such close quarters. Then, when I continued to come to the hospital to personally check on your progress, there started to grow in me such a fierce feeling of wanting to protect you. And from there I found I wanted to be with you, to talk to you—to be your companion, if you like. Then one day at Grove House you asked, ''Do I belong to someone?''. And while I fully appreciated just how very dreadful it must be for you to have absolutely no memory of family or friends, I knew right then that it did not matter who you were. You were mine and I was in love with you.'

Larch clearly remembered it. It was shortly after he had taken her to Grove House. 'You've loved me since then?' she asked in wonderment.

'I've been enchanted by you,' he confessed. 'I nearly told you as much that Sunday we took a walk around the village. I just couldn't stop myself from kissing you. And for my sins made myself scarce the next week, while I tried to get myself under control. By then, sweet love, I found that my love for you included a need to hold you in my arms, to kiss and embrace you. Which meant that the only way I could cope was to not let you get close. I came home at the end of that week…'

'It was a Friday, two weeks ago,' Larch recalled without effort. 'You were a pig,' she said lovingly.

'Oh, I was,' he thoroughly agreed. 'Until I saw I had upset you. I came after you and held you in my arms—and wanted to hold you like that for evermore.'

'Why couldn't you?'

'You loved me then?'

'I loved you then,' Larch answered.

'When? Since when?' he demanded.

'Since that day I got my memory back,' she answered instantly. 'We were having dinner that night, you and me, and—I just knew I was in love with you. It was just there, and whether I wanted it or not it was not going to go away.'

'Oh, my darling,' he murmured, and held her close up against him while he lingeringly kissed her. Her heart was pounding anew when Tye pulled back. 'That's why,' he said.

'That's why what?' she asked, completely mesmerised by the warmth of feeling, that hint of passion in his kiss.

'You asked why couldn't I hold you for ever,' he reminded her. 'That's why. You still had two weeks to go before you saw Miles—I was beginning to feel the strain.'

'Oh, love,' she whispered.

'It was only a week later that I was kissing you again, while at the same time assuring you that I would never take advantage of your innocence.'

'You are a spoilsport,' she teased, and loved it that she could.

'Talk like that is going to get you into very serious trouble,' he threatened with a humorous growl, but went on, 'It was around then that my normal logical thinking processes started to become clouded.'

'*Clouded?*' she repeated. Tye struck her as a man whose thought processes never got fogged up. 'I know I've been up to my neck in confusion, but—you?'

'With what logic I could find, I had to make a decision,' he answered. 'I knew I loved you, and that I wanted you, but I had to decide not to do anything about it until Miles said you were completely recovered, completely well.'

'You wanted to hear that I was fully well before…'

'Before I could set about asking you out—not as my house guest but as my woman-friend. My intention had been to come with you today to see Miles, and as soon as he gave you a clean bill of health we'd go out for that celebratory dinner and I would begin my courting campaign.'

'Oh, Tye!' Larch sighed. 'And I ruined it for you by leaving Grove House!'

'And left me wondering if my plan to give you "personal" attention was ever going to get off the ground. What if you did not want my personal attention? It looked very much as if you didn't. And yet I just couldn't let you disappear out of my life.'

Larch stared at him open-mouthed. By the sound of it Tye had been in the same stewed-up world that she had. 'But you knew on Tuesday night, when, despite what you say, I did cling on to you, that I was—er—receptive.'

'Oh, my darling,' he breathed. 'When I left your room that night...'

'Why did you?' she asked, going a pretty shade of pink and adoring him when, seeing her colour, he smiled a tender smile. 'I mean, if *you* didn't think I was clinging...'

'I had to leave you, my love,' Tye said gently. 'I'd not many days before assured you I would never take advantage of you, yet there you were, inexperienced, in my arms—and still had a medical check to go through. Your health seemed fine to me—but what did I know? I wasn't trained to spot any small—'

'Oh, my poor love,' she interrupted softly. 'All that went through your head while you were telling me you had better go?'

He nodded. 'It was a torturous night,' he owned. 'But as I went through everything that was between us, every wonderful facet I knew of you, I suddenly began to hope. And all at once I was torn between wanting to believe, and being afraid to believe, what all my instincts were telling me.'

'That I might love you a little?'

His arms tightened around her. 'I tried to scoff at the notion, but again and again I seemed to come to the same conclusion. You didn't hate me; that was fairly certain.'

'You asked if I hated you when you came to my room on Wednesday morning,' she reminded him with a loving smile.

'I was unsure of my reception,' he said with a grin. 'Part

of me wanted to tell you straight away how it was with me, while at the same time I was afraid of rushing you. I wanted to ask you to throw some clothes on and come with me—while common sense tripped me up. I'd be involved with business for the next couple of days—what fun would that be for you? So it was back to my original plan.'

'Your plan to...'

'My plan to wait until Miles said you were completely well, and so gave me permission to come courting you.'

'Oh, Tye.' She could hardly believe any of this. It was all so marvellous. To her delight, Tye bent and kissed her in a way that was so filled with love she was speechless when he drew back.

He smiled into her eyes, but it took him several seconds before he remembered. 'Hmm—that was a couple of days ago. But I was impatient. Friday seemed an impossibly long way away. I tried to ring you—and discovered my wait was going to be even more stressful than I had imagined.'

'You went home—to Grove House.'

'I couldn't believe you'd gone!'

'I'm sorry.' She loved him so much she could not bear to think how her leaving the way she had must have hurt him. 'I love you,' she whispered, and reached up and kissed him.

More heart-stoppingly wonderful seconds passed as they kissed and held each other, then Tye was drawing back from her so he could see into her face. 'You said in your letter that you honestly didn't know what you would have done without me.' Larch looked into his grey eyes, her heart racing at the love and warmth in them for her.

'I meant every word,' she replied huskily.

'May I tell you then, my dear, my very dear, adorable Larch, that I am so deeply in love with you that I honestly don't know what *I* will do, without you in my life?'

'Tye.' She breathed his name.

He tenderly kissed her, then let go of her with one arm

while he found something in his pocket. 'Remember this?' he asked, and showed her his grandmother's ring.

It was a lovely memory. 'You haven't given it to Paulette yet?'

'I no longer intend to.'

'You—don't?' Larch queried.

He caught hold of her left hand. 'Until I can get you a ring of your choosing, would you wear this one?' he asked.

'What are you s-saying?' she asked tremulously, her insides all of a tremble once more.

Tye looked sincerely into her wide blue eyes. 'I'm saying, my darling, that I love you with all of my heart. That I cannot think of a life without you. And that I would like it very much if you would marry me.'

'You want to marry me?' she gasped. 'But—but—you once agreed it was highly unlikely that you would ever marry! You said so.'

'It would appear I'm better at putting up a smokescreen than I thought,' he answered with a smile. 'I knew then, as I said it, that I was having dinner with the woman I was hoping would be my wife.'

She was staring at him in amazement, tears very near. 'Oh, Tye,' she cried softly.

'Is that a yes or a no?' he asked, and only then did she notice the sudden look of strain on his face as he waited for her answer.

She smiled lovingly at him. 'We both know the ring fits,' she whispered.

And Tye slid the ring home on her engagement finger. 'I'm taking that as a yes,' he said. She was too full to speak, so nodded, and with a joyous smile breaking on his face, 'Come here,' he said, his voice gruff with emotion. But it was tenderly that he held her and kissed her—his fiancée.